EVERYMAN'S LIBRARY

994

ESSAYS
&
BELLES-LETTRES

Everyman, I will go with thee, and be thy guide,
In thy most need to go by thy side

SAMUEL JOHNSON, born at Lichfield in 1709, the son of a bookseller. His poverty induced him to leave Oxford before taking a degree. Became an usher and a school-teacher, but in 1737 went to London and devoted himself to journalism and literature generally. Made a number of important friendships, but it was not until 1762 that he became settled financially. Met Boswell, 1763. Died on 13th December 1784.

SAMUEL JOHNSON

THE RAMBLER

INTRODUCTION BY
S. C. ROBERTS

LONDON J. M. DENT & SONS LTD
NEW YORK E. P. DUTTON & CO INC

INTRODUCTION

IN 1737 Samuel Johnson and David Garrick rode together on horseback to London. 'In his visionary project of an academy,' writes Arthur Murphy, 'Johnson had probably wasted his wife's substance; and Garrick's father had little more than his half-pay. . . . In three or four years afterwards Garrick came forth with talents that astonished the publick . . . Johnson was left to toil in the humble walks of literature.'

The *Rambler* is one of the many products of this period of toil. It is true that by 1750 Johnson had established himself as a writer of competence and of some distinction. In addition to much hack-work for the *Gentleman's Magazine* (including his experience as a parliamentary reporter) he had published his *Life of Savage*; he had gained a *succès d'estime* by his poems *London* and *The Vanity of Human Wishes*; he had seen his play *Irene* produced by Garrick; and, above all, he had been selected by a large group of booksellers as the man to compile a *Dictionary of the English Language*.

But neither the approbation of his poetry nor the prospective fruits of lexicography would keep the wolf from the door, and Johnson who, in Hawkins's words, 'had entertained a resolution to become an author by profession' had to seek other modes of 'writing for bread.'

Nearly forty years before, the *Tatler* and the *Spectator* had come to an end and for Addison's prose Johnson had a deep admiration. 'Whoever,' he said, 'wishes to attain an English style . . . must give his days and nights to the volumes of Addison.' But for Johnson the *Rambler* was something more than a remunerative exercise in prose composition. He embarked upon the work with a prayer: 'Grant, I beseech Thee, that in this undertaking thy Holy Spirit may not be withheld from me, but that I may promote thy glory and the salvation of myself and others.' Such was the deeply sincere petition of Johnson the Moralist, and it is to be remembered that it was as a moralist that he primarily impressed his readers, and among them James Boswell.

About a month after their first encounter in Tom Davies's shop

Boswell was much gratified at supping with Johnson at the Mitre tavern. He preserved a full record of their conversation and at the end of it reflected: 'Had I but thought some years that I should pass an evening with the author of the *Rambler*!' Long before this meeting he had been a reader of Johnson's works and nowhere had he found more 'bark and steel for the mind' than in the *Rambler*, a copy of which he took with him on his continental tour. After commenting on Johnson's amazing universality of genius as a writer, he continues: 'His conversation, too, is as great as his writing.'

Later generations of readers have approached Johnson's writings very differently. Turning to them after the fascination of Boswell's brilliant reporting of Johnson in the tavern chair, they are moved to remark: 'His writing, alas, is not so good as his conversation.'

Thus, Macaulay: 'His books are written in a learned language ... when he wrote for publication, he did his sentences out of English into Johnsonese'; or Taine: 'His truths are too true; we already know his precepts by heart. We learn from him that life is short and that we ought to improve the few moments accorded to us. ... We remember that sermons are liked in England and that these essays are sermons.' Leslie Stephen, who had himself been a clergyman, puts it more gently: 'It is hardly desirable,' he writes, 'for a moralist to aim at originality in his precepts,' and although he deems the moralizing to be the best part of the *Rambler* he puts Johnson the writer far below Johnson the talker.

Macaulay's influence upon the literary taste of the nineteenth century was so profound that his dictum about 'Johnsonese' has been widely and uncritically accepted. But is 'Johnsonese' unbearable? Is it, in fact, wholly unpopular? The truth is that the reader loves his Johnsonese provided that it is served to him in small doses and served by James Boswell. If a phrase such as 'I can scarce check my risibility' had been part of a recorded conversation of Johnson it would have been frequently and pleasurably quoted; but since it occurs in a *Rambler* paper it is dubbed 'Johnsonese' and dismissed. Of course it must be admitted that Johnson's prose writing lacks the sharp vigour of his conversation. There is an element of thunder in both: from the printed pages comes the deep rumble, from the talk comes the flash and the explosion. Johnson was fully conscious of the distinction, which was, indeed, deliberate:

'The graces of writing and conversation are of different kinds; and though he who excels in one might have been, with opportunity and application, equally successful in the other, yet as many please by extemporary talk, though utterly unacquainted with the more accurate method and more laboured beauties which composition requires; so it is very possible that men wholly accustomed to works of study may be without that readiness of conception and affluence of language always necessary to colloquial entertainment.'

Here is the Rambler's own warning of what we are to expect from him—not colloquial entertainment, but more accurate method and more laboured beauties. His primary purpose was instruction in the great issues of human life; he made no attempt to satisfy contemporary curiosity and when, like all regular contributors to a journal, he found it difficult to think of a subject, he never seized upon a newspaper article or upon a newly published book as a peg on which to hang a moral tale. Perhaps the *Rambler* would have retained more interest for modern readers if he had. It would have been entertaining, for instance, if Johnson had given us his first thoughts on Gray's *Elegy* or on Smart's *Ode on the Immensity of the Supreme Being,* both of which were published in 1751.

But in 1750 Johnson was still feeling his way as a writer. In his second *Rambler* he wrote: 'There is nothing more dreadful to an author than neglect,' and in the following paper he remarked, with some bitterness, of critics: 'To these men it is necessary for a new author to find some means of recommendation. . . . I have heard how some have been pacified with claret and a supper and others laid asleep with the soft notes of flattery.' As always, Johnson was conscious of the vanity of human wishes, and especially in relation to literary ambition. In No. 145 of the *Rambler* he writes:

'It has been formerly imagined that he who intends the entertainment or instruction of others, must feel in himself some peculiar impulse of genius . . . and animate his efforts with the hope of raising a monument of learning which neither time nor envy shall be able to destroy. But the authors whom I am now endeavouring to recommend have been too long hackneyed in the ways of men to indulge the chimerical ambition of immortality. They have seldom any claim to the trade of writing, but that they have tried some other without success. They perceive no particular summons to composition, except the sound of the clock ... and about the opinion of posterity they have little solicitude, for their productions are seldom intended to remain in the world longer than a week.'

Critics may call this 'Johnsonese' if they will, but can they point to a finer exposition of the lot of 'those who retail their labours in periodical sheets'?

Similarly, Johnson had no illusions about the accumulations of literature. In *Rambler* No. 106 he writes: 'No place affords a more striking conviction of the vanity of human hopes than a publick library, ... of the innumerable authors whose performances are thus treasured up in magnificent obscurity, most are forgotten because they never deserved to be remembered.'

But although the struggles of the adventurer in literature (as Johnson described himself when he first came to London) are vividly portrayed in the pages of the *Rambler*, they are far from predominating the whole series of essays. Character sketches are frequent. One of them, that of Suspirius (No. 59), was the prototype of Croaker in Goldsmith's comedy *The Good-Natur'd Man* and, when the future of the play hung in the balance, it was Shuter's playing of the part of Croaker that determined its success. There are plenty of other characters, both of men and women, and the Rambler seems to have paid particular regard to marriageable, and married, couples. For the over-domesticated hostess he displays a keen dislike. Lady Bustle, for instance, is thus described in No. 51:

'She has no crime but luxury, nor any virtue but chastity. She has no desire to be praised but for her cookery, nor wishes any ill to the rest of mankind but that whenever they aspire to a feast their custards may be wheyish and their pie-crusts tough.'

A similar scorn is reserved for the omnivorously impartial collector (No. 82) with his lock of Cromwell's hair in a box turned from a piece of the royal oak and for the virtuoso who 'looked on all his associates as wretches of depraved taste and narrow notions.' To modern readers familiar with the lightness and whimsy of later essayists Johnson's satire may well seem to be applied with too heavy a hand. But again it must be recalled that the Rambler was primarily and deliberately what Boswell proclaimed him to be—'a majestic teacher of moral and religious wisdom.' Frequently he wrote of the minor foibles of humanity, but when the subject was a serious one he exemplified what he wrote in another context: 'Nothing can be more improper than ease and laxity of expression when the importance of the subject impresses solicitude.'

There is a grim humour in many of the essays, but Johnson is most deeply moved when he turns to the tragic side of the life around him. No essay is more impressive than his unsentimental picture of the prostitute's life drawn from the prostitute's point of view (Nos. 170, 171), and his protest against the death-sentence for robbery (No. 114) is one of many examples of the high Tory being well in advance of his time in liberal thinking:

'Death is ... of dreadful things the most dreadful. ... This terror should therefore be reserved as the last resort of authority, as the strongest and most operative of prohibitory sanctions. ... To equal robbery with murder is to reduce murder to robbery, to confound in common minds the gradations of iniquity and incite the commission of a greater crime to prevent the detection of a less.'

As a periodical essayist Johnson recognized that he was not, in the first instance, a favourite with the public. Less than five hundred copies of each *Rambler* were sold as separate essays, but when they were collected in book form they had a much wider sale and reached their twelfth edition in the year of Johnson's death. Like all collections of periodical essays, they are uneven, and Johnson himself would be the last man to expect that any one, in his own day or in ours, should read the *Rambler* continuously and in its entirety ('Sir, do you read books *through*?').

But those who profess and call themselves Johnsonians must not rest upon Boswell alone, and that man is little to be envied whose knowledge of Johnson will not be enriched and his affection deepened by a reading of a selection of essays from the *Rambler*.

S. C. R.

EDITOR'S NOTE

This selection of the *Rambler* essays is designed to show Dr Johnson as both moralist and critic: as moralist in the philosophical and religious spheres, as critic of literature and manners. His moods range from the contemplation of eternal truth to the grim humour of his contemporary scene.

The text used is that of the tenth edition, 6 vols. (1784). Spelling and punctuation have been modernized. No titles were prefixed to the original essays: those given here are based upon the list supplied by the edition of 1793 in Parsons's Select British Classics.

J. WARRINGTON.

1953.

BIBLIOGRAPHICAL NOTE

[For a full bibliography see W. P. Courtney and D. Nichol Smith, *A Bibliography of Samuel Johnson* (1915; enlarged edition, 1925).]

The following is a list of Johnson's principal works:

A Voyage to Abyssinia, by Father Jerome Lobo (translated from the French), 1735; *London: A Poem*, 1738; *Marmor Norfolcience: or an Essay on an Ancient Prophetical Inscription*, 1739; *A Complete Vindication of the Licensers of the Stage*, 1739; *The Life of Admiral Blake*, 1740; *The Life of Mr. Richard Savage*, 1744; *The Life of J. P. Barretier*, 1744; *Miscellaneous Observations on the Tragedy of Macbeth*, 1745; *The Plan of a Dictionary of the English Language*, 1747; *Prologue and Epilogue at the opening of Drury Lane*, 1747; *The Vanity of Human Wishes*, 1749; *Irene: A Tragedy*, 1749; *The Rambler*, 1750–2; *A New Prologue spoken by Mr. Garrick*, 1750; *A Dictionary of the English Language*, 1755; *The Prince of Abyssinia (Rasselas)*, 1759; *The Idler*, 1761; *The Plays of William Shakespeare*, 1765; *The False Alarm*, 1770; *Thoughts on the Late Transactions respecting Falkland's Islands*, 1771; *The Patriot*, 1774; *Taxation no Tyranny*, 1775; *A Journey to the Western Islands of Scotland*, 1775; *Prefaces to the Works of the English Poets*, 1779–81 (published separately as *Lives of the Poets*, 1781).

In addition Johnson wrote many prefaces to the works of others and a very large number of essays, poems, and reviews for the *Gentleman's Magazine*, the *Literary Magazine*, the *London Chronicle*, and other journals.

Of his posthumous works the most important are his Letters, now collected and edited by R. W. Chapman (1952); his Prayers and Meditations, first published in 1785 and frequently re-edited (e.g. by H. E. Savage, 1927); his Debates in Parliament (1787); an Account of his life to his eleventh year (1805); his Diary of a Journey into North Wales (ed. R. Duppa, 1816); his French Journal (ed. Tyson and Guppy, 1932); and the Sermons attributed to him and left for publication by John Taylor (1789).

There are several collected editions of Johnson's works, including that of Sir John Hawkins (1787); of Arthur Murphy (1792); of R. Lynam (1825); and the Oxford Edition (1825).

The standard edition of his collected Poems is that of Nichol Smith and McAdam (1941).

In addition to Boswell's *Journal of a Tour to the Hebrides* (1785) and *Life of Johnson* (1791), there are other contemporary authorities, including Sir John Hawkins's *Life* (1787), Mrs. Piozzi's *Anecdotes* (1786), Fanny Burney's Diary (1842–6), as well as other anecdotes, many of them assembled in Birkbeck Hill's *Johnsonian Miscellanies* (1897). Of the many modern works on Johnson, the following may be noted: T. B. Macaulay: *Essay on Boswell's Life* (1831) and article in the *Encyclopaedia Britannica*, 1856; T. Carlyle: *Essay on Boswell's Life*, 1832; L. Stephen: *Samuel Johnson*, 1878; F. Grant:

Life of Samuel Johnson, 1887; T. Seccombe: *The Age of Johnson*, 1899; W. Raleigh: *Six Essays on Johnson*, 1910; J. Bailey: *Dr. Johnson and his Circle*, 1913; S. C. Roberts: *The Story of Dr. Johnson*, 1919, and *Dr. Johnson*, 1935; P. H. Houston: *Dr. Johnson: A Study in Eighteenth-century Humanism*, 1923; C. Hollis: *Doctor Johnson*, 1928; J. W. Krutch: *Samuel Johnson*, 1944; R. W. Chapman: *Johnsonian and other Essays*, 1953.

CONTENTS

Numbers in parentheses are those of the original papers, and by which reference is generally made to the *Rambler* essays.

THE FIRST ADDRESS (1)

Tuesday, 20th March 1750

Cur tamen hoc libeat potius decurrere campo,
Per quem magnus equos auruncae flexit alumnus,
Si vacat, et placidi rationem admittitis, edam.

JUVENAL.

Why to expatiate in this beaten field;
Why arms oft us'd in vain, I mean to wield;
If time permit, and candour will attend,
Some satisfaction this essay may lend.

ELPHINSTON.

THE difficulty of the first address on any new occasion is felt by every man in his transactions with the world, and confessed by the settled and regular forms of salutation which necessity has introduced into all languages. Judgment was wearied with the perplexity of being forced upon choice where there was no motive to preference; and it was found convenient that some easy method of introduction should be established, which, if it warranted the allurement of novelty, might enjoy the security of prescription.

Perhaps few authors have presented themselves before the public without wishing that such ceremonial modes of entrance had been anciently established as might have freed them from those dangers which the desire of pleasing is certain to produce, and precluded the vain expedients of softening censure by apologies or rousing attention by abruptness.

The epic writers have found the proemial part of the poem such an addition to their undertaking, that they have almost unanimously adopted the first lines of Homer; and the reader needs only to be informed of the subject to know in what manner the poem will begin.

But this solemn repetition is hitherto the peculiar distinction of heroic poetry; it has never been legally extended to the lower orders of literature, but seems to be considered as an hereditary privilege to be enjoyed only by those who claim it from their alliance to the genius of Homer.

The rules which the injudicious use of this prerogative suggested to Horace may indeed be applied to the direction of candidates for inferior fame. It may be proper for all to remember, that they ought not to raise expectation which it is not in their power to satisfy, and that it is more pleasing to see smoke brightening into flame than flame sinking into smoke.

This precept has been long received, both from regard to the authority of Horace and its conformity to the general opinion of the world; yet there have been always some that thought it no deviation from modesty to recommend their own labours, and imagined themselves entitled by indisputable merit to an exemption from general restraints, and to elevations not allowed in common life. They perhaps believed that when, like Thucydides, they bequeathed to mankind 'κτῆμα ἐς ἀεί—an estate for ever,' it was an additional favour to inform them of its value.

It may, indeed, be no less dangerous to claim, on certain occasions, too little than too much. There is something captivating in spirit and intrepidity, to which we often yield as to a resistless power; nor can he reasonably expect the confidence of others who too apparently distrusts himself.

Plutarch, in his enumeration of the various occasions on which a man may without just offence proclaim his own excellencies, has omitted the case of an author entering the world; unless it may be comprehended under his general position—that a man may lawfully praise himself for those qualities which cannot be known but from his own mouth, as when he is among strangers, and can have no opportunity of an actual exertion of his powers. That the case of an author is parallel will scarcely be granted, because he necessarily discovers the degree of his merit to his judges when he appears at his trial. But it should be remembered, that unless his judges are inclined to favour him they will hardly be persuaded to hear the cause.

In love, the state which fills the heart with a degree of solicitude next that of an author, it has been held a maxim that success is most easily obtained by indirect and unperceived approaches. He who too soon professes himself a lover raises obstacles to his own wishes; and those whom disappointments have taught experience endeavour to conceal their passion till they believe their mistress wishes for the discovery. The same method, if it were practicable to writers, would save many complaints of the severity of the age and the caprices of criticism. If a man could glide imperceptibly into the favour of the public, and only proclaim his pretensions to literary honours when he is sure of not being rejected, he might commence author with better hopes, as his failings might escape contempt though he shall never attain much regard.

But since the world supposes every man that writes ambitious of applause, as some ladies have taught themselves to believe that every man intends love who expresses civility, the miscarriage of any endeavour in learning raises an unbounded contempt, indulged by most minds without scruple as an honest triumph over unjust claims and exorbitant expectations. The artifices of those who put themselves in this hazardous state have therefore been multiplied in proportion to their fear as well as their ambition, and are to be looked upon with more indulgence as they are incited at once by the two great movers of the human mind, the desire of good and the fear of evil. For who can wonder that, allured on one side and frightened on the other, some should endeavour to gain favour by bribing the judge with an appearance of respect which they do not feel, to excite compassion by confessing weakness of which they are not convinced, and others to attract regard by a show of openness and magnanimity, by a daring profession of their own deserts, and a public challenge of honours and rewards.

The ostentatious and haughty display of themselves has been the usual refuge of diurnal writers; in vindication of whose practice it may be said that what it wants in prudence is supplied by sincerity; and who at least may plead that if their boasts deceive any into the perusal of their performances, they defraud them of but little time.

> *Quid enim? Concurritur horae.*
> *Memento cito mors venit, aut victoria laeta.*
>
> HORACE.

> The battle join; and, in a moment's flight,
> Death, or a joyful conquest, ends the fight.
>
> FRANCIS.

The question concerning the merit of the day is soon decided; and we are not condemned to toil through half a folio to be convinced that the writer has broke his promise.

It is one among many reasons for which I purpose to endeavour the entertainment of my countrymen by a short essay on Tuesday and Saturday, that I hope not much to tire those whom I shall not happen to please; and if I am not commended for the beauty of my works, to be at least pardoned for their brevity. But whether my expectations are most fixed on pardon or praise I think it not necessary to discover; for having accurately weighed the reasons for arrogance and submission, I find them so nearly equiponderant, that my impatience to try the event of my first performance will not suffer me to attend any longer the trepidations of the balance.

There are, indeed, many conveniences almost peculiar to this method of publication, which may naturally flatter the author, whether he be confident or timorous. The man to whom the extent of his knowledge, or the sprightliness of his imagination, has in his own opinion already secured the praises of the world, willingly takes that way of displaying his abilities which will soonest give him an opportunity of hearing the voice of fame. It heightens his alacrity to think in how many places he shall hear what he is now writing read with ecstasies to-morrow. He will often please himself with reflecting that the author of a large treatise must proceed with anxiety lest, before the completion of his work, the attention of the public may have changed its object. But that he who is confined to no single topic may follow the national taste through all its variations, and catch the *aura popularis* the gale of favour, from what point soever it shall blow.

Nor is the prospect less likely to ease the doubts of the cautious and the terrors of the fearful. For to such the shortness of every single paper is a powerful encouragement. He that questions his abilities to arrange the dissimilar parts of an extensive plan, or fears to be lost in a complicated system, may yet hope to adjust a few pages without perplexity; and if, when he turns over the repositories of his memory, he finds his collection too small for a volume, he may yet have enough to furnish out an essay. He that would fear to lay out too much time upon an experiment of which he knows not the event persuades himself that a few days will show him what he is to expect from his learning and his genius. If he thinks his own judgment not sufficiently enlightened he may, by attending the remarks which every paper will produce, rectify his opinions. If he should with too little premeditation encumber himself by an unwieldy subject he can quit it without confessing his ignorance, and pass to other topics less dangerous or more tractable. And if he finds, with all his industry and all his artifices, that he cannot deserve regard, or cannot attain it, he may let the design fall at once and, without injury to others or himself, retire to amusements of greater pleasure or to studies of better prospect.

ON LOOKING INTO FUTURITY (2)

Saturday, 24th March 1750

Stare loco nescit, pereunt vestigia mille
Ante fugam, absentemque ferit gravis ungula campum.

STATIUS.

> Th' impatient courser pants in every vein,
> And pawing seems to beat the distant plain;
> Hills, vales, and floods appear already crost,
> And, ere he starts, a thousand steps are lost.

POPE.

THAT the mind of man is never satisfied with the objects immediately before it, but is always breaking away from the present moment and losing itself in schemes of future felicity; and that we forget the proper use of the time now in our power to provide for the enjoyment of that which, perhaps, may never be granted us, has been frequently remarked. And as this practice is a commodious subject of raillery to the gay and of declamation to the serious, it has been ridiculed with all the pleasantry of wit and exaggerated with all the amplifications of rhetoric. Every instance by which its absurdity might appear most flagrant has been studiously collected; it has been marked with every epithet of contempt, and all the tropes and figures have been called forth against it.

Censure is willingly indulged, because it always implies some superiority; men please themselves with imagining that they have made a deeper search or wider survey than others, and detected faults and follies which escape vulgar observation. And the pleasure of wantoning in common topics is so tempting to a writer that he cannot easily resign it: a train of sentiments generally received enables him to shine without labour, and to conquer without a contest. It is so easy to laugh at the folly of him who lives only in idea, refuses immediate ease for distant pleasures, and instead of enjoying the blessings of life lets life glide away in preparations to enjoy them. It affords such opportunities of triumphant exultation to exemplify the uncertainty of the human state, to rouse mortals from their dream and inform them of the silent celerity of time, that we may believe authors willing rather to transmit than examine so advantageous a principle, and more inclined to pursue a track so smooth and so flowery than attentively to consider whether it leads to truth.

This quality of looking forward into futurity seems the unavoidable condition of a being whose motions are gradual and whose life is progressive. As his powers are limited he must use means for the attainment of his ends, and intend first what he performs last. As, by continual advances from his first stage of existence he is perpetually varying the horizon of his prospects, he must always discover new motives of action, new excitements of fear, and allurements of desire.

The end, therefore, which at present calls forth our efforts will be found, when it is once gained, to be only one of the means to some remoter end. The natural flights of the human mind are not from pleasure to pleasure, but from hope to hope.

He that directs his steps to a certain point must frequently turn his eyes to that place which he strives to reach; he that undergoes the fatigue of labour must solace his weariness with the contemplation of its reward. In agriculture, one of the most simple and necessary employments, no man turns up the ground but because he thinks of the harvest, that harvest which blights may intercept, which inundations may sweep away, or which death or calamity may hinder him from reaping.

Yet as few maxims are widely received or long retained but for some conformity with truth and nature, it must be confessed that this caution against keeping our view too intent upon remote advantages is not without its propriety or usefulness, though it may have been recited with too much levity or enforced with too little distinction: for not to speak of that vehemence of desire which presses through right and wrong to its gratification, or that anxious inquietude which is justly chargeable with distrust of heaven, subjects too solemn for my present purpose; it frequently happens that, by indulging early the raptures of success, we forget the measures necessary to secure it, and suffer the imagination to riot in the fruition of some possible good till the time of obtaining it has slipped away.

There would, however, be few enterprises of great labour or hazard undertaken if we had not the power of magnifying the advantages which we persuade ourselves to expect from them. When the knight of La Mancha gravely recounts to his companion the adventures by which he is to signalize himself in such a manner that he shall be summoned to the support of empires, solicited to accept the heiress of the crown which he has preserved, have honours and riches to scatter about him, and an island to bestow on his worthy squire, very few readers, amidst their mirth or pity, can deny that they have admitted visions of the same kind; though they have not perhaps expected events equally strange, or by means equally inadequate. When we pity them we reflect on our own disappointments; and when we laugh our hearts inform us that he is not more ridiculous than ourselves, except that he tells what we have only thought.

The understanding of a man, naturally sanguine, may indeed be easily vitiated by the luxurious indulgence of hope, however necessary to the production of everything great or excellent, as some plants are destroyed by too open exposure to that sun which gives life and beauty to the vegetable world.

Perhaps no class of the human species requires more to be cautioned against this anticipation of happiness, than those that aspire to the name of authors. A man of lively fancy no sooner finds a hint moving in his mind than he makes momentaneous excursions to the press and to the world, and with a little encouragement from flattery pushes forward into future ages, and prognosticates the honours to be paid him when envy is extinct and faction forgotten, and those whom partiality now suffers to obscure him shall have given way to the triflers of as short duration as themselves.

Those who have proceeded so far as to appeal to the tribunal of succeeding times, are not likely to be cured of their infatuation; but all endeavours ought to be used for the prevention of a disease for which, when it has attained its height, perhaps no remedy will be found in the gardens of philosophy however she may boast her physic of the mind, her cathartics of vice, or lenitives of passion.

I shall, therefore, while I am yet but lightly touched with the symptoms of the writer's malady, endeavour to fortify myself against the infection, not without some weak hope that my preservatives may extend their virtue to others whose employment exposes them to the same danger.

> Laudis amore tumes? Sunt certa piacula, quae te
> Ter pure lecto poterunt recreare libello.

> Is fame your passion? Wisdom's powerful charm,
> If thrice read over, shall its force disarm.

FRANCIS.

It is the sage advice of Epictetus that a man should accustom himself often to think of what is most shocking and terrible, that by such reflections he may be preserved from too ardent wishes for seeming good and from too much dejection in real evil.

There is nothing more dreadful to an author than neglect, compared with which reproach hatred and opposition are names of happiness; yet this worst, this meanest fate, every one who dares to write has reason to fear.

> I nunc, et versus tecum meditare canoros.

> Go now, and meditate thy tuneful lays.

ELPHINSTON.

It may not be unfit for him who makes a new entrance into the lettered world, so far to suspect his own powers as to believe that he possibly may deserve neglect; that nature may not have qualified him much to enlarge or embellish knowledge, nor sent him forth entitled by indisputable superiority to regulate the conduct of the rest of mankind; that though the world must be granted to be yet in ignorance, he is not destined to dispel the cloud, nor to shine out as one of the luminaries of life.   For this suspicion every catalogue of a library will furnish sufficient reason; as he will find it crowded with names of men who, though now forgotten, were once no less enterprising or confident than himself, equally pleased with their own productions, equally caressed by their patrons, and flattered by their friends.

But though it should happen that an author is capable of excelling, yet his merit may pass without notice huddled in the variety of things and thrown into the general miscellany of life.   He that endeavours after fame by writing solicits the regard of a multitude fluctuating in pleasures or immersed in business without time for intellectual amusements; he appeals to judges prepossessed by passions or corrupted by prejudices, which preclude their approbation of any new performance.   Some are too indolent to read anything till its reputation is established; others too envious to promote that fame which gives them pain by its increase.   What is new is opposed because most are unwilling to be taught; and what is known is rejected because it is not sufficiently considered that men more frequently require to be reminded than informed.   The learned are afraid to declare their opinion early lest they should put their reputation in hazard; the ignorant always imagine themselves giving some proof of delicacy when they refuse to be pleased; and he that finds his way to reputation through all these obstructions must acknowledge that he is indebted to other causes besides his industry, his learning, or his wit.

CRITICISM: AN ALLEGORY (3)

Tuesday, 27th March 1750

Virtus, repulsae nescia sordidae,
Intaminatis fulget honoribus,
  Nec sumit aut ponit secures
  Arbitrio popularis aurae.

HORACE.

Undisappointed in designs,
With native honours virtue shines;
Nor takes up pow'r, nor lays it down,
As giddy rabbles smile or frown.

ELPHINSTON.

THE talk of an author is either to teach what is not known or to recommend known truths by his manner of adorning them; either to let new light in upon the mind and open new scenes to the prospect, or to vary the dress and situation of common objects so as to give them fresh grace and more powerful attractions; spread such flowers over the regions through which the intellect has already made its progress, as may tempt it to return and take a second view of things hastily passed over or negligently regarded.

Either of these labours is very difficult because, that they may not be fruitless, men must not only be persuaded of their errors but reconciled to their guide; they must not only confess their ignorance, but what is still less pleasing must allow that he from whom they are to learn is more knowing than themselves.

It might be imagined that such an employment was in itself sufficiently irksome and hazardous; that none would be found so malevolent as wantonly to add weight to the stone of Sisyphus; and that few endeavours would be used to obstruct those advances to reputation which must be made at such an expense of time and thought, with so great hazard in the miscarriage, and with so little advantage from the success.

Yet there is a certain race of men that either imagine it their duty or make it their amusement to hinder the reception of every work of learning or genius, who stand as sentinels in the avenues of fame, and value themselves upon giving Ignorance and Envy the first notice of a prey.

To these men, who distinguish themselves by the appellation of Critics, it is necessary for a new author to find some means of recommendation. It is probable that the most malignant of these persecutors might be somewhat softened and prevailed on for a short time to remit their fury. Having for this purpose considered many expedients, I find in the records of ancient times that Argus was lulled by music and Cerberus quieted with a sop; and am therefore inclined to believe that modern critics, who if they have not the eyes, have the watchfulness of Argus and can bark as loud as Cerberus, though perhaps they cannot bite with equal force, might be subdued by methods of the same kind. I have heard how some have been pacified with claret and a supper and others laid asleep with the soft notes of flattery.

Though the nature of my undertaking gives me sufficient reason to dread the united attacks of this virulent generation, yet I have not hitherto persuaded myself to take any measures for flight or treaty. For I am in doubt whether they can act against me by lawful authority, and suspect that they have presumed upon a forged commission, styled themselves the ministers of criticism, without any authentic evidence of delegation, and uttered their own determinations as the decrees of a higher judicature.

Criticism, from whom they derive their claim to decide the fate of writers, was the eldest daughter of Labour and of Truth; she was, at her birth, committed to the care of Justice and brought up by her in the palace of Wisdom. Being soon distinguished by the celestials for her uncommon qualities, she was appointed the governess of Fancy and empowered to beat time to the chorus of the Muses when they sung before the throne of Jupiter.

When the Muses condescended to visit this lower world, they came accompanied by Criticism, to whom, upon her descent from her native regions, Justice gave a sceptre to be carried aloft in her right hand, one end of which was tinctured with ambrosia and enwreathed with a golden foliage of amaranths and bays; the other end was encircled with cypress and poppies, and dipped in the waters of Oblivion. In her left hand she bore an unextinguishable torch manufactured by Labour and lighted by Truth, of which it was the particular quality immediately to show everything in its true form however it might be disguised to common eyes. Whatever Art could complicate, or Folly could confound, was upon the first gleam of the torch of Truth exhibited in its distinct parts and original simplicity. It darted through the labyrinths of sophistry, and showed at once all the absurdities to which they served for refuge. It pierced through the robes which Rhetoric often sold to Falsehood, and detected the disproportion of parts which artificial veils had been contrived to cover.

Thus furnished for the execution of her office, Criticism came down to survey the performances of those who professed themselves the votaries of the Muses. Whatever was brought before her she beheld by the steady light of the torch of Truth; and when her examination had convinced her that the laws of just writing had been observed, she touched it with the amaranthine end of the sceptre and consigned it over to immortality.

But it more frequently happened that in the works which required her inspection there was some imposture attempted; that false colours were laboriously laid; that some secret inequality was found between the words and sentiments, or some dissimilitude of the ideas and the original objects; that incongruities were linked together, or that some parts were of no use but to enlarge the appearance of the whole without contributing to its beauty, solidity, or usefulness.

Wherever such discoveries were made, and they were made whenever these faults were committed, Criticism refused the touch which conferred the sanction of immortality; and when the errors were frequent and gross, reversed the sceptre, and let drops of Lethe distil from the poppies and cypress, a fatal mildew, which immediately began to waste the work away till it was at last totally destroyed.

There were some compositions brought to the test in which when the strongest light was thrown upon them their beauties and faults appeared so equally mingled that Criticism stood with her sceptre poised in her hand, in doubt whether to shed lethe or ambrosia upon them. These at last increased to so great a number that she was weary of attending such doubtful claims, and, for fear of using improperly the sceptre of justice, referred the cause to be considered by Time.

The proceedings of Time, though very dilatory, were, some few caprices excepted, conformable to justice; and many who thought themselves secure by a short forbearance, have sunk under his scythe, as they were posting down with their volumes in triumph to futurity. It was observable that some were destroyed by little and little and others crushed for ever by a single blow.

Criticism having long kept her eye fixed steadily upon Time, was at last so well satisfied with his conduct that she withdrew from the earth with her patroness Astrea, and left prejudice and False Taste to ravage at large as the associates of Fraud and Mischief, contenting herself thenceforth to shed her influence from afar upon some select minds fitted for its reception by learning and by virtue.

Before her departure she broke her sceptre; of which the shivers that formed the ambrosial end were caught up by Flattery, and those that had been infected with the waters of Lethe were with equal haste seized by Malevolence. The followers of Flattery, to whom she distributed her part of the sceptre, neither had nor desired light, but touched indiscriminately whatever power or interest happened to exhibit. The companions of Malevolence were supplied by the Furies with a torch which had this quality peculiar to infernal lustre, that its light fell only upon faults.

> No light, but rather darkness visible,
> Serv'd only to discover sights of woe.

With these fragments of authority the slaves of Flattery and Malevolence marched out at the command of their mistresses, to confer immortality or condemn to oblivion. But the sceptre had now lost its power; and Time passes his sentence at leisure, without any regard to their determinations.

Tuesday, 10th April 1750

O qui perpetuâ mundum ratione gubernas,
Terrarum coelique sator!—
Disjice terrenae nebulas et pondera molis,
Atque tuo splendore mica!   Tu namque serenum,
Tu requies tranquilla piis.   Te cernere, finis,
Principium, vector, dux, semita, terminus, idem.

BOETHIUS.

O Thou, whose pow'r o'er moving worlds presides,
Whose voice created, and whose wisdom guides,
On darkling man in pure effulgence shine,
And clear the clouded mind with light divine.
'Tis thine alone to calm the pious breast
With silent confidence and holy rest;
From Thee, great God, we spring, to Thee we tend;
Path, motive, guide, original, and end.

THE love of Retirement has, in all ages, adhered closely to those minds which have been most enlarged by knowledge or elevated by genius.   Those who enjoyed everything generally supposed to confer happiness have been forced to seek it in the shades of privacy.   Though they possessed both power and riches, and were therefore surrounded by men who considered it as their chief interest to remove from them everything that might offend their ease or interrupt their pleasure, they have soon felt the languors of satiety, and found themselves unable to pursue the race of life without frequent respirations of intermediate solitude.

To produce this disposition, nothing appears requisite but quick sensibility and active imagination; for though not devoted to virtue or science, the man whose faculties enable him to make ready comparisons of the present with the past will find such a constant recurrence of the same pleasures and troubles, the same expectations and disappointments, that he will gladly snatch an hour of retreat to let his thoughts expatiate at large, and seek for that variety in his own ideas which the objects of sense cannot afford him.

Nor will greatness or abundance exempt him from the importunities of this desire, since, if he is born to think, he cannot restrain himself from a thousand inquiries and speculations which he must

13

pursue by his own reason, and which the splendour of his condition can only hinder. For those who are most exalted above dependence or control are yet condemned to pay so large a tribute of their time to custom, ceremony, and popularity, that, according to the Greek proverb, no man in the house is more a slave than the master.

When a king asked Euclid the mathematician whether he could not explain his art to him in a more compendious manner, he was answered that there was no royal way to geometry. Other things may be seized by might or purchased with money, but knowledge is to be gained only by study, and study to be prosecuted only in retirement.

These are some of the motives which have had power to sequester kings and heroes from the crowds that soothed them with flatteries or inspirited them with acclamations, but their efficacy seems confined to the higher mind and to operate little upon the common classes of mankind, to whose conceptions the present assemblage of things is adequate and who seldom range beyond those entertainments and vexations which solicit their attention by pressing on their senses.

But there is a universal reason for some stated intervals of solitude which the institutions of the Church call upon me, now especially, to mention; a reason, which extends as wide as moral duty or the hopes of divine favour in a future state; and which ought to influence all ranks of life and all degrees of intellect; since none can imagine themselves not comprehended in its obligation but such as determine to set their Maker at defiance by obstinate wickedness, or whose enthusiastic security of his approbation places them above external ordinances and all human means of improvement.

The great task of him who conducts his life by the precepts of religion is to make the future predominate over the present, to impress upon his mind so strong a sense of the importance of obedience to the divine will, of the value of the reward promised to virtue, and the terrors of the punishment denounced against crimes, as may overbear all the temptations which temporal hope or fear can bring in his way and enable him to bid equal defiance to joy and sorrow, to turn away at one time from the allurements of ambition and push forward at another against the threats of calamity.

It is not without reason that the apostle represents our passage through this stage of our existence by images drawn from the alarms and solicitude of a military life, for we are placed in such a state that almost everything about us conspires against our chief interest. We are in danger from whatever can get possession of our thoughts; all that can excite in us either pain or pleasure has a tendency to obstruct the way that leads to happiness, and either to turn us aside or retard our progress.

Our senses, our appetites, and our passions, are our lawful and faithful guides in most things that relate solely to this life; and therefore, by the hourly necessity of consulting them, we gradually sink into an implicit submission and habitual confidence. Every act of compliance with their motions facilitates a second compliance, every new step towards depravity is made with less reluctance than the former, and thus the descent to life merely sensual is perpetually accelerated.

The senses have not only that advantage over conscience, which things necessary must always have over things chosen, but they have likewise a kind of prescription in their favour. We feared pain much earlier than we apprehended guilt, and were delighted with the sensations of pleasure before we had capacities to be charmed with the beauty of rectitude. To this power, thus early established, and incessantly increasing, it must be remembered that almost every man has, in some part of his life, added new strength by a voluntary or negligent subjection of himself; for who is there that has not instigated his appetites by indulgence or suffered them by an unresisting neutrality to enlarge their dominion and multiply their demands?

From the necessity of dispossessing the sensitive faculties of the influence which they must naturally gain by this preoccupation of the soul, arises that conflict between opposite desires in the first endeavours after a religious life; which, however enthusiastically it may have been described, or however contemptuously ridiculed, will naturally be felt in some degree, though varied without end, by different tempers of mind and innumerable circumstances of health or condition, greater or less fervour, more or fewer temptations to relapse.

From the perpetual necessity of consulting the animal faculties in our provision for the present life, arises the difficulty of withstanding their impulses even in cases where they ought to be of no weight. For the motions of sense are instantaneous, its objects strike unsought, we are accustomed to follow its directions and therefore often submit to the sentence without examining the authority of the judge.

Thus it appears upon a philosophical estimate that supposing the mind, at any certain time, in an equipose between the pleasures of this life and the hopes of futurity, present objects falling more frequently into the scale would in time preponderate, and that our regard for an invisible state would grow every moment weaker, till at last it would lose all its activity and become absolutely without effect.

To prevent this dreadful event the balance is put into our own hands and we have power to transfer the weight to either side. The motives to a life of holiness are infinite, not less than the favour or anger of Omnipotence, not less than eternity of happiness or misery. But these can only influence our conduct as they gain our attention, which the business or diversions of the world are always calling off by contrary attractions.

The great art, therefore, of piety, and the end for which all religious rites seem to be instituted, is the perpetual renovation of the motives to virtue by a voluntary employment of our mind in the contemplation of its excellence, its importance, and its necessity, which, in proportion as they are more frequently and more willingly revolved, gain a more forcible and permanent influence till in time they become the reigning ideas and standing principles of action and the test by which everything proposed to the judgment is rejected or approved.

To facilitate this change of our affections it is necessary that we weaken the temptations of the world by retiring at certain seasons from it; for its influence arising only from its presence is much lessened when it becomes the object of solitary meditation. A constant residence amidst noise and pleasure inevitably obliterates the impressions of piety, and a frequent abstraction of ourselves into a state where this life, like the next, operates only upon the reason will reinstate religion in its just authority, even without those irradiations from above, the hope of which I have no intentions to withdraw from the sincere and the diligent.

This is that conquest of the world and of ourselves which has been always considered as the perfection of human nature; and this is only to be obtained by fervent prayer, steady resolutions, and frequent retirement from folly and vanity, from the cares of avarice and the joys of intemperance, from the lulling sounds of deceitful flattery and the tempting fight of prosperous wickedness.

FOLLY OF ANGER (11)

Tuesday, 24th April 1750

Non Dindymene, non adytis quatit
Mentem sacerdotum incola Pythius
    Non liber aeque, non acuta
    Sic geminant Corybantes aera,
Tristes ut irae.

HORACE.

Yet O! remember, nor the god of wine,
Nor Pythian Phoebus from his inmost shrine,
Nor Dindymene, nor her priests possest,
Can with their sounding cymbals shake the breast,
Like furious anger.

FRANCIS.

THE maxim which Periander of Corinth, one of the seven sages of Greece, left as a memorial of his knowledge and benevolence, was χόλου κράτει, *Be master of thy anger*. He considered Anger as the great disturber of human life, the chief enemy both of public happiness and private tranquillity, and thought that he could not lay on posterity a stronger obligation to reverence his memory than by leaving them a salutary caution against this outrageous passion.

To what latitude Periander might extend the word, the brevity of his precept will scarce allow us to conjecture. From anger in its full import, protracted into malevolence and exerted in revenge, arise, indeed, many of the evils to which the life of man is exposed. By anger operating upon power are produced the subversion of cities, the desolation of countries, the massacre of nations, and all those dreadful and astonishing calamities which fill the histories of the world and which could not be read at any distant point of time, when the passions stand neutral and every motive and principle is left to its natural force without some doubt of the truth of the relation, did we not see the same causes still tending to the same effects, and only acting with less vigour for want of the same concurrent opportunities.

But this gigantic and enormous species of anger falls not properly under the animadversion of a writer whose chief end is the regulation of common life, and whose precepts are to recommend

themselves by their general use.   Nor is this essay intended to
expose the tragical or fatal effects even of private malignity.   The
anger which I propose now for my subject is such as makes those
who indulge it more troublesome than formidable, and ranks them
rather with hornets and wasps than with basilisks and lions.   I
have therefore prefixed a motto which characterizes this passion,
not so much by the mischief that it causes as by the noise that it
utters.

There is in the world a certain class of mortals, known and
contentedly known by the appellation of *passionate men,* who
imagine themselves entitled by that distinction to be provoked on
every slight occasion, and to vent their rage in vehement and fierce
vociferations, in furious menaces and licentious reproaches.   Their
rage, indeed, for the most part fumes away in outcries of injury and
protestations of vengeance, and seldom proceeds to actual violence
unless a drawer or link-boy falls in their way; but they interrupt the
quiet of those that happen to be within the reach of their clamours,
obstruct the course of conversation, and disturb the enjoyment of
society.

Men of this kind are sometimes not without understanding or
virtue, and are therefore not always treated with the severity which
their neglect of the ease of all about them might justly provoke;
they have obtained a kind of prescription for their folly, and are
considered by their companions as under a predominant influence
that leaves them not masters of their conduct or language, as acting
without consciousness and rushing into mischief with a mist before
their eyes.   They are therefore pitied rather than censured, and their
sallies are passed over as the involuntary blows of a man agitated
by the spasms of a convulsion.

It is surely not to be observed without indignation, that men may
be found of minds mean enough to be satisfied with this treatment;
wretches who are proud to obtain the privilege of madmen, and
can, without shame and without regret, consider themselves as
receiving hourly pardons from their companions and giving them
continual opportunities of exercising their patience and boasting
their clemency.

Pride is undoubtedly the original of anger, but pride, like every
other passion, if it once breaks loose from reason, counteracts its
own purposes.   A passionate man, upon the review of his day, will
have very few gratifications to offer to his pride when he has considered how his outrages were caused, why they were borne, and
in what they are likely to end at last.

Those sudden bursts of rage generally break out upon small occasions, for life, unhappy as it is, cannot supply great evils as frequently as the man of fire thinks it fit to be enraged. Therefore the first reflection upon his violence must show him that he is mean enough to be driven from his post by every petty incident, that he is the mere slave of casualty, and that his reason and virtue are in the power of the wind.

One motive there is of these loud extravagancies, which a man is careful to conceal from others and does not always discover to himself. He that finds knowledge narrow and his arguments weak and by consequence his suffrage not much regarded, is sometimes in hope of gaining that attention by his clamours, which he cannot otherwise obtain, and is pleased with remembering that at least he made himself heard, that he had the power to interrupt those whom he could not confute, and suspend the decision which he could not guide.

Of this kind is the fury to which many men give way among their servants and domestics. They feel their own ignorance, they see their own insignificance, and therefore they endeavour by their fury to fright away contempt from before them, when they know it must follow them behind, and think themselves eminently masters when they see one folly tamely complied with, only lest refusal or delay should provoke them to a greater.

These temptations cannot but be owned to have some force. It is so little pleasing to any man to see himself wholly overlooked in the mass of things, that he may be allowed to try a few expedients for procuring some kind of supplemental dignity and use some endeavour to add weight, by the violence of his temper, to the lightness of his other powers. But this has now been long practised, and found upon the most exact estimate not to produce advantages equal to its inconveniences; for it appears not that a man can by uproar, tumult, and bluster, alter any one's opinion of his understanding or gain influence except over those whom fortune or nature have made his dependants.

He may, by a steady perseverance in his ferocity, fright his children and harass his servants, but the rest of the world will look on and laugh; and he will have the comfort at last of thinking that he lives only to raise contempt and hatred, emotions to which wisdom and virtue would be always unwilling to give occasion. He has contrived only to make those fear him, whom every reasonable being is endeavouring to endear by kindness, and must content himself with the pleasure of a triumph obtained by trampling on them who could not resist. He must perceive that the apprehension which his presence causes is not the awe of his virtue but the dread of his brutality, and that he has given up the felicity of being loved without gaining the honour of being reverenced.

But this is not the only ill consequence of the frequent indulgence of this blustering passion which a man, by often calling to his assistance, will teach in a short time to intrude before the summons, to rush upon him with resistless violence and without any previous notice of its approach. He will find himself liable to be inflamed at the first touch of provocation, and unable to retain his resentment till he has a full conviction of the offence, to proportion his anger to the cause, or to regulate it by prudence or by duty. When a man has once suffered his mind to be thus vitiated, he becomes one of the most hateful and unhappy beings. He can give no security to himself that he shall not, at the next interview, alienate by some sudden transport his dearest friend, or break out upon some slight contradiction into such terms of rudeness as can never be perfectly forgotten. Whoever converses with him lives with the suspicion and solicitude of a man that plays with a tame tiger, always under a necessity of watching the moment, in which the capricious savage shall begin to growl.

It is told by Prior, in a panegyric on the Duke of Dorset, that his servants used to put themselves in his way when he was angry because he was sure to recompense them for any indignities which he made them suffer.   This is the round of a passionate man's life; he contracts debts when he is furious, which his virtue, if he has virtue, obliges him to discharge at the return of reason.   He spends his time in outrage and acknowledgment, injury and reparation. Or if there be any who hardens himself in oppression and justifies the wrong because he has done it, his insensibility can make small part of his praise or his happiness; he only adds deliberate to hasty folly, aggravates petulance by contumacy, and destroys the only plea that he can offer for the tenderness and patience of mankind.

Yet even this degree of depravity we may be content to pity, because it seldom wants a punishment equal to its guilt.   Nothing is more despicable or more miserable than the old age of a passionate man.   When the vigour of youth fails him, and his amusements pall with frequent repetition, his occasional rage sinks by decay of strength into peevishness; that peevishness, for want of novelty and variety, becomes habitual; the world falls off from around him, and he is left, as Homer expresses it, φθινύθων φίλον χῆρ, to devour his own heart in solitude and contempt.

DOMESTIC SERVICE (12)

Saturday, 28th April 1750

—Miserum parva stipe focilat, ut pudibundos
Exercere sales inter convivia possit. . . .
. . . Tu mitis, et acri
Asperitate carens, positoque per omnia fastu,
Inter ut aequales, unus numeraris amicos,
Obsequiumque doces, et amorem quaeris amando.

De Laude Pisonis.

Unlike the ribald, whose licentious jest
Pollutes his banquet, and insults his guest;
From wealth and grandeur easy to descend,
Thou joy'st to lose the master in the friend:
We round thy board the cheerful menials see,
Gay with the smile of bland equality;
No social care the gracious lord disdains;
Love prompts to love, and rev'rence rev'rence gains.

Sir,

As you seem to have devoted your labours to virtue I cannot forbear to inform you of one species of cruelty with which the life of a man of letters, perhaps, does not often make him acquainted; and which, as it seems to produce no other advantage to those that practise it than a short gratification of thoughtless vanity, may become less common when it has been once exposed in its various forms and its full magnitude.

I am the daughter of a country gentleman, whose family is numerous, and whose estate, not at first sufficient to supply us with affluence, has been lately so much impaired by an unsuccessful lawsuit, that all the younger children are obliged to try such means as their education affords them for procuring the necessaries of life. Distress and curiosity concurred to bring me to London, where I was received by a relation with the coldness which misfortune generally finds. A week, a long week, I lived with my cousin before the most vigilant inquiry could procure us the least hopes of a place, in which time I was much better qualified to bear all the vexations of servitude. The first two days she was content to pity me, and only wished I had not been quite so well bred; but people must comply with their circumstances. This lenity, however, was soon at an end, and for the remaining part of the week I heard every hour of the pride of my family, the obstinacy of my father, and of people better born than myself that were common servants.

At last, on Saturday noon, she told me, with very visible satisfaction, that Mrs. Bombasine, the great silk-mercer's lady, wanted a maid, and a fine place it would be, for there would be nothing to do but to clean my mistress's room, get up her linen, dress the young ladies, wait at tea in the morning, take care of a little miss just come from nurse, and then sit down to my needle. But madam was a woman of great spirit, and would not be contradicted, and therefore I should take care, for good places were not easily to be got.

With these cautions I waited on Madam Bombasine, of whom the first sight gave me no ravishing ideas. She was two yards round the waist, her voice was at once loud and squeaking, and her face brought to my mind the picture of the full moon. 'Are you the young woman,' says she, 'that are come to offer yourself? It is strange, when people of substance want a servant, how soon it is the town-talk: but they know they shall have a bellyful that live with me. Not like people at the other end of the town, we dine at one o'clock. But I never take anybody without a character; what friends do you come of?' I then told her that my father was a gentleman and that we had been unfortunate. 'A great misfortune, indeed, to come to me, and have three meals a day! So your father was a gentleman, and you are a gentlewoman, I suppose —such gentlewomen!' 'Madam, I did not mean to claim any exemptions, I only answered your inquiry.' 'Such gentlewomen! People should set their children to good trades and keep them off the parish. Pray go to the other end of the town, there are gentlewomen if they would pay their debts: I am sure we have lost enough by gentlewomen.' Upon this her broad face grew broader with triumph, and I was afraid she would have taken me for the pleasure of continuing her insult; but, happily, the next word was: 'Pray, Mrs. Gentlewoman, troop downstairs.' You may believe I obeyed her.

I returned and met with a better reception from my cousin than I expected; for while I was out she had heard that Mrs. Standish, whose husband had lately been raised from a clerk in an office to be commissioner of the excise, had taken a fine house and wanted a maid.

To Mrs. Standish I went, and after having waited six hours was at last admitted to the top of the stairs, when she came out of her room with two of her company. There was a smell of punch. 'So, young woman, you want a place; whence do you come?'

'From the country, madam.' 'Yes, they all come out of the country! And what brought you to town, a bastard? Where do you lodge? At the Seven Dials? What, you never heard of the foundling house?' Upon this they all laughed so obstreperously that I took the opportunity of sneaking off in the tumult.

I then heard of a place at an elderly lady's. She was at cards; but in two hours, I was told, she would speak to me. She asked me if I could keep an account, and ordered me to write. I wrote two lines out of some book that lay by her. She wondered what people meant to breed up poor girls to write at that rate. 'I suppose, Mrs. Flirt, if I was to see your work it would be fine stuff! You may walk. I will not have love-letters written from my house to every young fellow in the street.'

Two days after I went on the same pursuit to Lady Lofty, dressed, as I was directed, in what little ornaments I had, because she had lately got a place at court. Upon the first sight of me she turns to the woman that showed me in: 'Is this the lady that wants a place? Pray, what place would you have, miss? A maid of honour's place? Servants nowadays!' 'Madam, I heard you wanted——' 'Wanted what? Somebody finer than myself! A pretty servant, indeed. I should be afraid to speak to her. I suppose, Mrs. Mynx, these fine hands cannot bear wetting. A servant indeed! Pray move off—I am resolved to be the head person in this house. You are ready dressed, the taverns will be open.'

I went to inquire for the next place in a clean linen gown, and heard the servant tell his lady there was a young woman, but he saw she would not do. I was brought up, however. 'Are you the trollop that has the impudence to come for my place? What, you have hired that nasty gown and are come to steal a better!' 'Madam, I have another, but being obliged to walk——' 'Then these are your manners, with your blushes and your courtesies, to come to me in your worst gown.' 'Madam, give me leave to wait upon you in my other.' 'Wait on me, you saucy slut! Then you are sure of coming—I could not let such a drab come near me. Here, you girl, that came up with her, have you touched her? If you have, wash your hands before you dress me. Such trollops! Get you down. What, whimpering? Pray walk.'

I went away with tears, for my cousin had lost all patience. However, she told me that, having a respect for my relations, she was willing to keep me out of the street, and would let me have another week.

The first day of this week I saw two places. At one I was asked where I had lived. And upon my answer was told by the lady that people should qualify themselves in ordinary places, for she should never have done if she was to follow girls about. At the other house I was a smirking hussey, and that sweet face I might make money of. For her part, it was a rule with her never to take any creature that thought herself handsome.

The three next days were spent in Lady Bluff's entry, where I waited six hours every day for the pleasure of seeing the servants peep at me and go away laughing. 'Madam will stretch her small shanks in the entry; she will know the house again.' At sunset the two first days I was told that my lady would see me to-morrow, and on the third, that her woman stayed.

My week was now near its end, and I had no hopes of a place. My relation, who always laid upon me the blame of every miscarriage, told me that I must learn to humble myself, and that all great ladies had particular ways; that if I went on in that manner, she could not tell who would keep me; she had known many that had refused places sell their clothes and beg in the streets.

It was to no purpose that the refusal was declared by me to be never on my side; I was reasoning against interest and against stupidity. And therefore I comforted myself with the hope of succeeding better in my next attempt, and went to Mrs. Courtly, a very fine lady who had routs at her house, and saw the best company in town.

I had not waited two hours before I was called up, and found Mr. Courtly and his lady at piquet in the height of good humour. This I looked on as a favourable sign and stood at the lower end of the room in expectation of the common questions. At last Mr. Courtly called out, after a whisper: 'Stand facing the light, that one may see you.' I changed my place, and blushed. They frequently turned their eyes upon me, and seemed to discover many subjects of merriment; for, at every look, they whispered and laughed with the most violent agitations of delight. At last Mr. Courtly cried out: 'Is that colour your own, child?' 'Yes,' says the lady, 'if she has not robbed the kitchen hearth.' This was so happy a conceit that it renewed the storm of laughter and they threw down their cards in hopes of better sport. The lady then called me to her, and began, with an affected gravity, to inquire what I could do? 'But first turn about, and let us see your fine shape. Well, what are you fit for, Mrs. Mum? You would find your tongue, I suppose, in the kitchen.' 'No, no,' says Mr. Courtly, 'the girl's a good girl yet; but I am afraid a brisk young fellow, with fine tags on his shoulder—— Come, child, hold up your head; what? you have stole nothing.' 'Not yet,' says the lady, 'but she hopes to steal your heart quickly.' Here was a laugh of happiness and triumph, prolonged by the confusion which I could no longer repress. At last the lady recollected herself: 'Stole! no—but if I had her, I should watch her; for that downcast eye. Why cannot you look people in the face?' 'Steal!' says her husband, 'she would steal nothing but perhaps a few ribbons before they were left off by her lady.' 'Sir,' answered I, 'why should you, by supposing me a thief, insult one from whom you had received no injury?' 'Insult!' says the lady. 'Are you come here to be a servant, you fancy baggage, and talk of insulting? What will this world come to if a gentleman may not jest with a servant. Well, such servants! pray begone, and see when you will have the honour to be so insulted again. Servants insulted—a fine time—— Insulted! Get downstairs, you slut, or the footman shall insult you.'

The last day of the last week was now coming, and my kind cousin talked of sending me down in the wagon, to preserve me from bad courses. But in the morning she came and told me that she had one trial more for me. Euphemia wanted a maid, and perhaps I might do for her; for, like me, she must fall her crest, being forced to lay down her chariot upon the loss of half her fortune by bad securities, and with her way of giving her money to everybody that pretended to want it, she could have little beforehand; therefore I might serve her; for, with all her fine sense, she must not pretend to be nice.

I went immediately and met at the door a young gentlewoman, who told me she had herself been hired that morning, but that she was ordered to bring any that offered upstairs. I was accordingly introduced to Euphemia, who, when I came in, laid down her book and told me that she sent for me, not to gratify an idle curiosity but lest my disappointment might be made still more grating by incivility; that she was in pain to deny anything, much more what was no favour; that she saw nothing in my appearance which did not make her wish for my company; but that another, whose claims might perhaps be equal, had come before me. The thought of being so near to such a place, and missing it, brought tears into my eyes, and my sobs hindered me from returning my acknowledgments. She rose up confused, and supposing by my concern that I was distressed, placed me by her, and made me tell my story; which when she had heard, she put two guineas into my hand,

ordering me to lodge near her and make use of her table till she
could provide for me.   I am now under her protection, and know
not how to show my gratitude better than by giving this account to
the *Rambler*.

ZOSIMA.

DUTY OF SECRECY (13)

Tuesday, 1st May 1750

Commissumque teges et vino tortus et irâ.

HORACE.

And let not wine or anger wrest
Th' intrusted secret from your breast.

FRANCIS.

IT is related by Quintus Curtius, that the Persians always conceived
an invincible contempt of a man who had violated the laws of
secrecy, for they thought that however he might be deficient in the
qualities requisite to actual excellence, the negative virtues at least
were in his power, and though he perhaps could not speak well if
he was to try, it was still easy for him not to speak.

In forming this opinion of the easiness of secrecy, they seem to
have considered it as opposed not to treachery but loquacity, and
to have conceived the man whom they thus censured not frighted
by menaces to reveal, or bribed by promises to betray, but incited by
the mere pleasure of talking or some other motive equally trifling,
to lay open his heart without reflection, and to let whatever he knew
slip from him, only for want of power to retain it.   Whether, by
their settled and avowed scorn of thoughtless talkers, the Persians
were able to diffuse to any great extent the virtue of taciturnity, we
are hindered by the distances of those times from being able to discover, there being very few memoirs remaining of the court of
Persepolis, nor any distinct accounts handed down to us of their
office clerks, their ladies of the bedchamber, their attorneys, their
chambermaids or their footmen.   In these latter ages, though the
old animosity against a prattler is still retained, it appears wholly to
have lost its effects upon the conduct of mankind.   For secrets are
so seldom kept, that it may with some reason be doubted whether
the ancients were not mistaken in their first postulate, whether the
quality of retention be so generally bestowed, and whether a secret

has not some subtle volatility by which it escapes imperceptibly at the smallest vent, or some power of fermentation by which it expands itself so as to burst the heart that will not give it way.

Those that study either the body or the mind of man very often find the most specious and pleasing theory falling under the weight of contrary experience; and instead of gratifying their vanity by inferring effects from causes, they are always reduced at last to conjecture causes from effects. That it is easy to be secret the speculatist can demonstrate in his retreat, and therefore thinks himself justified in placing confidence. The man of the world knows that, whether difficult or not, it is uncommon, and therefore finds himself rather inclined to search after the reason of this universal failure in one of the most important duties of society.

The vanity of being known to be trusted with a secret is generally one of the chief motives to disclose it; for however absurd it may be thought to boast an honour by an act which shows that it was conferred without merit, yet most men seem rather inclined to confess the want of virtue than of importance, and more willingly show their influence, though at the expense of their probity, than glide through life with no other pleasure than the private consciousness of fidelity, which, while it is preserved, must be without praise except from the single person who tries and knows it.

There are many ways of telling a secret, by which a man exempts himself from the reproaches of his conscience and gratifies his pride without suffering himself to believe that he impairs his virtue. He tells the private affairs of his patron or his friend only to those from whom he would not conceal his own; he tells them to those who have no temptation to betray the trust, or with a denunciation of a certain forfeiture of his friendship if he discovers that they become public.

Secrets are very frequently told in the first ardour of kindness or of love, for the sake of proving by so important a sacrifice sincerity or tenderness; but with this motive, though it be strong in itself, vanity concurs, since every man desires to be most esteemed by those whom he loves, or with whom he converses, with whom he passes his hours of pleasure, and to whom he retires from business and from care.

When the discovery of secrets is under consideration there is always a distinction carefully to be made between our own and those of another, those of which we are fully masters as they affect only our own interest, and those which are reposited with us in trust and involve the happiness of convenience of such as we have no right to expose to hazard.   To tell our own secrets is generally folly, but that folly is without guilt; to communicate those with which we are entrusted is always treachery, and treachery for the most part combined with folly.

There have indeed been some enthusiastic and irrational zealots for friendship, who have maintained and perhaps believed that one friend has a right to all that is in possession of another, and that therefore it is a violation of kindness to exempt any secret from this boundless confidence.   Accordingly, a late female minister of state has been shameless enough to inform the world that she used, when she wanted to extract anything from her sovereign, to remind her of Montaigne's reasoning, who has determined that to tell a secret to a friend is no breach of fidelity, because the number of persons trusted is not multiplied, a man and his friend being virtually the same.

That such a fallacy could be imposed upon any human understanding, or that an author could have advanced a position so remote from truth and reason, any other way than as a declaimer, to show to what extent he could stretch his imagination, and with what strength he could press his principle, would scarcely have been credible, had not this lady kindly shown us how far weakness may be deluded, or indolence amused.   But since it appears that even this sophistry has been able with the help of a strong desire to repose in quiet upon the understanding of another, to mislead honest intentions, and an understanding not contemptible, it may not be superfluous to remark that those things which are common among friends are only such as either possesses in his own right and can alienate or destroy without injury to any other person.   Without this limitation confidence must run on without end, the second person may tell the secret to the third upon the same principle as he received it from the first, and the third may hand it forward to a fourth till at last it is told in the round of friendship to them from whom it was the first intention to conceal it.

The confidence which Caius has of the faithfulness of Titius is nothing more than an opinion which himself cannot know to be true, and which Claudius who first tells his secret to Caius may know to be false; and therefore the trust is transferred by Caius, if he reveal what has been told him to one from whom the person originally concerned would have withheld it.   And whatever may be the event, Caius has hazarded the happiness of his friend without necessity and without permission, and has put that trust in the hand of fortune which was given only to virtue.

All the arguments upon which a man who is telling the private affairs of another may ground his confidence of security, he must upon reflection know to be uncertain, because he finds them without effect upon himself. When he is imagining that Titius will be cautious from a regard to his interest, his reputation, or his duty, he ought to reflect that he is himself at that instant acting in opposition to all these reasons, and revealing what interest, reputation, and duty direct him to conceal.

Everyone feels that in his own case he should consider the man incapable of trust who believed himself at liberty to tell whatever he knew to the first whom he should conclude deserving of his confidence. Therefore Caius, in admitting Titius to the affairs imparted only to himself, must know that he violates his faith, since he acts contrary to the intention of Claudius, to whom that faith was given. For promises of friendship are, like all others, useless and vain unless they are made in some known sense, adjusted and acknowledged by both parties.

I am not ignorant that many questions may be started relating to the duty of secrecy, where the affairs are of public concern, where subsequent reasons may arise to alter the appearance and nature of the trust; that the manner in which the secret was told may change the degree of obligation; and that the principles upon which a man is chosen for a confidant may not always equally constrain him. But these scruples, if not too intricate, are of too extensive consideration for my present purpose, nor are they such as generally occur in common life; and though casuistical knowledge be useful in proper hands, yet it ought by no means to be carelessly exposed, since most will use it rather to lull than awaken their own consciences; and the threads of reasoning, on which truth is suspended, are frequently drawn to such subtlety that common eyes cannot perceive, and common sensibility cannot feel them.

The whole doctrine as well as practice of secrecy is so perplexing and dangerous, that next to him who is compelled to trust I think him unhappy who is chosen to be trusted; for he is often involved in scruples without the liberty of calling in the help of any other understanding; he is frequently drawn into guilt under the appearance of friendship and honesty; and sometimes subjected to suspicion by the treachery of others who are engaged without his knowledge in the same schemes. For he that has one confidant has generally more, and when he is at last betrayed, is in doubt on whom he shall fix the crime.

The rules, therefore, that I shall propose concerning secrecy, and from which I think it not safe to deviate without long and exact deliberation, are: Never to solicit the knowledge of a secret.　Not willingly, nor without many limitations, to accept such confidence when it is offered.　When a secret is once admitted, to consider the truth as of a very high nature, important as society and sacred as truth, and therefore not to be violated for any incidental convenience, or slight appearance of contrary fitness.

AN AUTHOR'S WRITING AND CONVERSATION CONTRASTED (14)

Saturday, 5th March 1750

. . . Nil fuit unquam
Sic dispar sibi. . . .

HORACE.

Sure such a various creature ne'er was known.

FRANCIS.

AMONG the many inconsistencies which folly produces or infirmity suffers in the human mind, there has often been observed a manifest and striking contrariety between the life of an author and his writings; and Milton, in a letter to a learned stranger by whom he had been visited, with great reason congratulates himself upon the consciousness of being found equal to his own character, and having preserved in a private and familiar interview that reputation which his works had procured him.

Those whom the appearance of virtue or the evidence of genius have tempted to a nearer knowledge of the writer in whose performances they may be found, have indeed had frequent reason to repent their curiosity: the bubble that sparkled before them has become common water at the touch; the phantom of perfection has vanished when they wished to press it to their bosom.　They have lost the pleasure of imagining how far humanity may be exalted, and perhaps felt themselves less inclined to toil up the steeps of virtue when they observe those who seem best able to point the way loitering below, as either afraid of the labour or doubtful of the reward.

It has been long the custom of the oriental monarchs to hide themselves in gardens and palaces, to avoid the conversation of

mankind, and to be known to their subjects only by their edicts.
The same policy is no less necessary to him that writes than to him
that governs; for men would not more patiently submit to be taught
than commanded, by one known to have the same follies and weaknesses with themselves.   A sudden intruder into the closet of an
author would perhaps feel equal indignation with the officer who,
having long solicited admission into the presence of Sardanapalus,
saw him not consulting upon laws, inquiring into grievances, or
modelling armies, but employed in feminine amusement, and
directing the ladies in their work.

It is not difficult to conceive, however, that for many reasons a
man writes much better than he lives.   For, without entering into
refined speculations, it may be shown much easier to design than to
perform.   A man proposes his schemes of life in a state of abstraction and disengagement, except from the enticements of hope, the
solicitations of affection, the importunities of appetite, or the
depressions of fear, and is in the same state with him that teaches
upon land the art of navigation, to whom the sea is always smooth
and the wind always prosperous.

The mathematicians are well acquainted with the difference
between pure science, which has to do only with ideas, and the
application of its laws to the use of life, in which they are con-
strained to submit to the imperfection of matter and the influence
of accidents.   Thus in moral discussions it is to be remembered
that many impediments obstruct our practice, which very easily
give way to theory.   The speculatist is only in danger of erroneous
reasoning, but the man involved in life has his own passions and
those of others to encounter, and is embarrassed with a thousand
inconveniences, which confound him with variety of impulse, and
either perplex or obstruct his way.   He is forced to act without
deliberation, and obliged to choose before he can examine; he is
surprised by sudden alterations of the state of things, and changes
his measures according to superficial appearances; he is led by
others, either because he is indolent or because he is timorous; he is
sometimes afraid to know what is right, and sometimes finds friends
or enemies diligent to deceive him.

We are, therefore, not to wonder that most fail, amidst tumult
and snares and danger, in the observance of those precepts which
they laid down in solitude, safety, and tranquillity, with a mind
unbiased and with liberty unobstructed.   It is the condition of
our present state to see more than we can attain; the exactest vigilance and caution can never maintain a single day of unmingled

innocence, much less can the utmost efforts of incorporated mind reach the summits of speculative virtue.

It is, however, necessary for the idea of perfection to be proposed, that we may have some object to which our endeavours are to be directed; and he that is most deficient in the duties of life makes some atonement for his faults if he warns others against his own failings, and hinders, by the salubrity of his admonitions, the contagion of his example.

Nothing is more unjust, however common, than to charge with hypocrisy him that expresses zeal for those virtues which he neglects to practise; since he may be sincerely convinced of the advantages of conquering his passions, without having yet obtained the victory, as a man may be confident of the advantages of a voyage or a journey, without having courage of industry to undertake it, and may honestly recommend to others those attempts which he neglects himself.

The interest which the corrupt part of mankind have in hardening themselves against every motive to amendment, has disposed them to give to these contradictions, when they can be produced against the cause of virtue, that weight which they will not allow them in any other case. They see men act in opposition to their interest, without supposing that they do not know it. Those who give way to the sudden violence of passion, and forsake the most important pursuits for petty pleasures, are not supposed to have changed their opinions or to approve their own conduct. In moral or religious questions alone they determine the sentiments by the actions, and charge every man with endeavouring to impose upon the world whose writings are not confirmed by his life. They never consider that they themselves neglect or practise something, every day, inconsistently with their own settled judgment; nor discover that the conduct of the advocates for virtue can little increase, or lessen, the obligations of their dictates. Argument is to be invalidated only by argument, and is in itself of the same force, whether or not it convinces him by whom it is proposed.

Yet since this prejudice, however unreasonable, is always likely to have some prevalence, it is the duty of every man to take care lest he should hinder the efficacy of his own instructions. When he desires to gain the belief of others, he should show that he believes himself; and when he teaches the fitness of virtue by his reasonings, he should, by his example, prove its possibility. This much at least may be required of him, that he shall not act worse than others because he writes better, nor imagine that, by the merit of his genius, he may claim indulgence beyond mortals of the lower classes, and be excused for want of prudence or neglect of virtue.

Bacon, in his history of the winds, after having offered something to the imagination as desirable, often proposes lower advantages in its place to the reason as attainable. The same method may be sometimes pursued in moral endeavours, which this philosopher has observed in natural inquiries. Having first set positive and absolute excellence before us, we may be pardoned though we sink down to humbler virtue, trying, however, to keep our point always in view, and struggling not to lose ground though we cannot gain it.

It is recorded of Sir Matthew Hale, that he for a long time concealed the consecration of himself to the stricter duties of religion, lest, by some flagitious and shameful action he should bring piety into disgrace. For the same reason it may be prudent for a writer who apprehends that he shall not enforce his own maxims by his domestic character, to conceal his name, that he may not injure them.

There are, indeed, a greater number whose curiosity to gain a more familiar knowledge of successful writers, is not so much prompted by an opinion of their power to improve as to delight, and who expect from them not arguments against vice, or dissertations on temperance or justice, but flights of wit, and sallies of pleasantry, or at least acute remarks, nice distinctions, justness of sentiment, and elegance of diction.

This expectation is indeed specious and probable, and yet such is the fate of all human hopes, that it is very often frustrated, and those who raise admiration by their books, disgust by their company. A man of letters for the most part spends, in the privacies of study, that season of life in which the manners are to be softened into ease, and polished into elegance, and when he has gained knowledge enough to be respected, has neglected the minuter acts by which he might have pleased. When he enters life, if his temper is soft and timorous, he is diffident and bashful, from the knowledge of his defects; or if he was born with spirit and resolution, he is ferocious and arrogant, from the consciousness of his merit: he is either dissipated by the awe of company, and unable to recollect his reading, and arrange his arguments; or he is hot and dogmatical, quick in opposition and tenacious in defence, disabled by his own violence, and confused by his haste to triumph.

The graces of writing and conversation are of different kinds,

and though he who excels in one might have been with opportunities and application equally successful in the other, yet as many
please by extemporary talk, though utterly unacquainted with the
more accurate method and more laboured beauties which composition requires; so it is very possible that men, wholly accustomed to works of study, may be without that readiness of conception and affluence of language, always necessary to colloquial
entertainment.   They may want address to watch the hints which
conversation offers for the display of their particular attainments, or
they may be so much unfurnished with matter on common subjects,
that discourse not professedly literary glides over them as heterogeneous bodies, without admitting their conceptions to mix in the
circulation.

A transition from an author's book to his conversation, is too
often like an entrance into a large city after a distant prospect.
Remotely, we see nothing but spires of temples and turrets of
palaces, and imagine it the residence of splendour, grandeur, and
magnificence; but, when we have passed the gates, we find it
perplexed with narrow passages, disgraced with despicable cottages,
embarrassed with obstructions, and clouded with smoke.

MISERIES OF LITERARY EMINENCE (16)

Saturday, 12th *May* 1750

Multis dicendi copia torrens,
Et sua mortifera est facundia.

JUVENAL.

Some who the depths of eloquence have found,
In that unnavigable stream were drown'd.

DRYDEN.

SIR,

I am the modest young man whom you favoured with your
advice in a late paper; and as I am very far from suspecting that you
foresaw the numberless inconveniences which I have, by following
it, brought upon myself, I will lay my condition open before you,
for you seem bound to extricate me from the perplexities in which
your counsel, however innocent in the intention, has contributed to
involve me.

You told me, as you thought to my comfort, that a writer might
easily find means of introducing his genius to the world, for the

presses of England were open. This I have now fatally experienced;
the press is indeed open.

> Facilis descensus Averni,
> Noctes atque dies patet atri janua Ditis.

> The gates of hell are open night and day;
> Smooth the descent, and easy is the way.
>
> DRYDEN.

The means of doing hurt to ourselves are always at hand. I
immediately sent to a printer and contracted with him for an
impression of several thousand of my pamphlet. While it was at
the press I was seldom absent from the printing-house, and continually urged the workmen to haste by solicitations, promises,
and rewards. From the day all other pleasures were excluded by
the delightful employment of correcting the sheets; and from the
night sleep was generally banished by anticipation of the happiness
which every hour was bringing nearer.

At last the time of publication approached, and my heart beat
with the raptures of an author. I was above all little precautions
and, in defiance of envy or of criticism, set my name upon the title,
without sufficiently considering that what has once passed the press
is irrevocable, and that though the printing-house may properly be
compared to the infernal regions for the facility of its entrance and
the difficulty with which authors return from it, yet there is this
difference, that a great genius can never return to his former state
by a happy draught of the waters of oblivion.

I am now, Mr. Rambler, known to be an author, and am condemned, irreversibly condemned, to all the miseries of high reputation. The first morning after publication, my friends assembled
about me; I presented each, as is usual, with a copy of my book.
They looked into the first pages, but were hindered by their
admiration from reading further. The first pages are indeed very
elaborate. Some passages they particularly dwelt upon, as more
eminently beautiful than the rest; and some delicate strokes and
secret elegancies I pointed out to them, which had escaped their
observation. I then begged of them to forbear their compliments,
and invited them, I could do no less, to dine with me at a tavern.
After dinner the book was resumed; but their praises very often so
much overpowered my modesty, that I was forced to put about the
glass, and had often no means of repressing the clamours of their
admiration but by thundering to the drawer for another bottle.

Next morning another set of my acquaintance congratulated me upon my performance, with such importunity of praise, that I was again forced to obviate their civilities by a treat. On the third day I had yet a greater number of applauders to put to silence in the same manner; and on the fourth those whom I had entertained the first day came again, having, in the perusal of the remaining part of the book, discovered so many forcible sentences and masterly touches that it was impossible for me to bear the repetition of their commendations. I therefore persuaded them once more to adjourn to the tavern and choose some other subject, on which I might share in the conversation. But it was not in their power to withhold their attention from my performance, which had so entirely taken possession of their minds that no entreaties of mine could change their topic, and I was obliged to stifle, with claret, that praise which neither my modesty could hinder nor my uneasiness repress.

The whole week was thus spent in a kind of literary revel, and I have now found that nothing is so expensive as great abilities, unless there is joined with them an insatiable eagerness of praise. For to escape from the pain of hearing myself exalted above the greatest names dead and living of the learned world, it has already cost me two hogsheads of port, fifteen gallons of arrack, ten dozen of claret, and five-and-forty bottles of champagne.

I was resolved to stay at home no longer, and therefore rose early and went to the coffee-house, but found that I had now made myself too eminent for happiness, and that I was no longer to enjoy the pleasure of mixing, upon equal terms, with the rest of the world. As soon as I enter the room I see part of the company raging with envy which they endeavour to conceal, sometimes with the appearance of laughter and sometimes with that of contempt. But the disguise is such that I can discover the secret rancour of their hearts; and as envy is deservedly its own punishment, I frequently indulge myself in tormenting them with my presence.

But though there may be some slight satisfaction received from the mortification of my enemies, yet my benevolence will not suffer me to take any pleasure in the terrors of my friends. I have been cautious, since the appearance of my work, not to give myself more premeditated airs of superiority than the most rigid humility might allow. It is indeed not impossible that I may sometimes have laid down my opinion in a manner that showed a consciousness of my ability to maintain it, or interrupted the conversation when I saw its tendency, without suffering the speaker to waste his time in explaining his sentiments; and indeed I did indulge myself for two days in a custom of drumming with my fingers when the company began to lose themselves in absurdities or to encroach upon subjects which I knew them unqualified to discuss. But I generally acted with great appearance of respect, even to those whose stupidity I pitied in my heart. Yet, notwithstanding this exemplary moderation, so universal is the dread of uncommon powers, and such the unwillingness of mankind to be made wiser, that I have now for some days found myself shunned by all my acquaintance. If I knock at a door nobody is at home, if I enter a coffee-house I have the box to myself. I live in the town like a lion in his desert, or an eagle on his rock, too great for friendship or society, and condemned to solitude by unhappy elevation and dreaded ascendancy.

Nor is my character only formidable to others, but burdensome to myself. I naturally love to talk without much thinking, to scatter my merriment at random, and to relax my thoughts with ludicrous remarks and fanciful images; but such is now the importance of my opinion that I am afraid to offer it lest, by being established too hastily into a maxim, it should be the occasion of error to half the nation; and such is the expectation with which I am attended, when I am going to speak, that I frequently pause to reflect whether what I am about to utter is worthy of myself.

This, sir, is sufficiently miserable, but there are still greater calamities behind. You must have read in Pope and Swift how men of parts have had their closets rifled and their cabinets broke open at the instigation of piratical booksellers for the profit of their works; and it is apparent that there are many prints now sold in the shops of men whom you cannot suspect of sitting for that purpose, and whose likenesses must have been certainly stolen when their names made their faces vendible. These considerations at first put me on my guard, and I have indeed found sufficient reason for my caution, for I have discovered many people examining my countenance with a curiosity that showed their intention to draw it. I immediately left the house but find the same behaviour in another.

Others may be persecuted but I am haunted. I have good reason to believe that eleven painters are now dogging me, for they know that he who can get my face first will make his fortune. I often change my wig and wear my hat over my eyes, by which I hope somewhat to confound them, for you know it is not fair to sell my face without admitting me to share the profit.

I am, however, not so much in pain for my face as for my papers, which I dare neither carry with me nor leave behind. I have indeed taken some measures for their preservation, having put them in an iron chest and fixed a padlock upon my closet. I change my lodgings five times a week, and always remove at the dead of night.

Thus I live, in consequence of having given too great proofs of a predominant genius, in the solitude of a hermit with the anxiety of a miser and the caution of an outlaw. Afraid to show my face lest it should be copied, afraid to speak lest I should injure my character, and to write lest my correspondents should publish my letters; always uneasy lest my servants should steal my papers for the sake of money, or my friends for that of the public. This it is to soar above the rest of mankind; and this representation I lay before you, that I may be informed how to divest myself of the laurels which are so cumbersome to the wearer, and descend to the enjoyment of that quiet from which I find a writer of the first class so fatally debarred.

MISELLUS.

CONTEMPLATION OF DEATH (17)

Tuesday, 15th May 1750

Me non oracula certum,
Sed mors certa facit.

LUCAN.

Let those weak minds, who live in doubt and fear,
To juggling priests for oracles repair;
One certain hour of death to each decreed,
My fixt, my certain soul from doubt has freed.

ROWE.

IT is recorded of some eastern monarch, that he kept an officer in his house whose employment it was to remind him of his mortality, by calling out every morning at a stated hour: 'Remember, prince, that thou shalt die.' And the contemplation of the frailness and uncertainty of our present state appeared of so much importance to Solon of Athens that he left this precept to future ages: 'Keep thine eye fixed upon the end of life.'

A frequent and attentive prospect of that moment which must put a period to all our schemes and deprive us of all our acquisitions, is indeed of the utmost efficacy to the just and rational regulation of our lives; nor would ever anything wicked, or often anything absurd, be undertaken or prosecuted by him who should begin every day with a serious reflection that he is born to die.

The disturbers of our happiness in this world are our desires, our griefs, and our fears, and to all these the consideration of mortality is a certain and adequate remedy. Think, says Epictetus, frequently on poverty, banishment, and death, and thou wilt then never indulge violent desires, or give up thy heart to mean sentiments. οὐδὲν οὐδεποε τατεινὸν ἐνθυμήσῃ, οὐπ τε ἄγαν ἐπιθυμήσεις τινὸς.

That the maxim of Epictetus is founded on just observation will easily be granted, when we reflect how that vehemence of eagerness after the common objects of pursuit is kindled in our minds. We represent to ourselves the pleasures of some future possession, and suffer our thoughts to dwell attentively upon it till it has wholly engrossed the imagination and permits us not to conceive any happiness but its attainment, or any misery but its loss. Every other satisfaction which the bounty of providence has scattered over life is neglected as inconsiderable in comparison of the great object which we have placed before us, and is thrown from us as encumbering our activity, or trampled under foot as standing in our way.

Every man has experienced how much of this ardour has been remitted when a sharp or tedious sickness has set death before his eyes. The extensive influence of greatness, the glitter of wealth, the praises of admirers, and the attendance of supplicants, have appeared vain and empty things when the last hour seemed to be approaching; and the same appearance they would always have, if the same thought was always predominant. We should then find the absurdity of stretching out our arms incessantly to grasp that which we cannot keep, and wearing out our lives in endeavours to add new turrets to the fabric of ambition, when the foundation itself is shaking, and the ground on which it stands is mouldering away.

All envy is proportionate to desire. We are uneasy at the attainments of another, according as we think our own happiness would be advanced by the addition of that which he withholds from us; and therefore whatever depresses immoderate wishes will, at the same time, set the heart free from the corrosion of envy and exempt us from that vice, which is, above most others, tormenting to ourselves, hateful to the world, and productive of mean artifices and sordid projects. He that considers how soon he must close his life, will find nothing of so much importance as to close it well; and therefore look with indifference upon whatever is useless to that purpose. Whoever reflects frequently upon the uncertainty of his own duration, will find out that the state of others is not more permanent, and that what can confer nothing on himself very desirable, cannot so much improve the condition of a rival as to make him much superior to those from whom he has carried the prize, a prize too mean to deserve a very obstinate opposition.

Even grief, that passion to which the virtuous and tender mind is particularly subject, will be obviated or alleviated by the same thoughts. It will be obviated if all the blessings of our condition are enjoyed with a constant sense of this uncertain tenure. If we remember that whatever we possess is to be in our hands but a very little time, and that the little which our most lively hopes can promise us, may be made less by ten thousand accidents, we shall not much repine at a loss of which we cannot estimate the value, but of which, though we are not able to tell the least amount, we know, with sufficient certainty the greatest, and are convinced that the greatest is not much to be regretted.

But if any passion has so much usurped our understanding as not to suffer us to enjoy advantages with the moderation prescribed by reason, it is not too late to apply this remedy, when we find ourselves sinking under sorrow and inclined to pine for that which is irrecoverably vanished. We may then usefully revolve the uncertainty of our own condition and the folly of lamenting that from which, if it had stayed a little longer, we should ourselves have been taken away.

With regard to the sharpest and most melting sorrow, that which arises from the loss of those whom we have loved with tenderness, it may be observed that friendship between mortals can be contracted on no other terms than that one must some time mourn for the other's death: and this grief will always yield to the survivor one consolation proportionate to his affliction; for the pain, whatever it be, that he himself feels his friend has escaped.

Nor is fear, the most overbearing and resistless of all our passions, less to be temperated by this universal medicine of the mind. The frequent contemplation of death, as it shows the vanity of all human good, discovers likewise the lightness of all terrestrial evil, which certainly can last no longer than the subject upon which it acts and, according to the old observation, must be shorter as it is more violent. The most cruel calamity which misfortune can produce must, by the necessity of nature, be quickly at an end.

The soul cannot long be held in prison, but will fly away, and leave a lifeless body to human malice.

Ridetque sui ludibria trunci.

And soaring mocks the broken frame below.

The utmost that we can threaten to one another is that death which, indeed, we may precipitate but cannot retard, and from which, therefore, it cannot become a wise man to buy a reprieve at the expense of virtue, since he knows not how small a portion of time he can purchase, but knows that, whether short or long, it will be made less valuable by the remembrance of the price at which it has been obtained. He is sure that he destroys his happiness but is not sure that he lengthens his life.

The known shortness of life, as it ought to moderate our passions, may likewise, with equal propriety, contract our designs. There is not time for the most forcible genius, and most active industry, to extend its effects beyond a certain sphere. To project the conquest of the world is the madness of mighty princes; to hope for excellence in every science has been the folly of literary heroes; and both have found at last that they have panted for a height of eminence denied to humanity, and have lost many opportunities of making themselves useful and happy by a vain ambition of obtaining a species of honour which the eternal laws of providence have placed beyond the reach of man.

The miscarriages of the great designs of princes are recorded in the histories of the world but are of little use to the bulk of mankind, who seem very little interested in admonitions against errors which they cannot commit. But the fate of learned ambition is a proper subject for every scholar to consider; for who has not had occasion to regret the dissipation of great abilities in a boundless multiplicity of pursuits, to lament the sudden desertion of excellent designs upon the offer of some other subject made inviting by its novelty, and to observe the inaccuracy and deficiencies of works left unfinished by too great an extension of the plan?

It is always pleasing to observe how much more our minds can conceive than our bodies can perform; yet it is our duty, while we continue in this complicated state, to regulate one part of our composition by some regard to the other. We are not to indulge our corporeal appetites with pleasures that impair our intellectual vigour, nor gratify our minds with schemes which we know our lives must fail in attempting to execute. The uncertainty of our duration ought at once to set bounds to our designs, and add incitements to our industry; and when we find ourselves inclined either to immensity in our schemes or sluggishness in our endeavours, we may either check, or animate ourselves by recollecting, with the father of physic, *that art is long, and life is short.*

UNHAPPINESS IN MARRIAGE (18)

Saturday, 19th May 1750

Illic matre carentibus
Privignis mulier temperat innocens,
Nec dotata regit virum
Conjux, nec nitido fidit adulteo.
Dos est magna parentum
Virtus, et metuens alterius tori
Certo foedere castitas.

HORACE.

Not there the guiltless step-dame knows
The baleful draught for orphans to compose;
No wife high-portion'd rules her spouse,
Or trusts her effenc'd lover's faithless vows:
The lovers there for dow'ry claim
The father's virtue, and the spotless fame,
Which dares not break the nuptial tie.

FRANCIS.

THERE is no observation more frequently made by such as employ themselves in surveying the conduct of mankind, than that marriage, though the dictate of nature and the institution of Providence, is yet very often the cause of misery, and that those who enter into that state can seldom forbear to express their repentance and their envy of those whom either chance or caution hath withheld from it.

This general unhappiness has given occasion to many sage maxims among the serious, and smart remarks among the gay. The moralist and the writer of epigrams have equally shown their abilities upon it: some have lamented and some have ridiculed it; but as the faculty of writing has been chiefly a masculine endowment, the reproach of making the world miserable has been always thrown upon the women, and the grave and the merry have equally thought themselves at liberty to conclude either with declamatory complaints or satirical censures of female folly or fickleness, ambition or cruelty, extravagance or lust.

Led by such number of examples and incited by my share in the common interest, I sometimes venture to consider this universal grievance, having endeavoured to divest my heart of all partiality and place myself as a kind of neutral being between the sexes, whose clamours, being equally vented on both sides with all the vehemence of distress, all the apparent confidence of justice, and all the indignation of injured virtue, seem entitled to equal regard. The men have indeed by their superiority of writing, been able to collect the evidence of many ages and raise prejudices in their favour by the venerable testimonies of philosophers, historians, and poets; but the pleas of the ladies appeal to passions of more forcible operation than the reverence of antiquity. If they have not so great names on their side, they have stronger arguments; it is to little purpose that Socrates or Euripides are produced against the sighs of softness and the tears of beauty. The most frigid and inexorable judge would, at least, stand suspended between equal powers, as Lucan was perplexed in the determination of the cause, where the deities were on one side and Cato on the other.

But I who have long studied the severest and most abstracted philosophy have now, in the cool maturity of life, arrived to such command over my passions that I can hear the vociferations of either sex without catching any of the fire from those that utter them. For I have found, by long experience, that a man will sometimes rage at his wife when in reality his mistress has offended him; and a lady complain of the cruelty of her husband when she has no other enemy than bad cards. I do not suffer myself to be any longer imposed upon by oaths on one side or fits on the other; nor when the husband hastens to the tavern and the lady retires to her closet am I always confident that they are driven by their miseries, since I have sometimes reason to believe that they purpose not so much to sooth their sorrows as to animate their fury. But how little credit soever may be given to particular accusations, the general accumulation of the charge shows, with too much evidence, that married persons are not very often advanced in felicity; and, therefore, it may be proper to examine at what avenues so many evils have made their way into the world. With this purpose, I have reviewed the lives of my friends who have been least successful in connubial contracts, and attentively considered by what motives they were incited to marry, and by what principles they regulated their choice.

One of the first of my acquaintances that resolved to quit the unsettled thoughtless condition of a batchelor was Prudentius, a man of slow parts, but not without knowledge or judgment in things which he had leisure to consider gradually before he determined them. Whenever we met at a tavern, it was his province to settle the scheme of our entertainment, contract with the cook, and inform us when we had called for wine to the sum originally proposed. This grave considerer found by deep meditation that a man was no loser by marrying early, even though he contented himself with a less fortune; for estimating the exact worth of annuities, he found that, considering the constant diminution of the value of life with the probable fall of the interest of money, it was not worse to have ten thousand pounds at the age of two-and-twenty years than a much larger fortune at thirty; for many opportunities, says he, occur of improving money, which if a man misses he may not afterwards recover.

Full of these reflections he threw his eyes about him, not in search of beauty or elegance, dignity or understanding, but of a woman with ten thousand pounds. Such a woman in a wealthy part of the kingdom it was not very difficult to find: and by artful management with her father, whose ambition was to make his daughter a gentlewoman, my friend got her, as he boasted to us in confidence two days after his marriage, for a settlement of seventy-three pounds a year less than her fortune might have claimed, and less than he would himself have given if the fools had been but wise enough to delay the bargain.

Thus, at once delighted with the superiority of his parts and the augmentation of his fortune, he carried Furia to his own house, in which he never afterwards enjoyed one hour of happiness. For Furia was a wretch of mean intellect, violent passions, a strong voice, and low education, without any sense of happiness but that which consisted in eating and counting money. Furia was a scold. They agreed in the desire of wealth, but with this difference, that Prudentius was for growing rich by gain, Furia by parsimony. Prudentius would venture his money with chances very much in his favour; but Furia, very wisely observing that what they had was, while they had it, *their own*, thought all traffic too great a hazard, and was for putting it out at low interest upon good security. Prudentius ventured, however, to insure a ship at a very unreasonable price, but happening to lose his money was so tormented with the clamours of his wife that he never durst try a second experiment. He has now grovelled seven-and-forty years under Furia's direction, who never once mentioned him, since his bad luck, by any other name than that of *the insurer*.

The next that married from our society was Florentius. He happened to see Zephyretta in a chariot at a horse-race, danced with her at night, was confirmed in his first ardour, waited on her next morning, and declared himself her lover. Florentius had not knowledge enough of the world to distinguish between the flutter of coquetry and the sprightliness of wit, or between the smile of allurement and that of cheerfulness. He was soon waked from his rapture by conviction that his pleasure was but the pleasure of a day. Zephyretta had in four-and-twenty hours spent her stock of repartee, gone round the circle of her airs, and had nothing remaining for him but childish insipidity, or for her herself but the practice of the same artifices upon new men.

Melissus was a man of parts, capable of enjoying and of improving life. He had passed through the various scenes of gaiety with that indifference and possession of himself, natural to men who have something higher and nobler in their prospect. Retiring to spend the summer in a village little frequented, he happened to lodge in the same house with Ianthe, and was unavoidably drawn to some acquaintance which her wit and politeness soon invited him to improve. Having no opportunity of any other company, they were always together, and as they owed their pleasures to each other they began to forget that any pleasure was enjoyed before their meeting. Melissus, from being delighted with her company, quickly began to be uneasy in her absence, and being sufficiently convinced of the force of her understanding, and finding, as he imagined, such a conformity of temper as declared them formed for each other, addressed her as a lover, after no very long courtship obtained her for his wife, and brought her next winter to town in triumph.

Now began their infelicity. Melissus had only seen her in one scene, where there was no variety of objects to produce the proper excitements to contrary desires. They had both loved solitude and reflection, where there was nothing but solitude and reflection to be loved; but when they came into public life Ianthe discovered those passions which accident rather than hypocrisy had hitherto concealed. She was, indeed, not without the power of thinking, but was wholly without the exertion of that power when either gaiety or splendour played on her imagination. She was expensive in her diversions, vehement in her passions, insatiate of pleasure however dangerous to her reputation, and eager of applause by whomsoever it might be given. This was the wife which Melissus the philosopher found in his retirement, and from whom he expected an associate in his studies and an assistant to his virtues.

Prosapius, upon the death of his younger brother, that the family might not be extinct, married his housekeeper, and has ever since been complaining to his friends that mean notions are instilled into his children, that he is ashamed to sit at his own table, and that his house is uneasy to him for want of suitable companions.

Avaro, master of a very large estate, took a woman of bad reputation, recommended to him by a rich uncle who made that marriage the condition on which he should be his heir. Avaro now wonders to perceive his own fortune, his wife's, and his uncle's, insufficient to give him that happiness which is to be found only with a woman of virtue.

I intend to treat in more papers on this important article of life, and shall therefore make no reflection upon these histories, except that all whom I have mentioned failed to obtain happiness for want of considering that marriage is the strictest tie of perpetual friendship; that there can be no friendship without confidence, and no confidence without integrity; and that he must expect to be wretched who pays to beauty, riches, or politeness, that regard which only virtue and piety can claim.

AFFECTATION (20)

Saturday, 26th May 1750

Ad populum phaleras, ego te intus, et in cute novi.

PERSIUS.

Such pageantry be to the people shown;
There boast thy horse's trappings and thy own:
I know thee to thy bottom; from within
Thy shallow centre to thy utmost skin.

DRYDEN.

AMONG the numerous stratagems by which pride endeavours to recommend folly to regard, there is scarcely one that meets with less success than affectation or a perpetual disguise of the real character by fictitious appearances, whether it be that every man hates falsehood, from the natural congruity of truth to his faculties of reason, or that every man is jealous of the honour of his understanding and thinks his discernment consequentially called in question whenever anything is exhibited under a borrowed form.

This aversion from all kinds of disguise, whatever be its cause, is universally diffused and incessantly in action; nor is it necessary that to exasperate detestation or excite contempt any interest should be invaded or any competition attempted; it is sufficient that there is an intention to deceive, an intention which every heart swells to oppose, and every tongue is busy to detect.

This reflection was awakened in my mind by a very common practice among my correspondents, of writing under characters which they cannot support, which are of no use to the explanation or enforcement of that which they describe or recommend, and which, therefore, since they assume them only for the sake of displaying their abilities, I will advise them for the future to forbear as laborious without advantage.

It is almost a general ambition of those who favour me with their advice for the regulation of my conduct, or their contribution for the assistance of my understanding, to affect the style and the names of ladies. And I cannot always withhold some expression of anger, like Sir Hugh in the comedy, when I happen to find that a woman has a beard. I must therefore warn the gentle Phyllis that she send me no more letters from the Horse Guards, and require of Belinda that she be content to resign her pretensions to female elegance till she has lived three weeks without hearing the politics of Batson's coffee-house. I must indulge myself in the liberty of observation that there were some allusions in Chloris's production sufficient to show that Bracton and Plowden are her favourite authors, and that Euphelia has not been long enough at home to wear out all the traces of the phraseology which she learned in the expedition to Carthagena.

Among all my female friends there was none who gave me more trouble to decipher her true character than Penthesilea, whose letter lay upon my desk three days before I could fix upon the real writer. There was a confusion of images and medley of barbarity which held me long in suspense, till by perseverance I disentangled the perplexity, and found that Penthesilea is the son of a wealthy stock-jobber who spends his morning under his father's eye in Change-Alley, dines at a tavern in Covent Garden, passes his evening in the playhouse, and parts of the night at a gaming-table, and, having learned the dialects of these various regions, has mingled them all in a studied composition.

When Lee was once told by a critic that it was very easy to write like a madman, he answered that it was difficult to write like a madman but easy enough to write like a fool; and I hope to be excused by my kind contributors if, in imitation of this great author, I presume to remind them that it is much easier not to write like a man than to write like a woman.

I have, indeed, some ingenious well-wishers who, without departing from their sex, have found very wonderful appellations. A very smart letter has been sent me from a puny ensign, signed Ajax Telamonius; another, in recommendation of a new treatise upon cards, from a gamester who calls himself Sesostris; and another, upon the improvement of the fishery, from Diocletian. But as these seem only to have picked up their appellations by chance, without endeavouring at any particular imposture, their improprieties are rather instances of blunder than of affectation, and are, therefore, not equally fitted to inflame the hostile passions; for it is not folly but pride, not error but deceit, which the world means to persecute when it raises the full cry of nature to hunt down affectation.

The hatred which dissimulation always draws upon itself is so great, that if I did not know how much cunning differs from wisdom, I should wonder that any men have so little knowledge of their own interest as to aspire to wear a mask for life; to try to impose upon the world a character to which they feel themselves void of any just claim; and to hazard their quiet, their fame, and even their profit, by exposing themselves to the danger of that reproach, malevolence, and neglect, which such a discovery as they have always to fear will certainly bring upon them.

It might be imagined that the pleasure of reputation should consist in the satisfaction of having our opinion of our own merit confirmed by the suffrage of the public; and that to be extolled for a quality which a man knows himself to want should give him no other happiness than to be mistaken for the owner of an estate over which he chances to be travelling. But he who subsists upon affectation knows nothing of this delicacy: like a desperate adventurer in commerce, he takes up reputation upon trust, mortgages possessions which he never had, and enjoys to the fatal hour of bankruptcy, though with a thousand terrors and anxieties, the unnecessary splendour of borrowed riches.

Affectation is to be always distinguished from hypocrisy, as being the art of counterfeiting those qualities which we might, with innocence and safety, be known to want. Thus, the man who, to carry on any fraud or to conceal any crime, pretends to rigours of devotion and exactness of life, is guilty of hypocrisy; and his guilt is greater, as the end, for which he puts on the false appearance, is more pernicious. But he that with an awkward address and unpleasing countenance boasts of the conquests made by him among the ladies, and counts over the thousands which he might have possessed if he would have submitted to the yoke of matrimony, is chargeable only with affectation. Hypocrisy is the necessary burthen of villainy, affectation part of the chosen trappings of folly; the one completes a villain, the other only finishes a fop. Contempt is the proper punishment of affectation, and detestation the just consequence of hypocrisy.

With the hypocrite it is not at present my intention to expostulate, though even he might be taught the excellency of virtue by the necessity of seeming to be virtuous; but the man of affectation may, perhaps, be reclaimed by finding how little he is likely to gain by perpetual constraint and incessant vigilance, and how much more securely he might make his way to esteem by cultivating real than displaying counterfeit qualities.

Everything future is to be estimated by a wise man in proportion to the probability of attaining it and its value when attained; and neither of these considerations will much contribute to the encouragement of affectation. For if the pinnacles of fame be, at best, slippery, how unsteady must his footing be who stands upon pinnacles without foundation! If praise be made, by the inconstancy and maliciousness of those who must confer it, a blessing which no man can promise himself from the most conspicuous merit and vigorous industry, how faint must be the hope of gaining it when the uncertainty is multiplied by the weakness of the pretensions! He that pursues fame with just claims trusts his happiness to the winds; but he that endeavours after it by false merit has to fear not only the violence of the storm, but the leaks of his vessel. Though he should happen to keep above water for a time by the help of a soft breeze and a calm sea, at the first gust he must inevitably founder, with this melancholy reflection, that, if he would have been content with his natural station he might have escaped his calamity. Affectation may possibly succeed for a time, and a man may, by great attention, persuade others that he really has the qualities which he presumes to boast; but the hour will come when he should exert them, and then whatever he enjoyed in praise he must suffer in reproach.

Applause and admiration are by no means to be counted among the necessaries of life, and therefore any indirect arts to obtain them have very little claim to pardon or compassion. There is scarcely any man without some valuable or improvable qualities, by which he might always secure himself from contempt. And perhaps exemption from ignominy is the most eligible reputation, as freedom from pain is, among some philosophers, the definition of happiness.

If we therefore compare the value of the praise obtained by fictitious excellence, even while the cheat is yet undiscovered, with that kindness which every man may suit by his virtue, and that esteem to which most men may rise by common understanding steadily and honestly applied, we shall find that when from the adscititious happiness all the deductions are made by fear and casualty, there will remain nothing equiponderant to the security of truth. The state of the possessor of humble virtues to the affector of great excellencies is that of a small cottage of stone to the palace raised with ice by the Empress of Russia: it was for a time splendid and luminous, but the first sunshine melted it to nothing.

ANXIETIES OF LITERATURE (21)

Tuesday, 29th May 1750

Terra salutiferas herbas, eademque nocentes,
    Nutrit; et urticae proxima saepe rosa est.

OVID.

Our bane and physic the same earth bestows,
And near the noisome nettle blooms the rose.

EVERY man is prompted by the love of himself to imagine that he possesses some qualities superior, either in kind or in degree, to those which he sees allotted to the rest of the world; and whatever apparent disadvantages he may suffer in the comparison with others, he has some invisible distinctions, some latent reserve of excellence, which he throws into the balance, and by which he generally fancies that it is turned in his favour.

The studious and speculative part of mankind always seem to consider the fraternity as placed in a state of opposition to those who are engaged in the tumult of public business, and have pleased themselves from age to age with celebrating the felicity of their own condition, and with recounting the perplexity of politics, the dangers of greatness, the anxieties of ambition, and the miseries of riches.

Among the numerous topics of declamation that their industry has discovered on this subject there is none which they press with greater efforts, or on which they have more copiously laid out their reason and their imagination, than the instability of high stations and the uncertainty with which the profits and honours are possessed that must be acquired with so much hazard, vigilance, and labour.

This they appear to consider as an irrefragable argument against the choice of the statesman and the warrior, and swell with confidence or victory, thus furnished by the muses with the arms which never can be blunted and which no art or strength of their adversaries can elude or resist.

It was well known by experience to the nations which employed elephants in war that, though by the terror of their bulk and the violence of their impression they often threw the enemy into disorder, yet there was always danger in the use of them very nearly equivalent to the advantage; for if their first charge could be supported, they were easily driven back upon their confederates; they then broke through the troops behind them, and made no less havoc in the precipitation of their retreat than in the fury of their onset.

I know not whether those who have so vehemently urged the inconveniences and danger of an active life have not made use of arguments that may be retorted with equal force upon themselves; and whether the happiness of a candidate for literary fame be not subject to the same uncertainty with that of him who governs provinces, commands armies, presides in the senate, or dictates in the cabinet.

That eminence of learning is not to be gained without labour at least equal to that which any other kind of greatness can require, will be allowed by those who wish to elevate the character of a scholar since they cannot but know that every human acquisition is valuable in proportion to the difficulty employed in its attainment. And that those who have gained the esteem and veneration of the world by their knowledge or their genius are by no means exempt from the solicitude which any other kind of dignity produces, may be conjectured from the innumerable artifices which they make use of to degrade a superior, to repress a rival, or obstruct a follower; artifices so gross and mean as to prove evidently how much a man may excel in learning without being either more wise or more virtuous than those whose ignorance he pities or despises.

Nothing therefore remains by which the student can gratify his desire of appearing to have built his happiness on a more firm basis than his antagonist, except the certainty with which his honours are enjoyed. The garlands gained by the heroes of literature must be gathered from summits equally difficult to climb with those that bear the civic or triumphal wreaths. They must be worn with equal envy and guarded with equal care from those hands that are always employed in efforts to tear them away. The only remaining hope is that their verdure is more lasting, and that they are less likely to fail by time, or less obnoxious to the blasts of accident.

Even this hope will receive very little encouragement from the examination of the history of learning, or observation of the fate of scholars in the present age. If we look back into past times we find innumerable names of authors once in high reputation, read perhaps by the beautiful, quoted by the witty, and commended by the grave, but of whom we now know only that they once existed. If we consider the distribution of literary fame in our own time, we shall find it a possession of very uncertain tenure: sometimes bestowed by a sudden caprice of the public, and again transferred to a new favourite for no other reason than that he is new; sometimes refused to long labour and eminent desert, and sometimes granted to very slight pretensions; lost sometimes by security and negligence, and sometimes by too diligent endeavours to retain it.

A successful author is equally in danger of the diminution of his fame whether he continues or ceases to write. The regard of the public is not to be kept but by tribute, and the remembrance of past service will quickly languish unless successive performances frequently revive it. Yet in every new attempt there is new hazard, and there are few who do not, at some unlucky time, injure their own characters by attempting to enlarge them.

There are many possible causes of that inequality which we may so frequently observe in the performances of the same man, from the influence of which no ability or industry is sufficiently secured, and which have so often sullied the splendour of genius, that the wit, as well as the conqueror, may be properly cautioned not to indulge his pride with too early triumphs, but to defer to the end of life his estimate of happiness.

> Ultima semper
> Expectanda dies homini, dicique beatus
> Ante obitum nemo, supremaque funera debet.

> But no frail man, however great or high,
> Can be concluded blest before he die.
>
> ADDISON.

Among the motives that urge an author to undertakings by which his reputation is impaired, one of the most frequent must be mentioned with tenderness because it is not to be counted among his follies, but his miseries. It very often happens that the works of learning or of wit are performed at the direction of those by whom they are to be rewarded: the writer has not always the choice of his subject, but is compelled to accept any task which is thrown before him, without much consideration of his own convenience and without time to prepare himself by previous studies.

Miscarriages of this kind are likewise frequently the consequences of that acquaintance with the great, which is generally considered as one of the chief privileges of literature and genius. A man who has once learned to think himself exalted by familiarity with those whom nothing but their birth, or their fortunes, or such stations as are seldom gained by moral excellence, set above him, will not be long without submitting his understanding to their conduct. He will suffer them to prescribe the course of his studies and employ him for their own purposes either of diversion or interest. His desire of pleasing those whose favour he has weakly made necessary to himself will not suffer him always to consider how little he is qualified for the work imposed. Either his vanity will tempt him to conceal his deficiencies, or that cowardice, which always encroaches fast upon such as spend their lives in the company of persons higher than themselves, will not leave him resolution to assert the liberty of choice.

But, though we suppose that a man by his fortune can avoid the necessity of dependence, and by his spirit can repel the usurpations of patronage, yet he may easily, by writing long, happen to write ill. There is a general succession of effects in which contraries are produced by periodical vicissitudes. Labour and care are rewarded with success, success produces confidence, confidence relaxes industry, and negligence ruins that reputation which accuracy has raised.

He that happens not to be lulled by praise into supineness, may be animated by it to undertakings above his strength, or incited to fancy himself alike qualified for every kind of composition, and able to comply with the public taste through all its variations. By some opinion like this many men have been engaged at an advanced age in attempts which they had not time to complete, and, after a few weak efforts, sunk into the grave with vexation to see the rising generation gain ground upon them. From these failures the highest genius is not exempt: that judgment which appears so penetrating, when it is employed upon the works of others, very often fails where interest or passion can exert their power. We are blinded in examining our own labours by innumerable prejudices. Our juvenile compositions please us because they bring to our minds the remembrance of youth. Our latter performances we are ready to esteem because we are unwilling to think that we have made no improvement. What flows easily from the pen charms us because we read with pleasure that which flatters our opinion of our own powers. What was composed with great struggles of the mind we do not easily reject, because we cannot bear that so much labour should be fruitless. But the reader has none of these prepossessions, and wonders that the author is so unlike himself, without considering that the same soil will, with different culture, afford different products.

CONTRARIETY OF CRITICISM (23)

Tuesday, 5th June 1750

Tres mihi convivae prope dissentire videntur:
Poscentur vario multum diversa palato.

HORACE.

Three guests I have, dissenting at the feast
Requiring each to gratify his taste
With different food.

FRANCIS.

THAT every man should regulate his actions by his own conscience, without any regard to the opinions of the rest of the world, is one of the first precepts of moral prudence, justified not only by the suffrage of reason, which declares that none of the gifts of heaven are to lie useless, but by the voice likewise of experience, which will soon inform us that, if we make the praise or blame of others the rule of our conduct, we shall be distracted by a boundless variety of irreconcilable judgments, be held in perpetual suspense between contrary impulses, and consult for ever without determination.

I know not whether, for the same reason, it is not necessary for an author to place some confidence in his own skill, and to satisfy himself in the knowledge that he has not deviated from the established law of composition, without submitting his works to frequent examinations before he gives them to the public, or endeavouring to secure success by a solicitous conformity to advice and criticism.

It is, indeed, quickly discoverable that consultation and compliance can conduce little to the perfection of any literary performance; for whoever is so doubtful of his own abilities as to encourage the remarks of others will find himself every day embarrassed with new difficulties, and will harass his mind in vain with the hopeless labour of uniting heterogeneous ideas, digesting independent hints, and collecting into one point the several rays of borrowed light emitted often with contrary directions.

Of all authors, those who retail their labours in periodical sheets would be most unhappy if they were much to regard the censures or the admonitions of their readers: for, as their works are not sent into the world at once, but by small parts in gradual succession, it is always imagined by those who think themselves qualified to give instructions that they may yet redeem their former failings by hearkening to better judges, and supply the deficiencies of their plan by the help of the criticisms which are so liberally afforded.

I have had occasion to observe, sometimes with vexation and sometimes with merriment, the different temper with which the same man reads a printed and manuscript performance. When a book is once in the hands of the public it is considered as permanent and unalterable; and the reader, if he be free from personal prejudices, takes it up with no other intention than of pleasing or instructing himself. He accommodates his mind to the author's design, and, having no interest in refusing the amusement that is offered him, never interrupts his own tranquillity by studied cavils, or destroys his satisfaction in that which is already well, by an anxious inquiry how it might be better, but is often contented without pleasure and pleased without perfection.

But if the same man be called to consider the merit of a production yet unpublished, he brings an imagination heated with objections to passages which he has yet never heard. He invokes all the powers of criticism, and stores his memory with Taste and Grace, Purity and Delicacy, Manners and Unities, sounds which, having been once uttered by those that understood them, have since been re-echoed without meaning and kept up to the disturbance of the world by a constant repercussion from one coxcomb to another. He considers himself as obliged to show by some proof of his abilities that he is not consulted to no purpose, and therefore watches every opening for objection, and looks round for every opportunity to propose some specious alteration. Such opportunities a very small degree of sagacity will enable him to find; for in every work of imagination the disposition of parts, the insertion of incidents, and use of decorations may be varied a thousand ways with equal propriety; and, as in things nearly equal that will always seem best to every man which he himself produces, the critic, whose business is only to propose without the care of execution, can never want the satisfaction of believing that he has suggested very important improvements, nor the power of enforcing his advice by arguments which, as they appear convincing to himself, either his kindness or his vanity will press obstinately and importunately, without suspicion that he may possibly judge too hastily in favour of his own advice, or inquiry whether the advantage of the new scheme be proportionate to the labour.

It is observed by the younger Pliny that an orator ought not so much to select the strongest arguments which his cause admits, as to employ all which his imagination can afford. For, in pleading, those reasons are of most value which will most affect the judges; and the judges, says he, will be always most touched with that which they had before conceived. Every man who is called to give his opinion of a performance decides upon the same principle: he first suffers himself to form expectations, and then is angry at his disappointment. He lets his imagination rove at large, and wonders that another, equally unconfined in the boundless ocean of possibility, takes a different course.

But though the rule of Pliny be judiciously laid down, it is not applicable to the writer's cause, because there always lies an appeal from domestic criticism to a higher judicature, and the public, which is never corrupted nor often deceived, is to pass the last sentence upon literary claims.

Of the great force of preconceived opinions I had many proofs when I first entered upon this weekly labour. My readers having, from the performances of my predecessors, established an idea of unconnected essays to which they believed all future authors under a necessity of conforming, were impatient of the least deviation from their system, and numerous remonstrances were accordingly made by each as he found his favourite subject omitted or delayed. Some were angry that the *Rambler* did not, like the *Spectator*, introduce himself to the acquaintance of the public by an account of his own birth and studies, an enumeration of his adventures, and a description of his physiognomy. Others soon began to remark that he was a solemn, serious, dictatorial writer, without sprightliness or gaiety, and called out with vehemence for mirth and humour. Another admonished him to have a special eye upon the various clubs of this great city, and informed him that much of the *Spectator's* vivacity was laid out upon such assemblies. He has been censured for not imitating the politeness of his predecessors, having hitherto neglected to take the ladies under his protection, and give them rules for the just opposition of colours and the proper dimensions of ruffles and pinners. He has been required by one to fix a particular censure upon those matrons who play at cards with spectacles. And another is very much offended whenever he meets with a speculation in which naked precepts are comprised without the imitation of examples and characters.

I make not the least question that all these monitors intend the promotion of my design and the instruction of my readers; but they do not know, or do not reflect, that an author has a rule of choice peculiar to himself, and selects those subjects which he is best qualified to treat by the course of his studies or the accidents of his life; that some topics of amusement have been already treated with too much success to invite a competition; and that he who endeavours to gain many readers must try various arts of invitation, essay every avenue of pleasure, and make frequent changes in his methods of approach.

I cannot but consider myself amidst this tumult of criticism as a ship in a poetical tempest, impelled at the same time by opposite winds and dashed by the waves from every quarter, but held upright by the contrariety of the assailants, and secured in some measure by multiplicity of distress. Had the opinion of my censurers been unanimous, it might perhaps have overset my resolution; but since I find them at variance with each other, I can, without scruple, neglect them and endeavour to gain the favour of the public by following the direction of my own reason, and indulging the sallies of my own imagination.

Saturday, 23rd June 1750

Illi mors gravis incubat,
Qui notus nimis omnibus,
Ignotus moritur sibi.

SENECA.

To him, alas, to him, I fear,
The face of death will terrible appear,
Who in his life, flatt'ring his senseless pride,
By being known to all the world beside,
Does not himself, when he is dying know,
Nor what he is, nor whither he's to go.

I HAVE shown in a late essay to what errors men are hourly betrayed by a mistaken opinion of their own powers and a negligent inspection of their own character. But as I then confined my observations to common occurrences and familiar scenes, I think it proper to inquire how far a nearer acquaintance with ourselves is necessary to our preservation from crimes as well as follies, and how much the attentive study of our own minds may contribute to secure to us the approbation of that Being to whom we are accountable for our thoughts and our actions, and whose favour must finally constitute our total happiness.

If it be reasonable to estimate the difficulty of any enterprise by frequent miscarriages, it may justly be concluded that it is not easy for a man to know himself. For wheresoever we turn our view, we shall find almost all with whom we converse so nearly as to judge of their sentiments indulging more favourable conceptions of their own virtue than they have been able to impress upon others, and congratulating themselves upon degrees of excellence which their fondest admirers cannot allow them to have attained.

Those representations of imaginary virtue are generally considered as arts of hypocrisy and as snares laid for confidence and praise. But I believe the suspicion often unjust. Those who thus propagate their own reputation only extend the fraud by which they have been themselves deceived. For this failing is incident to numbers who seem to live without designs, competitions, or pursuits; it appears on occasions which promise no accession of honour or of profit, and to persons from whom very little is to be hoped or feared. It is, indeed, not easy to tell how far we may be blinded by the love of ourselves, when we reflect how much a secondary passion can cloud our judgment, and how few faults a man in the first raptures of love can discover in the person or conduct of his mistress.

To lay open all the sources from which error flows in upon him who contemplates his own character would require more exact knowledge of the human heart than, perhaps, the most acute and laborious observers have acquired. And since falsehood may be diversified without end, it is not unlikely that every man admits an imposture in some respect peculiar to himself, as his views have been accidentally directed, or his ideas particularly combined.

Some fallacies, however, there are, more frequently insidious, which it may, perhaps, not be useless to detect, because though they are not gross they may be fatal, and because nothing but attention is necessary to defeat them.

One sophism by which men persuade themselves that they have those virtues which they really want is formed by the substitution of single acts for habits. A miser who once relieved a friend from the danger of a prison suffers his imagination to dwell for ever upon his own heroic generosity; he yields his heart up to indignation at those who are blind to merit or insensible to misery, and who can please themselves with the enjoyment of that wealth which they never permit others to partake. From any censures of the world or reproaches of his conscience he has an appeal to action and to knowledge; and though his whole life is a course of rapacity and avarice, he concludes himself to be tender and liberal because he has once performed an act of liberality and tenderness.

As a glass which magnifies objects by the approach of one end to the eye lessens them by the application of the other, so vices are extenuated by the inversion of that fallacy by which virtues are augmented. Those faults which we cannot conceal from our own notice are considered, however frequent, not as habitual corruptions or settled practices, but as casual failures and single lapses. A man who has, from year to year, set his country to sale, either for the gratification of his ambition or resentment, confesses that the heat of party now and then betrays the severest virtue to measures that cannot be seriously defended. He that spends his days and nights in riot and debauchery owns that his passions often-times overpower his resolution. But each comforts himself that his faults are not without precedent, for the best and the wisest men have given way to the violence of sudden temptations.

There are men who always confound the praise of goodness with the practice, and who believe themselves mild and moderate, charitable and faithful, because they have exerted their eloquence in commendation of mildness, fidelity, and other virtues. This is an error almost universal among those that converse much with dependants, with such whose fear or interest disposes them to a seeming reverence for any declamation, however enthusiastic, and submission to any boast, however arrogant. Having none to recall their attention to their lives, they rate themselves by the goodness of their opinions, and forget how much more easily men may show their virtue in their talk than in their actions.

The tribe is likewise very numerous of those who regulate their lives not by the standard of religion but the measure of other men's virtue; who lull their own remorse with the remembrance of crimes more atrocious than their own, and seem to believe that they are not bad while another can be found worse.

For escaping these and a thousand other deceits many expedients have been proposed. Some have recommended the frequent consultation of a wise friend admitted to intimacy and encouraged to sincerity. But this appears a remedy by no means adapted to general use, for in order to secure the virtue of one it presupposes more virtue in two than will generally be found. In the first such a desire of rectitude and amendment as may incline him to hear his own accusation from the mouth of him whom he esteems and by whom, therefore, he will always hope that his faults are not discovered; and in the second such zeal and honesty as will make him content for his friend's advantage to lose his kindness.

A long life may be passed without finding a friend in whose understanding and virtue we can equally confide, and whose opinion we can value at once for its justness and sincerity. A weak man, however honest, is not qualified to judge. A man of the world, however penetrating, is not fit to counsel. Friends are often chosen for similitude of manners, and therefore each palliates the other's failings because they are his own. Friends are tender and unwilling to give pain, or they are interested and fearful to offend.

These objections have inclined others to advise that he who would know himself should consult his enemies, remember the reproaches that are vented to his face, and listen for the censures that are uttered in private. For his great business is to know his faults, and those malignity will discover and resentment will reveal. But this precept may be often frustrated; for it seldom happens that rivals or opponents are suffered to come near enough to know our conduct with so much exactness as that conscience should allow and reflect the accusation. The charge of an enemy is often totally false, and commonly so mingled with falsehood, that the mind takes advantage from the failure of one part to discredit the rest, and never suffers any disturbance afterward from such partial reports.

Yet it seems that enemies have been always found by experience the most faithful monitors; for adversity has ever been considered as the state in which a man most easily becomes acquainted with himself, and this effect it must produce by withdrawing flatterers, whose business it is to hide our weaknesses from us, or by giving loose to malice and licence to reproach, or at least by cutting off those pleasures which called us away from meditation on our conduct, and repressing that pride which too easily persuades us that we merit whatever we enjoy.

Part of these benefits it is in every man's power to procure to himself by assigning proper portions of his life to the examination of the rest, and by putting himself frequently in such a situation of retirement and abstraction as may weaken the influence of external objects. By this practice he may obtain the solitude of adversity without its melancholy, its instructions without its censures, and its sensibility without its perturbations.

The necessity of setting the world at a distance from us when we are to take a survey of ourselves has sent many from high stations to the severities of a monastic life. And, indeed, every man deeply engaged in business, if all regard to another state be not extinguished, must have the conviction, though, perhaps, not the resolution of Valdesso, who, when he solicited Charles V to dismiss him, being asked whether he retired upon disgust, answered that he laid down his commission for no other reason but because 'there ought to be some time for sober reflection between the life of a soldier and his death.'

There are few conditions which do not entangle us with sublunary hopes and fears, from which it is necessary to be at intervals disencumbered, that we may place ourselves in His presence who views effects in their causes and actions in their motives; that we may, as Chillingworth expresses it, consider things as if there were no other beings in the world but God and ourselves; or, to use language yet more awful, may commune with our own hearts, and be still.

Death, says Seneca, falls heavy upon him who is too much

known to others and too little to himself; and Pontanus, a man celebrated among the early restorers of literature, thought the study of our own hearts of so much importance, that he has recommended it from his tomb. *Sum* Joannes Jovianus Pontanus, *quem amave-runt bonae musae, suspexerunt viri probi, honestaverunt reges domini; iam scis qui sim, vel qui potius fuerim; ego vero te, hospes, noscere in tenebris nequeo, sed teipsum ut noscas rogo.* 'I am Pontanus, beloved by the powers of literature, admired by men of worth, and dignified by the monarchs of the world. Thou knowest now who I am, or more properly who I was. For thee, stranger, I who am in darkness cannot know thee, but I entreat thee to know thyself.'

I hope every reader of this paper will consider himself as engaged to the observation of a precept which the wisdom and virtue of all ages have concurred to endorse, a precept dictated by philosophers, inculcated by poets, and ratified by saints.

FOLLY OF ANTICIPATING MISFORTUNE (29)

Tuesday, 26th June 1750

Prudens futuri temporis exitum
Caliginosa nocte premit deus,
    Ridetque si mortalis ultra
        Fas trepidet——

HORACE.

But God has wisely hid from human sight
    The dark decrees of future fate,
And sown their seeds in depth of night;
He laughs at all the giddy turns of state,
    When mortals search too soon, and fear too late.

DRYDEN.

THERE is nothing recommended with greater frequency among the gayer poets of antiquity than the secure possession of the present hour, and the dismission of all the cares which intrude upon our quiet or hinder, by importunate perturbations, the enjoyment of those delights which our condition happens to set before us.

The ancient poets are, indeed, by no means unexceptionable teachers of morality: their precepts are to be always considered as the sallies of a genius, intent rather upon giving pleasure than instruction, eager to take every advantage of insinuation, and, provided the passions can be engaged on its side, very little solicitous about the suffrage of reason.

The darkness and uncertainty through which the heathens were compelled to wander in the pursuit to happiness may, indeed, be alleged as an excuse for many of their seducing invitations to immediate enjoyment, which the moderns, by whom they have been imitated, have not to plead.   It is no wonder that such as had no promise of another state should eagerly turn their thoughts upon the improvement of that which was before them.   But surely those who are acquainted with the hopes and fears of eternity might think it necessary to put some restraint upon their imagination, and reflect that by echoing the songs of the ancient bacchanals and transmitting the maxims of past debauchery, they not only prove that they want invention, but virtue, and submit to the servility of imitation only to copy that of which the writer, if he was to live now, would often be ashamed.

Yet as the errors and follies of a great genius are seldom without some radiations of understanding, by which meaner minds may be enlightened, the incitements to pleasure are, in these authors, generally mingled with such reflections upon life as well deserve to be considered distinctly from the purposes for which they are produced, and to be treasured up as the settled conclusions of extensive observation, acute sagacity, and mature experience.

It is not without true judgment that on these occasions they often warn their readers against inquiries into futurity and solicitude about events which lie hid in causes yet unactive and which time has not brought forward into the view of reason.   An idle and thoughtless resignation to chance, without any struggle against calamity or endeavour after advantage, is indeed below the dignity of a reasonable being, in whose power Providence has put a great part even of his present happiness; but it shows an equal ignorance of our proper sphere, to harass our thoughts with conjectures about things not yet in being.   How can we regulate events of which we yet know not whether they will ever happen?   And why should we think with painful anxiety about that on which our thoughts can have no influence?

It is a maxim commonly received that a wise man is never surprised; and perhaps this exemption from astonishment may be imagined to proceed from such a prospect into futurity as gave previous intimation of those evils which often fall unexpected upon others that have less foresight. But the truth is that things to come, except when they approach very nearly, are equally hidden from men of all degrees of understanding; and if a wise man is not amazed at sudden occurrences, it is not that he has thought more, but less, upon futurity. He never considered things not yet existing as the proper objects of his attention; he never indulged dreams till he was deceived by their phantoms; nor ever realized nonentities to his mind. He is not surprised because he is not disappointed, and he escapes disappointment because he never forms any expectations.

The concern about things to come that is so justly censured is not the result of those general reflections on the variableness of fortune, the uncertainty of life, and the universal insecurity of all human acquisitions, which must always be suggested by the view of the world; but such a desponding anticipation of misfortune as fixes the mind upon scenes of gloom and melancholy, and makes fear predominate in every imagination.

Anxiety of this kind is nearly of the same nature with jealousy in love and suspicion in the general commerce of life. A temper which keeps the man always in alarms disposes him to judge of everything in a manner that least favours his own quiet, fills him with perpetual stratagems of counteraction, wears him out in schemes to obviate evils which never threatened him, and at length, perhaps, contributes to the production of those mischiefs of which it had raised such dreadful apprehensions.

It has been usual in all ages for moralists to repress the swellings of vain hope by representations of the innumerable casualties to which life is subject, and by instances of the unexpected defeat of the wisest schemes of policy and sudden subversions of the highest eminences of greatness. It has, perhaps, not been equally observed that all these examples afford the proper antidote to fear as well as to hope, and may be applied with no less efficacy as consolations to the timorous than as restraints to the proud.

Evil is uncertain in the same degree as good, and for the reason that we ought not to hope too securely, we ought not to fear with too much dejection. The state of the world is continually changing, and none can tell the result of the next vicissitude. Whatever is afloat in the stream of time may, when it is very near us, be driven away by an accidental blast which shall happen to cross the general course of the current. The sudden accidents by which the powerful are depressed may fall upon those whose malice we fear, and the greatness by which we expect to be overborne may become another proof of the false flatteries of fortune.   Our enemies may become weak or we grow strong before our encounter, or we may advance against each other without ever meeting. There are, indeed, natural evils which we can flatter ourselves with no hopes of escaping, and with little of delaying; but of the ills which are apprehended from human malignity or the opposition of rival interests, we may always alleviate the terror by considering that our persecutors are weak and ignorant and mortal like ourselves.

The misfortunes which arise from the concurrence of unhappy incidents should never be suffered to disturb us before they happen, because if the breast be once laid open to the dread of mere possibilities of misery, life must be given a prey to dismal solicitude, and quiet must be lost for ever.

It is remarked by old Cornaro that it is absurd to be afraid of the natural dissolution of the body, because it must certainly happen, and can, by no caution or artifice, be avoided.   Whether this sentiment be entirely just I shall not examine; but certainly, if it be improper to fear events which must happen, it is yet more evidently contrary to right reason to fear those which may never happen and which, if they should come upon us, we cannot resist.

As we ought not to give way to fear any more than indulgence to hope, because the objects both of fear and hope are yet uncertain, so we ought not to trust the representations of one more than of the other, because they are both equally fallacious: as hope enlarges happiness, fear aggravates calamity.   It is generally allowed that no man ever found the happiness of possession proportionate to that expectation which incited his desire and invigorated his pursuit. Nor has any man found the evils of life so formidable in reality as they were described to him by his own imaginations.   Every species of distress brings with it some peculiar supports, some unforeseen means of resisting, or power of enduring.   Taylor justly blames some pious persons who indulge their fancies too much, set themselves by the force of imagination in the place of the ancient martyrs and confessors, and question the validity of their own faith because they shrink at the thoughts of flames and tortures. It is, says he, sufficient that you are able to encounter the temptations which now assault you.   When God sends trials He may send strength.

All fear is in itself painful, and when it conduces not to safety is painful without use.   Every consideration, therefore, by which groundless terrors may be removed adds something to human happiness. It is likewise not unworthy of remark that in proportion as our cares are employed upon the future they are abstracted from the present, from the only time which we can call our own, and of which if we neglect the duties, to make provision against visionary attacks, we shall certainly counteract our own purpose. For he, doubtless, mistakes his true interest who thinks that he can increase his safety when he impairs his virtue.

VANITY OF STOICISM (32)

Saturday, 7th July 1750

ὅσά τε δαιμονίῃσι τύχαις βροτοὶ ἄλγε' ἔχουσιν,
ὧν ἂν μοῖραν ἔχῃς, πράως φέρε, μηδ' ἀγανάκτει
'ιᾶσθαι δὲ πρέπει κάθ' ὅσον δυνῇ.

PYTHAGORAS.

Of all the woes that load the mortal state,
Whate'er thy portion, mildly meet thy fate;
But ease it as thou canst.

ELPHINSTON.

So large a part of human life passes in a state contrary to our natural desires, that one of the principal topics of moral instruction is the art of bearing calamities. And such is the certainty of evil, that it is the duty of every man to furnish his mind with those principles that may enable him to act under it with decency and propriety.

The sect of ancient philosophers that boasted to have carried this necessary science to the highest perfection were the Stoics, or scholars of Zeno, whose wild enthusiastic virtue pretended to an exemption from the sensibilities of unenlightened mortals, and who proclaimed themselves exalted by the doctrines of their sect above the reach of those miseries which embitter life to the rest of the world. They therefore removed pain, poverty, loss of friends, exile, and violent death from the catalogue of evils, and passed, in their haughty style, a kind of irreversible decree by which they forbade them to be counted any longer among the objects of terror or anxiety, or to give any disturbance to the tranquillity of a wise man.

This edict was, I think, not universally observed; for though one of the more resolute, when he was tortured by a violent disease, cried out that, let pain harass him to its utmost power, it should never force him to consider it as other than indifferent and neutral, yet all had not stubbornness to hold out against their senses. For a weaker pupil of Zeno is recorded to have confessed in the anguish of the gout, that he now found pain to be an evil.

It may, however, be questioned whether these philosophers can be very properly numbered among the teachers of patience. For if pain be not an evil, there seems no instruction requisite how it may be borne; and therefore when they endeavour to arm their followers with arguments against it, they may be thought to have given up their first position. But such inconsistencies are to be expected from the greatest understandings when they endeavour to grow eminent by singularity and employ their strength in establishing opinions opposite to nature.

The controversy about the reality of external evils is now at an end. That life has many miseries, and that those miseries are, sometimes at least, equal to all the powers of fortitude, is now universally confessed. And therefore it is useful to consider not only how we may escape them, but by what means those which either the accidents of affairs or the infirmities of nature must bring upon us may be mitigated and lightened; and how we may make those hours less wretched which the condition of our present existence will not allow to be very happy.

The cure for the greatest part of human miseries is not radical, but palliative. Infelicity is involved in corporeal nature and interwoven with our being. All attempts, therefore, to decline it wholly are useless and vain: the armies of pain send their arrows against us on every side, the choice is only between those which are more or less sharp, or tinged with poison of greater or less malignity; and the strongest armour which reason can supply will only blunt their points, but cannot repel them.

The great remedy which heaven has put in our hands is patience, by which, though we cannot lessen the torments of the body, we can in a great measure preserve the peace of the mind, and shall suffer only the natural and genuine force of an evil without heightening its acrimony or prolonging its effects.

There is indeed nothing more unsuitable to the nature of man in any calamity than rage and turbulence, which, without examining whether they are not sometimes impious, are at least always offensive and incline others rather to hate and despise than to pity and assist us. If what we suffer has been brought upon us by ourselves, it is observed by an ancient poet that patience is eminently our duty, since no one should be angry at feeling that which he has deserved.

> Leniter ex merito quicquid patiare ferendum est.

> Let pain deserv'd without complaint be borne.

And surely, if we are conscious that we have not contributed to our own sufferings, if punishment upon innocence or disappointment happens to industry and prudence, patience, whether more necessary or not, is much easier, since our pain is then without aggravation, and we have not the bitterness of remorse to add to the asperity of misfortune.

In those evils which are allotted to us by Providence, privation of any of the senses, or old age, it is always to be remembered that impatience can have no present effect but to deprive us of the consolations which our condition admits by driving away from us those by whose means, conversation, or advice, we might be amused or helped; and that with regard to futurity, it is yet less to be justified, since, without lessening the pain, it cuts off the hope of that reward, which He by whom it is inflicted will confer upon them that bear it well.

In all evils which admit a remedy impatience is to be avoided because it wastes that time and attention in complaints that, if properly applied, might remove the cause. Turenne, among the acknowledgments which he used to pay in conversation to the memory of those by whom he had been instructed in the art of war, mentioned one with honour who taught him not to spend his time in regretting any mistake which he had made, but to set himself immediately and vigorously to repair it.

Patience and submission are very carefully to be distinguished from cowardice and indolence. We are not to repine, but we may lawfully struggle; for the calamities of life, like the necessities of nature, are calls to labour and exercises of diligence. When we feel any pressure of distress, we are not to conclude that we can only obey the will of Heaven by languishing under it, any more than when we perceive the pain of thirst we are to imagine that water is prohibited. Of misfortune it never can be certainly known whether, as proceeding from the hand of God, it is an act of favour or of punishment. But since all the ordinary dispensations of Providence are to be interpreted according to the general analogy of things, we may conclude that we have a right to remove one inconvenience as well as another; that we are only to take care lest we purchase ease with guilt; and that our Maker's purpose, whether of reward or severity, will be answered by the labours which He lays us under the necessity of performing.

This duty is not more difficult in any state than in diseases intensely painful, which may indeed suffer such exacerbations as seem to strain the powers of life to their utmost stretch and leave very little of the attention vacant to precept or reproof. In this state the nature of man requires some indulgence, and every extravagance but impiety may be easily forgiven him. Yet, lest we should think ourselves too soon entitled to the mournful privileges of irresistible misery, it is proper to reflect that the utmost anguish which human wit can contrive, or human malice can inflict, has been borne with constancy; and that if the pains of disease be, as I believe they are, sometimes greater than those of artificial torture, they are therefore in their own nature shorter, the vital frame is quickly broken, or the union between soul and body is for a time suspended by insensibility, and we soon cease to feel our maladies when they once become too violent to be borne. I think there is some reason for questioning whether the body and mind are not so proportioned that the one can bear all that can be inflicted on the other, whether virtue cannot stand its ground as long as life, and whether a soul well principled will not be separated sooner than subdued.

In calamities which operate chiefly on our passions, such as diminution of fortune, loss of friends, or declension of character, the chief danger of impatience is upon the first attack, and many expedients have been contrived, by which the blow may be broken. Of these the most general precept is, not to take pleasure in anything of which it is not in our power to secure the possession to ourselves. This counsel, when we consider the enjoyment of any terrestrial advantage as opposite to a constant and habitual solicitude for future felicity, is undoubtedly just and delivered by that authority which cannot be disputed; but in any other sense is it not like advice not to walk lest we should stumble, or not to see lest our eyes should light upon deformity? It seems to me reasonable to enjoy blessings with confidence as well as to resign them with submission, and to hope for the continuance of good which we possess without insolence or voluptuousness, as for the restitution of that which we lose without despondency or murmurs.

The chief security against the fruitless anguish of impatience must arise from frequent reflection on the wisdom and goodness of the God of nature, in whose hands are riches and poverty, honour and disgrace, pleasure and pain, and life and death. A settled conviction of the tendency of everything to our good, and of the possibility of turning miseries into happiness by receiving them rightly, will incline us to bless the name of the Lord, whether He gives or takes away.

FEMALE COWARDICE (34)

Saturday, 14th July 1750

Non sine vano
Aurarum et silvae metu.

HORACE.

Alarm'd with ev'ry rising gale,
In ev'ry wood, in ev'ry vale.

ELPHINSTON.

I HAVE been censured for having hitherto dedicated so few of my speculations to the ladies; and indeed the moralist whose instructions are accommodated only to one-half of the human species must be confessed not sufficiently to have extended his views. Yet it is to be considered that masculine duties afford more room for counsels and observations, as they are less uniform and connected with things more subject to vicissitude and accident. We therefore find that in philosophical discourses which teach by precept, or historical narratives that instruct by example, the peculiar virtues or faults of women fill but a small part; perhaps generally too small, for so much of our domestic happiness is in their hands, and their influence is so great upon our earliest years, that the universal interest of the world requires them to be well instructed in their province. Nor can it be thought proper that the qualities by which so much pain or pleasure may be given should be left to the direction of chance.

I have therefore willingly given a place in my paper to a letter, which perhaps may not be wholly useless to them whose chief ambition is to please, as it shows how certainly the end is missed by absurd and injudicious endeavours at distinction.

TO THE 'RAMBLER'

SIR,
    I am a young gentleman at my own disposal, with a considerable

estate; and having passed through the common forms of education, spent some time in foreign countries, and made myself distinguished since my return in the politest company, I am now arrived at that part of life in which every man is expected to settle and provide for the continuation of his lineage. I withstood for some time the solicitations and remonstrances of my aunts and uncles, but at last was persuaded to visit Anthea, an heiress whose land lies contiguous to mine, and whose birth and beauty are without objection. Our friends declared that we were born for each other. All those on both sides who had no interest in hindering our union contributed to promote it, and were conspiring to hurry us into matrimony before we had any opportunity of knowing one another. I was, however, too old to be given away without my own consent, and having happened to pick up an opinion which to many of my relations seemed extremely odd, that a man might be unhappy with a large estate, determined to obtain a nearer knowledge of the person with whom I was to pass the remainder of my time. To protract the courtship was by no means difficult, for Anthea had a wonderful facility of evading questions which I seldom repeated, and of barring approaches which I had no great eagerness to press.

Thus the time passed away in visits and civilities without any ardent professions of love or formal offers of settlements. I often attended her to public places, in which, as is well known, all behaviour is so much regulated by custom, that very little insight can be gained into the private character, and therefore I was not yet able to inform myself of her humour and inclinations.

At last I ventured to propose to her to make one of a small party and spend a day in viewing a seat and gardens a few miles distant. And having, upon her compliance, collected the rest of the company, I brought, at the hour, a coach which I had borrowed from an acquaintance, having delayed to buy one myself till I should have an opportunity of taking the lady's opinion for whose use it was intended. Anthea came down, but as she was going to step into the coach started back with great appearance of terror, and told us that she durst not enter, for the shocking colour of the lining had so much the air of the mourning coach in which she followed her aunt's funeral three years before, that she should never have her poor dear aunt out of her head.

I knew that it was not for lovers to argue with their mistresses; I therefore sent back the coach, and got another more gay. Into this we all entered; the coachman began to drive; and we were amusing ourselves with the expectation of what we should see, when, upon a small inclination of the carriage, Anthea screamed out that we were overthrown. We were obliged to fix all our attention upon her, which she took care to keep up by renewing her outcries at every corner where we had occasion to turn. At intervals she entertained us with fretful complaints of the uneasiness of the coach, and obliged me to call several times on the coachman to take care and drive without jolting. The poor fellow endeavoured to please us, and therefore moved very slowly till Anthea found out that this pace would only keep us longer on the stones and desired that I would order him to make more speed. He whipped his horses, the coach jolted again, and Anthea very complaisantly told us how much she repented that she made one of our company.

At last we got into the smooth road, and began to think our difficulties at an end, when, on a sudden, Anthea saw a brook before us, which she could not venture to pass. We were therefore obliged to alight that we might walk over the bridge; but when we came to it we found it so narrow that Anthea durst not set her foot upon it, and was content, after long consultation, to call the coach back, and with innumerable precautions, terrors, and lamentations, crossed the brook.

It was necessary, after this delay, to mend our pace, and directions were accordingly given to the coachman, when Anthea informed us that it was common for the axle to catch fire with a quick motion, and begged of me to look out every minute, lest we should all be consumed. I was forced to obey and give her, from time to time, the most solemn declarations that all was safe and that I hoped we should reach the place without losing our lives either by fire or water.

Thus we passed on, over ways soft and hard, with more or with less speed, but always with new vicissitudes of anxiety. If the ground was hard we were jolted, if soft we were sinking. If we went fast we should be overturned, if slowly we should never reach the place. At length she saw something which she called a cloud, and began to consider that at that time of the year it frequently thundered. This seemed to be the capital terror, for after that the coach was suffered to move on; and no danger was thought too dreadful to be encountered, provided she could get into a house before the thunder.

Thus our whole conversation passed in dangers and cares and fears and consolations and stories of ladies dragged in the mire, forced to spend all the night on a heath, drowned in rivers or burnt with lightning; and no sooner had a hairbreadth escape set us free from one calamity but we were threatened with another.

At length we reached the house where we intended to regale ourselves, and I proposed to Anthea the choice of a great number of dishes which the place, being well provided for entertainment, happened to afford. She made some objection to everything that was offered. One thing she hated at that time of the year, another she could not bear since she had seen it spoiled at Lady Feedwell's table, another she was sure they could not dress at this house, and another she could not touch without French sauce. At last she fixed her mind upon salmon, but there was no salmon in the house. It was, however, procured with great expedition, and when it came to the table she found that her fright had taken away her stomach, which indeed she thought was no great loss, for she could never believe that anything at an inn could be cleanly got.

Dinner was now over, and the company proposed (for I was now past the condition of making overtures) that we should pursue our original design of visiting the gardens. Anthea declared that she could not imagine what pleasure we expected from the sight of a few green trees and a little gravel and two or three pits of clear water; that for her part she hated walking till the cool of the evening, and thought it very likely to rain, and again wished that she had stayed at home. We then reconciled ourselves to our disappointment and began to talk on common subjects, when Anthea told us that since we came to see gardens she would not hinder our satisfaction. We all rose and walked through the enclosures for some time with no other trouble than the necessity of watching lest a frog should hop across the way, which Anthea told us would certainly kill her if she should happen to see him.

Frogs, as it fell out, there were none; but when we were within a furlong of the gardens Anthea saw some sheep and heard the wether clink his bell, which she was certain was not hung upon him for nothing, and therefore no assurances nor entreaties could prevail upon her to go a step further. She was sorry to disappoint the company, but her life was dearer to her than ceremony.

We came back to the inn, and Anthea now discovered that there was no time to be lost in returning, for the night would come upon us, and a thousand misfortunes might happen in the dark. The horses were immediately harnessed, and Anthea, having wondered what could seduce her to stay so long, was eager to set out. But we had now a new scene of terror. Every man we saw was a robber, and we were ordered sometimes to drive hard lest a traveller whom we saw behind should overtake us, and sometimes to stop lest we should come up to him who was passing before us. She alarmed many an honest man by begging him to spare her life as he passed by the coach, and drew me into fifteen quarrels with persons who increased her fright by kindly stopping to inquire whether they could assist us. At last we came home, and she told her company next day what a pleasant ride she had been taking.

I suppose, Sir, I need not inquire of you what deductions may be made from this narrative, nor what happiness can arise from the society of that woman who mistakes cowardice for elegance, and imagines all delicacy to consist in refusing to be pleased.

I am, &c.

A MARRIAGE OF CONVENIENCE (35)

Tuesday, 17th July 1750

Non pronuba Juno,
Non Hymenaeus adest, non illi Gratia lecto.
OVID.

Without connubial Juno's aid they wed;
Nor Hymen nor the Graces bless the bed.

ELPHINSTON.

TO THE 'RAMBLER'

SIR,

As you have hitherto delayed the performance of the promise by which you gave us reason to hope for another paper upon matrimony, I imagine you desirous of collecting more materials than your own experience or observation can supply: and I shall therefore lay candidly before you an account of my own entrance into the conjugal state.

I was about eight-and-twenty years old, when, having tried the diversions of the town till I began to be weary, and being awakened into attention to more serious business by the failure of an attorney to whom I had implicitly trusted the conduct of my fortune, I resolved to take my estate into my own care, and methodize my whole life according to the strictest rules of economical prudence.

In pursuance of this scheme I took leave of my acquaintance, who dismissed me with numberless jests upon my new system, having first endeavoured to divert me from a design so little worthy of a man of wit by ridiculous accounts of the ignorance and rusticity into which many had sunk in their retirements after having distinguished themselves in taverns and playhouses, and given hopes of rising to uncommon eminence among the gay part of mankind.

When I came first into the country, which, by a neglect not uncommon among young heirs, I had never seen since the death of my father, I found everything in such confusion, that, being utterly without practice in business, I had great difficulties to encounter in disentangling the perplexities of my circumstances. They, however, gave way to diligent application, and I perceived that the advantage of keeping my own accounts would very much overbalance the time which they could require.

I had now visited my tenants, surveyed my land, and repaired the old house which for some years had been running to decay. These proofs of pecuniary wisdom began to recommend me as a sober, judicious, thriving gentleman to all my graver neighbours of the country, who never failed to celebrate my management in opposition to Thriftless and Latterwit, two smart fellows who had estates in the same part of the kingdom, which they visited now and then in a frolic, to take up their rents beforehand, debauch a milk-maid, make a feast for the village, and tell stories of their own intrigues, and then rode post back to town to spend their money.

It was doubtful, however, for some time, whether I should be able to hold my resolution; but a short perseverance removed all suspicions. I rose every day in reputation by the decency of my conversation and the regularity of my conduct, and was mentioned with great regard at the assizes as a man very fit to be put in commission for the peace.

During the confusion of my affairs and the daily necessity of visiting farms, adjusting contracts, letting leaves, and superintending repairs, I found very little vacuity in my life, and therefore had not many thoughts of marriage. But, in a little time the tumult of business subsided, and the exact method which I had established enabled me to dispatch my accounts with the same facility. I had therefore now upon my hands the art of finding means to spend my time without falling back into the poor amusement which I had hitherto indulged, or changing them for the sports of the field which I saw pursued with too much eagerness by the gentlemen of the country, that they were indeed the only pleasures in which I could promise myself any partaker.

The inconvenience of this situation naturally disposed me to wish for a companion; and the known value of my estate, with my reputation for frugality and prudence, easily gained me admission into every family. For I soon found that no inquiry was made after any other virtue, nor any testimonial necessary, but of my freedom from incumbrances and my care of what they termed the 'main chance.' I saw, not without indignation, the eagerness with which the daughters, wherever I came, were set out to show; nor could I consider them in a state much different from prostitution when I found them ordered to play their airs before me and to exhibit, by some seeming chance, specimens of their music, their work, or their housewifery. No sooner was I placed at table than the young lady was called upon to pay me some civility or other. Nor could I find means of escaping, from either father or mother, some account of their daughter's excellencies, with a declaration that they were now leaving the world and had no business on this side the grave but to see their children happily disposed of; that she whom I had been pleased to compliment at table was indeed the chief pleasure of their age, so good, so dutiful, so great a relief to her mamma in the care of the house, and so much her papa's favourite for her cheerfulness and wit, that it would be with the last reluctance that they should part; but to a worthy gentleman in the neighbourhood, whom they might often visit, they would not so far consult their own gratification as to refuse her; and their tenderness should be shown in her fortune whenever a suitable settlement was proposed.

As I knew these overtures not to proceed from any preference of me before another equally rich, I could not but look with pity on young persons condemned to be set to auction and made cheap by injudicious commendations. For how could they know themselves offered and rejected a hundred times without some loss of that soft elevation and maiden dignity so necessary to the completion of female excellence?

I shall not trouble you with a history of the stratagems practised upon my judgment, or the allurements tried upon my heart, which, if you have in any part of your life been acquainted with rural politics, you will easily conceive. Their arts have no great variety, they think nothing worth their care but money, and, supposing its influence the same upon all the world, seldom endeavour to deceive by any other means than false computations.

I will not deny that, by hearing myself loudly commended for my discretion, I began to set some value upon my character, and was unwilling to lose my credit by marrying for love. I therefore resolved to know the fortune of the lady whom I should address, before I inquired after her wit, delicacy, or beauty.

This determination led me to Mitissa, the daughter of Chrysophilus, whose person was at least without deformity, and whose manners were free from reproach, as she had been bred up at a distance from all common temptations. To Mitissa, therefore, I obtained leave from her parents to pay my court, and was referred by her again to her father, whose direction she was resolved to follow. The question then was only what should be settled. The old gentleman made an enormous demand, with which I refused to comply. Mitissa was ordered to exert her power. She told me that if I could refuse her papa I had no love for her; that she was an unhappy creature, and that I was a perfidious man. Then she burst into tears and fell into fits. All this, as I was no passionate lover, had little effect. She next refused to see me, and because I thought myself obliged to write in terms of distress they had once hopes of starving me into measures. But finding me inflexible, the father complied with my proposal and told me he liked me the more for being so good at a bargain.

I was now married to Mitissa, and was to experience the happiness of a match made without passion. Mitissa soon discovered that she was equally prudent with myself, and had taken a husband only to be at her own command, and to have a chariot at her own call. She brought with her an old maid recommended by her mother, who taught her all the arts of domestic management, and was on every occasion her chief agent and directress. They soon invented one reason or other to quarrel with all my servants, and either prevailed on me to turn them away, or treated them so ill that they left me of themselves, and always supplied their places with some brought from my wife's relations. Thus they established a family over which I had no authority, and which was in a perpetual conspiracy against me; for Mitissa considered herself as having a separate interest, and thought nothing her own but what she laid up without my knowledge. For this reason she brought me false accounts of the expenses of the house, joined with my tenants in complaints of hard times, and by means of a steward of her own took rewards for soliciting abatements of the rent. Her great hope is to outlive me that she may enjoy what she has thus accumulated, and therefore she is always contriving some improvements of her jointure land, and once tried to procure an injunction to hinder me from felling timber upon it for repairs. Her father and mother assist her in her projects, and are frequently hinting that she is ill used, and reproaching me with the presents that other ladies receive from their husbands.

Such, Sir, was my situation for seven years, till at last my patience was exhausted. And having one day invited her father to my house, I laid the state of my affairs before him, detected my wife in several of her frauds, turned out her steward, charged a constable with her maid, took my business in my own hands, reduced her to a settled allowance, and now write this account to warn others against marrying those whom they have no reason to esteem.

I am, &c.

DELIGHTS OF PASTORAL POETRY (36)

Saturday, 21st July 1750

ἅμ' ἕποντο νομῆες
Τερπόμενοι σύριγξι δόλον δ'οὔτι προνόησαν.

HOMER.

Piping on their reeds, the shepherds go
Nor fear an ambush, nor suspect a foe.

POPE.

THERE is scarcely any species of poetry that has allured more readers or excited more writers than the Pastoral. It is generally pleasing because it entertains the mind with representations of scenes familiar to almost every imagination, and of which all can equally judge whether they are well described. It exhibits a life to which we have been always accustomed to associate peace and leisure and innocence; and therefore we readily set open the heart for the admission of its images, which contribute to drive away cares and perturbations, and suffer ourselves, without resistance, to be transported to Elysian regions, where we are to meet with nothing but joy and plenty and contentment; where every gale whispers pleasure and every shade promises repose.

It has been maintained by some who love to talk of what they do not know that pastoral is the most ancient poetry; and, indeed, since it is probable that poetry is nearly of the same antiquity with rational nature, and since the life of the first man was certainly rural, we may reasonably conjecture that, as their ideas would necessarily be borrowed from those objects with which they were acquainted, their composures, being filled chiefly with such thoughts on the visible creation as must occur to the first observers, were pastoral hymns like those which Milton introduces the original pair singing in the day of innocence to the praise of their Maker.

For the same reason that pastoral poetry was the first employment of the human imagination, it is generally the first literary amusement of our minds. We have seen fields and meadows and groves from the time that our eyes opened upon life; and are pleased with birds and brooks and breezes much earlier than we engage among the actions and passions of mankind. We are therefore delighted with rural pictures because we know the original at an age when our curiosity can be very little awakened by descriptions of courts which we never beheld, or representations of passion which we never felt.

The satisfaction received from this kind of writing not only begins early, but lasts long. We do not, as we advance into the intellectual world, throw it away among other childish amusements and pastimes, but willingly return to it in any hour of indolence and relaxation. The images of true pastoral have always the power of exciting delight, because the works of nature, from which they are drawn, have always the same order and beauty, and continue to force themselves upon our thoughts, being at once obvious to the most careless regard, and more than adequate to the strongest reason and severest contemplation. Our inclination to stillness and tranquillity is seldom much lessened by long knowledge of the busy and tumultuary part of the world. In childhood we turn our thoughts to the country as to the region of pleasure, we recur to it in old age as a port of rest, and perhaps with that secondary and adventitious gladness which every man feels on reviewing those places, or recollecting those occurrences, that contributed to his youthful enjoyments, and bring him back to the prime of life when the world was gay with the bloom of novelty, when mirth wantoned at his side, and hope sparkled before him.

The sense of this universal pleasure has invited 'numbers without number' to try their skill in pastoral performances, in which they have generally succeeded after the manner of other imitators, transmitting the same images in the same combination from one to another, till he that reads the title of a poem may guess at the whole series of the composition. Nor will a man, after the perusal of thousands of these performances, find his knowledge enlarged with a single view of nature not produced before, or his imagination amused with any new application of those views to moral purposes.

The range of pastoral is indeed narrow, for though nature itself, philosophically considered, be inexhaustible, yet its general effects on the eye and on the ear are uniform and incapable of much variety of description.   Poetry cannot dwell upon the minuter distinctions by which one species differs from another without departing from that simplicity of grandeur which fills the imagination; nor dissect the latent qualities of things without losing its general power of gratifying every mind by recalling its conceptions.   However, as each age makes some discoveries and those discoveries are by degrees generally known, as new plants or mode of culture are introduced and by little and little become common, pastoral might receive from time to time small augmentations, and exhibit once in a century a scene somewhat varied.

But pastoral subjects have been often, like others, taken into the hands of those that were not qualified to adorn them, men to whom the face of nature was so little known, that they have drawn it only after their own imagination, and changed or distorted her features that their portraits might appear something more than servile copies from their predecessors.

Not only the images of rural life, but the occasions on which they can be properly produced, are few and general.   The state of a man confined to the employments and pleasures of the country is so little diversified, and exposed to so few of those accidents which produce perplexities, terrors, and surprises in more complicated transactions, that he can be shown but seldom in such circumstances as attract curiosity.   His ambition is without policy, and his love without intrigue.   He has no complaint to make of his rival but that he is richer than himself, nor any disasters to lament but a cruel mistress or a bad harvest.

The conviction of the necessity of some new source of pleasure induced Sannazarius to remove the scene from the fields to the sea, to substitute fishermen for shepherds, and derive his sentiments from the piscatory life; for which he has been censured by succeeding critics, because the sea is an object of terror, and by no means proper to amuse the mind and lay the passions asleep. Against this objection he might be defended by the established maxim that the poet has a right to select his images, and is no more obliged to show the sea in a storm than the land under an inundation, but may display all the pleasures and conceal the dangers of the water, as he may lay his shepherd under a shady beech without giving him an ague or letting a wild beast loose upon him.

There are, however, two defects in the piscatory eclogue which perhaps cannot be supplied. The sea, though in hot countries it is considered by those who live, like Sannazarius, upon the coast as a place of pleasure and diversion, has notwithstanding much less variety than the land, and therefore will be sooner exhausted by a descriptive writer. When he has once shown the sun rising or setting upon it, curled its waters with the vernal breeze, rolled the waves in gentle succession to the shore, and enumerated the fish sporting in the shallows, he has nothing remaining but what is common to all other poetry, the complaint of a nymph for a drowned lover, or the indignation of a fisher that his oysters are refused and Mycon's accepted.

Another obstacle to the general reception of this kind of poetry is the ignorance of maritime pleasures in which the greater part of mankind must always live. To all the inland inhabitants of every region the sea is only known as an immense diffusion of waters over which men pass from one country to another and in which life is frequently lost. They have, therefore, no opportunity of tracing in their own thoughts the descriptions of winding shores and calm bays, nor can look on the poem on which they are mentioned with other sensations than on a sea chart or the metrical geography of Dionysius.

This defect Sannazarius was hindered from perceiving by writing in a learned language to readers generally acquainted with the works of nature; but if he had made his attempt in any vulgar tongue, he would soon have discovered how vainly he had endeavoured to make that loved which was not understood.

I am afraid it will not be found easy to improve the pastorals of antiquity by any great additions or diversifications. Our descriptions may indeed differ from those of Virgil, as an English from an Italian summer, and, in some respects, as modern from ancient life; but as nature is in both countries nearly the same, and as poetry has to do rather with the passions of men, which are uniform, than their customs, which are changeable, the varieties which time or place can furnish will be inconsiderable: and I shall endeavour to show in the next paper how little the latter ages have contributed to the improvement of the rustic muse.

PRINCIPLES OF PASTORAL POETRY

Tuesday, 24th July 1750

Canto quae solitus, si quando armenta vocabat,
Amphion Dircaeus.

VIRGIL.

Such strains I sing as once Amphion play'd,
When list'ning flocks the powerful call obeyed.

ELPHINSTON.

IN writing or judging of Pastoral Poetry, neither the authors nor critics of latter times seem to have paid sufficient regard to the originals left us by antiquity, but have entangled themselves with unnecessary difficulties by advancing principles which, having no foundation in the nature of things, are wholly to be rejected from a species of composition in which, above all others, mere nature is to be regarded.

It is therefore necessary to inquire after some more distinct and exact idea of this kind of writing. This may, I think, be easily found in the pastorals of Virgil, from whose opinion it will not appear very safe to depart if we consider that every advantage of nature and of fortune concurred to complete his productions; that he was born with great accuracy and severity of judgment, enlightened with all the learning of one of the brightest ages, and embellished with the elegance of the Roman court; that he employed his powers rather in improving than inventing, and therefore must have endeavoured to recompense the want of novelty by exactness; that, taking Theocritus for his original, he found pastoral far advanced towards perfection, and that having so great a rival, he must have proceeded with uncommon caution.

If we search the writings of Virgil for the true definition of a pastoral, it will be found 'a poem in which any action or passion is represented by its effects upon a country life.' Whatsoever, therefore, may, according to the common course of things, happen in the country may afford a subject for a pastoral poet.

In this definition it will immediately occur to those who are versed in the writings of the modern critics that there is no mention of the golden age. I cannot indeed easily discover why it is thought necessary to refer descriptions of a rural state to remote times, nor can I perceive that any writer has consistently preserved the Arcadian manners and sentiments. The only reason, that I have read, on which this rule has been founded is that according to the customs of modern life it is improbable that shepherds should be capable of harmonious numbers or delicate sentiments; and therefore the reader must exalt his ideas of the pastoral character by carrying his thoughts back to the age in which the care of herds and flocks was the employment of the wisest and greatest men.

These reasoners seem to have been led into their hypothesis by considering pastoral, not in general as a representation of rural nature and consequently as exhibiting the ideas and sentiments of those (whoever they are) to whom the country affords pleasure or employment, but simply as a dialogue or narrative of men actually tending sheep and busied in the lowest and most laborious offices. From whence they very readily concluded, since characters must necessarily be preserved, that either the sentiments must sink to the level of the speakers or the speakers must be raised to the height of the sentiments.

In consequence of these original errors a thousand precepts have been given, which have only contributed to perplex and confound. Some have thought it necessary that the imaginary manners of the golden age should be universally preserved, and have therefore believed, that nothing more could be admitted in pastoral than lilies and roses and rocks and streams, among which are heard the gentle whispers of chaste fondness or the soft complaints of amorous impatience. In pastoral, as in other writings, chastity of sentiment ought doubtless to be observed, and purity of manners to be represented, not because the poet is confined to the images of the golden age, but because, having the subject in his own choice, he ought always to consult the interest of virtue.

These advocates for the golden age lay down other principles not very consistent with their general plan. For they tell us, that to support the character of the shepherd it is proper that all refinement should be avoided, and that some slight instances of ignorance should be interspersed. Thus the shepherd in Virgil is supposed to have forgot the name of Anaximander, and in Pope the term Zodiac is too hard for a rustic apprehension. But if we place our shepherds in their primitive condition, we may give them learning among their other qualifications; and if we suffer them to allude at all to things of latter existence, which perhaps cannot with any great propriety be allowed, there can be no danger of making them speak with too much accuracy, since they conversed with divinities and transmitted to succeeding ages the arts of life.

Other writers, having the mean and despicable condition of a shepherd always before them, conceive it necessary to degrade the language of pastoral by obsolete terms and rustic words, which they very learnedly called Doric, without reflecting that they thus became authors of a mangled dialect which no human being ever could have spoken, that they may as well refine the speech as the sentiments of their personages, and that none of the inconsistencies which they endeavour to avoid is greater than that of joining elegance of thought with coarseness of diction. Spenser begins one of his pastorals with studied barbarity.

> Diggon Davie, I bid her good day;
> Or, Diggon her is, or I missay.
> *Dig.* Her was her while it was day-light,
> But now her is a most wretched wight.

What will the reader imagine to be the subject on which speakers like these exercise their eloquence? Will he not be somewhat disappointed when he finds them met together to condemn the corruptions of the church of Rome? Surely, at the same time that a shepherd learns theology, he may gain some acquaintance with his native language.

Pastoral admits of all ranks of persons, because persons of all ranks inhabit the country. It excludes not, therefore, on account of the characters necessary to be introduced, any elevation or delicacy of sentiment. Those ideas only are improper which, not owing their original to rural objects, are not pastoral. Such is the exclamation in Virgil:

> Nunc scio quid sit Amor, duris in cautibus illum
> Ismarus, aut Rhodope, aut extremi Garamantes,
> Nec generis nostri puerum nec sanguinis, edunt;

> I know thee, Love, in desarts thou wert bred,
> And at the dugs of savage tygers fed;
> Alien of birth, usurper of the plains.

> DRYDEN.

which Pope, endeavouring to copy, was carried to still greater impropriety.

> I know thee, Love, wild as the raging main,
> More fierce than tygers on the Libyan plain,
> Thou wert from Aetna's burning entrails torn,
> Begot in tempests, and in thunders born!

Sentiments like these, as they have no existence in nature, are indeed of little value in any poem; but in pastoral they are particularly liable to censure, because it wants that exaltation above common life which in tragic or heroic writings often reconciles us to bold flights and daring figures.

Pastoral being the *representation of an action or passion, by its effects upon a country life*, has nothing peculiar but its confinement to rural imagery, without which it ceases to be pastoral. This is its true characteristic, and this it cannot lose by any dignity of sentiment or beauty of diction. The Pollio of Virgil, with all its elevation, is a composition truly bucolic, though rejected by the critics; for all the images are either taken from the country or from the religion of the age common to all parts of the empire.

The Silenus is indeed of a more disputable kind because, though the scene lies in the country, the song being religious and historical, had been no less adapted to any other audience or place. Neither can it well be defended as a fiction, for the introduction of a god seems to imply the golden age, and yet he alludes to many subsequent transactions, and mentions Gallus, the poet's contemporary.

It seems necessary to the perfection of this poem, that the occasion which is supposed to produce it be at least not inconsistent with a country life, or less likely to interest those who have retired into places of solitude and quiet than the more busy part of mankind. It is therefore improper to give the title of a pastoral to verses in which the speakers, after the slight mention of their flocks, fall to complaints of errors in the church and corruptions in the government, or to lamentations of the death of some illustrious person whom when once the poet has called a shepherd he has no longer any labour upon his hands, but can make the clouds weep and lilies wither and the sheep hang their heads, without art or learning, genius or study.

It is part of Claudian's character of his rustic that he computes his time not by the succession of consuls, but of harvests. Those who pass their days in retreats distant from the theatres of business are always least likely to hurry their imagination with public affairs.

The facility of treating actions or events in the pastoral style has incited many writers from whom more judgment might have been expected to put the sorrow or the joy which the occasion required into the mouth of Daphne or of Thyrsis; and as one absurdity must naturally be expected to make way for another, they have written with an utter disregard both of life and nature, and filled their productions with mythological allusions, with incredible fictions, and with sentiments which neither passion nor reason could have dictated since the change which religion has made in the whole system of the world.

MEDIOCRITY:[1] A FABLE (38)

Saturday, 28th July 1750

Auream quisquis mediocritatem
Diligit, tutus caret obsoleti
Sordibus tecti, caret invidendâ
Sobrius aulâ.

                                        HORACE.

The man within the golden mean,
Who can his boldest wish contain,
Securely views the ruin'd cell,
Where sordid want and sorrow dwell;
And in himself serenely great,
Declines an envied room of state.

                                        FRANCIS.

AMONG many parallels which men of imagination have drawn between the natural and moral state of the world, it has been observed that happiness, as well as virtue, consists in mediocrity; that to avoid every extreme is necessary even to him who has no other care than to pass through the present state with ease and safety; and that the middle path is the road of security, on either side of which are not only the pitfalls of vice but the precipices of ruin.

Thus the maxim of Cleobulus the Lindian, μέτιρον ἄριστον, *Mediocrity is best*, has been long considered as an universal principle, extended through the whole compass of life and nature. The experience of every age seems to have given it new confirmation, and to show that nothing, however specious or alluring, is pursued with propriety or enjoyed with safety, beyond certain limits.

Even the gifts of nature, which may truly be considered as the most solid and durable of all terrestrial advantages, are found, when they exceed the middle point, to draw the possessor into many

---

[1] The word here has no disparaging sense. It means rather 'the middle way,' in the sense of 'nothing in excess.'

calamities easily avoided by others that have been less bountifully enriched or adorned. We see every day women perish with infamy by having been too willing to set their beauty to show, and others, though not with equal guilt or misery, yet with very sharp remorse, languishing in decay, neglect, and obscurity for having rated their youthful charms at too high a price. And, indeed, if the opinion of Bacon be thought to deserve much regard, very few sighs would be vented for eminent and superlative elegance of form. 'For beautiful women,' says he, 'are seldom of any great accomplishments, because they, for the most part, study behaviour rather than virtue.'

Health and vigour and a happy constitution of the corporeal frame are of absolute necessity to the enjoyment of the comforts and to the performance of the duties of life, and requisite in yet a greater measure to the accomplishment of anything illustrious or distinguished. Yet even these, if we can judge by their apparent consequences, are sometimes not very beneficial to those on whom they are most liberally bestowed. They that frequent the chambers of the sick will generally find the sharpest pains and most stubborn maladies among them whom confidence of the force of nature formerly betrayed to negligence and irregularity; and that superfluity of strength, which was once their boast and their snare, has often, in the latter part of life, no other effect than it continues them long in impotence and anguish.

The gifts of nature are, however, always blessings in themselves and to be acknowledged with gratitude to Him that gives them, since they are, in their regular and legitimate effects, productive of happiness, and prove pernicious only by voluntary corruption or idle negligence. And as there is little danger of pursuing them with too much ardour or anxiety, because no skill or diligence can hope to procure them, the uncertainty of their influence upon our lives is mentioned not to depreciate their real value, but to repress the discontent and envy to which the want of them often gives occasion in those who do not enough suspect their own frailty nor consider how much less is the calamity of not possessing great powers than of not using them aright.

Of all those things that make us superior to others there is none so much within the reach of our endeavours as riches, nor anything more eagerly or constantly desired. Poverty is an evil always in our view, an evil complicated with so many circumstances of uneasiness and vexation, that every man is studious to avoid it. Some degree of riches is therefore required, that we may be exempt from the gripe of necessity. When this purpose is once attained we naturally wish for more, that the evil which is regarded with so much horror may be yet at a greater distance from us; as he that has once felt or dreaded the paw of a savage will not be at rest till they are parted by some barrier which may take away all possibility of a second attack.

To this point, if fear be not unreasonably indulged, Cleobulus would, perhaps, not refuse to extend his mediocrity. But it almost always happens that the man who grows rich changes his notions of poverty, states his wants by some new measure, and from flying the enemy that pursued him bends his endeavours to overtake those whom he sees before him. The power of gratifying his appetites increases their demands; a thousand wishes crowd in upon him, importunate to be satisfied, and vanity and ambition open prospects to desire, which still grow wider as they are more contemplated.

Thus in time want is enlarged without bounds, an eagerness for increase of possessions deluges the soul, and we sink into the gulfs of insatiability only because we do not sufficiently consider that all real need is very soon supplied, and all real danger of its invasion easily precluded; that the claims of vanity, being without limits, must be denied at last; and that the pain of repressing them is less pungent before they have been long accustomed to compliance.

Whosoever shall look heedfully upon those who are eminent for their riches will not think their condition such as that he should hazard his quiet, and much less his virtue, to obtain it. For all that great wealth generally gives, above a moderate fortune, is more room for the freaks of caprice, and more privilege for ignorance and vice, a quicker succession of flatteries, and a larger circle of voluptuousness.

There is one reason seldom remarked, which makes riches less desirable. Too much wealth is very frequently the occasion of poverty. He whom the wantonness of abundance has once softened easily sinks into neglect of his affairs; and he that thinks he can afford to be negligent is not far from being poor. He will soon be involved in perplexities which his inexperience will render insurmountable; he will fly for help to those whose interest it is that he should be more distressed, and will be at last torn to pieces by the vultures that always hover over fortunes in decay.

When the plains of India were burnt up by a long continuance of drought, Hamet and Raschid, two neighbouring shepherds, faint with thirst, stood at the common boundary of their grounds, with their flocks and herds panting around them, and in extremity of distress prayed for water. On a sudden the air was becalmed, the birds ceased to chirp, and the flocks to bleat. They turned their eyes every way, and saw a being of mighty stature advancing through the valley, whom they knew upon his nearer approach to be the Genius of distribution. In one hand he held the sheaves of plenty and in the other the sabre of destruction The shepherds stood trembling, and would have retired before him, but he called to them with a voice gentle as the breeze that plays in the evening among the spices of Sabaea: 'Fly not from your benefactor, children of the dust! I am come to offer you gifts which only your own folly can make vain. You here pray for water, and water I will bestow: let me know with how much you will be satisfied. Speak not rashly; consider, that of whatever can be enjoyed by the body excess is no less dangerous than scarcity. When you remember the pain of thirst do not forget the danger of suffocation. Now, Hamet, tell me your request.'

'O Being, kind and beneficent,' says Hamet, 'let thine eye pardon my confusion. I entreat a little brook, which in summer shall never be dry and in winter never overflow.' 'It is granted,' replies the Genius; and immediately he opened the ground with his sabre, and a fountain bubbling up under their feet scattered its rills over the meadows. The flowers renewed their fragrance, the trees spread a greener foliage, and the flock and herds quenched their thirst.

Then turning to Raschid, the Genius invited him likewise to offer his petition. 'I request,' says Raschid, 'that thou wilt turn the Ganges through my grounds, with all his waters, and all their inhabitants.' Hamet was struck with the greatness of his neighbour's sentiments, and secretly repined in his heart that he had not made the same petition before him, when the Genius spoke: 'Rash man, be not insatiable! Remember, to thee that is nothing which thou canst not use; and how are thy wants greater than the wants of Hamet?' Raschid repeated his desire and pleased himself with the mean appearance that Hamet would make in the presence of the proprietor of the Ganges. The Genius then retired towards the river, and the two shepherds stood waiting the event. As Raschid was looking with contempt upon his neighbour on a sudden was heard the roar of torrents, and they found by the mighty stream that the mounds of the Ganges were broken. The flood rolled forward into the lands of Raschid, his plantations were torn up, his flocks overwhelmed, he was swept away before it, and a crocodile devoured him.

UNHAPPINESS OF WOMEN (39)

Tuesday, 31st July 1750

Infelix . . . nulli bene nupta marito.

AUSONIUS.

Unblest, still doom'd to wed with misery.

THE condition of the female sex has been frequently the subject of compassion to medical writers, because their constitution of body is such that every state of life brings its peculiar deseases. They are placed, according to the proverb, between Scylla and Charybdis, with no other choice than of dangers equally formidable; and, whether they embrace marriage or determine upon a single life, are exposed, in consequence of their choice, to sickness, misery, and death.

It were to be wished that so great a degree of natural infelicity might not be increased by adventitious and artificial miseries, and that beings whose beauty we cannot behold without admiration, and whose delicacy we cannot contemplate without tenderness, might be suffered to enjoy every alleviation of their sorrows. But, however it has happened, the custom of the world seems to have been formed in a kind of conspiracy against them, though it does not appear but they had themselves an equal share in its establishment; and prescriptions which, by whomsoever they were begun, are now of long continuance, and by consequence of great authority seem to have almost excluded them from content, in whatsoever condition they shall pass their lives.

If they refuse the society of men, and continue in that state which is reasonably supposed to place happiness most in their own power, they seldom give those that frequent their conversation any exalted notions of the blessing of liberty. For whether it be that they are angry to see with what inconsiderate eagerness other heedless females rush into slavery or with what absurd vanity the married ladies boast the change of their condition and condemn the heroines who endeavour to assert the natural dignity of their sex; whether they are conscious that, like barren countries, they are free, only because they were never thought to deserve the trouble of a conquest or imagine that their sincerity is not always unsuspected when they declare their contempt of men, it is certain that they generally appear to have some great and incessant cause of uneasiness, and that many of them have at last been persuaded by powerful rhetoricians to try the life which they had so long contemned, and put on the bridal ornaments at a time when they least became them.

What are the real causes of the impatience which the ladies discover in a virgin state I shall perhaps take some other occasion to examine. That it is not to be envied for its happiness appears from the solicitude with which it is avoided, from the opinion universally prevalent among the sex that no woman continues long in it but because she is not invited to forsake it, from the disposition always shown to treat old maids as the refuse of the world, and from the willingness with which it is often quitted at last by those whose experience has enabled them to judge at leisure and decide with authority.

Yet such is life, that whatever is proposed it is much easier to find reasons for rejecting than embracing. Marriage, though a certain security from the reproach and solitude of antiquated virginity, has yet, as it is usually conducted, many disadvantages that take away much from the pleasure which society promises and might afford if pleasures and pains were honestly shared and mutual confidence inviolably preserved.

The miseries, indeed, which many ladies suffer under conjugal vexations are to be considered with great pity, because their husbands are often not taken by them as objects of affection, but forced upon them by authority and violence or by persuasion and importunity, equally resistless when urged by those whom they have been always accustomed to reverence and obey; and it very seldom appears that those who are thus despotic in the disposal of their children pay any regard to their domestic and personal felicity, or think it so much to be inquired whether they will be happy, as whether they will be rich.

It may be urged, in extenuation of this crime which parents, not in any other respect to be numbered with robbers and assassins, frequently commit, that, in their estimation, riches and happiness are equivalent terms. They have passed their lives with no other wish than that of adding acre to acre and filling one bag after another, and imagine the advantage of a daughter sufficiently considered when they have secured her a large jointure and given her reasonable expectations of living in the midst of those pleasures with which she had seen her father and mother solacing their age.

There is an economical oracle received among the prudential part of the world, which advises fathers to marry their daughters lest they should marry themselves. By which I suppose it is implied that women left to their own conduct generally unite themselves with such partners as can contribute very little to their felicity. Who was the author of this maxim, or with what intention it was originally uttered, I have not yet discovered; but imagine that, however solemnly it may be transmitted or however implicitly received, it can confer no authority which nature has denied: it cannot license Titius to be unjust lest Caia should be imprudent, nor give right to imprison for life lest liberty should be ill employed.

That the ladies have sometimes incurred imputations which might naturally produce edicts not much in their favour must be confessed by their warmest advocates; and I have indeed seldom observed that, when the tenderness or virtue of their parents has preserved them from forced marriage and left them at large to choose their own path in the labyrinth of life, they have made any great advantage of their liberty. They commonly take the opportunity of independence to trifle away youth, and lose their bloom in a hurry of diversions, recurring in a succession too quick to leave room for any settled reflection. They see the world without gaining experience, and at last regulate their choice by motives trifling as those of a girl, or mercenary as those of a miser.

Melanthia came to town upon the death of her father with a very large fortune and with the reputation of a much larger. She was therefore followed and caressed by many men of rank and by some of understanding; but having an insatiable desire of pleasure, she was not at leisure from the park, the gardens, the theatres, visits, assemblies, and masquerades to attend seriously to any proposal, but was still impatient for a new flatterer, and neglected marriage as always in her power; till in time her admirers fell away, wearied with expense, disgusted at her folly, or offended by her inconstancy. She heard of concerts to which she was not invited, and was more than once forced to sit still at an assembly for want of a partner. In this distress chance threw in her way Philotryphus, a man vain, glittering, and thoughtless as herself, who had spent a small fortune in equipage and dress, and was shining in the last suit for which his tailor would give him credit. He had been long endeavouring to retrieve his extravagance by marriage, and therefore soon paid his court to Melanthia, who after some weeks of insensibility saw him at a ball and was wholly overcome by his performance in a minuet. They married. But a man cannot always dance, and Philotryphus had no other method of pleasing.

However, as neither was in any great degree vicious, they live together with no other unhappiness than vacuity of mind and that tastelessness of life which proceeds from a satiety of juvenile pleasures, and an utter inability to fill their place by nobler employments. As they have known the fashionable world at the same time, they agree in their notions of all those subjects on which they ever speak; and being able to add nothing to the ideas of each other, are not much inclined to conversation, but very often join in one wish, 'That they could sleep more, and think less.'

Argyris, after having refused a thousand offers, at last consented to marry Cotylus, the younger brother of a duke, a man without elegance of mien, beauty of person, or force of understanding, who, while he courted her, could not always forbear allusions to her birth and hints how cheaply she would purchase an alliance to so illustrious a family. His conduct from the hour of his marriage has been insufferably tyrannical, nor has he any other regard to her than what arises from his desire that her appearance may not disgrace him. Upon this principle, however, he always orders that she should be gaily dressed and splendidly attended; and she has, among all her mortifications, the happiness to take place of her eldest sister.

MISERY OF A MODISH LADY (42)

Saturday, 11th August 1750

Mihi tarda fluunt ingrataque tempora.

HORACE.

How heavily my time revolves along!

ELPHINSTON.

TO THE 'RAMBLER'

MR. RAMBLER,

I am no great admirer of grave writings, and therefore very frequently lay your papers aside before I have read them through. Yet I cannot but confess that by slow degrees you have raised my opinion of your understanding, and that, though I believe it will be long before I can be prevailed upon to regard you with much kindness, you have, however, more of my esteem than those whom I sometimes make happy with opportunities to fill my tea-pot or pick up my fan. I shall therefore choose you for the confidant of my distresses, and ask your counsel with regard to the means of conquering or escaping them, though I never expect from you any of that softness and pliancy which constitutes the perfection of a companion for the ladies, as in the place where I now am I have recourse to the mastiff for protection, though I have no intention of making him a lapdog.

My mamma is a very fine lady who has more numerous and more frequent assemblies at her house than any other person in the same quarter of the town. I was bred from my earliest infancy in a perpetual tumult of pleasure, and remember to have heard of little else than messages, visits, playhouses, and balls, of the awkwardness of one woman, and the coquetry of another, the charming convenience of some rising fashion, the difficulty of playing a new game, the incidents of a masquerade, and the dresses of a court-night. I knew before I was ten years old all the rules of paying and receiving visits, and to how much civility every one of my acquaintance was entitled, and was able to return, with the proper degree of reserve or of vivacity the stated and established answer to every compliment. So that I was very soon celebrated as a wit and a beauty, and had heard before I was thirteen all that is ever said to a young lady. My mother was generous to so uncommon a degree as to be pleased with my advance into life, and allowed me, without envy or reproof, to enjoy the same happiness with herself, though most women about her own age were very angry to see young girls so forward, and many fine gentlemen told her how cruel it was to throw new chains upon mankind and to tyrannize over them at the same time with her own charms and those of her daughter.

I have now lived two-and-twenty years, and have passed of each year nine months in town and three at Richmond. So that my time has been spent uniformly in the same company and the same amusements, except as fashion has introduced new diversions, or the revolutions of the gay world have afforded new successions of wits and beaux. However, my mother is so good an economist of pleasure that I have no spare hours upon my hands. For every morning brings some new appointment, and every night is hurried away by the necessity of making our appearance at different places, and of being with one lady at the opera and with another at the card-table.

When the time came of setting our scheme of felicity for the summer it was determined that I should pay a visit to a rich aunt in a remote county. As you know, the chief conversation of all tea-tables in the spring arises from a communication of the manner in which time is to be passed till winter. It was a great relief to the barrenness of our topics to relate the pleasures that were in store for me, to describe my uncle's seat with the park and gardens, the charming walks and beautiful waterfalls; and every one told me how much she envied me and what satisfaction she had once enjoyed in a situation of the same kind.

As we are all credulous in our own favour and willing to imagine some latent satisfaction in anything which we have not experienced, I will confess to you without restraint that I had suffered my head to be filled with expectations of some nameless pleasure in a rural life, and that I hoped for the happy hour that should set me free from noise and flutter and ceremony, dismiss me to the peaceful shade, and lull me in content and tranquillity. To solace myself under the misery of delay I sometimes heard a studious lady of my acquaintance read pastorals, I was delighted with scarce any talk but of leaving the town, and never went to bed without dreaming of groves and meadows and frisking lambs.

At length I had all my clothes in a trunk, and saw the coach at the door. I sprung in with ecstasy, quarrelled with my maid for being too long in taking leave of the other servants, and rejoiced as the ground grew less which lay between me and the completion of my wishes. A few days brought me to a large old house, encompassed on three sides with woody hills and looking from the front on a gentle river, the sight of which renewed all my expectations of pleasure and gave me some regret for having lived so long without the enjoyment which these delightful scenes were now to afford me. My aunt came out to receive me, but in a dress so far removed from the present fashion that I could scarcely look upon her without laughter, which would have been no kind requital for the trouble which she had taken to make herself fine against my arrival. The night and the next morning were driven along with inquiries about our family. My aunt then explained our pedigree and told me stories of my great-grandfather's bravery in the civil wars. Nor was it less than three days before I could persuade her to leave me to myself.

At last economy prevailed. She went in the usual manner about her own affairs, and I was at liberty to range in the wilderness and sit by the cascade. The novelty of the objects about me pleased me for a while; but after a few days they were new no longer, and I soon began to perceive that the country was not my element, that shades and flowers and lawns and waters had very soon exhausted all their power of pleasing, and that I had not in myself any fund of satisfaction with which I could supply the loss of my customary amusements.

I unhappily told my aunt in the first warmth of our embraces that I had leave to stay with her ten weeks. Six only are yet gone, and how shall I live through the remaining four? I go out and return; I pluck a flower and throw it away; I catch an insect, and when I have examined its colours, see it at liberty; I fling a pebble into the water and see one circle spread after another. When it chances to rain I walk in the great hall and watch the minute hand upon the dial, or play with a litter of kittens which the cat happens to have brought in a lucky time.

My aunt is afraid I shall grow melancholy, and therefore encourages the neighbouring gentry to visit us. They came at first with great eagerness to see the fine lady from London, but when we met we had no common topic on which we could converse. They had no curiosity after plays, operas, or music: and I find as little satisfaction from their accounts of the quarrels or alliances of families whose names, when once I can escape, I shall never hear. The women have now seen me, know how my gown is made, and are satisfied; the men are generally afraid of me, and say little because they think themselves not at liberty to talk rudely.

Thus am I condemned to solitude. The day moves slowly forward, and I see the dawn with uneasiness because I consider that night is at a great distance. I have tried to sleep by a brook but find its murmurs ineffectual; so that I am forced to be awake at least twelve hours, without visits, without cards, without laughter, and without flattery. I walk because I am disgusted with sitting still, and sit down because I am weary with walking. I have no motive to action, nor any object of love or hate or fear or inclination. I cannot dress with spirit, for I have neither rival nor admirer. I cannot dance without a partner, nor be kind or cruel without a lover.

Such is the life of Euphelia, and such it is likely to continue for a month to come. I have not yet declared against existence, nor called upon the destinies to cut my thread; but I have sincerely resolved not to condemn myself to such another summer nor too hastily to flatter myself with happiness. Yet I have heard, Mr. Rambler, of those who never thought themselves so much at ease as in solitude, and cannot but suspect it to be some way or other my own fault that, without great pain either of mind or body, I am thus weary of myself, that the current of youth stagnates, and that I am

languishing in a dead calm for want of some external impulse. I
shall therefore think you a benefactor to our sex if you will teach
me the art of living alone. For I am confident that a thousand and
a thousand and a thousand ladies who affect to talk with ecstasies of
the pleasures of the country are, in reality, like me, longing for the
winter and wishing to be delivered from themselves by company
and diversion.

I am, Sir, yours,
Euphelia.

PRECIPITATION (43)

Tuesday, 14th August 1750

Flumine perpetuo torrens solet acrius ire,
Sed tamen haec brevis est, illa perennis aqua.

Ovid.

In course impetuous soon the torrent dries,
The brook a constant peaceful stream supplies.

F. Lewis.

It is observed by those who have written on the constitution of the
human body and the original of these diseases by which it is
afflicted that every man comes into the world morbid; that there is
no temperature so exactly regulated but that some humour is fatally
predominant; and that we are generally impregnated in our first
entrance upon life with the seeds of that malady which in time shall
bring us to the grave.

This remark has been extended by others to the intellectual
faculties. Some that imagine themselves to have looked with
more than common penetration into human nature have endeavoured to persuade us that each man is born with a mind formed
peculiarly for certain purposes, and with desires unalterably determined to particular objects, from which the attention cannot be long
diverted, and which alone, as they are well or ill pursued, must
produce the praise or blame, the happiness or misery, of his future
life.

This position has not, indeed, been hitherto proved with
strength proportionate to the assurance with which it has been
advanced, and perhaps will never gain much prevalence by a close
examination.

If the doctrine of innate ideas be itself disputable, there seems to be little hope of establishing an opinion which supposes that even complications of ideas have been given us at our birth, and that we are made by nature ambitious or covetous before we know the meaning of either power or money.

Yet as every step in the progression of existence changes our position with respect to the things about us so as to lay us open to new assaults and particular dangers, and subjects us to inconveniences from which any other situation is exempt—as a public or a private life, youth and age, wealth and poverty, have all some evil closely adherent, which cannot wholly be escaped but by quitting the state to which it is annexed and submitting to the encumbrances of some other condition—so it cannot be denied that every difference in the structure of the mind has its advantages and its wants, and that failures and defects inseparable from humanity, however the powers of understanding be extended or contracted, there will on one side or the other always be an avenue to error and miscarriage.

There seems to be some souls suited to great and others to little employments; some formed to soar aloft and take in wide views, and others to grovel on the ground and confine their regard to a narrow sphere. Of these the one is always in danger of becoming useless by a daring negligence, the other by a scrupulous solicitude. The one collects many ideas but confused and indistinct, the other is busied in minute accuracy, but without compass and without dignity.

The general error of those who possess powerful and elevated understandings is that they form schemes of too great extent and flatter themselves too hastily with success. They feel their own force to be great, and, by the complacency with which every man surveys himself, imagine it still greater. They therefore look out for undertakings worthy of their abilities, and engage in them with very little precaution, for they imagine that without premeditated measures they shall be able to find expedients in all difficulties. They are naturally apt to consider all prudential maxims as below their regard, to treat with contempt those securities and resources which others know themselves obliged to provide, and disdain to accomplish their purposes by established means and common gradations.

Precipitation, thus incited by the pride of intellectual superiority, is very fatal to great designs. The resolution of the combat is seldom equal to the vehemence of the charge. He that meets with an opposition which he did not expect loses his courage. The violence of his first onset is succeeded by a lasting and unconquerable languor; miscarriage makes him fearful of giving way to new hopes; and the contemplation of an attempt in which he has fallen below his own expectations is painful and vexatious. He therefore naturally turns his attention to more pleasing objects, and habituates his imagination to other entertainments till, by slow degrees, he quits his first pursuit and suffers some other project to take possession of his thoughts, in which the same ardour of mind promises him again certain success, and which disappointments of the same kind compel him to abandon.

Thus too much vigour in the beginning of an undertaking often intercepts and prevents the steadiness and perseverance always necessary in the conduct of a complicated scheme where many interests are to be connected, many movements to be adjusted, and the joint effort of distinct and independent powers to be directed to a single point. In all important events which have been suddenly brought to pass chance has been the agent rather than reason; and therefore, however those who seemed to preside in the transaction may have been celebrated by such as loved or feared them, succeeding times have commonly considered them as fortunate rather than prudent. Every design in which the connection is regularly traced from the first motion to the last must be formed and executed by calm intrepidity, and requires not only courage which danger cannot turn aside, but constancy which fatigues cannot weary and contrivance which impediments cannot exhaust.

All the performances of human art at which we look with praise or wonder are instances of the resistless force of perseverance. It is by this that the quarry becomes a pyramid and that distant countries are united with canals. If a man was to compare the effect of a single stroke of the pick-axe or of one impression of the spade with the general design and last result, he would be overwhelmed by the sense of their disproportion. Yet those petty operations, incessantly continued, in time surmount the greatest difficulties, and mountains are levelled, and oceans bounded, by the slender force of human beings.

It is therefore of the utmost importance that those who have any intention of deviating from the beaten roads of life and acquiring a reputation superior to names hourly swept away by time among the refuse of fame should add to their reason and their spirit the power of persisting in their purposes, acquire the art of sapping what they cannot batter, and the habit of vanquishing obstinate resistance by obstinate attacks.

The student who would build his knowledge on solid foundations and proceed by just degrees to the pinnacles of truth is directed by the great philosopher of France to begin by doubting of his own existence. In like manner, whoever would complete any arduous or intricate enterprise should, as soon as his imagination can cool after the first blaze of hope, place before his own eyes every possible embarrassment that may retard or defeat him. He should first question the probability of success, and then endeavour to remove the objections that he has raised. It is proper, says old Markham, to exercise your horse on the more inconvenient side of the course, that if he should in the race be forced upon it, he may not be discouraged. And Horace advises his poetical friend to consider every day as the last which he shall enjoy, because that will always give pleasure which we receive beyond our hopes. If we alarm ourselves beforehand with more difficulties than we really find, we shall be animated by unexpected facility with double spirit; and if we find our cautions and fears justified by the consequences, there will, however, happen nothing against which provision has not been made, no sudden shock will be received, nor will the main scheme be disconcerted.

There is, indeed, some danger lest he that too scrupulously balances probabilities, and too perspicaciously foresees obstacles, should remain always in a state of inaction, without venturing upon attempts on which he may perhaps spend his labour without advantage. But previous despondence is not the fault of those for whom this essay is designed. They who require to be warned against precipitation will not suffer more fear to intrude into their contemplations than is necessary to allay the effervescence of an agitated fancy. As Descartes has kindly shown how a man may prove to himself his own existence, if once he can be prevailed upon to question it, so the ardent and adventurous will not be long without finding some plausible extenuation of the greatest difficulties. Such, indeed, is the uncertainty of all human affairs, that security and despair are equal follies; and as it is presumption and arrogance to anticipate triumphs it is weakness and cowardice to prognosticate miscarriages. The numbers that have been stopped in their career of happiness are sufficient to show the uncertainty of human foresight; but there are not wanting contrary instances of such success obtained against all appearances as may warrant the boldest flights of genius if they are supported by unshaken perseverance.

CAUSES OF MARITAL DISAGREEMENT (45)

Tuesday, 21st August 1750

Ἥπερ μεγίστη γίγνεται σωτηρία,
ὅταν γύνη πρὸς ἄνδρα μὴ διχοστάτῃ,
νῦν δ'ἔχθρα πάντα.

EURIPIDES.

This is the chief felicity of life,
That concord smile on the connubial bed;
But now 'tis hatred all.

TO THE 'RAMBLER'

Sir,

Though in the dissertations which you have given us on marriage very just cautions are laid down against the common causes of infelicity, and the necessity of having in that important choice the first regard to virtue is carefully inculcated, yet I cannot think the subject so much exhausted but that a little reflection would present to the mind many questions, in the discussion of which great numbers are interested, and many precepts which deserve to be more particularly and forcibly impressed.

You seem, like most of the writers that have gone before you, to have allowed as an uncontested principle that marriage is generally unhappy. But I know not whether a man who professes to think for himself, and concludes from his own observations, does not depart from his character when he follows the crowd thus implicitly and receives maxims without recalling them to a new examination, especially when they comprise so wide a circuit of life and include such variety of circumstances. As I have an equal right with others to give my opinion of the objects about me, and a better title to determine concerning that state which I have tried than many who talk of it without experience, I am unwilling to be restrained by mere authority from advancing what, I believe, an accurate view of the world will confirm, that marriage is not commonly unhappy otherwise than as life is unhappy; and that most of those who complain of connubial miseries have as much satisfaction as their nature would have admitted, or their conduct procured, in any other condition.

It is, indeed, common to hear both sexes repine at their change, relate the happiness of their earlier years, blame the folly and rashness of their own choice, and warn those whom they see coming into the world against the same precipitance and infatuation. But it is to be remembered that the days which they so much wish to call back are the days not only of celibacy but of youth, the days of novelty and improvement, of ardour and of hope, of health and vigour of body, of gaiety and lightness of heart. It is not easy to surround life with any circumstances in which youth will not be delightful; and I am afraid that, whether married or unmarried, we shall find the vesture of terrestrial existence more heavy and cumbrous the longer it is worn.

That they censure themselves for the indiscretion of their choice is not a sufficient proof that they have chosen ill, since we see the same discontent at every other part of life which we cannot change. Converse with almost any man grown old in a profession, and you will find him regretting that he did not enter into some different course to which he too late finds his genius better adapted or in which he discovers that wealth and honour are more easily attained. 'The merchant,' says Horace, 'envies the soldier, and the soldier recounts the felicity of the merchant; the lawyer, when his clients harass him, calls out for the quiet of the countryman; and the countryman, when business calls him to town, proclaims that there is no happiness but amidst opulence and crowds.' Every man recounts the inconveniences of his own station, and thinks those of any other less because he has not felt them. Thus the married praise the ease and freedom of a single state, and the single fly to marriage from the weariness of solitude. From all our observations we may collect with certainty that misery is the lot of man, but cannot discover in what particular condition it will find most alleviations, or whether all external appendages are not, as we use them, the causes either of good or ill.

Whoever feels great pain naturally hopes for ease from change of posture. He changes it and finds himself equally tormented. And of the same kind are the expedients by which we endeavour to obviate or elude those uneasinesses to which mortality will always be subject. It is not likely that the married state is eminently miserable, since we see such numbers, whom the death of their partners has set free from it, entering it again.

Wives and husbands are, indeed, incessantly complaining of each other; and there would be reason for imagining that almost every house was infested with perverseness or oppression beyond human sufferance, did we not know upon how small occasions some minds burst out into lamentations and reproaches, and how naturally every animal revenges his pain upon those who happen to be near, without any nice examination of its cause. We are always willing to fancy ourselves within a little of happiness; and when, with repeated efforts, we cannot reach it, persuade ourselves that it is intercepted by an ill-paired mate, since, if we could find any other obstacle, it would be our own fault that it was not removed.

Anatomists have often remarked that though our diseases are sufficiently numerous and severe, yet when we inquire into the structure of the body the tenderness of some parts, the minuteness of others, and the immense multiplicity of animal functions that must concur to the healthful and vigorous exercise of all our powers, there appears reason to wonder rather that we are preserved so long than that we perish so soon, and that our frame subsists for a single day or hour without disorder, rather than that it should be broken or obstructed by violence of accidents or length of time.

The same reflection arises in my mind upon observation of the manner in which marriage is frequently contracted. When I see the avaricious and crafty taking companions to their tables and their beds without any inquiry but after farms and money, or the giddy and thoughtless uniting themselves for life to those whom they have only seen by the light of tapers at a ball; when parents make articles for their children without inquiring after their consent; when some marry for heirs to disappoint their brothers, and others throw themselves into the arms of those whom they do not love because they have found themselves rejected where they were more solicitous to please; when some marry because their servants cheat them, some because they squander their own money, some because their houses are pestered with company, some because they will live like other people, and some only because they are sick of themselves, I am not so much inclined to wonder that marriage is sometimes unhappy, as that it appears so little loaded with calamity; and cannot but conclude that society has something in itself eminently agreeable to human nature when I find its pleasures so great that even the ill choice of a companion can hardly overbalance them.

By the ancient custom of the Muscovites the men and women never saw each other till they were joined beyond the power of parting. It may be suspected that by this method many unsuitable matches were produced and many tempers associated that were not qualified to give pleasure to each other. Yet, perhaps, among a people so little delicate, where the paucity of gratifications and the uniformity of life gave no opportunity for imagination to interpose its objections, there was not much danger of capricious dislike, and while they felt neither cold nor hunger they might live quietly together without any thought of the defects of one another.

Amongst us, whom knowledge has made nice and affluence wanton, there are, indeed, more cautions requisite to secure tranquillity. And yet if we observe the manner in which those converse who have singled out each other for marriage, we shall, perhaps, not think that the Russians lost much by their restraint. For the whole endeavour of both parties during the time of courtship is to hinder themselves from being known, and to disguise their natural temper and real desires in hypocritical imitation, studied compliance, and continued affectation. From the time that their love is avowed neither sees the other but in a mask, and the cheat is managed often on both sides with so much art, and discovered afterwards with so much abruptness, that each has reason to suspect that some transformation has happened on the wedding-night, and that by a strange imposture one has been courted and another married.

I desire you, therefore, Mr. Rambler, to question all who shall hereafter come to you with matrimonial complaints concerning their behaviour in the time of courtship, and inform them that they are neither to wonder nor repine when a contract begun with fraud has ended in disappointment.

I am, &c.

Tuesday, 28th August 1750

Quanquam his solatiis acquiescam, debilitor et frangor eadem illa
humanitate quae me, ut hoc ipsum permitterem, induxit, non ideo
tamen velim durior fieri: nec ignoro alios hujusmodi casus nihil
amplius vocare quam damnum: eoque sibi magnos homines et
sapientes videri. Qui an magni sapientesque sint, nescio: homines
non sunt. Hominis est enim affici dolore, sentire: resistere tamen,
et solatia admittere; non solatiis non egere.

PLINY.

These proceedings have afforded me some comfort in my distress; notwithstanding which, I am still dispirited, and unhinged by the same
motives of humanity that induced me to grant such indulgences.
However, I by no means wish to become less susceptible of tenderness. I know these kind of misfortunes would be estimated by
other persons only as common losses, and from such sensations they
would conceive themselves great and wise men. I shall not determine either their greatness or their wisdom; but I am certain they
have no humanity. It is the part of a man to be affected with grief;
to feel sorrow, at the same time, that he is to resist it, and to admit of
comfort.

EARL OF ORRERY.

OF the passions with which the mind of man is agitated it may be
observed that they naturally hasten towards their own extinction by
inciting and quickening the attainment of their objects. Thus fear
urges our flight, and desire animates our progress; and if there are
some which perhaps may be indulged till they outgrow the good
appropriated to their satisfaction, as it is frequently observed of
avarice and ambition, yet their immediate tendency is to some
means of happiness really existing and generally within the prospect. The miser always imagines that there is a certain sum that
will fill his heart to the brim; and every ambitious man, like King
Pyrrhus, has an acquisition in his thoughts that is to terminate his
labours, after which he shall pass the rest of his life in ease or gaiety,
in repose or devotion.

Sorrow is perhaps the only affection of the breast that can be
excepted from this general remark, and it therefore deserves the
particular attention of those who have assumed the arduous province of preserving the balance of the mental constitution. The

other passions are diseases indeed, but they necessarily direct us to their proper cure. A man at once feels the pain, and knows the medicine, to which he is carried with greater haste as the evil which requires it is more excruciating, and cures himself by unerring instinct as the wounded stags of Crete are related by Aelian to have recourse to vulnerary herbs. But for sorrow there is no remedy provided by nature. It is often occasioned by accidents irreparable, and dwells upon objects that have lost or changed their existence. It requires what it cannot hope, that the laws of the universe should be repealed, that the dead should return, or the past should be recalled.

Sorrow is not that regret for negligence or error which may animate us to future care or activity, or that repentance of crimes for which, however irrevocable, our Creator has promised to accept it as an atonement. The pain which arises from these causes has very salutary effects, and is every hour extenuating itself by the reparation of those miscarriages that produce it. Sorrow is properly that state of the mind in which our desires are fixed upon the past without looking forward to the future, an incessant wish that something were otherwise than it has been, a tormenting and harassing want of some enjoyment or possession which we have lost and which no endeavours can possibly regain. Into such anguish many have sunk upon some sudden diminution of their fortune, an unexpected blast of their reputation, or the loss of children or of friends. They have suffered all sensibility of pleasure to be destroyed by a single blow, have given up for ever the hopes of substituting any other object in the room of that which they lament, resigned their lives to gloom and despondency, and worn themselves out in unavailing misery.

Yet so much is this passion the natural consequence of tenderness and endearment, that, however painful and however useless, it is justly reproachful not to feel it on some occasions. And so widely and constantly has it always prevailed, that the laws of some nations and the customs of others have limited a time for the external appearances of grief caused by the dissolution of close alliances and the breach of domestic union.

It seems determined by the general suffrage of mankind that sorrow is to a certain point laudable, as the offspring of love, or at least pardonable as the effect of weakness; but that it ought not to be suffered to increase by indulgence, but must give way after a stated time to social duties and the common avocations of life. It is at first unavoidable, and therefore must be allowed, whether with or without our choice. It may afterwards be admitted as a decent and affectionate testimony of kindness and esteem. Something will be extorted by nature, and something may be given to the world. But all beyond the bursts of passion or the forms of solemnity is not only useless, but culpable; for we have no right to sacrifice to the vain longings of affection that time which Providence allows us for the task of our station.

Yet it too often happens that sorrow, thus lawfully entering, gains such a firm possession of the mind, that it is not afterwards to be ejected. The mournful ideas, first violently impressed and afterwards willingly received, so much engross the attention as to predominate in every thought, to darken gaiety, and perplex ratiocination. An habitual sadness seizes upon the soul, and the faculties are chained to a single object which can never be contemplated but with hopeless uneasiness.

From this state of dejection it is very difficult to rise to cheerfulness and alacrity, and therefore many who have laid down rules of intellectual health think preservatives easier than remedies, and teach us not to trust ourselves with favourite enjoyments, not to indulge the luxury of fondness, but to keep our minds always suspended in such indifference that we may change the objects about us without emotion.

An exact compliance with this rule might, perhaps, contribute to tranquillity, but surely it would never produce happiness. He that regards none so much as to be afraid of losing them must live for ever without the gentle pleasures of sympathy and confidence. He must feel no melting fondness, no warmth of benevolence, nor any of those honest joys which nature annexes to the power of pleasing. And, as no man can justly claim more tenderness than he pays, he must forfeit his share in that officious and watchful kindness which love only can dictate, and those lenient endearments by which love only can soften life. He may justly be overlooked and neglected by such as have more warmth in their heart; for who would be the friend of him whom, with whatever assiduity he may be courted and with whatever services obliged, his principles will not suffer to make equal returns, and who, when you have exhausted all the instances of goodwill, can only be prevailed on not to be an enemy?

An attempt to preserve life in a state of neutrality and indifference is unreasonable and vain. If by excluding joy we could shut out grief, the scheme would deserve very serious attention. But since, however we may debar ourselves from happiness, misery will find its way at many inlets, and the assaults of pain will force our regard, though we may withhold it from the invitations of pleasure, we may surely endeavour to raise life above the middle point of apathy at one time, since it will necessarily sink below it at another.

But though it cannot be reasonable not to gain happiness for fear of losing it, yet it must be confessed that in proportion to the pleasure of possession will be for some time our sorrow for the loss. It is therefore the province of the moralist to inquire whether such pains may not quickly give way to mitigation. Some have thought that the most certain way to clear the heart from its embarrassment is to drag it by force into scenes of merriment. Others imagine that such a transition is too violent, and recommend rather to soothe it into tranquillity by making it acquainted with miseries more dreadful and afflictive, and diverting to the calamities of others the regard which we are inclined to fix too closely upon our own misfortunes.

It may be doubted whether either of those remedies will be sufficiently powerful. The efficacy of mirth it is not always easy to try, and the indulgence of melancholy may be suspected to be one of those medicines which will destroy if it happens not to cure.

The safe and general antidote against sorrow is employment. It is commonly observed that among soldiers and seamen, though there is much kindness there is little grief. They see their friend fall without any of that lamentation which is indulged in security and idleness, because they have no leisure to spare from the care of themselves. And whoever shall keep his thoughts busy will find himself equally unaffected with irretrievable losses.

Time is observed generally to wear out sorrow, and its effects might doubtless be accelerated by quickening the succession and enlarging the variety of objects.

> Si tempore longo
> Leniri poterit luctus, tu sperne morari,
> Qui sapiet sibi tempus erit.
>
> GROTIUS.

> 'Tis long ere time can mitigate your grief;
> To wisdom fly, she quickly brings relief.
>
> F. LEWIS.

Sorrow is a kind of rust of the soul, which every new idea contributes in its passage to scour away. It is the putrefaction of stagnant life, and is remedied by exercise and motion.

A COUNTRY HOUSEWIFE (51)

Tuesday, 10th September 1750

Stultus labor est ineptiarum.

MARTIAL.

How foolish is the toil of trifling cares!

ELPHINSTON.

TO THE 'RAMBLER'

SIR,

As you have allowed a place in your paper to Euphelia's letters from the country, and appear to think no form of human life unworthy of your attention, I have resolved, after many struggles with idleness and diffidence, to give you some account of my entertainment in this sober season of universal retreat, and to describe to you the employments of those who look with contempt on the pleasures and diversions of polite life, and employ all their powers of censure and invective upon the uselessness, vanity, and folly of dress, visits, and conversation.

When a tiresome and vexatious journey of four days had brought me to the house where invitation, regularly sent for seven years together, had at last induced me to pass the summer, I was surprised after the civilities of my first reception, to find, instead of the leisure and tranquillity which a rural life always promises, and, if well conducted, might always afford, a confused wildness of care and a tumultuous hurry of diligence, by which every face was clouded and every motion agitated. The old lady who was my father's relation was, indeed, very full of the happiness which she received from my visit, and, according to the forms of obsolete breeding, insisted that I should recompense the long delay of my company with a promise not to leave her till winter. But amidst all her kindness and caresses she very frequently turned her head aside and whispered with anxious earnestness some order to her daughters, which never failed to send them out with unpolite precipitation. Sometimes her impatience would not suffer her to stay behind. She begged my pardon, she must leave me for a moment: she went, and returned and sat down again, but was again disturbed by some new care, dismissed her daughters with the same trepidation, and followed them with the same countenance of business and solicitude.

However I was alarmed at this show of eagerness and disturbance, and however my curiosity was excited by such busy preparations as naturally promised some great event, I was yet too much a stranger to gratify myself with inquiries. But finding none of the family in mourning, I pleased myself with imagining that I should rather see a wedding than a funeral.

At last we sat down to supper, when I was informed that one of the young ladies, after whom I thought myself obliged to inquire, was under a necessity of attending some affair that could not be neglected. Soon afterward my relation began to talk of the regularity of her family and the inconvenience of London hours; and at last let me know that they had purposed that night to go to bed sooner than was usual because they were to rise early in the morning to make cheese-cakes. This hint sent me to my chamber, to which I was accompanied by all the ladies, who begged me to excuse some large sieves of leaves and flowers that covered two-thirds of the floor, for they intended to distil them when they were dry, and they had no other room that so conveniently received the rising sun.

The scent of the plants hindered me from rest; and therefore I rose early in the morning with a resolution to explore my new habitation. I stole unperceived by my busy cousins into the garden, where I found nothing either more great or elegant than in the same number of acres cultivated for the market. Of the gardener I soon learned that this lady was the greatest manager in that part of the country, and that I was come hither at the time in which I might learn to make more pickles and conserves than could be seen at any other house a hundred miles round.

It was not long before her ladyship gave me sufficient opportunities of knowing her character, for she was too much pleased with her own accomplishments to conceal them, and took occasion, from some sweetmeats which she set next day upon the table, to discourse for two long hours upon robs and jellies; laid down the best methods of conserving, reserving, and preserving all sorts of fruit; told us with great contempt of the London lady in the neighbourhood, by whom these terms were very often confounded; and hinted how much she should be ashamed to set before company at her own house sweetmeats of so dark a colour as she had often seen at mistress Sprightly's.

It is, indeed, the great business of her life to watch the skillet on the fire, to see it simmer with the due degree of heat, and to snatch it off at the moment of projection. And the employments to which she has bred her daughters are to turn rose-leaves in the shade, to pick out the seeds of currants with a quill, to gather fruit without bruising it, and to extract bean-flower water for the skin. Such are the tasks with which every day since I came hither has begun and ended, to which the early hours of life are sacrificed, and in which that time is passing away which never shall return.

But to reason or expostulate are hopeless attempts. The lady has settled her opinions, and maintains the dignity of her own performances with all the firmness of stupidity accustomed to be flattered. Her daughters, having never seen any house but their own, believe their mother's excellence on her own word. Her husband is a mere sportsman who is pleased to see his table well furnished, and thinks the day sufficiently successful in which he brings home a leash of hares to be potted by his wife.

After a few days I pretended to want books, but my lady soon told me that none of her books would suit my taste. For the part she never loved to see young women give their minds or such follies, by which they would only learn to use hard words. She bred up her daughters to understand a house, and whoever should marry them, if they knew anything of good cookery, would never repent it.

There are, however, some things in the culinary science too sublime for youthful intellects, mysteries into which they must not be initiated till the years of serious maturity, and which are referred to the day of marriage, as the supreme qualification for connubial life. She makes an orange pudding which is the envy of all the neighbourhood and which she has hitherto found means of mixing and baking with such secrecy, that the ingredient to which it owes its flavour has never been discovered. She, indeed, conducts this great affair with all the caution that human policy can suggest. It is never known beforehand when this pudding will be produced. She takes the ingredients privately into her own closet, employs her maids and daughters in different parts of the house, orders the oven to be heated for a pie, and places the pudding in it with her own hands. The mouth of the oven is then stopped, and all inquiries are vain.

The composition of the pudding she has, however, promised Clarinda, that if she pleases her in marriage she shall be told without reserve. But the art of making English capers she has not yet persuaded herself to discover, but seems resolved that secret shall perish with her, as some alchemists have obstinately suppressed the art of transmuting metals.

I once ventured to lay my fingers on her book of receipts, which she left upon the table, having intelligence that a vessel of gooseberry wine had burst the hoops. But though the importance of the event sufficiently engrossed her care to prevent any recollection of the danger to which her secrets were exposed, I was not able to make use of the golden moments; for this treasure of hereditary knowledge was so well concealed by the manner of spelling used by her grandmother, her mother, and herself, that I was totally unable to understand it, and lost the opportunity of consulting the oracle for want of knowing the language in which its answers were returned.

It is, indeed, necessary, if I have any regard to her ladyship's esteem, that I should apply myself to some of these economical accomplishments. For I overheard her two days ago warning her daughters by my mournful example against negligence of pastry and ignorance in carving. 'For you saw,' said she, 'that, with all her pretensions to knowledge, she turned the partridge the wrong way when she attempted to cut it, and, I believe, scarcely knows the difference between paste raised and paste in a dish.'

The reason, Mr. Rambler, why I have laid Lady Bustle's character before you, is a desire to be informed whether, in your opinion, it is worthy of imitation, and whether I shall throw away the books which I have hitherto thought it my duty to read for *The Lady's Closet Opened, The Complete Servant Maid,* and *The Court Cook,* and resign all curiosity after right and wrong for the art of scalding damascenes without bursting them, and preserving the whiteness of pickled mushrooms.

Lady Bustle has, indeed, by this incessant application to fruits and flowers, contracted her cares into a narrow space and set herself free from many perplexities with which other minds are disturbed. She has no curiosity after the events of a war or the fate of heroes in distress; she can hear without the least emotion the ravage of a fire or devastations of a storm. Her neighbours grow rich or poor, come into the world or go out of it, without regard while she is pressing the jelly-bag or airing the state-room. But I cannot perceive that she is more free from disquiets than those whose understandings take a wider range. Her marigolds, when they are almost cured, are often scattered by the wind, the rain sometimes falls upon fruit when it ought to be gathered dry. While her artificial wines are fermenting her whole life is restlessness and anxiety. Her sweetmeats are not always bright, and the maid sometimes forgets the just proportions of salt and pepper when venison is to be baked. Her conserves mould, her wines sour, and pickles mother; and, like all the rest of mankind, she is every day mortified with the defeat of her schemes and the disappointment of her hopes.

With regard to vice and virtue she seems a kind of neutral being. She has no crime but luxury, nor any virtue but chastity. She has no desire to be praised but for her cookery, nor wishes any ill to the rest of mankind but that whenever they aspire to a feast their custards may be wheyish and their pie-crusts tough.

I am now very impatient to know whether I am to look on these ladies as the great patterns of our sex, and to consider conserves and pickles as the business of my life; whether the censures which I now suffer be just; and whether the brewers of wines and the distillers of washes have a right to look with insolence on the weakness of

CORNELIA.

A REMEDY FOR GRIEF (52)

Saturday, 15th September 1750

Quoties flenti Theseius heros
Siste modum, dixit, neque enim fortuna querenda
Sola tua est, similes aliorum respice casus,
Mitius ista feres.

OVID.

How oft in vain the son of Theseus said,
The stormy sorrows be with patience laid;
Nor are thy fortunes to be wept alone;
Weigh other's woes, and learn to bear thy own.

CATCOTT.

AMONG the various methods of consolation to which the miseries inseparable from our present state have given occasion it has been, as I have already remarked, recommended by some writers to put the sufferer in mind of heavier pressures and more excruciating calamities than those of which he has himself reason to complain.

This has in all ages been directed and practised; and, in conformity to this custom, Lipsius, the great modern master of the

E 994

Stoic philosophy, has, in his celebrated treatise on Steadiness of Hand, endeavoured to fortify the breast against too much sensibility of misfortune by enumerating the evils which have in former ages fallen upon the world, the devastation of wide-extended regions, the sack of cities, and massacre of nations. And the common voice of the multitude, uninstructed by precept and unprejudiced by authority, which, in questions that relate to the heart of man, is, in my opinion, more decisive than the learning of Lipsius, seems to justify the efficacy of this procedure. For one of the first comforts which one neighbour administers to another is a relation of the like infelicity combined with circumstances of greater bitterness.

But this medicine of the mind is like many remedies applied to the body, of which, though we see the effects, we are unacquainted with the manner of operation, and of which, therefore, some, who are unwilling to suppose anything out of the reach of their own sagacity, have been inclined to doubt whether they have really those virtues for which they are celebrated, and whether their reputation is not the mere gift of fancy, prejudice, and credulity.

Consolation, or comfort, are words which, in their proper acceptation, signify some alleviation of that pain to which it is not in our power to afford the proper and adequate remedy. They imply rather an augmentation of the power of bearing than a diminution of the burthen. A prisoner is relieved by him that sets him at liberty, but receives comfort from such as suggest considerations by which he is made patient under the inconvenience of confinement. To that grief which arises from a great loss he only brings the true remedy who makes his friend's condition the same as before; but he may be properly termed a comforter who by persuasion extenuates the pain of poverty, and shows, in the style of Hesiod, that half is more than the whole.

It is, perhaps, not immediately obvious how it can lull the memory of misfortune or appease the throbbings of anguish to hear that others are more miserable, others perhaps unknown or wholly indifferent, whose prosperity raises no envy, and whose fall can gratify no resentment. Some topics of comfort arising, like that which gave hope and spirit to the captive of Sesostris, from the perpetual vicissitudes of life and mutability of human affairs, may as properly raise the dejected as depress the proud, and have an immediate tendency to exhilarate and revive. But how can it avail the man who languishes in the gloom of sorrow, without prospect of emerging into the sunshine of cheerfulness, to hear that others are sunk yet deeper in the dungeon of misery, shackled with heavier chains, and surrounded with darker desperation.

The solace arising from this consideration seems, indeed, the weakest of all others, and is perhaps never properly applied but in cases where there is no place for reflections of more speedy and pleasing efficacy. But even from such calamities life is by no means free: a thousand ills incurable, a thousand losses irreparable, a thousand difficulties insurmountable are known, or will be known, by all the sons of men. Native deformity cannot be rectified, a dead friend cannot return, and the hours of youth trifled away in folly or lost in sickness cannot be restored.

Under the oppression of such melancholy it has been found useful to take a survey of the world, to contemplate the various scenes of distress in which mankind are struggling round us, and acquaint ourselves with the *terribiles visu formae*, the various shapes of misery, which make havoc of terrestrial happiness, range all corners almost without restraint, trample down our hopes at the hour of harvest, and when we have built our schemes to the top ruin their foundation.

The first effect of this meditation is that it furnishes a new employment for the mind and engages the passions on remoter objects, as kings have sometimes freed themselves from a subject too haughty to be governed and too powerful to be crushed by posting him in a distant province till his popularity has subsided or his pride been repressed. The attention is dissipated by variety, and acts more weakly upon any single part, as that torrent may be drawn off to different channels, which, pouring down in one collected body, cannot be resisted. This species of comfort is, therefore, unavailing in severe paroxysms of corporal pain, when the mind is every instant called back to misery, and in the first shock of any sudden evil; but will certainly be of use against encroaching melancholy and a settled habit of gloomy thoughts.

It is further advantageous as it supplies us with opportunities of making comparisons in our own favour. We know that very little of the pain or pleasure which does not begin and end in our senses is otherwise than relative. We are rich or poor, great or little, in proportion to the number that excel us or fall beneath us in any of these respects. And therefore a man whose uneasiness arises from reflection on any misfortune that throws him below those with whom he was once equal is comforted by finding that he is not yet lowest.

There is another kind of comparison, less tending towards the vice of envy, very well illustrated by an old poet whose system will not afford many reasonable motives to content. 'It is,' says he, 'pleasing to look from shore upon the tumults of a storm, and to see a ship struggling with the billows. It is pleasing, not because the pain of another can give us delight, but because we have a stronger impression of the happiness of safety.' Thus when we look abroad, and behold the multitudes that are groaning under evils heavier than those which we have experienced, we shrink back to our own state, and instead of repining that so much must be felt, learn to rejoice that we have not more to feel.

By this observation of the miseries of others fortitude is strengthened and the mind brought to a more extensive knowledge of her own powers. As the heroes of action catch the flame from one another, so they to whom Providence has allotted the harder task of suffering with calmness and dignity may animate themselves by the remembrance of those evils which have been laid on others, perhaps naturally as weak as themselves, and bear up with vigour and resolution against their own oppressions when they see it possible that more severe afflictions may be borne.

There is still another reason why, to many minds, the relation of other men's infelicity may give a lasting and continual relief. Some, not well instructed in the measures by which Providence distributes happiness, are perhaps misled by divines, who, as Bellarmine makes temporal prosperity one of the characters of the true Church, have represented wealth and ease as the certain concomitants of virtue and the unfailing result of the divine approbation. Such sufferers are dejected in their misfortunes, not so much for what they feel as for what they dread; not because they cannot support the sorrows or endure the wants of their present condition, but because they consider them as only the beginnings of more sharp and more lasting pains. To these mourners it is an act of the highest charity to represent the calamities which not only virtue has suffered, but virtue has incurred; to inform them that one evidence of a future state is the uncertainty of any present reward for goodness; and to remind them, from the highest authority, of the distresses and penury of men 'of whom the world was not worthy.'

DEATH-BED THE SCHOOL
OF WISDOM (54)

Saturday, 22nd September 1750

> Truditur dies die,
> Novaeque pergunt interire lunae;
> Tu secanda marmora
> Locas sub ipsum funus, et sepulchri
> Immemor struis domos.

HORACE.

> Day presses on the heels of day,
> And moons increase to their decay;
> But you, with thoughtless pride elate,
> Unconscious of impending fate,
> Command the pillar'd dome to rise,
> When lo! thy tomb forgotten lies.

FRANCIS.

TO THE 'RAMBLER'

SIR,

I have lately been called from a mingled life of business and amusement to attend the last hours of an old friend, an office which has filled me, if not with melancholy, at least with serious reflections, and turned my thoughts towards the contemplation of those subjects which, though of the utmost importance and of indubitable certainty, are generally secluded from our regard by the jollity of health, the hurry of employment, and even by the calmer diversions of study and speculation; or, if they become accidental topics of conversation and argument, yet rarely sink deep into the heart, but give occasion only to some subtleties of reasoning or elegancies of declamation which are heard, applauded, and forgotten.

It is, indeed, not hard to conceive how a man accustomed to extend his views through a long concatenation of causes and effects, to trace things from their origin to their period and compare means with ends may discover the weakness of human schemes, detect the fallacies by which mortals are deluded, show the insufficiency of wealth, honours, and power to real happiness, and please himself and his auditors with learned lectures on the vanity of life.

But though the speculatist may see and show the folly of terrestrial hopes, fears, and desires, every hour will give proofs that he never felt it. Trace him through the day or year, and you will find him acting upon principles which he has in common with the illiterate and unenlightened, angry and pleased like the lowest of the vulgar, pursuing with the same ardour the same designs, grasping with all the eagerness of transport those riches which he knows he cannot keep, and swelling with the applause which he has gained by proving that applause is of no value.

The only conviction that rushes upon the soul and takes away from our appetites and passions the power of resistance is to be found, where I have received it, at the bed of a dying friend. To enter this school of wisdom is not the peculiar privilege of geometricians. The most sublime and important precepts require no uncommon opportunities nor laborious preparations; they are enforced without the aid of eloquence, and understood without skill in analytic science. Every tongue can utter them, and every understanding can conceive them. He that wishes in earnest to obtain just sentiments concerning his condition, and would be intimately acquainted with the world, may find instructions on every side. He that desires to enter behind the scene, which every art has been employed to decorate and every passion labours to illuminate, and wishes to see life stripped of those ornaments which make it glitter on the stage and exposed in its natural meanness, impotence, and nakedness, may find all the delusion laid open in the chamber of disease. He will there find vanity divested of her robes, power deprived of her sceptre, and hypocrisy without her mask.

The friend whom I have lost was a man eminent for genius, and, like others of the same class, sufficiently pleased with acceptance and applause. Being caressed by those who have preferments and riches in their disposal, he considered himself as in the direct road of advancement, and had caught the flame of ambition by approaches to its object. But in the midst of his hopes, his projects, and his gaieties he was seized by a lingering disease, which, from its first stage, he knew to be incurable. Here was an end of all his visions of greatness and happiness: from the first hour that his health declined all his former pleasures grew tasteless. His friends expected to please him by those accounts of the growth of his reputation which were formerly certain of being well received; but they soon found how little he was now affected by compliments and how vainly they attempted by flattery to exhilarate the languor of weakness and relieve the solicitude of approaching death. Whoever would know how much piety and virtue surpass all external goods, might here have seen them weighed against each other, where all that gives motion to the active and elevation to the eminent, all that sparkles in the eye of hope and pants in the bosom of suspicion, at once became dust in the balance, without weight and without regard.   Riches, authority, and praise lose all their influence when they are considered as riches which to-morrow shall be bestowed upon another, authority which shall this night expire for ever, and praise which, however merited or however sincere, shall after a few moments be heard no more.

In those hours of seriousness and wisdom nothing appeared to raise his spirits or gladden his heart but the recollection of acts of goodness, not to excite his attention, but some opportunity for the exercise of the duties of religion.   Everything that terminated on this side of the grave was received with coldness and indifference, and regarded rather in consequence of the habit of valuing it than from any opinion that it deserved value.   It had little more prevalence over his mind than a bubble that was now broken, a dream from which he was awake.   His whole powers were engrossed by the consideration of another state, and all conversation was tedious that had not some tendency to disengage him from human affairs and to open his prospects into futurity.

It is now past, we have closed his eyes and heard him breathe the groan of expiration.   At the sight of this last conflict I felt a sensation never known to me before: a confusion of passions, an awful stillness of sorrow, a gloomy terror without a name.   The thoughts that entered my soul were too strong to be diverted and too piercing to be endured; but such violence cannot be lasting, the storm subsided in a short time, I wept, retired, and grew calm.

I have from that time frequently revolved in my mind the effects which the observation of death produces in those who are not wholly without the power and use of reflection.   For by far the greater part it is wholly unregarded, their friends and their enemies sink into the grave without raising any uncommon emotion or reminding them that they are themselves on the edge of the precipice and that they must soon plunge into the gulf of eternity.

It seems to me remarkable that death increases our veneration for the good and extenuates our hatred of the bad.   Those virtues which once we envied, as Horace observes, because they eclipsed our own, can now no longer obstruct our reputation, and we have therefore no interest to suppress their praise.   That wickedness which we feared for its malignity is now become impotent, and the man whose name filled us with alarm and rage and indignation can at last be considered only with pity or contempt.

When a friend is carried to his grave we at once find excuses for every weakness and palliations of every fault. We recollect a thousand endearments which before glided off our minds without impression, a thousand favours unrepaid, a thousand duties unperformed, and wish, vainly wish, for his return, not so much that we may receive, as that we may bestow, happiness and recompense that kindness which before we never understood.

There is not, perhaps, to a mind well instructed a more painful occurrence than the death of one whom we have injured without reparation. Our crime seems now irretrievable, it is indelibly recorded, and the stamp of fate is fixed upon it. We consider with the most afflictive anguish the pain which we have given and now cannot alleviate, and the losses which we have caused and now cannot repair.

Of the same kind are the emotions which the death of an emulator or competitor produces. Whoever had qualities to alarm our jealousy had excellence to deserve our fondness, and to whatever ardour of opposition interest may inflame us, no man ever outlived an enemy whom he did not then wish to have made a friend. Those who are versed in literary history know that the elder Scaliger was the redoubted antagonist of Cardan and Erasmus; yet at the death of each of his great rivals he relented and complained that they were snatched away from him before their reconciliation was completed.

> Tune etiam moreris? Ah! quid me linguis, Erasme,
>   Ante meus quam sit conciliatus amor?

> Art thou too fall'n? ere anger could subside
> And love return has great Erasmus died?

Such are the sentiments with which we finally review the effects of passion, but which we sometimes delay till we can no longer rectify our errors. Let us therefore make haste to do what we shall certainly at last wish to have done. Let us return the caresses of our friends, and endeavour by mutual endearments to heighten that tenderness which is the balm of life. Let us be quick to repent of injuries while repentance may not be a barren anguish, and let us open our eyes to every rival excellence, and pay early and willingly those honours which justice will compel us to pay at last.

ATHANATUS.

A GAY WIDOW'S IMPATIENCE (55)

Tuesday, 25th September 1750

Maturo proprior desine funeri
    Inter ludere virgines,
Et stellis maculam spargere candidis:
    Non siquid Pholoen satis
Et te, Chlori, decet.

HORACE.

Now near to death that comes but slow,
Now thou art stepping down below;
Sport not amongst the blooming maids,
But think on ghosts and empty shades:
What suits with Pholoe in her bloom,
Gray Chloris, will not thee become;
A bed is different from a tomb.

CREECH.

TO THE 'RAMBLER'

SIR,

I have been but a little time conversant in the world, yet I have already had frequent opportunities of observing the little efficacy of remonstrance and complaint which, however extorted by oppression or supported by reason, are detested by one part of the world as rebellion, censured by another as peevishness, by some heard with an appearance of compassion, only to betray any of those sallies of vehemence and resentment which are apt to break out upon encouragement, and by others passed over with indifference and neglect as matters in which they have no concern and which, if they should endeavour to examine or regulate, they might draw mischief upon themselves.

Yet since it is no less natural for those who think themselves injured to complain than for others to neglect their complaints, I shall venture to lay my case before you, in hopes that you will enforce my opinion if you think it just, or endeavour to rectify my sentiments if I am mistaken. I expect at least that you will divest yourself of partiality, and that, whatever your age or solemnity may be, you will not with the dotard's insolence pronounce me ignorant and foolish, perverse and refractory, only because you perceive that I am young.

My father, dying when I was but ten years old, left me and a brother two years younger than myself to the care of my mother, a woman of birth and education, whose prudence or virtue he had no reason to distrust. She felt for some time all the sorrow which nature calls forth upon the final separation of persons dear to one another; and as her grief was exhausted by its own violence it subsided into tenderness for me and my brother, and the year of mourning was spent in caresses, consolations, and instruction in celebration of my father's virtues, in professions of perpetual regard to his memory, and hourly instances of such fondness as gratitude will not easily suffer me to forget.

But when the term of this mournful felicity was expired and my mother appeared again without the ensigns of sorrow the ladies of her acquaintance began to tell her, upon whatever motives, that it was time to live like the rest of the world, a powerful argument which is seldom used to a woman without effect. Lady Giddy was incessantly relating the occurrences of the town, and Mrs. Gravely told her privately, with great tenderness, that it began to be publicly observed how much she over-acted her part, and that most of her acquaintance suspected her hope of procuring another husband to be the true ground of all that appearance of tenderness and piety.

All the officiousness of kindness and folly was busied to change her conduct. She was at one time alarmed with censure, and at another fired with praise. She was told of balls where others shone only because she was absent, of new comedies to which all the town was crowding, and of many ingenious ironies by which domestic diligence was made contemptible.

It is difficult for virtue to stand alone against fear on one side and pleasure on the other, especially when no actual crime is proposed, and prudence itself can suggest many reasons for relaxation and indulgence. My mamma was at last persuaded to accompany Miss Giddy to a play. She was received with a boundless profusion of compliments and attended home by a very fine gentleman. Next day she was with less difficulty prevailed on to play at Mrs. Gravely's, and came home gay and lively; for the distinctions that had been paid her awakened her vanity, and good luck had kept her principles of frugality from giving her disturbance. She now made her second entrance into the world, and her friends were sufficiently industrious to prevent any return to her former life. Every morning brought messages of invitation, and every evening was passed in places of diversion, from which she for some time complained that she had rather be absent. In a short time she began to feel the happiness of acting without control, of being unaccountable for her hours, her expenses, and her company, and learned by degrees to drop an expression of contempt or pity at the mention of ladies whose husbands were suspected of restraining their pleasures or their play, and confessed that she loved to go and come as she pleased.

I was still favoured with some incidental precepts and transient endearments, and was now and then fondly kissed for smiling like my papa. But most part of her morning was spent in comparing the opinion of her maid and milliner, contriving some variation in her dress, visiting shops, and sending compliments; and the rest of the day was too short for visits, cards, plays, and concerts.

She now began to discover that it was impossible to educate children properly at home. Parents could not have them always in their sight; the society of servants was contagious; company produced boldness and spirit; emulation excited industry; and a large school was naturally the first step into the open world. A thousand other reasons she alleged, some of little force in themselves but so well seconded by pleasure, vanity, and idleness, that they soon overcame all the remaining principles of kindness and piety, and both I and my brother were dispatched to boarding-schools.

How my mamma spent her time when she was thus disburthened I am not able to inform you, but I have reason to believe that trifles and amusements took still faster hold of her heart. At first she visited me at school and afterwards wrote to me; but in a short time both her visits and her letters were at an end, and no other notice was taken of me than to remit money for my support.

When I came home at the vacation I found myself coldly received with an observation that 'this girl will presently be a woman.' I was, after the usual stay, sent to school again, and overheard my mother say as I was a-going: 'Well, now I shall recover.'

In six months more I came again, and with the usual childish alacrity was running to my mother's embrace when she stopped me with exclamations at the suddenness and enormity of my growth, having, she said, never seen anybody shoot up so much at my age. She was sure no other girls spread at that rate, and she hated to have children look like women before their time. I was disconcerted, and retired without hearing anything more than: 'Nay, if you are angry, madam Steeple, you may walk off.'

When once the forms of civility are violated there remains little hope of return to kindness or decency. My mamma made this appearance of resentment a reason for continuing her malignity, and poor Miss Maypole, for that was my appellation, was never mentioned or spoken to but with some expression of anger or dislike.

She had yet the pleasure of dressing me like a child, and I know not when I should have been thought fit to change my habit had I not been rescued by a maiden sister of my father, who could not bear to see women in hanging-sleeves, and therefore presented me with brocade for a gown, for which I should have thought myself under great obligations, had she not accompanied her favour with some hints that my mamma might now consider her age and give me her ear-rings which she had shown long enough in public places.

I now left the school and came to live with my mamma, who considered me as a usurper that had seized the rights of a woman before they were due and was pushing her down the precipice of age that I might reign without a superior. While I am thus beheld with jealousy and suspicion you will readily believe that it is difficult to please. Every word and look is an offence. I never speak but I pretend to some qualities and excellencies which it is criminal to possess. If I am gay she thinks it early enough to coquette. If I am grave she hates a prude in bibs. If I venture into company I am in haste for a husband. If I retire to my chamber such matron-like ladies are lovers of contemplation. I am on one pretence or other generally excluded from her assemblies, nor am I ever suffered to visit at the same place with my mamma. Everyone wonders why she does not bring Miss more into the world, and when she comes home in vapours I am certain that she has heard either of my beauty or my wit, and expect nothing for the ensuing week but taunts and menaces, contradiction and reproaches.

That I live in a state of continual persecution only because I was born ten years too soon and cannot stop the course of nature or of time, but am unhappily a woman before my mother can willingly cease to be a girl. I believe you would contribute to the happiness of many families if, by any arguments or persuasions, you could make mothers ashamed of rivalling their children, if you could show them that though they may refuse to grow wise they must inevitably grow old, and that the proper solaces of age are not music and compliments but wisdom and devotion, that those who are so unwilling to quit the world will soon be driven from it, and that it is therefore their interest to retire while there yet remains a few hours for nobler employments.

> I am, &c.

THE DESIRE OF WEALTH (58)

Saturday, 6th October 1750

Improbae
Crescunt divitiae, tamen
Curtae nescio quid semper abest rei.

HORACE.

But, while in heaps his wicked wealth ascends,
    He is not of his wish possess'd;
There's something wanting still to make him bless'd.

FRANCIS.

As the love of money has been in all ages one of the passions that has given great disturbance to the tranquillity of the world, there is no topic more copiously treated by the ancient moralists than the folly of devoting the heart to the accumulation of riches. They who are acquainted with these authors need not be told how riches incite pity, contempt, or reproach whenever they are mentioned; with what numbers of examples the danger of large possessions is illustrated; and how all the powers of reason and eloquence have been exhausted in endeavours to eradicate a desire which seems to have entrenched itself too strongly in the mind to be driven out, and which, perhaps, had not lost its power even over those who declaimed against it, but would have broken out in the poet or the sage if it had been excited by opportunity and invigorated by the approximation of its proper object.

Their arguments have been, indeed, so unsuccessful, that I know not whether it can be shown that, by all the wit and reason which this favourite cause has called forth, a single convert was ever made; that even one man has refused to be rich, when to be rich was in his power, from the conviction of the greater happiness of a narrow fortune; or disburthened himself of wealth, when he had tried its inquietudes, merely to enjoy the peace and leisure and security of a mean and unenvied state.

It is true, indeed, that many have neglected opportunities of raising themselves to honours and to wealth, and rejected the kindest offers of fortune. But, however their moderation may be boasted by themselves or admired by such as only view them at a distance, it will be, perhaps, seldom found that they value riches less, but that they dread labour or danger more than others. They are unable to rouse themselves to action, to strain in the race of competition, or to stand the shock of contest; but though they therefore decline the toil of climbing, they nevertheless wish themselves aloft and would willingly enjoy what they dare not seize.

Others have retired from high stations, and voluntarily condemned themselves to privacy and obscurity. But even these will not afford many occasions of triumph to the philosopher; for they have commonly either quitted that only which they thought themselves unable to hold, and prevented disgrace by resignation, or they have been induced to try new measures by general inconstancy which always dreams of happiness in novelty, or by a gloomy disposition which is disgusted in the same degree with every state, and wishes every scene of life to change as soon as it is beheld. Such men found high and low stations equally unable to satisfy the wishes of a distempered mind, and were unable to shelter themselves in the closest retreat from disappointment, solicitude, and misery.

Yet though these admonitions have been thus neglected by those who either enjoyed riches or were able to procure them, it is not rashly to be determined that they are altogether without use. For since far the greatest part of mankind must be confined to conditions comparatively mean, and placed in situations from which they naturally look up with envy to the eminences before them, those writers cannot be thought ill employed that have administered remedies to discontent almost universal by showing that what we cannot reach may very well be forborne, that the inequality of distribution at which we murmur is for the most part less than it seems, and that the greatness which we admire at a distance has much fewer advantages and much less splendour when we are suffered to approach it.

It is the business of moralists to detect the frauds of fortune, and to show that she imposes upon the careless eye by a quick succession of shadows which will shrink to nothing in the gripe; that she disguises life in extrinsic ornaments which serve only for show and are laid aside in the hours of solitude and of pleasure; and that when greatness aspires either to felicity or to wisdom it shakes off those distinctions which dazzle the gazer and awe the supplicant.

It may be remarked that they whose condition has not afforded them the light of moral or religious instruction, and who collect all their ideas by their own eyes and digest them by their own understandings, seem to consider those who are placed in ranks of remote superiority as almost another and higher species of beings. As themselves have known little other misery than the consequences of want, they are with difficulty persuaded that where there is wealth there can be sorrow, or that those who glitter in dignity and glide along in affluence can be acquainted with pains and cares like those which lie heavy upon the rest of mankind.

This prejudice is, indeed, confined to the lowest meanness and the darkest ignorance; but it is so confined only because others have been shown its folly and its falsehood, because it has been opposed in its progress by history and philosophy and hindered from spreading its infection by powerful preservatives.

The doctrine of the contempt of wealth, though it has not been able to extinguish avarice or ambition or suppress that reluctance with which a man passes his days in a state of inferiority, must at least have made the lower conditions less grating and wearisome, and has consequently contributed to the general security of life by hindering that fraud and violence, rapine and circumvention, which must have been produced by an unbounded eagerness of wealth arising from an unshaken conviction that to be rich is to be happy.

Whoever finds himself incited by some violent impulse of passion to pursue riches as the chief end of being must surely be so much alarmed by the successive admonitions of those whose experience and sagacity have recommended them as the guides of mankind, as to stop and consider whether he is about to engage in an undertaking that will reward his toil, and to examine, before he rushes to wealth through right and wrong, what it will confer when he has acquired it; and this examination will seldom fail to repress his ardour and retard his violence.

Wealth is nothing in itself. It is not useful but when it departs from us; its value is found only in that which it can purchase, which, if we suppose it put to its best use by those that possess it, seems not much to deserve the desire or envy of a wise man. It is certain that, with regard to corporal enjoyment, money can neither open new avenues to pleasure nor block up the passages of anguish. Disease and infirmity still continue to torture and enfeeble, perhaps exasperated by luxury or promoted by softness. With respect to the mind, it has rarely been observed that wealth contributes much to quicken the discernment, enlarge the capacity, or elevate the imagination, but may, by hiring flattery or laying diligence asleep, confirm error and harden stupidity.

Wealth cannot confer greatness, for nothing can make that great which the decree of nature has ordained to be little. The bramble may be placed in a hot-bed, but can never become an oak. Even royalty itself is not able to give that dignity which it happens not to find, but oppresses feeble minds though it may elevate the strong. The world has been governed in the name of kings, whose existence has scarcely been perceived by any real effects beyond their own palaces.

When, therefore, the desire of wealth is taking hold of the heart let us look round and see how it operates upon those whose industry or fortune has obtained it. When we find them oppressed with their own abundance, luxurious without pleasure, idle without ease, impatient and querulous in themselves, and despised or hated by the rest of mankind, we shall soon be convinced that if the real wants of our condition are satisfied there remains little to be sought with solicitude or desired with eagerness.

SUSPIRIUS THE HUMAN SCREECH-OWL (59)

Tuesday, 9th October 1750

Est aliquid fatale malum per verba levare,
  Hoc querulum Halcyonenque Procnen facit:
Hoc erat in solo quare Paeantias antro
  Vox fatigaret Lemnia saxa sua.
Strangulat inclusus dolor atque exaestuat intus,
  Cogitur et vires multiplicare suas.

OVID.

Complaining oft, gives respite to our grief;
From hence the wretched Procne sought relief,
Hence the Paeantian chief his fate deplores,
And vents his sorrows to the Lemnian shores:
In vain by secrecy we would assuage
Our cares; conceal'd, they gather tenfold rage.

F. LEWIS.

IT is common to distinguish men by the names of animals which they are supposed to resemble. Thus a hero is frequently termed a lion, and a statesman a fox, an extortioner gains the appellation of vulture, and a fop the title of monkey. There is also among the various anomalies of character which a survey of the world exhibits a species of beings in human form which may be properly marked out as the screech-owls of mankind.

These screech-owls seem to be settled in an opinion that the great business of life is to complain, and that they were born for no other purpose than to disturb the happiness of others, to lessen the little comforts, and shorten the short pleasures of our condition by painful remembrances of the past or melancholy prognostics of the future.   Their only care is to crush the rising hope, to damp the kindling transport, and allay the golden hours of gaiety with the hateful dross of grief and suspicion.

To those whose weakness of spirits or timidity of temper subjects them to impressions from others, and who are apt to suffer by fascination and catch the contagion of misery, it is extremely unhappy to live within the compass of a screech-owl's voice; for it will often fill their ears in the hour of dejection, terrify them with apprehensions which their own thoughts would never have produced, and sadden by intruded sorrows the day which might have been passed in amusements or in business.   It will burthen the heart with unnecessary discontents, and weaken for a time that love of life which is necessary to the vigorous prosecution of any undertaking.

Though I have, like the rest of mankind, many failings and weaknesses, I have not yet, by either friends or enemies, been charged with superstition.   I never count the company which I enter, and I look at the new moon indifferently over either shoulder. I have, like most other philosophers, often heard the cuckoo without money in my pocket, and have been sometimes reproached as foolhardy for not turning down my eyes when a raven flew over my head.   I never go home abruptly because a snake crosses my way, nor have any particular dread of a climacterical year.   Yet I confess that, with all my scorn of old women and their tales, I consider it as an unhappy day when I happen to be greeted in the morning by Suspirius the screech-owl.

I have now known Suspirius fifty-eight years and four months, and have never yet passed an hour with him in which he has not made some attack upon my quiet.   When we were first acquainted his great topic was the misery of youth without riches, and whenever we walked out together he solaced me with a long enumeration of pleasures which, as they were beyond the reach of my fortune, were without the verge of my desires, and which I should never have considered as the objects of a wish, had not his unseasonable representations placed them in my sight.

Another of his topics is the neglect of merit, with which he never fails to amuse every man whom he sees not eminently fortunate.

If he meets with a young officer he always informs him of gentlemen whose personal courage is unquestioned and whose military skill qualifies them to command armies, that have, notwithstanding all their merit, grown old with subaltern commissions. For a genius in the church he is always provided with a curacy for life. The lawyer he informs of many men of great parts and deep study who have never had an opportunity to speak in the courts. And meeting Serenus the physician, 'Ah doctor,' says he, 'what, afoot still, when so many blockheads are rattling in their chariots? I told you seven years ago that you would never meet with encouragement, and I hope you will now take more notice when I tell you that your Greek and your diligence and your honesty will never enable you to live like yonder apothecary who prescribes to his own shop and laughs at the physician.'

Suspirius has in his time intercepted fifteen authors in their way to the stage; persuaded nine-and-thirty merchants to retire from a prosperous trade for fear of bankruptcy, broke off an hundred and thirteen matches by prognostications of unhappiness, and enabled the smallpox to kill nineteen ladies by perpetual alarms of the loss of beauty.

Whenever my evil stars bring us together he never fails to represent to me the folly of my pursuits, and informs me that we are much older than when we began our acquaintance, that the infirmities of decrepitude are coming fast upon me, that whatever I now get I shall enjoy but a little time, that fame is to a man tottering on the edge of the grave of very little importance, and that the time is at hand when I ought to look for no other pleasures than a good dinner and an easy chair.

Thus he goes on in his unharmonious strain, displaying present miseries and foreboding more, νυκτικόραξ ᾄδει θανατήφορος; every syllable is loaded with misfortune, and death is always brought nearer to the view. Yet, what always raises my resentment and indignation, I do not perceive that his mournful meditations have much effect upon himself. He talks and has long talked of calamities without discovering, otherwise than by the tone of his voice, that he feels any of the evils which he bewails or threatens, but has the same habit of uttering lamentations as others of telling stories, and falls into expressions of condolence for past or apprehensions of future mischiefs, as all men studious of their ease have recourse to those subjects upon which they can most fluently or copiously discourse.

It is reported of the Sybarites that they destroyed all their cocks

that they might dream out their morning dreams without disturbance.   Though I would not so far promote effeminacy as to propose the Sybarites for an example, yet since there is no man so
corrupt or foolish but something useful may be learned from him,
I could wish that, in imitation of a people not often to be copied,
some regulations might be made to exclude screech-owls from all
company as the enemies of mankind and confine them to some
proper receptacle where they may mingle sighs at leisure and
thicken the gloom of one another.

'Thou prophet of evil,' says Homer's Agamemnon, 'thou never
foretellest me good, but the joy of thy heart is to predict misfortunes.'
Whoever is of the same temper might there find the means of
indulging his thoughts and improving his vein of denunciation,
and the flock of screech-owls might hoot together without injury
to the rest of the world.

Yet, though I have so little kindness for this dark generation,
I am very far from intending to debar the soft and tender mind
from the privilege of complaining when the sigh rises from the
desire not of giving pain, but of gaining ease.   To hear complaints
with patience, even when complaints are vain, is one of the duties of
friendship; and though it must be allowed that he suffers most like
a hero that hides his grief in silence,

> Spem vultu simulat, premit altum corde dolorem.

> His outward smiles conceal'd his inward smart.

> DRYDEN.

yet it cannot be denied that he who complains acts like a man, like
a social being, who looks for help from his fellow creatures.   Pity
is to many of the unhappy a source of comfort in hopeless distresses,
as it contributes to recommend them to themselves by proving that
they have not lost the regard of others; and heaven seems to indi-
cate the duty even of barren compassion by inclining us to weep for
evils which we cannot remedy.

DIGNITY AND USES OF
BIOGRAPHY (60)

Saturday, 13th October 1750

Quid sit pulchrum, quid turpe, quid utile, quid non,
Plenius et melius Chrysippo et Crantore dicit.

HORACE.

Whose works the beautiful and base contain,
Of vice and virtue more instructive rules,
Than all the sober sages of the schools.

FRANCIS.

ALL joy or sorrow for the happiness or calamities of others is produced by an act of the imagination that realizes the event, however fictitious, or approximates it, however remote, by placing us for a time in the condition of him whose fortune we contemplate. So that we feel, while the deception lasts, whatever motions would be excited by the same good or evil happening to ourselves.

Our passions are therefore more strongly moved in proportion as we can more readily adopt the pains or pleasure proposed to our minds by recognizing them at once our own or considering them as naturally incident to our state of life. It is not easy for the most artful writer to give us an interest in happiness or misery which we think ourselves never likely to feel and with which we have never yet been made acquainted. Histories of the downfall of kingdoms and revolutions of empires are read with great tranquillity. The imperial tragedy pleases common auditors only by its pomp of ornament and grandeur of ideas; and the man whose faculties have been engrossed by business, and whose heart never fluttered but at the rise or fall of stocks, wonders how the attention can be seized or the affection agitated by a tale of love.

Those parallel circumstances and kindred images to which we readily conform our minds are, above all other writings, to be found in narratives of the lives of particular persons; and therefore no species of writing seems more worthy of cultivation than biography, since none can be more delightful or more useful, none can more certainly enchain the heart by irresistible interest, or more widely diffuse instruction to every diversity of condition.

The general and rapid narratives of history, which involve a thousand fortunes in the business of a day and complicate innumerable incidents in one great transaction, afford few lessons applicable to private life, which derives its comforts and its wretchedness from the right or wrong management of things which nothing but their frequency makes considerable—'Parva si non fiunt quotidie,' says Pliny—and which can have no place in those relations which never descend below the consultation of senates, the motions of armies, and the schemes of conspirators.

I have often thought that there has rarely passed a life of which a judicious and faithful narrative would not be useful. For not only every man has, in the mighty mass of the world, great numbers in the same condition with himself, to whom his mistakes and miscarriages, escapes and expedients, would be of immediate and apparent use, but there is such an uniformity in the state of man, considered apart from adventitious and separable decorations and disguises, that there is scarce any possibility of good or ill but is common to human kind. A great part of the time of those who are placed at the greatest distance by fortune or by temper must unavoidably pass in the same manner, and though, when the claims of nature are satisfied, caprice and vanity and accident begin to produce discriminations and peculiarities, yet the eye is not very heedful or quick which cannot discover the same causes still terminating their influence in the same effects, though sometimes accelerated, sometimes retarded, or perplexed by multiplied combinations. We are all prompted by the same motives, all deceived by the same fallacies, all animated by hope, obstructed by danger, entangled by desire, and seduced by pleasure.

It is frequently objected to relations of particular lives that they are not distinguished by any striking or wonderful vicissitudes. The scholar who passed his life among his books, the merchant who conducted only his own affairs, the priest whose sphere of action was not extended beyond that of his duty, are considered as no proper objects of public regard, however they might have excelled in their several stations, whatever might have been their learning, integrity, and piety. But this notion arises from false measures of excellence and dignity, and must be eradicated by considering that in the esteem of uncorrupted reason what is of most use is of most value.

It is, indeed, not improper to take honest advantages of prejudice and to gain attention by a celebrated name; but the business of the biographer is often to pass slightly over those performances and incidents which produce vulgar greatness, to lead the thoughts into domestic privacies, and display the minute details of daily life where exterior appendages are cast aside and men excel each other only by prudence and by virtue. The account of Thuanus is, with great propriety, said by its author to have been written that it might lay open to posterity the private and familiar character of that man, *cujus ingenium et candorum ex ipsius scriptis sunt olim semper miraturi,* whose candour and genius will to the end of time be by his writings preserved in admiration.

There are many invisible circumstances which, whether we read as inquirers after natural or moral knowledge, whether we intend to enlarge our science or increase our virtue, are more important than public occurrences. Thus Sallust, the great master of nature, has not forgot in his account of Cataline to remark that his walk was now quick and again slow, as an indication of a mind revolving something with violent commotion. Thus the story of Melanchthon affords a striking lecture on the value of time by informing us that when he made an appointment he expected not only the hour but the minute to be fixed, that the day might not run out in the idleness of suspense. And all the plans and enterprises of De Wit are now of less importance to the world than that part of his personal character which represents him as careful of his health and negligent of his life.

But biography has often been allotted to writers who seem very little acquainted with the nature of their task or very negligent about the performance. They rarely afford any other account than might be collected from public papers, but imagine themselves writing a life when they exhibit a chronological series of actions or preferments, and so little regard the manners or behaviour of their heroes, that more knowledge may be gained of a man's real character by a short conversation with one of his servants than from a formal and studied narrative begun with his pedigree and ended with his funeral.

If now and then they condescend to inform the world of particular facts, they are not always so happy as to select the most important. I know not well what advantage posterity can receive from the only circumstance by which Tickell has distinguished Addison from the rest of mankind, the irregularity of his pulse. Nor can I think myself overpaid for the time spent in reading the life of Malherbe by being enabled to relate, after the learned biographer, that Malherbe had two predominant opinions; one that the looseness of a single woman might destroy all her boast of ancient descent, the other that the French beggars made use very improperly and barbarously of the phrase *noble gentleman,* because either word included the sense of both.

There are, indeed, some natural reasons why these narratives are often written by such as were not likely to give much instruction or delight, and why most accounts of particular persons are barren and useless. If a life be delayed till interest and envy are at an end, we may hope for impartiality but must expect little intelligence. For the incidents which give excellence to biography are of a volatile and evanescent kind, such as soon escape the memory and are rarely transmitted by tradition. We know how few can portray a living acquaintance except by his most prominent and observable particularities and the grosser features of his mind; and it may be easily imagined how much of this little knowledge may be lost in imparting it, and how soon a succession of copies will lose all resemblance of the original.

If the biographer writes from personal knowledge and makes haste to gratify the public curiosity, there is danger lest his interest, his fear, his gratitude, or his tenderness overpower his fidelity and tempt him to conceal if not to invent. There are many who think it an act of piety to hide the faults or failings of their friends, even when they can no longer suffer by their detection. We therefore see whole ranks of characters adorned with uniform panegyric, and not to be known from one another but by extrinsic and casual circumstances. 'Let me remember,' says Hale, 'when I find myself inclined to pity a criminal, that there is likewise a pity due to the country.' If we owe regard to the memory of the dead, there is yet more respect to be paid to knowledge, to virtue, and to truth.

A YOUNG LADY LONGS FOR LONDON (62)

Saturday, 20th October 1750

Nunc ego Triptolemi cuperem conscendere currus,
  Misit in ignotam qui rude semen humum:
Nunc ego Medeae vellem fraenare dracones,
  Quos habuit fugiens arva, Corinthe, tua;
Nunc ego jactandas optarem sumere pennas,
  Sive tuas, Perseu; Daedale, sive tuas.

OVID.

Now would I mount his car, whose bounteous hand
First sow'd with teeming seed the furrow'd land:
Now to Medaea's dragons fix my reins,
That swiftly bore her from Corinthian plains;
Now on Daedalian waxen pinions stray,
Or those which wafted Perseus on his way.

F. LEWIS.

TO THE 'RAMBLER'

SIR,

  I am a young woman of a very large fortune which, if my parents would have been persuaded to comply with the rules and customs of the polite part of mankind, might long since have raised me to the highest honours of the female world.   But so strangely have they hitherto contrived to waste my life, that I am now on the borders of twenty without having ever danced but at our monthly assembly, or been toasted but among a few gentlemen of the neighbourhood, or seen any company in which it was worth a wish to be distinguished.

  My father having impaired his patrimony in soliciting a place at court at last grew wise enough to cease his pursuit; and, to repair the consequences of expensive attendance and negligence of his affairs, married a lady much older than himself, who had lived in the fashionable world till she was considered as an encumbrance upon parties of pleasure, and, as I can collect from incidental informations, retired from gay assemblies just time enough to escape the mortification of universal neglect.

  She was, however, still rich and not yet wrinkled.   My father was too distressfully embarrassed to think much on anything but the means of extrication; and though it is not likely that he wanted the delicacy which polite conversation will always produce in understandings not remarkably defective, yet he was contented with a match by which he might be set free from inconveniences that would have destroyed all the pleasures of imagination, and taken from softness and beauty the power of delighting.

As they were both somewhat disgusted with their treatment in the world, and married, though without any dislike of each other yet principally for the sake of setting themselves free from dependence on caprice or fashion, they soon retired into the country, and devoted their lives to rural business and diversions.

They had not much reason to regret the change of their situation; for their vanity, which had so long been tormented by neglect and disappointment, was here gratified with every honour that could be paid them. Their long familiarity with public life made them the oracles of all those who aspired to intelligence or politeness. My father dictated politics, my mother prescribed the mode; and it was sufficient to entitle any family to some consideration that they were known to visit at Mrs. Courtly's.

In this state they were, to speak in the style of novelists, made happy by the birth of your correspondent. My parents had no other child; I was therefore not browbeaten by a saucy brother, or lost in a multitude of coheiresses whose fortunes, being equal, would probably have conferred equal merit and procured equal regard; and as my mother was now old my understanding and my person had fair play, my inquiries were not checked, my advances towards importance were not repressed, and I was soon suffered to tell my own opinions and early accustomed to hear my own praises.

By these accidental advantages I was much exalted above the young ladies with whom I conversed, and was treated by them with great deference. I saw none who did not seem to confess my superiority and to be held in awe by the splendour of my appearance; for the fondness of my father made himself pleased to see me dressed, and my mother had no vanity nor expenses to hinder her from concurring with his inclinations.

Thus, Mr. Rambler, I lived without much desire after anything beyond the circle of our visits; and here I should have quietly continued to portion out my time among my books and my needle and my company, had not my curiosity been every moment excited by the conversation of my parents who, whenever they sit down to familiar prattle and endeavour the entertainment of each other, immediately transport themselves to London and relate some adventure in a hackney-coach, some frolic at a masquerade, some conversation in the Park, or some quarrel at an assembly; display the magnificence of a birth-night, relate the conquests of maids of honour, or give a history of diversions, shows, and entertainments which I had never known but from their accounts.

I am so well versed in the history of the gay world, that I can relate with great punctuality the lives of all the last race of wits and beauties; can enumerate with exact chronology the whole succession of celebrated singers, musicians, tragedians, comedians, and harlequins; can tell to the last twenty years all the changes of fashion; and am, indeed, a complete antiquary with respect to head-dresses, dances, and operas.

You will easily imagine, Mr. Rambler, that I could not hear these narratives for sixteen years together without suffering some impression and wishing myself nearer to those places where every hour brings some new pleasure and life is diversified with an unexhausted succession of felicity.

I indeed often asked my mother why she left a place which she recollected with so much delight, and why she did not visit London once a year, like some other ladies, and initiate me in the world by showing me its amusements, its grandeur, and its variety. But she always told me that the days which she had seen were such as will never come again; that all diversion is now degenerated; that the conversation of the present age is insipid, that their fashions are unbecoming, their customs absurd, and their morals corrupt; that there is no ray left of the genius which enlightened the times that she remembers; that no one who had seen or heard the ancient performers would be able to bear the bunglers of this despicable age; and that there is now neither politeness nor pleasure nor virtue in the world. She therefore assures me that she consults my happiness by keeping me at home, for I should now find nothing but vexation and disgust, and she should be ashamed to see me pleased with such fopperies and trifles as take up the thoughts of the present set of young people.

With this answer I was kept quiet for several years and thought it no great inconvenience to be confined to the country, till last summer a young gentleman and his sister came down to pass a few months with one of our neighbours. They had generally no great regard for the country ladies, but distinguished me by a particular complaisance; and, as we grew intimate, gave me such a detail of the elegance, the splendour, the mirth, the happiness of the town, that I am resolved to be no longer buried in ignorance and obscurity, but to share with other wits the joy of being admired, and divide with other beauties the empire of the world.

I do not find, Mr. Rambler, upon a deliberate and impartial comparison, that I am excelled by Belinda in beauty, in wit, in judgment, in knowledge, or in anything that a kind of gay, lively familiarity by which she mingled with strangers as with persons long acquainted, and which enables her to display her powers without any obstruction, hesitation, or confusion. Yet she can relate a thousand civilities paid to her in public, can produce, from a hundred lovers, letters filled with praises, protestations, ecstasies, and despair, has been handed by dukes to her chair, has been the occasion of innumerable quarrels, has paid twenty visits in an afternoon, been invited to six balls in an evening, and been forced to retire to lodgings in the country from the importunity of courtship and the fatigue of pleasure.

I tell you, Mr. Rambler, I will stay here no longer. I have at last prevailed upon my mother to send me to town, and shall set out in three weeks on the grand expedition. I intend to live in public and to crowd into the winter every pleasure which money can purchase and every honour which beauty can obtain.

But this tedious interval how shall I endure? Cannot you alleviate the misery of delay by some pleasing description of the entertainments of the town? I can read, I can talk, I can think of nothing else; and if you will not sooth my impatience, heighten my ideas, and animate my hopes, you may write for those who have more leisure, but are not to expect any longer the honour of being read by those eyes which are now intent only on conquest and destruction.

RHODOCLIA.

MAN'S HAPPINESS OR MISERY
AT HOME (68)

Saturday, 10th November 1750

Vivendum recte, cum propter plurima, tunc his
Praecipue causis, ut linguas mancipiorum
Contemnas; nam lingua mala pars pessima servi.

JUVENAL.

Let us live well: were it alone for this,
The baneful tongues of servants to despise:
Slander, that worst of poisons, ever finds
An easy entrance to ignoble minds.

HERVEY.

THE younger Pliny has very justly observed that of actions that
deserve our attention the most splendid are not always the greatest.
Fame and wonder and applause are not excited but by external and
adventitious circumstances, often distinct and separate from virtue
and heroism. Eminence of station, greatness of effect, and all the
favours of fortune must concur to place excellence in public view;
but fortitude, diligence, and patience, divested of their show, glide
unobserved through the crowd of life, and suffer and act, though
with the same vigour and constancy, yet without pity and without
praise.

This remark may be extended to all parts of life. Nothing is to
be estimated by its effect upon common eyes and common ears. A
thousand miseries make silent and invisible inroads on mankind,
and the heart feels innumerable throbs which never break into complaint. Perhaps, likewise, our pleasures are for the most part
equally secret, and most are borne up by some private satisfaction,
some internal consciousness, some latent hope, some peculiar prospect, which they never communicate but reserve for solitary hours
and clandestine meditation.

The main of life is, indeed, composed of small incidents and petty
occurrences: of wishes for objects not remote and grief for disappointments of no fatal consequence, of insect vexations which sting
us and fly away, impertinences which buzz awhile about us and are
heard no more, of meteorous pleasures which dance before us and
are dissipated, of compliments which glide off the soul like other

music and are forgotten by him that gave and him that received them.

Such is the general heap out of which every man is to cull his own condition; for, as the chemists tell us that all bodies are resolvable into the same elements and that the boundless variety of things arises from the different proportions of a very few ingredients, so a few pains and a few pleasures are all the materials of human life, and of these the proportions are partly allotted by Providence and partly left to the arrangement of reason and of choice.

As these are well or ill disposed, man is for the most part happy or miserable. For very few are involved in great events or have their thread of life entwisted with the chain of causes on which armies or nations are suspended; and even those who seem wholly busied in public affairs and elevated above low cares or trivial pleasures pass the chief part of their time in familiar and domestic scenes. From these they come into public life, to these they are every hour recalled by passions not to be suppressed, in these they have the reward of their toil, and to these at last they retire.

The great end of prudence is to give cheerfulness to those hours which splendour cannot gild and acclamation cannot exhilarate, those soft intervals of unbended amusement in which a man shrinks to his natural dimensions and throws aside the ornaments or disguises which he feels in privacy to be useless encumbrances and to lose all effect when they become familiar. To be happy at home is the ultimate result of all ambition, the end to which every enterprise and labour tends, and of which every desire prompts the prosecution.

It is, indeed, at home that every man must be known by those who would make a just estimate either of his virtue or felicity; for smiles and embroidery are alike occasional, and the mind is often dressed for show in painted honour and fictitious benevolence.

Every man must have found some whose lives in every house but their own was a continual series of hypocrisy, and who concealed under fair appearances bad qualities which, whenever they thought themselves out of the reach of censure, broke out from their restraint like winds imprisoned in their caverns, and whom everyone had reason to love but they whose love a wise man is chiefly solicitous to procure. And there are others who, without any show of general goodness, and without the attractions by which popularity is conciliated, are received among their own families as bestowers of happiness and reverenced as instructors, guardians, and benefactors.

The most authentic witnesses of any man's character are those who know him in his own family and see him without any restraint or rule of conduct but such as he voluntarily prescribes to himself. If a man carries virtue with him into his private apartments and takes no advantage of unlimited power or probable secrecy, if we trace him through the round of his time and find that his character, with those allowances which mortal frailty must always want, is uniform and regular, we have all the evidence of his sincerity that one man can have with regard to another: and, indeed, as hypocrisy cannot be its own reward, we may without hesitation determine that his heart is pure.

The highest panegyric, therefore, that private virtue can receive is the praise of servants. For, however vanity or insolence may look down with contempt on the suffrage of men undignified by wealth and unenlightened by education, it very seldom happens that they commend or blame without justice. Vice and virtue are easily distinguished. Oppression, according to Harrington's aphorism, will be felt by those that cannot see it; and, perhaps, it falls out very often that in moral questions the philosophers in the gown and in the livery differ not so much in their sentiments as in their language, and have equal power of discerning right though they cannot point it out to others with equal address.

There are very few faults to be committed in solitude or without some agents, partners, confederates, or witnesses. And therefore the servant must commonly know the secrets of a master who has any secrets to entrust; and failings merely personal are so frequently exposed by that security which pride and folly generally produce, and so inquisitively watched by that desire of reducing the inequalities of condition which the lower orders of the world will always feel, that the testimony of a menial domestic can seldom be considered as defective for want of knowledge. And though its impartiality may be sometimes suspected, it is at least as credible as that of equals, where rivalry instigates censure or friendship dictates palliations.

The danger of betraying our weakness to our servants and the impossibility of concealing it from them may be justly considered as one motive to a regular and irreproachable life. For no condition is more hateful or despicable than his who has put himself in the power of his servant, in the power of him whom, perhaps, he has first corrupted by making him subservient to his vices, and whose fidelity he therefore cannot enforce by any precepts of honesty or reason. It is seldom known that authority thus acquired is possessed without insolence, or that the master is not forced to confess by his tameness or forbearance that he has enslaved himself by some foolish confidence. And his crime is equally punished, whatever part he takes of the choice to which he is reduced; and he is, from that fatal hour in which he sacrificed his dignity to his passions, in perpetual dread of insolence or defamation, of a controller at home or an accuser abroad. He is condemned to purchase by continual bribes that secrecy which bribes never secured, and which, after a long course of submission, promises, and anxieties, he will find violated in a fit of rage or in a frolic of drunkenness.

To dread no eye and to suspect no tongue is the great prerogative of innocence, an exemption granted only to invariable virtue. But guilt has always its horrors and solicitudes; and, to make it yet more shameful and detestable, it is doomed often to stand in awe of those to whom nothing could give influence or weight but their power of betraying.

MISERIES OF OLD AGE (69)

Saturday, 1st December 1750

Rixatur de lana saepe caprina.

HORACE.

For nought tormented, she for nought torments.

ELPHINSTON.

MEN seldom give pleasure where they are not pleased themselves. It is necessary, therefore, to cultivate an habitual alacrity and cheerfulness, that in whatever state we may be placed by Providence, whether we are appointed to confer or receive benefits, to implore or to afford protection, we may secure the love of those with whom we transact. For though it is generally imagined that he who grants favours may spare any attention to his behaviour and that usefulness will always procure friends, yet it has been found that there is an art of granting requests (an art very difficult of attainment) that officiousness and liberality may be so adulterated as to lose the greater part of their effect that compliance may provoke, relief may harass, and liberality distress.

No disease of the mind can more fatally disable it from

benevolence, the chief duty of social beings, than ill humour or peevishness; for though it breaks not out in paroxysms of outrage, nor bursts into clamour, turbulence, and bloodshed, it wears out happiness by slow corrosion and small injuries incessantly repeated. It may be considered as the canker of life that destroys its vigour and checks its improvement, that creeps on with hourly depredations, and taints and vitiates what it cannot consume.

Peevishness, when it has been so far indulged as to outrun the motions of the will and discover itself without premeditation, is a species of depravity in the highest degree disgusting and offensive, because no rectitude of intention nor softness of address can ensure a moment's exemption from affront and indignity. While we are courting the favour of a peevish man and exerting ourselves in the most diligent civility an unlucky syllable displeases, an unheeded circumstance raffles and exasperates, and in the moment when we congratulate ourselves upon having gained a friend our endeavours are frustrated at once, and all our assiduity forgotten in the casual tumult of some trifling irritation.

This troublesome impatience is sometimes nothing more than the symptom of some deeper malady. He that is angry without daring to confess his resentment, or sorrowful without the liberty of telling his grief, is too frequently inclined to give vent to the fermentations of his mind at the first passages that are opened, and to let his passions boil over upon those whom accident throws in his way. A painful and tedious course of sickness frequently produces such an alarming apprehension of the least increase of uneasiness as keeps the soul perpetually on the watch, such a restless and incessant solicitude as no care or tenderness can appease and can only be pacified by the cure of the distemper and the removal of that pain by which it is excited.

Nearly approaching to this weakness is the captiousness of old age. When the strength is crushed, the senses dulled, and the common pleasures of life become insipid by repetition, we are willing to impute our uneasiness to causes not wholly out of our power, and please ourselves with fancying that we suffer by neglect, unkindness, or any evil which admits a remedy, rather than by the decays of nature which cannot be prevented or repaired. We therefore revenge our pains upon those on whom we resolve to charge them, and too often drive mankind away at the time we have the greatest need of tenderness and assistance.

But though peevishness may sometimes claim our compassion, as the consequence or concomitant of misery, it is very often found where nothing can justify or excuse its admission. It is frequently one of the attendants on the prosperous, and is employed by insolence in exacting homage or by tyranny in harassing subjection. It is the offspring of idleness or pride, of idleness anxious for trifles or pride unwilling to endure the least obstruction of her wishes. Those who have long lived in solitude, indeed, naturally contract this unsocial quality, because, having long had only themselves to please, they do not readily depart from their own inclinations. Their singularities therefore are only blameable when they have imprudently or morosely withdrawn themselves from the world. But there are others who have, without any necessity, nursed up this habit in their minds by making implicit submissiveness the condition of their favour, and suffering none to approach them but those who never speak but to applaud or move but to obey.

He that gives himself up to his own fancy and converses with none but such as he hires to lull him on the down of absolute authority, to sooth him with obsequiousness, and regale him with flattery, soon grows too slothful for the labour of contest, too tender for the asperity of contradiction, and too delicate for the coarseness of truth. A little opposition offends, a little restraint enrages, and a little difficulty perplexes him. Having been accustomed to see everything give way to his humour, he soon forgets his own littleness, and expects to find the world rolling at his beck and all mankind employed to accommodate and delight him.

Tetrica had a large fortune bequeathed to her by an aunt, which made her very early independent and placed her in a state of superiority to all about her. Having no superfluity of understanding, she was intoxicated by the flatteries of her maid, who informed her that ladies such as she had nothing to do but take pleasure their own way; that she wanted nothing from others, and had therefore no reason to value their opinion; that money was everything; and that they who thought themselves ill treated should look for better usage among their equals.

Warm with these generous sentiments, Tetrica came forth into the world, in which she endeavoured to force respect by haughtiness of mien and vehemence of language; but having neither birth, beauty, nor wit in any uncommon degree, she suffered such mortifications from those who thought themselves at liberty to return her insults, as reduced her turbulence to cooler malignity and taught her to practise her arts of vexation only where she might hope to tyrannize without resistance. She continued from her twentieth to her fifty-fifth year to torment all her inferiors with so much diligence, that she has formed a principle of disapprobation, and finds in every place something to grate her mind and disturb her quiet.

If she takes the air she is offended with the heat or cold, the glare of the sun, or the gloom of the clouds. If she makes a visit the room in which she is to be received is too light or too dark, or furnished with something which she cannot see without aversion. Her tea is never of the right sort. The figures on the china give her disgust. Where there are children she hates the gabble of brats. Where there are none she cannot bear a place without some cheerfulness and rattle. If many servants are kept in a house she never fails to tell how Lord Lavish was ruined by a numerous retinue; if few, she relates the story of an old miser that made his company wait on themselves. She quarrelled with one family because she had an unpleasant view from their windows, with another because the squirrel leaped within two yards of her, and with a third because she could not bear the noise of the parrot.

Of milliners and mantua-makers she is the proverbial torment. She compels them to alter their work, then to unmake it and contrive it after another fashion; then changes her mind and likes it better as it was at first; then will have a small improvement. Thus she proceeds till no profit can recompense the vexation: they at last leave the clothes at her house and refuse to serve her. Her maid, the only being that can endure her tyranny, professes to take her own course and hear her mistress talk. Such is the consequence of peevishness: it can be borne only when it is despised.

It sometimes happens that too close an attention to minute exactness or a too rigorous habit of examining everything by the standard of perfection vitiates the temper rather than improves the understanding, and teaches the mind to discern faults with unhappy penetration. It is incident likewise to men of vigorous imagination to please themselves too much with futurities and to fret because those expectations are disappointed which should never have been formed. Knowledge and genius are often enemies to quiet by suggesting ideas of excellence which men and the performances of men cannot attain. But let no man rashly determine that his unwillingness to be pleased is a proof of understanding, unless his superiority appears from less doubtful evidence. For though peevishness may sometimes justly boast its descent from learning or from wit, it is much oftener of base extraction, the child of vanity, and nursling of ignorance.

THE POWER OF NOVELTY (78)

Saturday, 15th December 1750

> Mors sola fatetur.
> Quantula sint hominum corpuscula.
>
> JUVENAL.

> Death only this mysterious truth unfolds,
> The mighty soul how small a body holds.
>
> DRYDEN.

CORPORAL sensation is known to depend so much upon novelty, that custom takes away from many things their power of giving pleasure or pain. Thus a new dress becomes easy by wearing it, and the palate is reconciled by degrees to dishes which at first disgusted it. That by long habit of carrying a burden we lose, in great part, our sensibility of its weight, any man may be convinced by putting on for an hour the armour of our ancestors; for he will scarcely believe that men would have had much inclination to marches and battles, encumbered and oppressed, as he will find himself, with the ancient panoply. Yet the heroes that overran regions and stormed towns in iron accoutrements, he knows not to have been bigger, and has no reason to imagine them stronger than the present race of men. He therefore must conclude that their peculiar powers were conferred only by peculiar habits, and that their familiarity with the dress of war enabled them to move in it with ease, vigour, and agility.

Yet it seems to be the condition of our present state that pain should be more fixed and permanent than pleasure. Uneasiness gives way by slow degrees and is long before it quits its possession of the sensory; but all our gratifications are volatile, vagrant, and easily dissipated. The fragrance of the jessamine bower is lost after the enjoyment of a few moments, and the Indian wanders among his native spices without any sense of their exhalations. It is, indeed, not necessary to show by many instances what all mankind confess by an incessant call for variety and restless pursuit of enjoyments which they value only because unpossessed.

Something similar or analogous may be observed in effects produced immediately upon the mind: nothing can strongly strike or affect us but what is rare or sudden. The most important events when they become familiar are no longer considered with wonder or solicitude, and that which at first filled up our whole attention and left no place for any other thought is soon thrust aside into some remote repository of the mind, and lies among other lumber of the memory overlooked and neglected. Thus far the mind resembles the body, but here the similitude is at an end.

The manner in which external force acts upon the body is very little subject to the regulation of the will. No man can at pleasure obtund or invigorate his senses, prolong the agency of any image traced upon the eye, or any sound infused into the ear. But our ideas are more subjected to choice: we can call them before us and command their stay, we can facilitate and promote their recurrence, we can either repress their intrusion or hasten their retreat. It is therefore the business of wisdom and virtue to select among numberless objects striving for our notice such as may enable us to exalt our reason, extend our views, and secure our happiness. But this choice is to be made with very little regard to rareness or frequency: for nothing is valuable merely because it is either rare or common, but because it is adapted to some useful purpose and enables us to supply some deficiency of our nature.

Milton has judiciously represented the father of mankind as seized with horror and astonishment at the sight of death exhibited to him on the Mount of Vision. For surely nothing can so much disturb the passions or perplex the intellects of man as the disruption of his union with visible nature, a separation from all that has hitherto delighted or engaged him, a change not only of the place but the manner of his being, an entrance into a state, not simply which he knows not but which perhaps he has not faculties to know, an immediate and perceptible communication with the Supreme Being, and, what is above all distressful and alarming, the final sentence and unalterable allotment.

Yet we, to whom the shortness of life has given frequent occasions of contemplating mortality, can without emotion see generations of men pass away, and are at leisure to establish modes of sorrow and adjust the ceremonial of death. We can look upon funeral pomp as a common spectacle in which we have no concern, and turn away from it to trifles and amusements without dejection of look or inquietude of heart.

It is, indeed, apparent from the constitution of the world that there must be a time for other thoughts; and a perpetual meditation upon the last hour, however it may become the solitude of a monastery, is inconsistent with many duties of common life. But surely the remembrance of death ought to predominate in our

minds as an habitual and settled principle, always operating though
not always perceived; and our attention should seldom wander so
far from our own condition as not to be recalled and fixed by sight
of an event which must soon, we know not how soon, happen
likewise to ourselves, and of which, though we cannot appoint the
time, we may secure the consequence.

Every instance of death may justly awaken our fears and quicken
our vigilance; but its frequency so much weakens its effect that we
are seldom alarmed unless some close connection is broken, some
scheme frustrated, or some hope defeated.   Many therefore seem
to pass on from youth to decrepitude without any reflection on the
end of life, because they are wholly involved within themselves,
and look on others only as inhabitants of the common earth without
any expectation of receiving good or intention of bestowing it.

Events of which we confess the importance excite little sensibility
unless they affect us more nearly than as sharers in the common
interest of mankind.   That desire which every man feels of being
remembered and lamented is often mortified when we remark how
little concern is caused by the eternal departure even of those who
have passed their lives with public honours and been distinguished
by extraordinary performances.   It is not possible to be regarded
with tenderness except by a few.   That merit which gives greatness
and renown diffuses its influence to a wide compass but acts weakly
on every single breast.   It is placed at a distance from common
spectators, and shines like one of the remote stars of which the light
reaches us but not the heat.   The wit, the hero, the philosopher,
whom their tempers or their fortunes have hindered from intimate
relations, die without any other effect than that of adding a new
topic to the conversation of the day.   They impress none with any
fresh conviction of the fragility of our nature because none had any
particular interest in their lives or was united to them by a reciprocation of benefits and endearments.

Thus it often happens that those who in their lives were applauded and admired are laid at last in the ground without the
common honour of a stone, because by those excellencies with
which many were delighted none had been obliged, and though
they had many to celebrate they had none to love them.

Custom so far regulates the sentiments, at least of common
minds, that I believe men may be generally observed to grow less
tender as they advance in age.   He who, when life was new, melted
at the loss of every companion can look in time without concern
upon the grave into which his last friend was thrown, and into

which himself is ready to fall. Not that he is more willing to die than formerly, but that he is more familiar to the death of others, and therefore is not alarmed so far as to consider how much nearer he approaches to his end. But this is to submit tamely to the tyranny of accident and to suffer our reason to lie useless. Every funeral may justly be considered as a summons to prepare for that state into which it shows us that we must some time enter; and the summons is more loud and piercing as the event of which it warns us is at less distance. To neglect at any time preparation for death is to sleep on our post at a siege, but to omit it in old age is to sleep at an attack.

It has always appeared to me one of the most striking passages in the visions of Quevedo which stigmatizes those as fools who complain that they failed of happiness by sudden death. 'How,' says he, 'can death be sudden to a being who always knew that he must die and that the time of his death was uncertain?'

Since business and gaiety are always drawing our attention away from a future state, some admonition is frequently necessary to recall it to our minds; and what can more properly renew the impression than the examples of mortality which every day supplies? The great incentive to virtue is the reflection that we must die. It will therefore be useful to accustom ourselves, whenever we see a funeral, to consider how soon we may be added to the number of those whose probation is past and whose happiness or misery shall endure for ever.

A COLLECTOR'S NARRATIVE (82)

Saturday, 29th December 1750

Omnia castor emit, sic fiet ut omnia vendat.

MARTIAL.

Who buys without discretion, buys to sell.

TO THE 'RAMBLER'

SIR,

It will not be necessary to solicit your goodwill by any formal preface when I have informed you that I have long been known as the most laborious and zealous virtuoso that the present age has had the honour of producing, and that inconveniences have been brought upon me by an unextinguishable ardour of curiosity and an unshaken perseverance in the acquisition of the productions of art and nature.

It was observed from my entrance into the world that I had something uncommon in my disposition and that there appeared in me very early tokens of superior genius. I was always an enemy to trifles: the playthings which my mother bestowed upon me I immediately broke that I might discover the method of their structure and the causes of their motions. Of all the toys with which children are delighted I valued only my coral, and as soon as I could speak asked, like Pieresc, innumerable questions which the maids about me could not resolve. As I grew older I was more thoughtful and serious, and, instead of amusing myself with puerile diversions, made collections of natural rarities, and never walked into the fields without bringing home stones of remarkable forms or insects of some uncommon species. I never entered an old house from which I did not take away the painted glass, and often lamented that I was not one of that happy generation who demolished the convents and monasteries and broke windows by law.

Being thus early possessed by a taste for solid knowledge, I passed my youth with very little disturbance from passions and appetites; and having no pleasure in the company of boys and girls who talked of plays, politics, fashions, or love, I carried on my inquiries with incessant diligence, and had amassed more stones, mosses, and shells than are to be found in many celebrated collections, at an age in which the greatest part of young men are studying under tutors or endeavouring to recommend themselves to notice by their dress, their air, and their levities.

When I was two-and-twenty years old I became, by the death of my father, possessed of a small estate in land with a very large sum of money in the public funds, and must confess that I did not much lament him, for he was a man of mean parts, bent rather upon growing rich than wise. He once fretted at the expense of only ten shillings which he happened to overhear me offering for the sting of a hornet, though it was a cold moist summer in which very few hornets had been seen. He often recommended to me the study of physic, 'in which,' said he, 'you may at once satisfy your curiosity after natural history and increase your fortune by benefiting mankind.' I heard him, Mr. Rambler, with pity; and as there was no prospect of elevating a mind formed to grovel, suffered him to please himself with hoping that I should some time follow his advice. For you know that there are men with whom, when they have once settled a notion in their heads, it is to very little purpose to dispute.

Being now left wholly to my own inclinations, I very soon enlarged the bounds of my curiosity, and contented myself no longer with such rarities as required only judgment and industry and, when once found, might be had for nothing. I now turned my thoughts to exotics and antiques, and became so well known for my generous patronage of ingenious men, that my levee was crowded with visitants, some to see my museum and others to increase its treasures by selling me whatever they had brought from other countries.

I had always a contempt for that narrowness of conception which contents itself with cultivating some single corner of the field of science. I took the whole region into my view and wished it of yet greater extent. But no man's power can be equal to his will. I was forced to proceed by slow degrees and to purchase what chance or kindness happened to present. I did not, however, proceed without some design or imitate the indiscretion of those who begin a thousand collections and finish none. Having been always a lover of geography I determined to collect the maps drawn in the rude and barbarous times before any regular surveys or just observations, and have, at a great expense, brought together a volume in which, perhaps, not a single country is laid down according to its true situation, and by which he that desires to know the errors of the ancient geographers may be amply informed.

But my ruling passion is patriotism. My chief care has been to procure the products of our own country; and as Alfred received the tribute of the Welsh in wolves' heads, I allowed my tenants to pay their rents in butterflies till I had exhausted the papilionaceous tribe. I then directed them to the pursuit of other animals, and obtained by this easy method most of the grubs and insects which land, air, or water can supply. I have three species of earthworms not known to the naturalists, have discovered a new ephemera, and can show four wasps that were taken torpid in their winter quarters. I have from my own ground the longest blade of grass upon record, and once accepted as a half-year's rent for a field of wheat an ear containing more grains than had been seen before upon a single stem.

One of my tenants so much neglected his own interest as to supply me in a whole summer with only two horse-flies, and those of little more than the common size; and I was upon the brink of seizing for arrears when his good fortune threw a white mole in his way, for which he was not only forgiven but rewarded.

These, however, were petty acquisitions, and made at small expense; nor should I have ventured to rank myself among the virtuosi without better claims. I have suffered nothing worthy the regard of a wise man to escape my notice. I have ransacked the old and the new world, and been equally attentive to past ages and the present. For the illustration of ancient history I can show a marble of which the inscription, though it is not now legible, appears, from some broken remains of the letters, to have been Tuscan, and therefore probably engraved before the foundation of Rome. I have two pieces of porphyry found among the ruins of Ephesus and three letters broken off by a learned traveller from the monuments of Persepolis, a piece of stone which paved the Areopagus of Athens, and a plate, without figures or characters, which was found at Corinth, and which I therefore believe to be that metal which was once valued before gold. I have sand gathered out of the Granicus, a fragment of Trajan's bridge over the Danube, some of the mortar which cemented the watercourse of Tarquin, a horseshoe broken on the Flaminian way, and a turf with five daisies dug from the field of Pharsalus.

I do not wish to raise the envy of unsuccessful collectors by too pompous a display of my scientific wealth, but cannot forbear to observe that there are few regions of the globe which are not honoured with some memorial in my cabinets. The Persian monarchs are said to have boasted the greatness of their empire by being served at their tables with drink from the Ganges and the Danube. I can show one vial of which the water was formerly an icicle on the crags of Caucasus, and another that contains what once was snow on the top of Atlas. In a third is dew brushed from a banana in the gardens of Ispahan, and in another brine that has rolled in the Pacific Ocean. I flatter myself that I am writing to a man who will rejoice at the honour which my labours have procured to my country; and therefore I shall tell you that Britain can, by my care, boast of a snail that has crawled upon the wall of China, a humming-bird which an American princess wore in her ear, the tooth of an elephant who carried the Queen of Siam, the skin of an ape that was kept in the palace of the Great Mogul, a ribbon that adorned one of the maids of a Turkish sultana, and a scimitar once wielded by a soldier of Abas the Great.

In collecting antiquities of every country I have been careful to choose only by intrinsic worth and real usefulness without regard to party or opinions. I have therefore a lock of Cromwell's hair in a box turned from a piece of the royal oak, and keep in the same drawer sand scraped from the coffin of King Richard and a commission signed by Henry VII. I have equal veneration for the ruff of Elizabeth and the shoe of Mary of Scotland, and should lose with like regret a tobacco-pipe of Raleigh and the stirrup of King James. I have paid the same price for a glove of Lewis and a thimble of Queen Mary, for a fur cap of the Czar and a boot of Charles of Sweden.

You will easily imagine that these accumulations were not made without some diminution of my fortune. For I was so well known to spare no cost, that at every sale some bid against me for hire, some for sport, and some for malice; and if I asked the price of anything it was sufficient to double the demand. For curiosity, trafficking thus with avarice, the wealth of India had not been enough; and I by little and little transferred all my money from the funds to my closet. Here I was inclined to stop and live upon my estate in literary leisure, but the sale of the Harleian collection shook my resolution. I mortgaged my land and purchased thirty medals which I could never find before. I have at length bought till I can buy no longer, and the cruelty of my creditors has seized my repository. I am therefore condemned to disperse what the labour of an age will not reassemble. I submit to that which cannot be opposed, and shall in a short time declare a sale. I have, while it is yet in my power, sent you a pebble picked up by Tavernier on the banks of the Ganges, for which I desire no other recompense than that you will recommend my catalogue to the public.

QUISQUILIUS.

THE COLLECTOR JUSTIFIED (83)

Tuesday, 1st January 1751

Nisi utile est quod facias stulta est gloria.

PHAEDRUS.

All useless science is an empty boast.

THE publication of the letter in my last paper has naturally led me to the consideration of that thirst after curiosities which often draws contempt and ridicule upon itself, but which is perhaps not otherwise blameable than as it wants those circumstantial recommendations which add lustre even to moral excellencies and are absolutely necessary to the grace and beauty of indifferent actions.

Learning confers so much superiority on those who possess it, that they might probably have escaped all censure had they been

able to agree among themselves.   But as envy and competition
have divided the republic of letters into factions, they have neglected the common interest.   Each has called in foreign aid and
endeavoured to strengthen his own cause by the frown of power,
the hiss of ignorance, and the clamour of popularity.   They have
all engaged in feuds till by mutual hostilities they demolished those
outworks which veneration had raised for their security, and
exposed themselves to barbarians by whom every region of science
is equally laid waste.

Between men of different studies and professions may be
observed a constant reciprocation of reproaches.   The collector of
shells and stones derides the folly of him who pastes leaves and
flowers upon paper, pleases himself with colours that are per-
ceptibly fading, and amasses with care what cannot be preserved.
The hunter of insects stands amazed that any man can waste his
short time upon lifeless matter while many tribes of animals yet
want their history.   Everyone is inclined not only to promote his
own study but to exclude all others from regard, and having heated
his imagination with some favourite pursuit, wonders that the rest of
mankind are not seized with the same passion.

There are, indeed, many subjects of study which seem but
remotely allied to useful knowledge and of little importance to
happiness or virtue; nor is it easy to forbear some sallies of merriment or expressions of pity when we see a man wrinkled with
attention and emaciated with solicitude in the investigation of
questions of which, without visible inconvenience, the world may
expire in ignorance.   Yet it is dangerous to discourage well-
intended labours or innocent curiosity: for he who is employed
in searches which by any deduction of consequences tend to the
benefit of life is surely laudable in comparison of those who spend
their time in counteracting happiness and filling the world with
wrong and danger, confusion and remorse.   No man can perform
so little as not to have reason to congratulate himself on his merits
when he beholds the multitudes that live in total idleness and have
never yet endeavoured to be useful.

It is impossible to determine the limits of inquiry or to foresee
what consequences a new discovery may produce.   He who suffers
not his faculties to lie torpid has a chance, whatever be his employment, of doing good to his fellow creatures.   The man that first
ranged the woods in search of medicinal springs, or climbed the
mountains for salutary plants, has undoubtedly merited the gratitude of posterity, how much soever his frequent miscarriages might

excite the scorn of his contemporaries. If what appears little be universally despised, nothing greater can be attained; for all that is great was at first little and rose to its present bulk by gradual accessions and accumulated labours.

Those who lay out time or money in assembling matter for contemplation are doubtless entitled to some degree of respect, though in a flight of gaiety it be easy to ridicule their treasure, or in a fit of sullenness to despise it. A man who thinks only on the particular object before him goes not away much illuminated by having enjoyed the privilege of handling the tooth of a shark or the paw of a white bear. Yet there is nothing more worthy of admiration to a philosophical eye than the structure of animals, by which they are qualified to support life in the elements or climates to which they are appropriated. And of all natural bodies it must be generally confessed that they exhibit evidences of infinite wisdom, bear their testimony to the supreme reason, and excite in the mind new raptures of gratitude and new incentives to piety.

To collect the productions of art and examples of mechanical science or manual ability is unquestionably useful, even when the things themselves are of small importance, because it is always advantageous to know how far the human powers have proceeded, and how much experience has found to be within the reach of diligence. Idleness and timidity often despair without being overcome and forbear attempts for fear of being defeated; and we may promote the invigoration of faint endeavours by showing what has been already performed. It may sometimes happen that the greatest efforts of ingenuity have been exerted in trifles. Yet the same principles and expedients may be applied to more valuable purposes, and the movements which put into action machines of no use but to raise the wonder of ignorance may be employed to drain fens or manufacture metals, to assist the architect or preserve the sailor.

For the utensils, arms, or dresses of foreign nations, which make the greatest part of many collections, I have little regard when they are valued only because they are foreign and can suggest no improvement of our own practice. Yet they are not all equally useless. Nor can it be always safely determined which should be rejected or retained, for they may sometimes unexpectedly contribute to the illustration of history and to the knowledge of the natural commodities of the country or of the genius and customs of its inhabitants.

Rarities there are of yet a lower rank, which owe their worth merely to accident, and which can convey no information nor satisfy any rational desire.   Such are many fragments of antiquity, as urns and pieces of pavement; and things held in veneration only for having been once the property of some eminent person, as the armour of King Henry; or for having been used on some remarkable occasion, as the lantern of Guy Fawkes.   The loss or preservation of these seems to be a thing indifferent, nor can I perceive why the possession of them should be coveted.   Yet, perhaps, even this curiosity is implanted by nature: and when I find Tully confessing of himself that he could not forbear at Athens to visit the walks and houses which the old philosophers had frequented or inhabited, and recollect the reverence which every nation, civil and barbarous, has paid to the ground where merit has been buried, I am afraid to declare against the general voice of mankind, and am inclined to believe that this regard, which we involuntarily pay to the meanest relic of a man great and illustrious, is intended as an incitement to labour and an encouragement to expect the same renown if it be sought by the same virtues. '

The virtuoso, therefore, cannot be said to be wholly useless. But perhaps he may be sometimes culpable for confining himself to business below his genius, and losing in petty speculations those hours by which, if he had spent them in nobler studies, he might have given new light to the intellectual world.   It is never without grief that I find a man capable of ratiocination or invention enlisting himself in this secondary class of learning.   For when he has once discovered a method of gratifying his desire of eminence by expense rather than by labour, and known the sweets of a life blessed at once with the ease of idleness and the reputation of knowledge, he will not easily be brought to undergo again the toil of thinking, or leave his toys and trinkets for arguments and principles, arguments which require circumspection and vigilance, and principles which cannot be obtained but by the drudgery of meditation.   He will gladly shut himself up for ever with his shells and medals like the companions of Ulysses who, having tasted the fruit of Lotos, would not, even by the hope of seeing their own country, be tempted again to the dangers of the sea.

> ἀλλ' αὐτοῦ βούλοντο μετ' ἀνδράσι Λωτοφάγοισι,
> λωτὸν ἐρεπτόμενοι, μενέμεν νόστου τε λαθέσθαι.

> Whoso tastes
> Insatiate riots in the sweet repasts;
> Nor other home nor other care intends,
> But quits his house, his country, and his friends.
>   POPE.

Collections of this kind are of use to the learned as heaps of stone and piles of timber are necessary to the architect. But to dig the quarry or to search the field requires not much of any quality beyond stubborn perseverance; and though genius must often lie inactive without this humble assistance, yet this can claim little praise because every man can afford it.

To mean understandings it is sufficient honour to be numbered amongst the lowest labours of learning; but different abilities must find different tasks. To hew stone would have been unworthy of Palladio, and to have rambled in search of shells and flowers had but ill suited with the capacity of Newton.

A YOUNG LADY'S IMPATIENCE
OF CONTROL (84)

Saturday, 5th January 1751

Cunarum fueras motor, Charideme, mearum,
　　Et pueri custos assiduusque comes.
Jam mihi nigrescunt tonsa sudaria barba,
Sed tibi non crevi: te noster villicus horret:
　　Te dispensator, te domus ipsa pavet.
Corripis, observas, quereris, suspiria ducis,
　　Et vix a ferulis abstinet iba manum.

MARTIAL.

You rock'd my cradle, were my guide
In youth, still tending at my side:
But now, dear Sir, my beard is grown,
Still I'm a child to thee alone.
Our steward, butler, cook, and all,
You fright; nay, e'en the very wall:
You pry, and frown, and growl, and chide,
And scarce will lay the rod aside.

F. LEWIS.

TO THE 'RAMBLER'

SIR,
　　You seem in all your papers to be an enemy to tyranny and to look with impartiality upon the world. I shall therefore lay my case before you, and hope by your decision to be set free from

unreasonable restraints and enabled to justify myself against the accusations which spite and peevishness produce against me.

At the age of five years I lost my mother; and my father, not being qualified to superintend the education of a girl, committed me to the care of his sister who instructed me with the authority, and, not to deny her what she may justly claim, with the affection of a parent. She had not very elevated sentiments or extensive views, but her principles were good and her intentions pure; and though some may practise more virtues, scarce any commit fewer faults.

Under this good lady I learned all the common rules of decent behaviour and standing maxims of domestic prudence, and might have grown up by degrees to a country gentlewoman without any thoughts of ranging beyond the neighbourhood, had not Flavia come down last summer to visit her relations in the next village. I was taken, of course, to compliment the stranger, and was at the first sight surprised at the unconcern with which she saw herself gazed at by the company whom she had never known before, at the carelessness with which she received compliments, and the readiness with which she returned them. I found she had something which I perceived myself to want, and could not but wish to be like her, at once easy and officious, attentive and unembarrassed. I went home, and for four days could think and talk of nothing but Miss Flavia, though my aunt told me that she was a forward flirt and thought herself wise before her time.

In a little time she repaid my visit and raised in my heart a new confusion of love and admiration. I soon saw her again, and still found new charms in her air, conversation, and behaviour. You, who have perhaps seen the world, may have observed that formality soon ceases between young persons. I know not how others are affected on such occasions, but I found myself irresistibly allured to friendship and intimacy by the familiar complaisance and airy gaiety of Flavia; so that in a few weeks I became her favourite, and all the time was passed with me that she could gain from ceremony and visit.

As she came often to me, she necessarily spent some hours with my aunt, to whom she paid great respect by low courtesies, submissive compliance, and soft acquiescence. But as I became gradually more accustomed to her manners I discovered that her civility was general, that there was a certain degree of deference shown by her to circumstances and appearances, that many went away flattered by her humility, whom she despised in her heart, that the influence of far the greater part of those with whom she conversed ceased with their presence, and that sometimes she did not remember the names of them whom, without any intentional insincerity or false commendation, her habitual civility had sent away with very high thoughts of their own importance.

It was not long before I perceived that my aunt's opinion was not of much weight in Flavia's deliberations, and that she was looked upon by her as a woman of narrow sentiments, without knowledge of books or observations on mankind. I had hitherto considered my aunt as entitled by her wisdom and experience to the highest reverence, and could not forbear to wonder that anyone so much younger should venture to suspect her of error or ignorance. But my surprise was without uneasiness; and being now accustomed to think Flavia always in the right, I readily learned from her to trust my own reason and to believe it possible that they who had lived longer might be mistaken.

Flavia had read much, and used so often to converse on subjects of learning, that she put all the men in the county to flight, except the old parson who declared himself much delighted with her company because she gave him opportunities to recollect the studies of his younger years, and by some mention of ancient story had made him rub the dust off his Homer which had lain unregarded in his closet. With Homer and a thousand other names familiar to Flavia I had no acquaintance, but began by comparing her accomplishments with my own, to repine at my education and wish that I had not been so long confined to the company of those from whom nothing but housewifery was to be learned. I then set myself to peruse such books as Flavia recommended, and heard her opinion of their beauties and defects. I saw new worlds hourly bursting upon my mind, and was enraptured at the prospect of diversifying life with endless entertainment.

The old lady finding that a large screen which I had undertaken to adorn with turkey work against winter made very slow advances, and that I had added in two months but three leaves to a flowered apron then in the frame, took the alarm, and with all the zeal of honest folly exclaimed against my new acquaintance who had filled me with idle notions and turned my head with books. But she had now lost her authority, for I began to find innumerable mistakes in her opinions and improprieties in her language; and therefore thought myself no longer bound to pay much regard to one who knew little beyond her needle and her dairy, and who professed to think that nothing more is required of a woman than to see that the house is clean and that the maids go to bed and rise at a certain hour.

She seemed, however, to look upon Flavia as seducing me, and to imagine that when her influence was withdrawn I should return to my allegiance. She therefore contented herself with remote hints and gentle admonitions intermixed with sage histories of the miscarriages of wit and disappointments of pride. But since she has found that, though Flavia is departed, I still persist in my new scheme, she has at length lost her patience. She snatches my book out of my hand, tears my paper if she finds me writing, burns Flavia's letters before my face when she can seize them, and threatens to lock me up and to complain to my father of my perverseness. 'If women,' she says, 'would but know their duty and their interest, they would be careful to acquaint themselves with family affairs, and many a penny might be saved; for while the mistress of the house is scribbling and reading, servants are junketing and linen is wearing out.' She then takes me round the rooms, shows me the worked hangings and chairs of tent-stitch, and asks whether all this was done with a pen and a book.

I cannot deny that I sometimes laugh and sometimes am sullen; but she has not delicacy enough to be much moved either with my mirth or my gloom, if she did not think the interest of the family endangered by this change of my manners. She had for some years marked out young Mr. Surly, an heir in the neighbourhood, remarkable for his love of fighting-cocks, as an advantageous match, and was extremely pleased with the civilities which he used to pay me till under Flavia's tuition I learned to talk of subjects which he could not understand. 'This,' he says, 'is the consequence of female study; girls grow too wise to be advised and too stubborn to be commanded.' But she is resolved to see who shall govern, and will thwart my humour till she breaks my spirit.

These menaces, Mr. Rambler, sometimes make me quite angry; for I have been sixteen these ten weeks, and think myself exempted from the dominion of a governess who has no pretensions to more sense or knowledge than myself. I am resolved, since I am as tall and as wise as other women, to be no longer treated like a girl. Miss Flavia has often told me that ladies of my age go to assemblies and routs without their mothers and their aunts. I shall therefore from this time leave asking advice and refuse to give accounts. I wish you would state the time at which young ladies may judge for themselves, which I am sure you cannot but think ought to begin before sixteen.   If you are inclined to delay it longer I shall have very little regard to your opinion.

My aunt often tells me of the advantages of experience and of the deference due to seniority; and both she and all the antiquated part of the world talk of the unreserved obedience which they paid to the commands of their parents and the undoubting confidence with which they listened to their precepts, of the terrors which they felt at a frown, and the humility with which they supplicated forgiveness whenever they had offended.   I cannot but fancy that this boast is too general to be true, and that the young and the old were always at variance.   I have, however, told my aunt that I will mend whatever she will prove to be wrong; but she replies that she has reasons of her own, and that she is sorry to live in an age when girls have the impudence to ask for proofs.

I beg once again, Mr. Rambler, to know whether I am not as wise as my aunt, and whether, when she presumes to check me as a baby, I may not pluck up a spirit and return her insolence.   I shall not proceed to extremities without your advice, which is therefore impatiently expected by

MYRTILLA.

PS. Remember I am past sixteen.

CAPRICES OF CRITICISM (93)

Tuesday, 5th February 1751

Experiar quid concedatur in illos
Quorum flaminia tegitur cinis atque latina.

JUVENAL.

More safely Truth to urge her claim presumes,
On names now found alone on books and tombs.

THERE are few books on which more time is spent by young students than on treatises which deliver the characters of authors, nor any which oftener deceive the expectations of the reader or fill his mind with more opinions which the progress of his studies and the increase of his knowledge oblige him to resign.

Baillet has introduced his collection of the decisions of the learned by an enumeration of the prejudices which mislead the critic and raise the passions in rebellion against the judgment.   His catalogue, though large, is imperfect; and who can hope to complete it? The beauties of writing have been observed to be often such as cannot, in the present state of human knowledge, be evinced by evidence or drawn out into demonstrations. They are therefore wholly subject to the imagination, and do not force their effects upon a mind preoccupied by unfavourable sentiments, nor overcome the counteraction of a false principle or of stubborn partiality.

To convince any man against his will is hard, but to please him against his will is justly pronounced by Dryden to be above the reach of human abilities. Interest and passion will hold out long against the closest siege of diagrams and syllogisms; but they are absolutely impregnable to imagery and sentiments, and will for ever bid defiance to the most powerful strains of Virgil or Homer, though they may give way in time to the batteries of Euclid or Archimedes.

In trusting, therefore, to the sentence of a critic, we are in danger not only from that vanity which exalts writers too often to the dignity of teaching what they are yet to learn from that negligence which sometimes steals upon the most vigilant caution and that fallibility to which the condition of nature has subjected every human understanding, but from a thousand extrinsic and accidental causes from everything which can excite kindness or malevolence, veneration or contempt.

Many of those who have determined with great boldness upon the various degrees of literary merit may be justly suspected of having passed sentence, as Seneca remarks of Claudius:

> Una tantum parte audita,
> Saepe et nulla,

without much knowledge of the cause before them. For it will not easily be imagined of Langbane, Borrichitus, or Rapin that they had very accurately perused all the books which they praise or censure; or that, even if nature and learning had qualified them for judges, they could read for ever with the attention necessary to just criticism. Such performances, however, are not wholly without their use, for they are commonly just echoes to the voice of fame, and transmit the general suffrage of mankind when they have no particular motives to suppress it.

Critics, like the rest of mankind, are very frequently misled by interest. The bigotry with which editors regard the authors whom they illustrate or correct has been generally remarked. Dryden was known to have written most of his critical dissertations only to recommend the work upon which he then happened to be employed; and Addison is suspected to have denied the expediency of poetical justice because his own Cato was condemned to perish in a good cause.

There are prejudices which authors, not otherwise weak or corrupt, have indulged without scruple; and, perhaps, some of them are so complicated with our natural affections that they cannot easily be disentangled from the heart. Scarce any can hear with impartiality a comparison between the writers of his own and another country. And though it cannot, I think, be charged equally on all nations that they are blinded with this literary patriotism, yet there are none that do not look upon their author with the fondness of affinity, and esteem them as well for the place of their birth as for their knowledge or their wit. There is, therefore, seldom much respect due to comparative criticism when the competitors are of different countries, unless the judge is of a nation equally indifferent to both. The Italians could not for a long time believe that there was any learning beyond the mountains, and the French seem generally persuaded that there are no wits or reasoners equal to their own. I can scarcely conceive that if Scaliger had not considered himself as allied to Virgil by being born in the same country he would have found his works so much superior to those of Homer, or have thought the controversy worthy of so much zeal, vehemence, and acrimony.

There is, indeed, one prejudice, and only one, by which it may be doubted whether it is any dishonour to be sometimes misguided. Criticism has so often given occasion to the envious and ill-natured of gratifying their malignity, that some have thought it necessary to recommend the virtue of candour without restriction, and to preclude all future liberty of censure. Writers possessed with this opinion are continually enforcing civility and decency, recommending to critics the proper diffidence of themselves, and inculcating the veneration due to celebrated names.

I am not of opinion that these professed enemies of arrogance and severity have much more benevolence or modesty than the rest of mankind, or that they feel in their own hearts any other intention than to distinguish themselves by their softness and delicacy. Some are modest because they are timorous, and some are lavish of praise because they hope to be repaid.

There is, indeed, some tenderness due to living writers when they attack none of those truths which are of importance to the happiness of mankind and have committed no other offence than that of betraying their own ignorance or dullness. I should think it cruelty to crush an insect who had provoked me only by buzzing in my ear, and would not willingly interrupt the dream of harmless stupidity or destroy the jest which makes its author laugh. Yet I am far from thinking this tenderness universally necessary. For he that writes may be considered as a kind of general challenger whom every one has a right to attack since he quits the common rank of life, steps forward beyond the lists, and offers his merit to the public judgment. To commence author is to claim praise, and no man can justly aspire to honour but at the hazard of disgrace.

But whatever be decided concerning contemporaries, whom he that knows the treachery of the human heart and considers how often we gratify our own pride or envy under the appearance of contending for elegance and propriety will find himself not much inclined to disturb, there can be no exemptions pleaded to secure them from criticism who can no longer suffer by reproach, and of whom nothing now remains but their writings and their names. Upon these authors the critic is, undoubtedly, at full liberty to exercise the strictest severity, since he endangers only his own fame, and, like Aeneas when he drew his sword in the infernal regions, encounters phantoms which cannot be wounded. He may, indeed, pay some regard to established reputation; but he can by that show of reverence consult only his own security, for all other motives are now at an end.

The faults of a writer of acknowledged excellence are more dangerous because the influence of his example is more extensive; and the interest of learning requires that they should be discovered and stigmatized before they have the sanction of antiquity conferred upon them and become precedents of indisputable authority.

It has, indeed, been advanced by Addison as one of the characteristics of a true critic, that he points out beauties rather than faults. But it is rather natural to a man of learning and genius to apply himself chiefly to the study of writers who have more beauties than faults to be displayed; for the duty of criticism is neither to depreciate nor dignify by partial representations, but to hold out the light of reason, whatever it may discover, and to promulgate the determinations of truth, whatever she shall dictate.

ADVICE TO UNMARRIED LADIES [1] (97)

Tuesday, 19th February 1751

Faecunda culpae secula nuptias
Primum inquinavere, et genus, et domos,
    Hoc fonte derivata clades
        In patriam populumque fluxit.

HORACE.

Fruitful of crimes, this age first stain'd
Their hapless offspring, and profan'd
The nuptial bed; from whence the woes,
Which various and unnumber'd rose
From this polluted fountain head,
O'er Rome and o'er the nations spread.

FRANCIS.

THE reader is indebted for this day's entertainment to an author from whom the age has received greater favours, who has enlarged the knowledge of human nature, and taught the passions to move at the command of virtue.

TO THE 'RAMBLER'

SIR,

When the *Spectator* was first published in single papers it gave me so much pleasure, that it is one of the favourite amusements of my age to recollect it; and when I reflect on the foibles of those times, as described in that useful work, and compare them with the vices now reigning among us, I cannot but wish that you would oftener take cognizance of the manners of the better half of the human species, that if your precepts and observations be carried down to posterity the *Spectators* may show to the rising generation what were the fashionable follies of their grandmothers, the *Rambler* of their mothers, and that from both they may draw instruction and warning.

When I read those *Spectators* which took notice of the misbehaviour of young women at church, by which they vainly hope to attract admirers, I used to pronounce such forward young women Seekers, in order to distinguish them by a mark of infamy from those who had patience and decency to stay till they were sought.

---

[1] This number was contributed by Samuel Richardson.

But I have lived to see such a change in the manners of women that I would now be willing to compound with them for that name, although I then thought it disgraceful enough if they would deserve no worse, since now they are too generally given up to negligence of domestic business, to idle amusements, and to wicked rackets without any settled view at all but of squandering time.

In the time of the *Spectator*, excepting sometimes an appearance in the ring, sometimes at a good and chosen play, sometimes on a visit at the house of a grave relation, the young ladies contented themselves to be found employed in domestic duties. For then routs, drums, balls, assemblies, and suchlike markets for women were not known.

Modesty and diffidence, gentleness and meekness, were looked upon as the appropriate virtues and characteristic graces of the sex. And if a forward spirit pushed itself into notice it was exposed in print as it deserved.

The churches were almost the only places where single women were to be seen by strangers. Men went thither expecting to see them, and perhaps too much for that only purpose.

But some good often resulted, however improper might be their motives. Both sexes were in the way of their duty. The man must be abandoned indeed who loves not goodness in another; nor were the young fellows of that age so wholly lost to a sense of right as pride and conceit has since made them affect to be. When, therefore, they saw a fair one whose decent behaviour and cheerful piety showed her earnest in her first duties, they had less doubt, judging politically only, that she would have a conscientious regard to her second.

With what ardour have I seen watched for the rising of a kneeling beauty; and what additional charms has devotion given to her recommunicated features.

The men were often the better for what they heard. Even a Saul was once found prophesying among the prophets whom he had set out to destroy. To a man thus put into good humour by a pleasing object religion itself looked more amiable. The men Seekers of the *Spectator*'s time loved the holy place for the object's sake, and loved the object for her suitable behaviour in it.

Reverence mingled with their love; and they thought that a young lady of such good principles must be addressed only by the man who at least made a show of good principles, whether his heart was yet quite right or not.

Nor did the young ladies behaviour at any time of the service lessen this reverence. Her eyes were her own, her ears the preacher's. Women are always most observed when they seem themselves least to observe or to lay out for observation. The eye of a respectful lover loves rather to receive confidence from the withdrawn eye of the fair one than to find itself obliged to retreat.

When a young gentleman's affection was thus laudably engaged he pursued its natural dictates. Keeping [a mistress] then was a rare, at least a secret and scandalous vice, and a wife was the summit of his wishes. Rejection was now dreaded and pre-engagements apprehended. A woman whom he loved, he was ready to think, must be admired by all the world. His fears, his uncertainties, increased his love.

Every inquiry he made into the lady's domestic excellence, which when a wife is to be chosen will surely not be neglected, confirmed him in his choice. He opens his heart to a common friend and honestly discovers the state of his fortune. His friend applies to those of the young lady, whose parents, if they approve his proposals, disclose them to their daughter.

She perhaps is not an absolute stranger to the passion of the young gentleman. His eyes, his assiduities, his constant attendance at a church, whither, till of late, he used seldom to come, and a thousand little observances that he paid her, had very probably first forced her to regard and then inclined her to favour him.

That a young lady should be in love and the love of the young gentleman undeclared is an heterodoxy which prudence and even policy must not allow. But thus applied to, she is all resignation to her parents. Charming resignation, which inclination opposes not.

Her relations applaud her for her duty, friends meet, points are adjusted, delightful perturbations and hopes and a few lover's fears, fill up the tedious space till an interview is granted. For the young lady had not made herself cheap at public places.

The time of interview arrives. She is modestly reserved, he is not confident. He declares his passion. The consciousness of her own worth and his application to her parents take from her any doubt of his sincerity; and she owns herself obliged to him for his good opinion. The inquiries of her friends into his character have taught her that his good opinion deserves to be valued.

She tacitly allows of his future visits. He renews them. The regard of each for the other is confirmed; and when he presses for the favour of her hand he receives a declaration of an entire acquiescence with her duty and a modest acknowledgment of esteem for him.

He applies to her parents, therefore, for a near day, and thinks himself under obligation to them for the cheerful and affectionate manner with which they receive his agreeable application.

With this prospect of future happiness the marriage is celebrated. Gratulations pour in from every quarter. Parents and relations on both sides, brought acquainted in the course of the courtship, can receive the happy couple with countenances illumined and joyful hearts.

The brothers, the sisters, the friends of one family are the brothers, the sisters, the friends of the other. Their two families thus made one are the world to the young couple.

Their home is the place of their principal delight, nor do they ever occasionally quit it but they find the pleasure of returning to it augmented in proportion to the time of their absence from it.

O Mr. Rambler, forgive the talkativeness of an old man. When I courted and married my Laetitia, then a blooming beauty, everything passed just so! But how is the case now? The ladies, maidens, wives, and widows are engrossed by places of open resort and general entertainment which fill every quarter of the metropolis and, being constantly frequented, make home irksome. Breakfasting-places, dining-places, routs, drums, concerts, balls, plays, operas, masquerades for the evening, and even for all night, and lately public sales of the goods of broken housekeepers, which the general dissoluteness of manners has contributed to make very frequent, come in as another seasonable relief to these modern time-killers.

In the summer there are in every country town assemblies: Tunbridge, Bath, Cheltenham, Scarborough! What expense of dress and equipage is required to qualify the frequenters for such emulous appearance!

By the natural infection of example the lowest people have places of sixpenny resort and gaming-tables for pence. Thus servants are now induced to fraud and dishonesty to support extravagance and supply their losses.

As to the ladies who frequent those public places, they are not ashamed to show their faces wherever men dare go, nor blush to try who shall stare most impudently or who shall laugh loudest on the public walks.

The men who would make good husbands, if they visit those places, are frighted at wedlock and resolve to live single except they are bought at a very high price. They can be spectators of all that passes, and, if they please, more than spectators, at the expense of others. The companion of an evening and the companion for life require very different qualifications.

Two thousand pounds in the last age, with a domestic wife, would go farther than ten thousand in this. Yet settlements are expected, that often, to a mercantile man especially, sink a fortune into uselessness; and pin-money is stipulated for, which makes a wife independent and destroys love by putting it out of a man's power to lay any obligation upon her that might engage gratitude and kindle affection. When to all this the card-tables are added, how can a prudent man think of marrying?

And when the worthy men know not where to find wives, must not the sex be left to the foplings, the coxcombs, the libertines of the age, whom they help to make such? And need even these wretches marry to enjoy the conversation of those who render their company so cheap?

And what, after all, is the benefit which the gay coquette obtains by her flutters? As she is approachable by every man without requiring I will not say incense or adoration, but even common complaisance, every fop treats her as upon the level, looks upon her light airs as invitations, and is on the watch to take the advantage. She has companions, indeed, but no lovers; for love is respectful and timorous. And where among all her followers will she find a husband?

Set, dear Sir, before the youthful, the gay, the inconsiderate, the contempt as well as the danger to which they are exposed. At one time or other women not utterly thoughtless will be convinced of the justice of your censure and the charity of your instruction.

But should your expostulations and reproofs have no effect upon those who are far gone in fashionable folly, they may be retailed from their mouths to their nieces (marriage will not often have entitled these to daughters), when they, the meteors of a day, find themselves elbowed off the stage of vanity by other flutterers. For the most admired women cannot have many Tunbridge, many Bath seasons to blaze in, since even fine faces often seen are less regarded than new faces. The proper punishment of showy girls for rendering themselves so impoliticly cheap.

I am, Sir,

Your sincere admirer, &c.

VANITY OF AN AUTHOR'S
EXPECTATIONS (106)

Saturday, 23rd March 1751

Opinionum commenta delet dies, naturae judicia confirmat.

CICERO.

Time obliterates the fictions of opinion, and confirms the decisions of
Nature.

IT is necessary to the success of flattery that it be accommodated to
particular circumstances or characters and enter the heart on that
side where the passions stand ready to receive it. A lady seldom
listens with attention to any praise but that of her beauty; a merchant always expects to hear of his influence at the bank, his
importance on the exchange, the height of his credit, and the extent
of his traffic; and the author will scarcely be pleased without
lamentations of the neglect of learning, the conspiracies against
genius, and the slow progress of merit, or some praises of the
magnanimity of those who encounter poverty and contempt in
the cause of knowledge and trust for the reward of their labours
to the judgment and gratitude of posterity.

An assurance of unfading laurels and immortal reputation is the
settled reciprocation of civility between amicable writers. To
raise monuments more durable than brass and more conspicuous
than pyramids has been long the common boast of literature. But
among the innumerable architects that erect columns to themselves
far the greater part, either for want of durable materials or of art to
dispose them, see their edifices perish as they are towering to completion; and those few that for a while attract the eye of mankind
are generally weak in the foundation and soon sink by the saps of
time.

No place affords a more striking conviction of the vanity of
human hopes than a public library. For who can see the wall
crowded on every side by mighty volumes, the works of laborious
meditation and accurate inquiry, now scarcely known but by the
catalogue, and preserved only to increase the pomp of learning
without considering how many hours have been wasted in vain
endeavours, how often imagination has anticipated the praises of
futurity, how many statues have risen to the eye of vanity, how

many ideal converts have elevated zeal, how often wit has exulted in the eternal infamy of his antagonists, and dogmatism has delighted in the gradual advances of his authority, the immutability of his decrees, and the perpetuity of his power.

> Non unquam dedit
> Documenta fors majora, quam fragili loco
> Starent superbi.

> Insulting chance ne'er call'd with louder voice,
> On swelling mortals to be proud no more.

Of the innumerable authors whose performances are thus treasured up in magnificent obscurity most are forgotten because they never deserved to be remembered, and owed the honours which they once obtained, not to judgment or to genius, to labour or to art, but to the prejudice of faction, the stratagem of intrigue, or the servility of adulation.

Nothing is more common than to find men whose works are now totally neglected mentioned with praises by their contemporaries as the oracles of their age and the legislators of science. Curiosity is naturally excited, their volumes after long inquiry are found, but seldom reward the labour of the search. Every period of time has produced these bubbles of artificial fame which are kept up awhile by the breath of fashion and then break at once and are annihilated. The learned often bewail the loss of ancient writers whose characters have survived their works; but perhaps if we could now retrieve them we should find them only the Granvilles, Montagus, Stepneys, and Sheffields of their time, and wonder by what infatuation or caprice they could be raised to notice.

It cannot, however, be denied, that many have sunk into oblivion, whom it were unjust to number with this despicable class. Various kinds of literary fame seem destined to various measures of duration. Some spread into exuberance with a very speedy growth, but soon wither and decay; some rise more slowly, but last long. Parnassus has its flowers of transient fragrance as well as its oaks of towering height and its laurels of eternal verdure.

Among those whose reputation is exhausted in a short time by its own luxuriance are the writers who take advantage of present incidents or characters which strongly interest the passions and engage universal attention. It is not difficult to obtain readers when we discuss a question which everyone is desirous to understand, which is debated in every assembly, and has divided the nation into parties; or when we display the faults or virtues of him whose public conduct has made almost every man his enemy or his friend. To the quick circulation of such productions all the motives of interest and vanity concur. The disputant enlarges his knowledge, the zealot animates his passion, and every man is desirous to inform himself concerning affairs so vehemently agitated and variously represented.

It is scarcely to be imagined through how many subordinations of interest the ardour of party is diffused, and what multitudes fancy themselves affected by every satire or panegyric on a man of eminence. Whoever has at any time taken occasion to mention him with praise or blame, whoever happens to love or hate any adherents, as he wishes to confirm his opinion and to strengthen his party, will diligently peruse every paper from which he can hope for sentiments like his own. An object, however small in itself, if placed near to the eye will engross all the rays of light; and a transaction, however trivial, swells into importance when it presses immediately on our attention. He that shall peruse the political pamphlets of any past reign will wonder why they were so eagerly read or so loudly praised. Many of the performances which had power to inflame factions and fill a kingdom with confusion have now very little effect upon a frigid critic; and the time is coming when the compositions of later hirelings shall be equally despised. In proportion as those who write on temporary subjects are exalted above their merit at first, they are afterwards depressed below it; nor can the brightest elegance of diction or most artful subtlety of reasoning hope for much esteem from those whose regard is no longer quickened by curiosity or pride.

It is, indeed, the fate of controvertists, even when they contend for philosophical or theological truth, to be soon laid aside and slighted. Either the question is decided, and there is no more place for doubt and opposition, or mankind despair of understanding it and grow weary of disturbance, content themselves with quiet ignorance, and refuse to be harassed with labours which they have no hopes of recompensing with knowledge.

The authors of new discoveries may surely expect to be reckoned among those whose writings are secure of veneration. Yet it often happens that the general reception of a doctrine obscures the books in which it was delivered. When any tenet is generally received and adopted as an incontrovertible principle, we seldom look back to the arguments upon which it was first established, or can bear that tediousness of deduction and multiplicity of evidence by which its author was forced to reconcile it to prejudice and fortify it in the weakness of novelty against obstinacy and envy.

It is well known how much of our philosophy is derived from Boyle's discovery of the qualities of the air. Yet of those who now adopt or enlarge his theory very few have read the detail of his experiments. His name is, indeed, reverenced, but his works are neglected. We are contented to know that he conquered his opponents, without inquiring what cavils were produced against him or by what proofs they were confuted.

Some writers apply themselves to studies boundless and inexhaustible, as experiments and natural philosophy. These are always lost in successive compilations as new advances are made and former observations become more familiar. Others spend their lives in remarks on language or explanations of antiquities, and only afford materials for lexicographers and commentators, who are themselves overwhelmed by subsequent collectors that equally destroy the memory of their predecessors by amplification, transposition, or contraction. Every new system of nature gives birth to a swam of expositors whose business is to explain and illustrate it, and who can hope to exist no longer than the founder of their sect preserves his reputation.

There are, indeed, few kinds of composition from which an author, however learned or ingenious, can hope a long continuance of fame. He who has carefully studied human nature and can well describe it may with most reason flatter his ambition. Bacon, among all his pretensions to the regard of posterity, seems to have pleased himself chiefly with his Essays, which come home to men's business and bosoms, and of which therefore he declares his expectation that they will live as long as books last. It may, however, satisfy an honest and benevolent mind to have been useful though less conspicuous; nor will he that extends his hope to higher rewards be so much anxious to obtain praise as to discharge the duty which Providence assigns him.

REPENTANCE (110)

Saturday, 6th April 1751

At nobis vitae dominum quaerentibus unum
Lux iter est, et clara dies, et gratia simplex.

PRUDENTIUS.

We thro' this maze of life one Lord obey;
Whose light and grace unerring lead the way.

F. LEWIS.

THAT to please the Lord and Father of the universe is the supreme interest of created and dependent beings, as it is easily proved, has been universally confessed. And since all rational agents are conscious of having neglected or violated the duties prescribed to them, the fear of being rejected or punished by God has always burdened the human mind. The expiation of crimes and renovation of the forfeited hopes of divine favour, therefore, constitutes a large part of every religion.

The various methods of propitiation and atonement which fear and folly have dictated, or artifice and interest tolerated, in the different parts of the world, however they may sometimes reproach or degrade humanity, at least show the general consent of all ages and nations in their opinion of the placability of the divine nature. That God will forgive may, indeed, be established as the first and fundamental truth of religion. For though the knowledge of His existence is the origin of philosophy, yet without the belief of His mercy it would have little influence upon our moral conduct. There could be no prospect of enjoying the protection or regard of Him whom the least deviation from rectitude made inexorable for ever; and every man would naturally withdraw his thoughts from the contemplation of a Creator whom he must consider as a governor too pure to be pleased and too severe to be pacified, as an enemy infinitely wise and infinitely powerful, whom he could neither deceive, escape, nor resist.

Where there is no hope there can be no endeavour. A constant and unfailing obedience is above the reach of terrestrial diligence; and therefore the progress of life could only have been the natural descent of negligent despair from crime to crime, had not the universal persuasion of forgiveness, to be obtained by proper means of reconciliation, recalled those to the paths of virtue whom their passions had solicited aside, and animated to new attempts and firmer perseverance those whom difficulty had discouraged or negligence surprised.

In times and regions so disjoined from each other that there can scarcely be imagined any communication of sentiments either by commerce or tradition has prevailed a general and uniform expectation of propitiating God by corporeal austerities, of anticipating His vengeance by voluntary inflictions, and appeasing His justice by a speedy and cheerful submission to a less penalty when a greater is incurred.

Incorporated minds will always feel some inclination towards exterior acts and ritual observances. Ideas not represented by sensible objects are fleeting, variable, and evanescent. We are not able to judge of the degree of conviction which operated at any particular time upon our own thoughts, but as it is recorded by some certain and definite effect. He that reviews his life in order to determine the probability of his acceptance with God, if he could once establish necessary proportion between crimes and sufferings, might securely rest upon his performance of the expiation. But while safety remains the reward only of mental purity he is always afraid lest he should decide too soon in his own favour, lest he should not have felt the pangs of true contrition, lest he should mistake satiety for detestation, or imagine that his passions are subdued when they are only sleeping.

From this natural and reasonable diffidence arose, in humble and timorous piety, a disposition to confound penance with repentance, to repose on human determinations, and to receive from some judicial sentence the stated and regular assignment of reconciliatory pain. We are never willing to be without resource, we seek in the knowledge of others a succour for our own ignorance, and are ready to trust any that will undertake to direct us when we have confidence in ourselves.

This desire to ascertain by some outward marks the state of the soul, and this willingness to calm the conscience by some settled method, have produced, as they are diversified in their effects by various tempers and principles, most of the disquisitions and rules, the doubts and solutions, that have embarrassed the doctrine of repentance, and perplexed tender and flexible minds with innumerable scruples concerning the necessary measures of sorrow and adequate degrees of self-abhorrence. And these rules, corrupted by fraud or debased by credulity, have, by the common resiliency of the mind from one extreme to another, incited others to an open contempt of all subsidiary ordinances, all prudential caution, and the whole discipline of regulated piety.

Repentance, however difficult to be practised, is, if it be explained without superstition, easily understood. Repentance is the relinquishment of any practice from the conviction that it has offended God. Sorrow and fear and anxiety are properly not parts but adjuncts of repentance; yet they are too closely connected with it to be easily separated, for they not only mark its sincerity but promote its efficacy.

No man commits any act of negligence or obstinacy, by which his safety or happiness in this world is endangered, without feeling the pungency of remorse. He who is fully convinced that he suffers by his own failure can never forbear to trace back his mis-carriage to its first cause, to image to himself a contrary behaviour, and to form involuntary resolutions against the like fault, even when he knows that he shall never again have the power of committing it. Danger considered as imminent naturally produces such trepidations of impatience as leave all human means of safety behind them. He that has once caught an alarm of terror is every moment seized with useless anxieties, adding one security to another, trembling with sudden doubts, and distracted by the perpetual occurrence of new expedients. If, therefore, he whose crimes have deprived him of the favour of God can reflect upon his conduct without disturbance or can at will banish the reflection, if he who considers himself as suspended over the abyss of eternal perdition only by the thread of life, which must soon part by its own weakness and which the wing of every minute may divide, can cast his eyes round him without shuddering with horror or panting with security, what can he judge of himself but that he is not yet awakened to sufficient conviction, since every loss is more lamented than the loss of the divine favour, and every danger more dreaded than the danger of final condemnation?

Retirement from the cares and pleasures of the world has been often recommended as useful to repentance. This at least is evident, that everyone retires whenever ratiocination and recollection are required on other occasions: and surely the retrospect of life, the disentanglement of actions complicated with innumerable circumstances and diffused in various relations, the discovery of the primary movements of the heart, and the extirpation of lusts and appetites deeply rooted and widely spread may be allowed to demand some secession from sport and noise and business and folly. Some suspension of common affairs, some pause of temporal pain and pleasure, is doubtless necessary to him that deliberates for eternity, who is forming the only plan in which miscarriage cannot be repaired, and examining the only question in which mistake cannot be rectified.

Austerities and mortifications are means by which the mind is invigorated and roused, by which the attractions of pleasure are interrupted, and the chains of sensuality are broken. It is observed by one of the fathers, that he who restrains himself in the use of things lawful, will never encroach upon things forbidden. Abstinence, if nothing more, is at least a cautious retreat from the utmost verge of permission, and confers that security which cannot be reasonably hoped by him that dares always to hover over the precipice of destruction, or delights to approach the pleasures which he knows it fatal to partake. Austerity is the proper antidote to indulgence. The diseases of the mind as well as body are cured by contraries, and to contraries we should readily have recourse, if we dreaded guilt as we dread pain.

The completion and sum of repentance is a change of life. That sorrow which dictates no caution, that fear which does not quicken our escape, that austerity which fails to rectify our affections, are vain and unavailing. But sorrow and terror must naturally precede reformation; for what other cause can produce it? He, therefore, that feels himself alarmed by his conscience, anxious for the attainment of a better state, and afflicted by the memory of his past faults, may justly conclude that the great work of repentance is begun, and hope by retirement and prayer, the natural and religious means of strengthening his conviction, to impress upon his mind such a sense of the divine presence as may overpower the blandishments of secular delights and enable him to advance from one degree of holiness to another till death shall set him free from doubt and contest, misery and temptation.

> What better can we do than prostrate fall
> Before Him reverent; and there confess
> Humbly our faults, and pardon beg with tears
> Wat'ring the ground, and with our sighs the air
> Frequenting, sent from hearts contrite in sign
> Of sorrow unfeign'd, and humiliation meek?

HYMENAEUS'S COURTSHIP [1] (113)

Tuesday, 16th April 1751

Uxorem, Posthume ducis?
Dic qua tisiphone, quibus exagitare colubris?

JUVENAL.

A sober man like thee to change his life!
What fury would possess thee with a wife?

DRYDEN.

TO THE 'RAMBLER'

SIR,

I know not whether it is always a proof of innocence to treat censure with contempt. We owe so much reverence to the wisdom of mankind as justly to wish that our own opinion of our merit may be ratified by the concurrence of other suffrages. And since guilt and infamy must have the same effect upon intelligences unable to pierce beyond external appearance, and influenced often rather by example than precept, we are obliged to refute a small charge lest we should countenance the crime which we have never committed. To turn away from an accusation with supercilious silence is equally in the power of him that is hardened by villainy and inspirited by innocence. The wall of brass which Horace erects upon a clear conscience may be sometimes raised by impudence or power; and we should always wish to preserve the dignity of virtue by adorning her with graces which wickedness cannot assume.

For this reason I have determined no longer to endure with either patient or sullen resignation a reproach which is, at least in my opinion, unjust, but will lay my case honestly before you that you or your readers may at length decide it.

Whether you will be able to preserve your boasted impartiality when you hear that I am considered as an adversary by half the female world you may surely pardon me for doubting, notwithstanding the veneration to which you may imagine yourself entitled by your age, your learning, your abstraction, or your virtue. Beauty, Mr. Rambler, has often overpowered the resolutions of the firm and the reasonings of the wise, roused the old to sensibility, and subdued the rigorous to softness.

[1] For the sequel see pp. 187–91, pp. 201–5, and pp. 253–6.

I am one of these unhappy beings who have been marked out as husbands for many different women, and deliberated a hundred times on the brink of matrimony. I have discussed all the nuptial preliminaries so often that I can repeat the forms in which jointures are settled, pin-money secured, and provisions for younger children ascertained, but am at last doomed by general consent to everlasting solitude, and excluded by an irreversible decree from all hopes of connubial felicity. I am pointed out by every mother as a man whose visits cannot be admitted without reproach, who raises hopes only to embitter disappointment, and makes offers only to seduce girls into a waste of that part of life in which they might gain advantageous matches and become mistresses and mothers.

I hope you will think that some part of this penal severity may justly be remitted when I inform you that I never yet professed love to a woman without sincere intentions of marriage; that I have never continued an appearance of intimacy from the hour that my inclination changed, but to preserve her whom I was leaving from the shock of abruptness or the ignominy of contempt; that I always endeavoured to give the ladies an opportunity of seeming to discard me; and that I never forsook a mistress for larger fortune or brighter beauty, but because I discovered some irregularity in her conduct or some depravity in her mind; not because I was charmed by another, but because I was offended by herself.

I was very early tired of that succession of amusements by which the thoughts of most young men are dissipated, and had not long glittered in the splendour of an ample patrimony before I wished for the calm of domestic happiness. Youth is naturally delighted with sprightliness and ardour, and therefore I breathed out the sighs of my first affection at the feet of the gay, the sparkling, the vivacious Ferocula. I fancied to myself a perpetual source of happiness in wit never exhausted and spirit never depressed; looked with veneration on her readiness of expedients, contempt of difficulty, assurance of address, and promptitude of reply; considered her as exempt by some prerogative of nature from the weakness and timidity of female minds; and congratulated myself upon a companion superior to all common troubles and embarrassments. I was, indeed, somewhat disturbed by the unshaken perseverance with which she enforced her demands of an unreasonable settlement; yet I should have consented to pass my life in union with her, had not my curiosity led me to a crowd gathered in the street where I found Ferocula, in the presence of hundreds, disputing for sixpence with a chairman. I saw her in so little need of assistance, that it was no breach of the laws of chivalry to forbear interposition, and I spared myself the shame of owning her acquaintance. I forgot some point of ceremony at our next interview, and soon provoked her to forbid me her presence.

My next attempt was upon a lady of great eminence for learning and philosophy. I had frequently observed the barrenness and uniformity of connubial conversation, and therefore thought highly of my own prudence and discernment when I selected from a multitude of wealthy beauties the deep-read Misothea, who declared herself the inexorable enemy of ignorant pertness and puerile levity, and scarcely condescended to make tea but for the linguist, the geometrician, the astronomer, or the poet. The queen of the Amazons was only to be gained by the hero who could conquer her in single combat; and Misothea's heart was only to bless the scholar who could overpower her by disputation. Amidst the fondest transports of courtship she could call for a definition of terms, and treated every argument with contempt that could not be reduced to regular syllogism. You may easily imagine that I wished this courtship at an end. But when I desired her to shorten my torments and fix the day of my felicity, we were led into a long conversation in which Misothea endeavoured to demonstrate the folly of attributing choice and self-direction to any human being. It was not difficult to discover the danger of committing myself for ever to the arms of one who might at any time mistake the dictates of passion or the calls of appetite for the decree of fate, or consider cuckoldom as necessary to the general system, as a link in the everlasting chain of successive causes. I therefore told her that destiny had ordained us to part, and that nothing should have torn me from her but the talons of necessity.

I then solicited the regard of the calm, the prudent, the economical Sophronia, a lady who considered wit as dangerous and learning as superfluous, and thought that the woman who kept her house clean and her accounts exact, took receipts for every payment, and could find them at a sudden call, inquired nicely after the condition of the tenants, read the price of stocks once a week, and purchased everything at the best market could want no accomplishments necessary to the happiness of a wise man. She discoursed with great solemnity on the care and vigilance which the superintendance of a family demands, observed how many were ruined by confidence in servants, and told me that she never expected honesty but from a strong chest and that the best store-keeper was the

mistress's eye.   Many such oracles of generosity she uttered, and
made every day new improvements in her schemes for the regulation of her servants and the distribution of her time.   I was convinced that whatever I might suffer from Sophronia I should escape
poverty, and we therefore proceeded to adjust the settlements
according to her own rule, 'fair and softly.'   But one morning her
maid came to me in tears to entreat my interest for a reconciliation
to her mistress, who had turned her out at night for breaking six
teeth of a tortoise-shell comb.   She had attended her lady from a
distant province, and, having not lived long enough to save much
money, was destitute among strangers and, though of a good
family, in danger of perishing in the streets or of being compelled
by hunger to prostitution.   I made no scruple of promising to
restore her, but upon my first application to Sophronia was
answered with an air, which called for approbation, that if she
neglected her own affairs I might suspect her of neglecting mine;
that the comb stood her in three half-crowns; that no servant
should wrong her twice; and that indeed she took the first opportunity of parting with Phillida because, though she was honest, her
constitution was bad, and she thought her very likely to fall sick.
Of our conference I need not tell you the effect.   It surely may be
forgiven me if on this occasion I forgot the decency of common
forms.

From two more ladies I was disengaged by finding that they
entertained my rivals at the same time and determined their choice
by the liberality of our settlements.   Another I thought myself
justified in forsaking because she gave my attorney a bribe to favour
her in the bargain; another because I could never soften her to
tenderness till she heard that most of my family had died young;
and another because, to increase her fortune by expectations, she
represented her sister as languishing and consumptive.

I shall in another letter give the remaining part of my history of
courtship.   I presume that I should hitherto have injured the
majesty of female virtue, had I not hoped to transfer my affection to
higher merit.

I am, &c.,

HYMENAEUS.

CRIME AND PUNISHMENT (114)

Saturday, 20th April 1751

Audi,
Nulla unquam de morte hominis cunctatio longa est.

JUVENAL.

When a man's life is in debate,
The judge can ne'er too long deliberate.

DRYDEN.

POWER and superiority are so flattering and delightful that, fraught with temptation and exposed to danger as they are, scarcely any virtue is so cautious, or any prudence so timorous, as to decline them. Even those that have most reverence for the laws of right are pleased with showing that not fear but choice regulates their behaviour, and would be thought to comply rather than obey. We love to overlook the boundaries which we do not wish to pass, and, as the Roman satirist remarks, 'He that has no design to take the life of another is yet glad to have it in his hands.'

From the same principle, tending yet more to degeneracy and corruption, proceeds the desire of investing lawful authority with terror and governing by force rather than persuasion. Pride is unwilling to believe the necessity of assigning any other reason than her own will, and would rather maintain the most equitable claims by violence and penalties than descend from the dignity of command to dispute and expostulation.

It may, I think, be suspected that this political arrogance has sometimes found its way into legislative assemblies and mingled with deliberations upon property and life. A slight perusal of the laws by which the measures of vindictive and coercive justice are established will discover so many disproportions between crimes and punishments, such capricious distinctions of guilt, and such confusion of remissness and severity as can scarcely be believed to have been produced by public wisdom, sincerely and calmly studious of public happiness.

The learned, the judicious, the pious Boerhaave relates that he never saw a criminal dragged to execution without asking himself: 'Who knows whether this man is not less culpable than me?' On the days when the prisons of this city are emptied into the grave let every spectator of the dreadful procession put the same question to his own heart. Few among those that crowd in thousands to the legal massacre and look with carelessness, perhaps with triumph, on the utmost exacerbations of human misery would then be able to return without horror and dejection. For who can congratulate himself upon a life passed without some act more mischievous to the peace or prosperity of others than the theft of a piece of money?

It has been always the practice when any particular species of robbery becomes prevalent and common, to endeavour its suppression by capital denunciations. Thus one generation of malefactors is commonly cut off and their successors are frighted into new expedients. The art of thievery is augmented with greater variety of fraud, and subtleized to higher degrees of dexterity and more occult methods of conveyance. The law then renews the pursuit in the heat of anger and overtakes the offender again with death. By this practice capital inflictions are multiplied, and crimes very different in their degrees of enormity are equally subjected to the severest punishment that man has the power of exercising upon man.

The lawgiver is undoubtedly allowed to estimate the malignity of an offence, not merely by the loss or pain which single acts may produce, but by the general alarm and anxiety arising from the fear of mischief and insecurity of possession. He therefore exercises the right which societies are supposed to have over the lives of those that compose them, not simply to punish a transgression but to maintain order and preserve quiet. He enforces those laws with severity that are most in danger of violation, as the commander of a garrison doubles the guard on that side which is threatened with the enemy.

This method has been long tried, but tried with so little success that rapine and violence are hourly increasing. Yet few seem willing to despair of its efficacy; and of those who employ their speculations upon the present corruption of the people some propose the introduction of more horrid, lingering, and terrific punishments, some are inclined to accelerate the executions, some to discourage pardons, and all seem to think that lenity has given confidence to wickedness and that we can only be rescued from the talons of robbery by inflexible rigour and sanguinary justice.

Yet since the right of setting an uncertain and arbitrary value upon life has been disputed, and since experience of past times gives us little reason to hope that any reformation will be effected by a periodical havoc of our fellow beings, perhaps it will not be useless to consider what consequences might arise from relaxations of the law and a more rational and equitable adoption of penalties to offences.

Death is, as one of the ancients observed, τὸ τῶν φοβερῶν φοβερώτατον, of dreadful things the most dreadful, an evil beyond which nothing can be threatened by sublunary power or feared from human enmity or vengeance. This terror should, therefore, be reserved as the last resort of authority, as the strongest and most operative of prohibitory sanctions, and placed before the treasure of life to guard from invasion what cannot be restored. To equal robbery with murder is to reduce murder to robbery, to confound in common minds the gradations of iniquity, and incite the commission of a greater crime, to prevent the detection of a less. If only murder were punished with death very few robbers would stain their hands in blood; but when by the last act of cruelty no new danger is incurred, and greater security may be obtained, upon what principle shall we bid them forbear?

It may be urged that the sentence is often mitigated to simple robbery. But surely this is to confess that our laws are unreasonable in our own opinion. And, indeed, it may be observed that all but murderers have at their last hour the common sensations of mankind pleading in their favour.

From this conviction of the inequality of the punishment to the offence proceeds the frequent solicitation of pardons. They who would rejoice at the correction of a thief are yet shocked at the thought of destroying him. His crime shrinks to nothing compared with his misery, and severity defeats itself by exciting pity.

The gibbet, indeed, certainly disables those who die upon it from infesting the community; but their death seems not to contribute more to the reformation of their associates than any other method of separation. A thief seldom passes much of his time in recollection or anticipation, but from robbery hastens to riot, and from riot to robbery, nor, when the grave closes upon his companion, has any other care than to find another.

The frequency of capital punishments, therefore, rarely hinders the commission of a crime, but naturally and commonly prevents its detection, and is, if we proceed only upon prudential principles, chiefly for that reason to be avoided. Whatever may be urged by casuists or politicians, the greater part of mankind, as they can never think that to pick the pocket and to pierce the heart is equally criminal, will scarcely believe that two malefactors so different in guilt can be justly doomed to the same punishment. Nor is the necessity of submitting the conscience to human laws so plainly evinced, so clearly stated, or so generally allowed, but that the pious, the tender, and the just will always scruple to concur with the community in an act which their private judgment cannot approve.

He who knows not how often rigorous laws produce total impunity, and how many crimes are concealed and forgotten for fear of hurrying the offender to that state in which there is no repentance, has conversed very little with mankind. And whatever epithets of reproach or contempt this compassion may incur from those who confound cruelty with firmness, I know not whether any wise man would wish it less powerful or less extensive.

If those whom the wisdom of our laws has condemned to die had been detected in their rudiments of robbery they might, by proper discipline and useful labour, have been disentangled from their habits : they might have escaped all the temptations to subsequent crimes, and passed their days in reparation and penitence. And detected they might all have been, had the prosecutors been certain that their lives would have been spared. I believe every thief will confess that he has been more than once seized and dismissed, and that he has sometimes ventured upon capital crimes because he knew that those whom he injured would rather connive at his escape than cloud their minds with the horrors of his death.

All laws against wickedness are ineffectual unless some will inform and some will prosecute. But till we mitigate the penalties for mere violations of property information will always be hated and prosecution dreaded. The heart of a good man cannot but recoil at the thought of punishing a slight injury with death, especially when he remembers that the thief might have procured safety by another crime from which he was restrained only by his remaining virtue.

The obligations to assist the exercise of public justice are indeed strong ; but they will certainly be overpowered by tenderness for life. What is punished with severity contrary to our ideas of adequate retribution will be seldom discovered ; and multitudes will be suffered to advance from crime to crime till they deserve death, because, if they had been sooner prosecuted, they would have suffered death before they deserved it.

This scheme of invigorating the laws by relaxation and extirpating wickedness by lenity is so remote from common practice, that I might reasonably fear to expose it to the public, could it be supported only by my own observations. I shall, therefore, by ascribing it to its author, Sir Thomas More, endeavour to procure it that attention which I wish always paid to prudence, to justice, and to mercy.

Tuesday, 23rd April 1751

Quaedam parva quidem, sed non toleranda maritis.

JUVENAL.

Some faults, tho' small, intolerable grow.

DRYDEN.

TO THE 'RAMBLER'

SIR,

I sit down, in pursuance of my late engagement, to recount the remaining part of the adventures that befell me in my long quest of conjugal felicity which, though I have not yet been so happy as to obtain it, I have at least endeavoured to deserve by unwearied diligence, without suffering from repeated disappointments any abatement of my hope or repression of my activity.

You must have observed in the world a species of mortals who employ themselves in promoting matrimony, and, without any visible motive of interest or vanity, without any discoverable impulse of malice or benevolence, without any reason but that they want objects of attention and topics of conversation, are incessantly busy in procuring wives and husbands. They fill the ears of every single man and woman with some convenient match, and, when they are informed of your age and fortune, offer a partner of life with the same readiness and the same indifference as a salesman, when he has taken measure by his eye, fits his customer with a coat.

It might be expected that they should soon be discouraged from this officious interposition by resentment or contempt, and that every man should determine the choice, on which so much of his happiness must depend, by his own judgment and observation. Yet it happens that as these proposals are generally made with a show of kindness, they seldom provoke anger, but are at worst heard with patience and forgotten. They influence weak minds to approbation; for many are sure to find in a new acquaintance whatever qualities report has taught them to expect; and in more powerful and active understandings they excite curiosity, and sometimes, by a lucky chance, bring persons of similar tempers within the attraction of each other.

I was known to possess a fortune and to want a wife, and

therefore was frequently attended by these hymeneal solicitors, with whose importunity I was sometimes diverted and sometimes perplexed. For they contended for me as vultures for a carcass, each employing all his eloquence and all his artifices to enforce and promote his own scheme, from the success of which he was to receive no other advantage than the pleasure of defeating others equally eager and equally industrious.

An invitation to sup with one of those busy friends made me by a concerted chance acquainted with Camilla, by whom it was expected that I should be suddenly and irresistibly enslaved. The lady, whom the same kindness had brought without her own concurrence into the lists of love, seemed to think me at least worthy of the honour of captivity, and exerted the power, both of her eyes and wit, with so much art and spirit, that though I had been too often deceived by appearances to devote myself irrevocably at the first interview, yet I could not suppress some raptures of admiration and flutters of desire. I was easily persuaded to make nearer approaches, but soon discovered that a union with Camilla was not too much to be wished. Camilla professed a boundless contempt for the folly, levity, ignorance, and impertinence of her own sex, and very frequently expressed her wonder that men of learning or experience could submit to trifle away life with beings incapable of solid thought. In mixed companies she always associated with the men, and declared her satisfaction when the ladies retired. If any short excursion into the country was proposed she commonly insisted upon the exclusion of women from the party because where they were admitted the time was wasted in frothy compliments, weak indulgences, and idle ceremonies. To show the greatness of her mind she avoided all compliance with the fashion, and to boast the profundity of her knowledge mistook the various textures of silk, confounded tabbies with damasks, and sent for ribbons by wrong names. She despised the commerce of stated visits, a farce of empty form without instruction, and congratulated herself that she never learned to write message cards. She often applauded the noble sentiment of Plato, who rejoiced that he was born a man rather than a woman, proclaimed her approbation of Swift's opinion that women are only a higher species of monkeys, and confessed that when she considered the behaviour or heard the conversation of her sex she could not but forgive the Turks for suspecting them to want souls.

It was the joy and pride of Camilla to have provoked, by this insolence, all the rage of hatred and all the persecutions of calumny ;

nor was she ever more elevated with her own superiority than when she talked of female anger and female cunning. Well, says she, has nature provided that such virulence should be disabled by folly and such cruelty be restrained by impotence.

Camilla doubtless expected that what she lost on one side she should gain on the other, and imagined that every male heart would be open to a lady who made such generous advances to the borders of virility. But man, ungrateful man, instead of springing forward to meet her, shrunk back at her approach. She was persecuted by the ladies as a deserter, and at best received by the men only as a fugitive. I, for my part, amused myself awhile with her fopperies; but novelty soon gave way to detestation, for nothing out of the common order of nature can be long borne. I had no inclination to a wife who had the ruggedness of a man without his force, and the ignorance of a woman without her softness. Nor could I think my quiet and honour to be entrusted to such audacious virtue as was hourly courting danger and soliciting assault.

My next mistress was Nitella, a lady of gentle mien and soft voice, always speaking to approve and ready to receive direction from those with whom chance had brought her into company. In Nitella I promised myself an easy friend with whom I might loiter away the day without disturbance or altercation. I therefore soon resolved to address her, but was discouraged from prosecuting my courtship by observing that her apartments were superstitiously regular, and that, unless she had notice of my visit, she was never to be seen. There is a kind of anxious cleanliness which I have always noted as the characteristic of a slattern. It is the superfluous scrupulosity of guilt, dreading discovery and shunning suspicion; it is the violence of an effort against habit, which, being impelled by external motives, cannot stop at the middle point.

Nitella was always tricked out rather with nicety than elegance, and seldom could forbear to discover by her uneasiness and constraint that her attention was burdened and her imagination engrossed. I therefore concluded that, being only occasionally and ambitiously dressed, she was not familiarized to her own ornaments. There are so many competitors for the fame of cleanliness that it is not hard to gain information of those that fail from those that desire to excel. I quickly found that Nitella passed her time between finery and dirt, and was always in a wrapper, night-cap, and slippers when she was not decorated for immediate show.

I was then led by my evil destiny to Charybdis, who never neglected an opportunity of seizing a new prey when it came within her reach. I thought myself quickly made happy by her permission to attend her to public places, and pleased my own vanity with imagining the envy which I should raise in a thousand hearts by appearing as the acknowledged favourite of Charybdis. She soon after hinted her intention to take a ramble for a fortnight into a part of the kingdom which she had never seen. I solicited the happiness of accompanying her, which, after a short reluctance, was indulged me. She had no other curiosity in her journey than after all possible means of expense, and was every moment taking occasion to mention some delicacy which I knew it my duty upon such notices to procure.

After our return, being now more familiar, she told me, whenever we met, of some new diversion. At night she had notice of a charming company that would breakfast in the gardens, and in the morning had been informed of some new song in the opera, some new dress at the playhouse, or some performer at a concert whom she longed to hear. Her intelligence was such that there never was a show to which she did not summon me on the second day; and, as she hated a crowd and could not go alone, I was obliged to attend at some intermediate hour and pay the price of a whole company. When we passed the streets she was often charmed with some trinket in the toy-shops, and from moderate desires of seals and snuff-boxes rose by degrees to gold and diamonds. I now began to find the smile of Charybdis too costly for a private purse, and added one more to six-and-forty lovers whose fortune and patience her rapacity had exhausted.

Imperia then took possession of my affections, but kept them only for a short time. She had newly inherited a large fortune; and having spent the early part of her life in the perusal of romances, brought with her into the world the pride of Cleopatra, expected nothing less than vows, altars, and sacrifices, and thought her charms dishonoured and her power infringed by the softest opposition to her sentiments or the smallest transgression of her commands. Time might indeed cure this species of pride in a mind not naturally undiscerning and vitiated only by false representations; but the operations of time are slow, and I therefore left her to grow wiser at leisure or to continue in error at her own expense.

Thus I have hitherto, in spite of myself, passed my life in frozen celibacy. My friends, indeed, often tell me that I flatter my imagination with higher hopes than human nature can gratify, that I dress up an ideal charmer in all the radiance of perfection, and then enter the world to look for the same excellence in corporeal beauty.   But surely, Mr. Rambler, it is not madness to hope for some terrestrial lady unstained with the spots which I have been describing.   At least I am resolved to pursue my search; for I am so far from thinking meanly of marriage, that I believe it able to afford the highest happiness decreed to our present state.   And if after all these miscarriages I find a woman that fills up my expectation you shall hear once more from,

Yours, &c.,
HYMENAEUS.

A YOUNG TRADER'S ATTEMPT TO POLITENESS [1] (116)

Saturday, 27th April 1751

Optat ephippia bos; piger optat arare caballus.

HORACE.

Thus the slow ox would gaudy trappings claim;
The sprightly horse would plough.

FRANCIS.

TO THE 'RAMBLER'

SIR,
I was the second son of a country gentleman by the daughter of a wealthy citizen of London.   My father, having by his marriage freed the estate from a heavy mortgage and paid his sisters their portions, thought himself discharged from all obligation to further thought and entitled to spend the rest of his life in rural pleasures. He therefore spared nothing that might contribute to the completion of his felicity.   He procured the best guns and horses that the kingdom could supply, paid large salaries to his groom and huntsman, and became the envy of the country for the discipline of his hounds.   But above all his other attainments he was eminent for a breed of pointers and setting-dogs which by long and vigilant cultivation he had so much improved that not a partridge or heath-cock could rest in security, and game of whatever species that dared

<hr>

[1] For the sequel see pp. 205–8.

to light upon his manor was beaten down by his shot or covered with his nets.

My elder brother was very early initiated in the chase, and at an age when other boys are creeping like snails unwillingly to school, he could wind the horn, beat the bushes, bound over hedges, and swim rivers. When the huntsman one day broke his leg he supplied his place with equal abilities, and came home with the scut in his hat amidst the acclamations of the whole village. I, being either delicate or timorous, less desirous of honour, or less capable of sylvan heroism, was always the favourite of my mother because I kept my coat clean and my complexion free from freckles, and did not come home, like my brother, mired and tanned, nor carry corn in my hat to the horse, nor bring dirty curs into the parlour.

My mother had not been taught to amuse herself with books, and being much inclined to despise the ignorance and barbarity of the country ladies, disdained to learn their sentiments or conversation, and had made no addition to the notions which she had brought from the precincts of Cornhill. She was therefore always recounting the glories of the City, enumerating the succession of mayors, celebrating the magnificence of the banquets at Guildhall, and relating the civilities paid her at the companies' feasts by men of whom some are now made aldermen, some have fined for sheriffs, and none are worth less than forty thousand pounds. She frequently displayed her father's greatness: told of the large bills which he had paid at sight, of the sums for which his word would pass upon the Exchange, the heaps of gold which he used on Saturday night to toss about with a shovel, the extent of his warehouse, and the strength of his doors, and, when she relaxed her imagination with lower subjects, described the furniture of their country house or repeated the wit of the clerks and porters.

By these narratives I was fired with the splendour and dignity of London and of trade. I therefore devoted myself to a shop, and warmed my imagination from year to year with inquiries about the privileges of a freeman, the power of the common council, the dignity of a wholesale dealer, and the grandeur of mayoralty, to which my mother assured me that many had arrived who began the world with less than myself.

I was very impatient to enter into a path which led to such honour and felicity, but was forced for a time to endure some repression of my eagerness, for it was my grandfather's maxim that 'a young man seldom makes much money who is out of his time before two-and-twenty.' They thought it necessary, therefore, to keep me at home till the proper age without any other employment than that of learning merchants' accounts and the art of regulating books. But at length the tedious days elapsed: I was transplanted to town, and, with great satisfaction to myself, bound to a haberdasher.

My master, who had no conception of any virtue, merit, or dignity but that of being rich, had all the good qualities which naturally arise from a close and unwearied attention to the main chance. His desire to gain wealth was so well tempered by the vanity of showing it, that, without any other principle of action, he lived in the esteem of the whole commercial world, and was always treated with respect by the only men whose good opinion he valued or solicited, those who were universally allowed to be richer than himself.

By his instructions I learned in a few weeks to handle a yard with great dexterity, to wind tape neatly upon the ends of my fingers, and to make up parcels with exact frugality of paper and pack-thread; and soon caught from my fellow apprentices the true grace of a counter-bow, the careless air with which a small pair of scales is to be held between the fingers, and the vigour and sprightliness with which the box, after the ribbon had been cut, is returned into its place. Having no desire of any higher employment, and therefore applying all my powers to the knowledge of my trade, I was quickly master of all that could be known, became a critic in small wares, contrived new variations of figures and new mixtures of colours, and was sometimes consulted by the weavers when they projected fashions for the ensuing spring.

With all these accomplishments, in the fourth year of my apprenticeship I paid a visit to my friends in the country, where I expected to be received as a new ornament of the family, and consulted by the neighbouring gentlemen as a master of pecuniary knowledge, and by the ladies as an oracle of the mode. But unhappily, at the first public table to which I was invited appeared a student in the Temple and an officer of the Guards, who looked upon me with a smile of contempt which destroyed at once all my hopes of distinction, so that I durst hardly raise my eyes for fear of encountering their superiority of mien. Nor was my courage revived by any opportunities of displaying my knowledge; for the templar entertained the company for part of the day with historical narratives and political observations, and the colonel afterwards detailed the adventures of a birth-night, told the claims and expectations of the courtiers, and gave an account of assemblies, gardens, and diversions. I, indeed, essayed to fill up a pause in a parliamentary debate with a faint mention of trade and Spaniards, and once attempted with some warmth to correct a gross mistake about a silver breast-knot. But neither of my antagonists seemed to think a reply necessary: they resumed their discourse without emotion, and again engrossed the attention of the company. Nor did one of the ladies appear desirous to know my opinion of her dress or to hear how long the carnation shot with white, that was then new amongst them, had been antiquated in town.

As I knew that neither of these gentlemen had more money than myself, I could not discover what had depressed me in their presence nor why they were considered by others as more worthy of attention and respect, and therefore resolved when we met again to rouse my spirit and force myself into notice. I went very early to the next weekly meeting, and was entertaining a small circle very successfully with a minute representation of my lord-mayor's show when the colonel entered careless and gay, sat down with a kind of unceremonious civility, and, without appearing to intend any interruption, drew my audience away to the other part of the room, to which I had not the courage to follow them. Soon after came in the lawyer, not indeed with the same attraction of mien, but with greater powers of language; and by one or other the company was so happily amused that I was neither heard nor seen, nor was able to give any other proof of my existence than that I put round the glass and was in my turn permitted to name the toast.

My mother, indeed, endeavoured to comfort me in my vexation by telling me that perhaps these showy talkers were hardly able to pay every one his own; that he who has money in his pocket needs not care what any man says of him; that if I minded my trade the time will come when lawyers and soldiers would be glad to borrow out of my purse; and that it is fine when a man can set his hands to his sides and say he is worth forty thousand pounds every day of the year. These and many more such consolations and encouragements I received from my good mother, which, however, did not much allay my uneasiness. For having by some accident heard that the country ladies despised her as a cit, I had therefore no longer much reverence for her opinions, but considered her as one whose ignorance and prejudice had hurried me, though without ill intentions, into a state of meanness and ignominy from which I could not find any possibility of rising to the rank which my ancestors had always held.

I returned, however, to my master, and busied myself among

thread and silks and laces, but without my former cheerfulness and alacrity. I had now no longer any felicity in contemplating the exact disposition of my powdered curls, the equal plaits of my ruffles, or the glossy blackness of my shoes; nor heard with my former elevation those compliments which ladies sometimes condescended to pay me upon my readiness in twisting a paper or counting out the change. The term of Young Man, with which I was sometimes honoured as I carried a parcel to the door of a coach, tortured my imagination. I grew negligent of my person and sullen in my temper, often mistook the demands of the customers, treated their caprices and objections with contempt, and received and dismissed them with surly silence.

My master was afraid lest the shop should suffer by this change of my behaviour and therefore, after some expostulations, posted me in the warehouse, and preserved me from the danger and reproach of desertion to which my discontent would certainly have urged me had I continued any longer behind the counter.

In the sixth year of my servitude my brother died of drunken joy for having run down a fox that had baffled all the packs in the province. I was now heir, and with the hearty consent of my master commenced gentleman. The adventures in which my new character engaged me shall be communicated in another letter, by, Sir,

Yours, &c.,

MISOCAPELUS.

ADVANTAGES OF LIVING IN A GARRET (117)

Tuesday, 30th April 1751

Ὄσσαν ἐπ᾽ Ὀλύμπῳ μέμασαν θέμεν, αὐτὰρ ἐπ᾽ Ὄσσῃ
Πήλιον ἐινοσίφυλλον ἵν᾽ οὐρανὸς ἀμβατὸς εἴη

HOMER.

The gods they challenge, and affect the skies;
Heav'd on Olympus tott'ring Ossa stood;
On Ossa, Pelion nods with all his wood.

POPE.

TO THE 'RAMBLER'

SIR,

Nothing has more retarded the advancement of learning than the disposition of vulgar minds to ridicule and vilify what they cannot comprehend. All industry must be excited by hope; and as the student often proposes no other reward to himself than praise, he is easily discouraged by contempt and insult. He who brings with him into a clamorous multitude the timidity of recluse speculation, and has never hardened his front in public life, or accustomed his passions to the vicissitudes and accidents, the triumphs and defeats of mixed conversation, will blush at the stare of petulant incredulity and suffer himself to be driven by a burst of laughter from the fortresses of demonstration. The mechanist will be afraid to assert before hardy contradiction the possibility of tearing down bulwarks with a silkworm's thread, and the astronomer of relating the rapidity of light, the distance of the fixed stars, and the height of the lunar mountains.

If I could by any efforts have shaken off this cowardice I had not sheltered myself under a borrowed name nor applied to you for the means of communicating to the public the theory of a garret, a subject which, except some slight and transient strictures, has been hitherto neglected by those who were best qualified to adorn it, either for want of leisure to prosecute the various researches in which a nice discussion must engage them, or because it requires such diversity of knowledge and such extent of curiosity as is scarcely to be found in any single intellect; or, perhaps, others foresaw the tumults which would be raised against them, and confined their knowledge to their own breasts and abandoned prejudice and folly to the direction of chance.

That the professors of literature generally reside in the highest storeys has been immemoriably observed. The wisdom of the ancients was well acquainted with the intellectual advantages of an elevated situation. Why else were the Muses stationed on Olympus or Parnassus by those who could with equal right have raised them bowers in the vale of Tempe, or erected their altars among the flexures of Meander? Why was Jove himself nursed upon a mountain? Or why did the goddesses, when the prize of beauty was contested, try the cause upon the top of Ida? Such were the fictions by which the great masters of the earlier ages endeavoured to inculcate to posterity the importance of a garret, which, though they had been long obscured by the negligence and ignorance of succeeding times, were well enforced by the celebrated symbol of Pythagoras—

ἀνεμῶν πνεόντων τὴν ἠχὼ προσχύνει—

when the wind blows, worship its echo. This could not but be understood by his disciples as an inviolable injunction to live in a garret, which I have found frequently visited by the echo and the wind. Nor was the tradition wholly obliterated in the age of Augustus, for Tibullus evidently congratulates himself upon his garret, not without some allusion to the Pythagorean precept—

> Quam juvat immites ventos audire cubantem
> Aut, gelidas hibernus aquas cum fuderit auster,
>   Securum somnos, imbre juvante, sequi!

> How sweet in sleep to pass the careless hours,
> Lull'd by the beating winds and dashing show'rs!

And it is impossible not to discover the fondness of Lucretius, an earlier writer, for a garret in his description of the lofty towers of serene learning and of the pleasure with which a wise man looks down upon the confused and erratic state of the world moving below him.

> Sed nil dulcius est, bene quam munita tenere
> Edita doctrina sapientum templa serena;
> Despicere unde queas alios, passimque videre
> Errare, atque viam palenteis quaerer vitae.

> 'Tis sweet thy lab'ring steps to guide
> To virtue's heights, with wisdom well supply'd,
> And all the magazines of learning fortify'd;
> From thence to look below on human kind,
> Bewilder'd in the maze of life, and blind.

DRYDEN.

The institution has, indeed, continued to our own time. The garret is still the usual receptacle of the philosopher and poet; but this, like many ancient customs, is perpetuated only by an accidental imitation, without knowledge of the original reason for which it was established.

Causa latet; res est notissima.

The cause is secret, but th' effect is known.

ADDISON.

Conjectures have, indeed, been advanced concerning these habitations of literature, but without much satisfaction to the judicious inquirer. Some have imagined that the garret is generally chosen by the wits as most easily rented, and concluded that no man rejoices in his aerial abode but on the days of payment. Others suspect that a garret is chiefly convenient as it is remoter than any other part of the house from the outer door, which is often observed to be infested by visitants who talk incessantly of beer or linen or a coat, and repeat the same sounds every morning, and sometimes again in the afternoon, without any variation except that they grow daily more importunate and clamorous, and raise their voices in time from mournful murmurs to raging vociferations. This eternal monotony is always detestable to a man whose chief pleasure is to enlarge his knowledge and vary his ideas. Others talk of freedom from noise and abstraction from common business or amusements; and some, yet more visionary, tell us that the faculties are enlarged by open prospects and that the fancy is more at liberty when the eye ranges without confinement.

These conveniences may perhaps all be found in a well-chosen garret; but surely they cannot be supposed sufficiently important to have operated invariably upon different climates, distant ages, and separate nations. Of an universal practice there must still be presumed an universal cause which, however recondite and abstruse, may be perhaps reserved to make me illustrious by its discovery and you by its promulgation.

It is universally known that the faculties of the mind are invigorated or weakened by the state of the body, and that the body is in a great measure regulated by the various compressions of the ambient element. The effects of the air in the production or cure of corporeal maladies have been acknowledged from the time of Hippocrates; but no man has yet sufficiently considered how far it may influence the operations of the genius, though every day affords instances of local understanding, of wits and reasoners, whose faculties are adapted to some single spot, and who, when they are removed to any other place, sink at once into silence and stupidity. I have discovered by a long series of observations that invention and elocution suffer great impediments from dense and impure vapours, and that the tenuity of a defecated air at a proper distance from the surface of the earth accelerates the fancy and sets at liberty those intellectual powers which were before shackled by too strong attraction and unable to expand themselves under the pressure of a gross atmosphere. I have found dullness to quicken into sentiment in a thin ether, as water, though not very hot, boils in a receiver partly exhausted; and heads, in appearance empty, have teemed with notions upon rising ground, as the flaccid sides of a football would have swelled out into stiffness and extension.

For this reason I never think myself qualified to judge decisively of any man's faculties whom I have only known in one degree of elevation, but take some opportunity of attending him from the cellar to the garret, and try upon him all the various degrees of rarefaction and condensation, tension, and laxity. If he is neither vivacious aloft nor serious below I then consider him as hopeless; but as it seldom happens that I do not find the temper to which the texture of his brain is fitted, I accommodate him in time with a tube of mercury, first marking the point most favourable to his intellects according to rules which I have long studied, and which I may, perhaps, reveal to mankind in a complete treatise of barometrical pneumatology.

Another cause of the gaiety and sprightliness of the dwellers in garrets is probably the increase of that vertiginous motion with which we are carried round by the diurnal revolution of the earth. The power of agitation upon the spirits is well known. Every man has felt his heart lightened in a rapid vehicle or on a galloping horse; and nothing is plainer than that he who towers to the fifth storey is whirled through more space by every circumrotation than another that grovels upon the ground floor. The nations between the tropics are known to be fiery, inconstant, inventive, and fanciful, because, living at the utmost length of the earth's diameter, they are carried about with more swiftness than those whom nature has placed nearer to the poles. And therefore, as it becomes a wise man to struggle with the inconveniences of his country, whenever celerity and acuteness are requisite, we must actuate our languor by taking a few turns round the centre in a garret.

If you imagine that I ascribe to air and motion effects which they cannot produce, I desire you to consult your own memory and consider whether you have never known a man acquire reputation in his garret, which, when fortune or a patron had placed him upon the first floor, he was unable to maintain, and who never recovered his former vigour of understanding till he was restored to his original situation.   That a garret will make every man a wit I am very far from supposing.   I know there are some who would continue blockheads even on the summit of the Andes or on the peak of Teneriffe.   But let not any man be considered as unimprovable till this potent remedy has been tried; for perhaps he was formed to be great only in a garret, as the joiner of Aretaeus was rational in no other place but his own shop.

I think a frequent removal to various distances from the centre so necessary to a just estimate of intellectual abilities, and consequently of so great use in education, that if I hoped that the public could be persuaded to so expensive an experiment, I would propose that there should be a cavern dug and a tower erected, like those which Bacon describes in Solomon's house, for the expansion and concentration of understanding according to the exigence of different employments or constitutions.   Perhaps some that fume away in meditations upon time and space in the tower might compose tables of interest at a certain depth, and he that upon level ground stagnates in silence or creeps in narrative might, at the height of half a mile, ferment into merriment, sparkle with repartee, and froth with declamation.

Addison observes that we may find the heat of Virgil's climate in some lines of his Georgic.   So, when I read a composition I immediately determine the height of the author's habitation.   As an elaborate performance is commonly said to smell of the lamp, my commendation of a noble thought, a sprightly sally, or a bold figure is to pronounce it fresh from the garret, an expression which would break from me upon the perusal of most of your papers, did I not believe that you sometimes quit the garret and ascend into the cock-loft.

HYPERTATUS.

Tuesday, 7th May 1751

Iliacos intra muros peccatur, et extra.

HORACE.

Faults lay on either side the Trojan towers.

ELPHINSTON.

TO THE 'RAMBLER'

SIR,

As, notwithstanding all that wit or malice or pride or prudence will be able to suggest, men and women must at last pass their lives together. I have never, therefore, thought those writers friends to human happiness, who endeavour to excite in either sex a general contempt or suspicion of the other. To persuade them who are entering the world and looking abroad for a suitable associate that all are equally vicious or equally ridiculous, that they who trust are certainly betrayed, and they who esteem are always disappointed, is not to awaken judgment, but to inflame temerity. Without hope there can be no caution. Those who are convinced that no reason for preference can be found will never harass their thoughts with doubt and deliberation. They will resolve, since they are doomed to misery, that no needless anxiety shall disturb their quiet. They will plunge at hazard into the crowd, and snatch the first hand that shall be held toward them.

That the world is overrun with vice cannot be denied; but vice, however predominant, has not yet gained an unlimited dominion. Simple and unmingled good is not in our power, but we may generally escape a greater evil by suffering a less; and therefore those who undertake to initiate the young and ignorant in the knowledge of life should be careful to inculcate the possibility of virtue and happiness and to encourage endeavours by prospects of success.

You, perhaps, do not suspect that these are the sentiments of one who has been subject for many years to all the hardships of antiquated virginity, has been long accustomed to the coldness of neglect and the petulance of insult, has been mortified in full assemblies by inquiries after forgotten fashions, games long disused, and wits and beauties of ancient renown, has been invited, with malicious importunity, to the second wedding of many acquaintances, has been ridiculed by two generations of coquettes in whispers intended to be heard, and been long considered by the airy and gay as too venerable for familiarity and too wise for pleasure. It is indeed natural for injury to provoke anger, and by continual repetition to produce an habitual asperity; yet I have hitherto struggled with so much vigilance against my pride and my resentment, that I have preserved my temper uncorrupted. I have not yet made it any part of my employment to collect sentences against marriage, nor am inclined to lessen the number of the few friends whom time has left me by obstructing that happiness which I cannot partake and venting my vexation in censures of the forwardness and indiscretion of girls or the inconstancy, tasteless-ness, and perfidy of men.

It is, indeed, not very difficult to bear that condition to which we are not condemned by necessity, but induced by observation and choice. And therefore I, perhaps, have never yet felt all the malignity with which a reproach edged with the appellation of old maid swells some of those hearts in which it is infixed. I was not condemned in my youth to solitude, either by indigence or deformity, nor passed the earlier part of life without the flattery of courtship and the joys of triumph. I have danced the round of gaiety amidst the murmurs of envy and gratulations of applause, been attended from pleasure to pleasure by the great, the sprightly, and the vain, and seen my regard solicited by the obsequiousness of gallantry, the gaiety of wit, and the timidity of love. If, therefore, I am yet a stranger to nuptial happiness I suffer only the conse-quences of my own resolves, and can look back upon the succession of lovers whose addresses I have rejected without grief and without malice.

When my name first began to be inscribed upon glasses I was honoured with the amorous professions of the gay Venustulus, a gentleman who, being the only son of a wealthy family, had been educated in all the wantonness of expense and softness of effemin-ancy. He was beautiful in his person and easy in his address, and therefore soon gained upon my eye at an age when the sight is very little overruled by the understanding. He had not any power in himself of gladdening or amusing, but supplied his want of con-versation by treats and diversions; and his chief art of courtship was to fill the mind of his mistress with parties, rambles, music, and shows. We were often engaged in short excursions to gardens and seats, and I was for a while pleased with the care which Venustulus discovered in securing me from any appearance of danger or possibility of mischance. He never failed to recommend caution to his coachman or to promise the waterman a reward if he landed us safe, and always contrived to return by daylight for fear of robbers. This extraordinary solicitude was represented for a time as the effect of his tenderness for me, but fear is too strong for continued hypocrisy. I soon discovered that Venustulus had the cowardice as well as elegance of a female. His imagination was perpetually clouded with terrors, and he could scarcely refrain from screams and outcries at any accidental surprise. He durst not enter a room if a rat was heard behind the wainscot, nor cross a field where the cattle were frisking in the sunshine. The least breeze that waved upon the river was a storm, and every clamour in the street was a cry of fire. I have seen him lose his colour when my squirrel had broke his chain, and was forced to throw water in his face on the sudden entrance of a black cat. Compassion once obliged me to drive away with my fan a beetle that kept him in distress, and chide off a dog that yelped at his heels, to which he would gladly have given up me to facilitate his own escape. Women naturally expect defence and protection from a lover or a husband, and therefore you will not think me culpable in refusing a wretch who would have burdened life with unnecessary fears and flown to me for that succour which it was his duty to have given.

My next lover was Fungosa, the son of a stock-jobber, whose visits my friends, by the importunity of persuasion, prevailed upon me to allow. Fungosa was no very suitable companion; for having been bred in a counting-house he spoke a language unintelligible in any other place. He had no desire of any reputation but that of an acute prognosticator of the changes in the funds; nor had any means of raising merriment but by telling how somebody was overreached in a bargain by his father. He was, however, a youth of great sobriety and prudence, and frequently informed us how carefully he would improve my fortune. I was not in haste to conclude the match, but was so much awed by my parents that I durst not dismiss him, and might perhaps have been doomed for ever to the grossness of pedlary and the jargon of usury, had not a fraud been discovered in the settlement, which set me free from the persecution of grovelling pride and pecuniary impudence.

I was afterwards six months without any particular notice, but at last became the idol of the glittering Flosculus, who prescribed the mode of embroidery to all the fops of his time and varied at pleasure the cock of every hat and the sleeve of every coat that appeared in fashionable assemblies.   Flosculus made some impression upon my heart by a compliment which few ladies can hear without emotion: he commended my skill in dress, my judgment in suiting colours, and my art in disposing ornaments.   But Flosculus was too much engaged by his own elegance to be sufficiently attentive to the duties of a lover or to please with varied praise an ear made delicate by riot of adulation.   He expected to be repaid part of his tribute, and stayed away three days because I neglected to take notice of a new coat.   I quickly found that Flosculus was rather a rival than an admirer, and that we should probably live in a perpetual struggle of emulous finery and spend our lives in stratagems to be first in the fashion.

I had soon after the honour at a feast of attracting the eyes of Dentatus, one of those human beings whose only happiness is to dine.   Dentatus regaled me with foreign varieties, told me of measures that he had laid for procuring the best cook in France, and entertained me with bills of fare, prescribed the arrangement of dishes, and taught me two sauces invented by himself.   At length, such is the uncertainty of human happiness, I declared my opinion too hastily upon a pie made under his own direction; after which he grew so cold and negligent that he was easily dismissed.

Many other lovers, or pretended lovers, I have had the honour to lead awhile in triumph.   But two of them I drove from me by discovering that they had no taste or knowledge in music.   Three I dismissed because they were drunkards, two because they paid their addresses at the same time to other ladies, and six because they attempted to influence my choice by bribing my maid.   Two more I discarded at the second visit for obscene allusions, and five for drollery on religion.   In the latter part of my reign I sentenced two to a perpetual exile for offering me settlements by which the children of a former marriage would have been injured, four for representing falsely the value of their estates, three for concealing their debts, and one for raising the rent of a decrepit tenant.

I have now sent you a narrative which the ladies may oppose to the tale of Hymenaeus.   I mean not to depreciate the sex which has produced poets and philosophers, heroes and martyrs: but will not suffer the rising generation of beauties to be dejected by partial satire, or to imagine that those who censured them have not likewise their follies and their vices.   I do not yet believe happiness unattainable in marriage, though I have never yet been able to find a man with whom I could prudently venture an inseparable union.

It is necessary to expose faults, that their deformity may be seen; but the reproach ought not to be extended beyond the crime, nor either sex to be condemned because some women, or men, are indelicate or dishonest.

I am, &c.

TRANQUILLA.

THE YOUNG TRADER TURNED GENTLEMAN (123)

Tuesday, 21st May 1751

Quo semel est imbuta recens, servabit odorem
Testa dit.

HORACE.

What season'd first the vessel, keeps the taste.

CREECH.

TO THE 'RAMBLER'

SIR,

Though I have so long found myself deluded by projects of honour and distinction that I often resolve to admit them no more into my heart, yet, how determinately soever excluded, they always recover by force or stratagem; and whenever, after the shortest relaxation of vigilance, reason and caution return to their charge, they find hope again in possession with all her train of pleasures dancing about her.

Even while I am preparing to write a history of disappointed expectations I cannot forbear to flatter myself that you and your readers are impatient for my performance, and that the sons of learning have laid down several of your late papers with discontent when they found that Misocapelus had delayed to continue his narrative.

But the desire of gratifying the expectations that I have failed is not the only motive of this relation which, having once promised it, I think myself no longer at liberty to forbear. For however I may have wished to clear myself from every other adhesion of trade, I hope I shall be always wise enough to retain my punctuality, and, amidst all my new arts of politeness, continue to despise negligence and detest falsehood.

When the death of my brother had dismissed me from the duties of a shop I considered myself as restored to the rights of my birth and entitled to the rank and reception which my ancestors obtained. I was, however, embarrassed with many difficulties at my first re-entrance into the world; for my haste to be a gentleman inclined me to precipitate measures, and every accident that forced me back towards my old station was considered by me as an obstruction of my happiness.

It was with no common grief and indignation that I found my former companions still daring to claim my notice, and the journey-men and apprentices sometimes pulling me by the sleeve as I was walking in the street, and, without any terror of my new sword which was, notwithstanding, of an uncommon size, inviting me to partake of a bottle at the old house, and entertaining me with histories of the girls in the neighbourhood. I had always in my official state been kept in awe by lace and embroidery, and imagined that to fright away these unwelcome familiarities nothing was necessary but that I should by splendour of dress proclaim my reunion with a higher rank. I therefore sent for my tailor, ordered a suit with twice the usual quantity of lace, and, that I might not let my persecutors increase their confidence by the habit of accosting me, stayed at home till it was made.

This week of confinement I passed in practising a forbidding frown, a smile of condescension, a slight salutation, and an abrupt departure, and in four mornings was able to turn upon my heel with so much levity and sprightliness that I made no doubt of discouraging all public attempts upon my dignity. I therefore issued forth in my new coat with a resolution of dazzling intimacy to a fitter distance, and pleased myself with the timidity and reverence which I should impress upon all who had hitherto presumed to harass me with their freedom. But whatever was the cause, I did not find myself received with any new degree of respect. Those whom I intended to drive from me ventured to advance with the usual phrases of benevolence, and those whose acquaintance I solicited grew more supercilious and reserved. I began soon to repent the expense by which I had procured no advantage, and to suspect that a shining dress, like a weighty weapon, has no force in itself, but owes all its efficacy to him that wears it.

Many were the mortifications and calamities which I was condemned to suffer in my initiation to politeness. I was so much tortured by the incessant civilities of my companions, that I never passed through that region of the city but in a chair with the curtains drawn, and at last left my lodgings and fixed myself in the verge of the court. Here I endeavoured to be thought a gentleman just returned from his travels, and was pleased to have my landlord believe that I was in some danger from importunate creditors. But this scheme was quickly defeated by a formal deputation sent to offer me, though I had now retired from business, the freedom of my company.

I was now detected in trade, and therefore resolved to stay no longer. I hired another apartment and changed my servants. Here I lived very happily for three months, and, with secret satisfaction, often overheard the family celebrating the greatness and felicity of the esquire; though the conversation seldom ended without some complaint of my covetousness or some remark upon my language or my gait. I now began to venture into the public walks and to know the faces of nobles and beauties, but could not observe without wonder, as I passed by them, how frequently they were talking of a tailor. I longed, however, to be admitted to conversation, and was somewhat weary of walking in crowds without a companion, yet continued to come and go with the rest till a lady whom I endeavoured to protect in a crowded passage as she was about to step into her chariot thanked me for my civility and told me that as she had often distinguished me for my modest and respectful behaviour, whenever I set up for myself I might expect to see her among my first customers.

Here was an end of my ambulatory projects. I indeed sometimes entered the walks again, but was always blasted by this destructive lady whose mischievous generosity recommended me to her acquaintance. Being therefore forced to practise my adscititious character upon another stage, I betook myself to a coffee-house frequented by wits, among whom I learned in a short time the cant of criticism, and talked so loudly and volubly of nature and manners and sentiment and diction and similies and contrasts and action and pronunciation, that I was often desired to lead the hiss and clap, and was feared and hated by the players and the poets. Many a sentence have I hissed which I did not understand, and many a groan have I uttered when the ladies were weeping in the boxes. At last a malignant author, whose performance I had persecuted through the nine nights, wrote an epigram upon Tape the critic, which drove me from the pit for ever.

My desire to be a fine gentleman still continued. I therefore, after a short suspense, chose a new set of friends at the gaming-table, and was for some time pleased with the civility and openness with which I found myself treated.   I was indeed obliged to play, but, being naturally timorous and vigilant, was never surprised into large sums.   What might have been the consequence of long familiarity with these plunderers I had not an opportunity of knowing; for one night the constables entered and seized us, and I was once more compelled to sink into my former condition by sending for my old master to attest my character.

When I was deliberating to what new qualifications I should aspire I was summoned into the country by an account of my father's death.   Here I had hopes of being able to distinguish myself and to support the honour of my family.   I therefore bought guns and horses, and, contrary to the expectation of the tenants, increased the salary of the huntsman.   But when I entered the field it was soon discovered that I was not destined to the glories of the chase.   I was afraid of thorns in the thicket and of dirt in the marsh, I shivered on the brink of a river while the sportsmen crossed it, and trembled at the sight of a five-bar gate.   When the sport and danger were over I was still equally disconcerted, for I was effeminate though not delicate, and could only join a feebly whispering voice in the clamours of their triumph.

A fall by which my ribs were broken soon recalled me to domestic pleasures, and I exerted all my art to obtain the favour of the neighbouring ladies.   But whenever I came there was always some unlucky conversation upon ribbons, fillets, pins, or threads, which drove all my stock of compliments out of my memory and overwhelmed me with shame and dejection.

Thus I passed the ten first years after the death of my brother, in which I have learned at last to repress that ambition which I could never gratify.   Instead of wasting more of my life in vain endeavours after accomplishments, which if not early acquired no endeavours can obtain, I shall confine my care to those higher excellencies which are in every man's power, and though I cannot enchant affection by elegance and ease, hope to secure esteem by honesty and truth.

I am, &c.,

MISOCAPELUS.

FOLLY OF COWARDICE AND
INACTIVITY (129)

Tuesday, 11th June 1751

Nunc, o nunc, Daedale, dixit,
Materiam, qua sis ingeniosus, habes.

OVID.

Now Daedalus, behold, by fate assign'd,
A task proportion'd to thy mighty mind!

MORALISTS like other writers, instead of casting their eyes abroad
in the living world and endeavouring to form maxims of practice
and new hints of theory, content their curiosity with that secondary
knowledge which books afford, and think themselves entitled to
reverence by a new arrangement of an ancient system or new
illustration of established principles. The sage precepts of the
first instructors of the world are transmitted from age to age with
little variation, and echoed from one author to another, not perhaps
without some loss of their original force at every repercussion.

I know not whether any other reason than this idleness of imitation can be assigned for that uniform and constant partiality by
which some vices have hitherto escaped censure and some virtues
wanted recommendation. Nor can I discover why else we have
been warned only against part of our enemies while the rest have
been suffered to steal upon us without notice; why the heart has on
one side been doubly fortified, and laid open on the other to the
incursions of error and the ravages of vice.

Among the favourite topics of moral declamation may be
numbered the miscarriages of imprudent boldness and the folly of
attempts beyond our power. Every page of every philosopher is
crowded with examples of temerity that sunk under burthens which
she laid upon herself, and called out enemies to battle by whom she
was destroyed.

Their remarks are too just to be disputed and too salutary to be
rejected. But there is likewise some danger lest timorous prudence
should be inculcated till courage and enterprise are wholly repressed, and the mind congealed in perpetual inactivity by the fatal
influence of frigorific wisdom.

Every man should, indeed, carefully compare his force with his undertaking. For though we ought not to love only for our own sakes, and though therefore danger or difficulty should not be avoided merely because we may expose ourselves to misery or disgrace, yet it may be justly required of us not to throw away our lives upon inadequate and hopeless designs, since we might by a just estimate of our abilities become more useful to mankind.

There is an irrational contempt of danger which approaches nearly to the folly, if not the guilt, of suicide; there is a ridiculous perseverance in impracticable schemes which is justly punished with ignominy and reproach. But in the wide regions of probability, which are the proper province of prudence and election, there is always room to deviate on either side of rectitude without rushing against apparent absurdity. And according to the inclinations of nature or the impressions of precept the daring and the cautious may move in different directions without touching upon rashness or cowardice.

That there is a middle path which it is every man's duty to find and to keep is unanimously confessed. But it is likewise acknowledged that this middle path is so narrow that it cannot easily be discovered, and so little beaten that there are no certain marks by which it can be followed. The care, therefore, of all those who conduct others has been that whenever they decline into obliquities they should tend towards the side of safety.

It can, indeed, raise no wonder that temerity has been generally censured; for it is one of the vices with which few can be charged, and which therefore great numbers are ready to condemn. It is the vice of noble and generous minds, the exuberance of magnanimity, and the ebullition of genius, and is therefore not regarded with much tenderness, because it never flatters us by that appearance of softness and imbecility which is commonly necessary to conciliate compassion. But if the same attention had been applied to the search of arguments against the folly of presupposing impossibilities and anticipating frustration, I know not whether many would not have been roused to usefulness, who, having been taught to confound prudence with timidity, never ventured to excel lest they should unfortunately fail.

It is necessary to distinguish our own interest from that of others, and that distinction will perhaps assist us in fixing the just limits of caution and adventurousness. In an undertaking that involves the happiness or the safety of many we have certainly no right to hazard more than is allowed by those who partake the danger. But where only ourselves can suffer by miscarriage we are not confined within such narrow limits. And still less is the reproach of temerity when numbers will receive advantage by success and only one be incommoded by failure.

Men are generally willing to hear precepts by which ease is favoured; and as no resentment is raised by general representation of human folly, even in those who are most eminently jealous of comparative reputation, we confess without reluctance that vain man is ignorant of his own weakness and therefore frequently presumes to attempt what he can never accomplish. But it ought likewise to be remembered that a man is no less ignorant of his own powers, and might perhaps have accomplished a thousand designs which the prejudices of cowardice restrained him from attempting.

It is observed in the golden verses of Pythagoras that 'power is never far from necessity.' The vigour of the human mind quickly appears when there is no longer any place for doubt and hesitation, when diffidence is absorbed in the sense of danger, or overwhelmed by some resistless passion. We then soon discover that difficulty is, for the most part, the daughter of idleness; that the obstacles with which our way seemed to be obstructed were only phantoms which we believed real because we durst not advance to a close examination; and we learn that it is impossible to determine without experience how much constancy may endure or perseverance perform.

But whatever pleasure may be found in the review of distresses when art or courage has surmounted them, few will be persuaded to wish that they may be awakened by want or terror to the conviction of their own abilities. Everyone should therefore endeavour to invigorate himself by reason and reflection, and determine to exert the latent force that nature may have reposited in him, before the hour of exigence comes upon him and compulsion shall torture him to diligence. It is below the dignity of a reasonable being to owe that strength to necessity which ought always to act at the call of choice, or to need any other motive to industry than the desire of performing his duty.

Reflections that may drive away despair cannot be wanting to him who considers how much life is now advanced beyond the state of naked, undisciplined, uninstructed nature. Whatever has been effected for convenience or elegance while it was yet unknown was believed impossible, and therefore would never have been attempted, had not some, more daring than the rest, adventured to bid defiance to prejudice and censure. Nor is there yet any reason to doubt the same labour would be rewarded with the same success.

There are qualities in the products of nature yet undiscovered, and combinations in the powers of art yet untried. It is the duty of every man to endeavour that something may be added by his industry to the hereditary aggregate of knowledge and happiness. To add much can indeed be the lot of few, but to add something, however little, everyone may hope. And of every honest endeavour it is certain that, however unsuccessful, it will be at last rewarded.

HISTORY OF A BEAUTY [1] (130)

Saturday, 15th June 1751

Non sic prata novo vere decentia
Aestatis calidae dispoliat vapor,
Saevit solstitio cum medius dies;
Ut fulgor teneris qui radiat genis
Momento rapitur.

SENECA.

Not faster in the summer's ray
The spring's frail beauty fades away,
Than anguish and decay consume
The smiling virgin's rosy bloom.

ELPHINSTON.

TO THE 'RAMBLER'

SIR,

You have very lately observed that in the numerous subdivisions of the world every class and order of mankind have joys and sorrows of their own. We all feel hourly pain and pleasure from events which pass unheeded before other eyes, but can scarcely communicate our perceptions to minds preoccupied by different objects, any more than the delight of well-disposed colours or harmonious sounds can be imparted to such as want the sense of hearing or of sight.

I am so strongly convinced of the justness of this remark, and have on so many occasions discovered with how little attention pride looks upon calamity of which she thinks herself not in danger, and indolence listens to complaint when it is not echoed by her own remembrance, that though I am about to lay the occurrences of my

[1] For the sequel see pp. 224–7.

life before you, I question whether you will condescend to peruse my narrative or, without the help of some female speculist, be able to understand it.

I was born a beauty.   From the dawn of reason I had my regard turned wholly upon myself, nor can recollect anything earlier than praise and admiration.   My mother, whose face had luckily advanced her to a condition above her birth, thought no evil so great as deformity.   She had not the power of imagining any other defect than a cloudy complexion or disproportionate features, and therefore contemplated me as an assemblage of all that could raise envy or desire, and predicted with triumphant fondness the extent of my conquests and the number of my slaves.

She never mentioned any of my young acquaintance before me but to remark how much they fell below my perfection; how one would have had a fine face, but that her eyes were without lustre; how another struck the sight at a distance, but wanted my hair and teeth at a nearer view; another disgraced an elegant shape with a brown skin; some had short fingers, and others dimples in a wrong place.

As she expected no happiness nor advantage but from beauty, she thought nothing but beauty worthy of her care; and her maternal kindness was chiefly exercised in contrivances to protect me from any accident that might deface me with a scar or stain me with a freckle.   She never thought me sufficiently shaded from the sun or screened from the fire.   She was severe or indulgent with no other intention than the preservation of my form.   She excused me from work lest I should learn to hang down my head or harden my finger with a needle.   She snatched away my book because a young lady in the neighbourhood had made her eyes red with reading by a candle.   But she would scarcely suffer me to eat lest I should spoil my shape, nor to walk lest I should swell my ankle with a sprain.   At night I was accurately surveyed from head to foot lest I should have suffered any diminution of my charms in the adventures of the day, and was never permitted to sleep till I had passed through the cosmetic discipline, part of which was a regular lustration performed with bean-flower water and May-dews.   My hair was perfumed with variety of unguents, by some of which it was to be thickened and by others to be curled.   The softness of my hands was secured by medicated gloves, and my bosom rubbed with a pomade prepared by my mother, of virtue to discuss pimples and clear discolorations.

I was always called up early because the morning air gives a freshness to the cheeks; but I was placed behind a curtain in my mother's chamber, because the neck is easily tanned by the rising sun. I was then dressed with a thousand precautions, and again heard my own praises and triumphed in the compliments and prognostications of all that approached me.

My mother was not so much prepossessed with an opinion of my natural excellencies as not to think some cultivation necessary to their completion. She took care that I should want none of the accomplishments included in female education or considered necessary in fashionable life. I was looked upon in my ninth year as the chief ornament of the dancing-master's ball, and Mr. Ariet used to reproach his other scholars with my performances on the harpsichord. At twelve I was remarkable for playing my cards with great elegance of manner and accuracy of judgment.

At last the time came when my mother thought me perfect in my exercises and qualified to display in the open world those accomplishments which had yet only been discovered in select parties or domestic assemblies. Preparations were therefore made for my appearance on a public night, which she considered as the most important and critical moment of my life. She cannot be charged with neglecting any means of recommendation or leaving anything to chance which prudence could ascertain. Every ornament was tried in every position, every friend was consulted about the colour of my dress, and the mantua-makers were harassed with directions and alterations.

At last the night arrived from which my future life was to be reckoned. I was dressed and sent out to conquer with a heart beating like that of an old knight errant at his first sally. Scholars have told me of a Spartan matron who, when she armed her son for battle, bade him bring back his shield or be brought upon it. My venerable parent dismissed me to a field, in her opinion of equal glory, with a command to show that I was her daughter and not to return without a lover.

I went, and was received like other pleasing novelties with a tumult of applause. Every man who valued himself upon the graces of his person or the elegance of his address crowded about me, and wit and splendour contended for my notice. I was delightfully fatigued with incessant civilities, which were made more pleasing by the apparent envy of those whom my presence exposed to neglect, and returned with an attendant equal in rank and wealth to my utmost wishes, and from this time stood in the first rank of beauty, was followed by gazers in the Mall, celebrated in the papers of the day, imitated by all who endeavoured to rise into fashion, and censured by those whom age or disappointment forced to retire.

My mother, who pleased herself with the hopes of seeing my exaltation, dressed me with all the exuberance of finery, and, when I represented to her that a fortune might be expected proportionate to my appearance, told me that she should scorn the reptile who could inquire after the fortune of a girl like me. She advised me to prosecute my victories, and time would certainly bring me a captive who might deserve the honour of being enchained for ever.

My lovers were indeed so numerous that I had no other care than that of determining to whom I should seem to give the preference. But having been steadily and industriously instructed to preserve my heart from any impressions which might hinder me from consulting my interest, I acted with less embarrassment because my choice was regulated by principles more clear and certain than the caprice of approbation. When I had singled out one from the rest as more worthy of encouragement I proceeded in my measures by the rules of art; and yet, when the ardour of the first visits was spent, generally found a sudden declension of my influence. I felt in myself the want of some power to diversify amusement and enliven conversation, and could not but suspect that my mind failed in performing the promises of my face. This opinion was soon confirmed by one of my lovers, who married Lavinia, with less beauty and fortune than mine, because he thought a wife ought to have qualities which might make her amiable when her bloom was past.

The vanity of my mother would not suffer her to discover any defect in one that had been formed by her instructions and had all the excellence which she herself could boast. She told me that nothing so much hindered the advancement of women as literature and wit, which generally frightened away those that could make the best settlements and drew about them a needy tribe of poets and philosophers that filled their heads with wild notions of content and contemplation and virtuous obscurity. She therefore enjoined me to improve my minuet step with a new French dancing master and wait the event of the next birth-night.

I had now almost completed my nineteenth year. If my charms had lost any of their softness it was more than compensated by additional dignity; and if the attractions of innocence were impaired their place was supplied by the arts of allurement. I was therefore preparing for a new attack without any abatement of my

confidence when in the midst of my hopes and schemes I was
seized by that dreadful malady which has so often put a sudden end
to the tyranny of beauty. I recovered my health after a long confinement; but when I looked again on that face which had been
often flushed with transport at its own reflection, and saw all that I
had learned to value, all that I had endeavoured to improve, all
that had procured me honours or praises, irrecoverably destroyed
I sunk at once into melancholy and despondence. My pain was
not much consoled or alleviated by my mother, who grieved that
I had not lost my life together with my beauty and declared that
she thought a young woman divested of her charms had nothing
for which those who loved her could desire to save her from the
grave.

Having thus continued my relation to the period from which my
life took a new course, I shall conclude it in another letter if by
publishing this you show any regard for the correspondence of,
Sir, &c.,

VICTORIA.

DESIRE OF GAIN UNIVERSAL (131)

Tuesday, 18th June 1751

Fatis accede deisque,
Et cole felices; miseros fuge. Sidera coelo
Ut distant, flamma mari, sic utile recto.

LUCAN.

Still follow where auspicious fates invite;
Caress the happy, and the wretched flight.
Sooner shall jarring elements unite,
Than truth with gain, than interest with right.

F. LEWIS.

THERE is scarcely any sentiment in which, amidst the innumerable
varieties of inclination that nature or accident have scattered in the
world, we find greater numbers concurring than in the wish for
riches; a wish indeed so prevalent, that it may be considered as
universal and transcendental, as the desire in which all other desires
are included, and of which the various purposes which actuate
mankind are only subordinate species and different modifications.

Wealth is the general centre of inclination, the point to which all minds preserve an invariable tendency, from which they afterwards diverge in numberless directions. Whatever is the remote or ultimate design, the immediate care is to be rich; and in whatever enjoyment we intend finally to acquiesce, we seldom consider it as attainable but by the means of money. Of wealth, therefore, all unanimously confess the value, nor is there any disagreement but about the use.

No desire can be formed which riches do not assist to gratify. He that places his happiness in splendid equipage or numerous dependants, in refined praise or popular acclamations, in the accumulation of curiosities or the revels of luxury, in splendid edifices or wide plantations, must still either by birth or acquisition possess riches. They may be considered as the elemental principles of pleasure which may be combined with endless diversity, as the essential and necessary substance of which only the form is left to be adjusted by choice.

The necessity of riches being thus apparent, it is not wonderful that almost every mind has been employed in endeavours to acquire them; that multitudes have vied in arts by which life is furnished with accommodations, and which therefore mankind may reasonably be expected to reward.

It had indeed been happy if this predominant appetite had operated only in concurrence with virtue by influencing none but those who were zealous to deserve what they were eager to possess and had abilities to improve their own fortunes by contributing to the ease or happiness of others. To have riches and to have merit would then have been the same, and success might reasonably have been considered as a proof of excellence.

But we do not find that any of the wishes of men keep a stated proportion to their powers of attainment. Many envy and desire wealth who can never procure it by honest industry or useful knowledge. They therefore turn their eyes about to examine what other methods can be found of gaining that which none, however impotent or worthless, will be content to want.

A little inquiry will discover that there are nearer ways to profit than through the intricacies of art or up the steeps of labour. What wisdom and virtue scarcely receive at the close of life as the recompense of long toil and repeated efforts is brought within the reach of subtlety and dishonesty by more expeditious and compendious measures. The wealth of credulity is an open prey to falsehood, and the possessions of ignorance and imbecility are easily stolen away by the conveyances of secret artifice or seized by the gripe of unresisted violence.

It is likewise not hard to discover that riches always procure protection for themselves, that they dazzle the eyes of inquiry, divert the celerity of pursuit, or appease the ferocity of vengeance. When any man is incontestably known to have large possessions very few think it requisite to inquire by what practices they were obtained. The resentment of mankind rages only against the struggles of feeble and timorous corruption, but when it has surmounted the first opposition it is afterwards supported by favour and animated by applause.

The prospect of gaining speedily what is ardently desired, and the certainty of obtaining by every accession of advantage an addition of security, have so far prevailed upon the passions of mankind, that the peace of life is destroyed by a general and incessant struggle for riches. It is observed of gold, by an old epigrammatist, that to have it is to be in fear, and to want it is to be in sorrow. There is no condition which is not disquieted either with the care of gaining or of keeping money; and the race of man may be divided in a political estimate between those who are practising fraud and those who are repelling it.

If we consider the present state of the world it will be found that all confidence is lost among mankind, that no man ventures to act, where money can be endangered, upon the faith of another. It is impossible to see the long scrolls in which every contract is included, with all their appendages of seals and attestation, without wondering at the depravity of those beings who must be restrained from violation of promise by such formal and public evidences, and precluded from equivocation and subterfuge by such punctilious minuteness. Among all the satires to which folly and wickedness have given occasion none is equally severe with a bond or a settlement.

Of the various arts by which riches may be obtained the greater part are at the first view irreconcilable with the laws of virtue. Some are openly flagitious and practised not only in neglect but in defiance of faith and justice, and the rest are on every side so entangled with dubious tendencies and so beset with perpetual temptations, that very few, even of those who are not yet abandoned, are able to preserve their innocence, or can produce any other claim to pardon than that they have deviated from the right less than others, and have sooner and more diligently endeavoured to return.

One of the chief characteristics of the golden age, of the age in which neither care nor danger had intruded on mankind, is the community of possessions. Strife and fraud were totally excluded, and every turbulent passion was stilled by plenty and equality. Such were indeed happy times; but such times can return no more. Community of possession must include spontaneity of production; for what is obtained by labour will be of right the property of him by whose labour it is gained. And while a rightful claim to pleasure or to affluence must be procured either by slow industry or uncertain hazard, there will always be multitudes whom cowardice or impatience incite to more safe and more speedy methods, who strive to pluck the fruit without cultivating the tree, and to share the advantages of victory without partaking the danger of the battle.

In latter ages the conviction of the danger to which virtue is exposed while the mind continues open to the influence of riches has determined many to vows of perpetual poverty. They have suppressed desire by cutting off the possibility of gratification, and secured their peace by destroying the enemy whom they had no hope of reducing to quiet subjection. But by debarring themselves from evil they have rescinded many opportunities of good. They have too often sunk into inactivity and uselessness, and though they have forborne to injure society have not fully paid their contributions to its happiness.

While riches are so necessary to present convenience and so much more easily obtained by crimes than virtues, the mind can only be secured from yielding to the continual impulse of covetousness by the preponderation of unchangeable and eternal motives. Gold will turn the intellectual balance when weighed only against reputation, but will be light and ineffectual when the opposite scale is charged with justice, veracity, and piety.

DIFFICULTY OF EDUCATING A YOUNG NOBLEMAN[1] (132)

Saturday, 22nd June 1751

Dociles imitandis
Turpibus ac pravis omnes sumus.

JUVENAL.

The mind of mortals, in perverseness strong,
Imbibes with dire docility the wrong.

MR. RAMBLER,

I was bred a scholar, and after the usual course of education found it necessary to employ for the support of life that learning which I had almost exhausted my little fortune in acquiring. The lucrative professions drew my regard with equal attraction; each presented ideas which excited my curiosity, and each imposed duties which terrified my apprehension.

There is no temper more unpropitious to interest than desultory application and unlimited inquiry, by which the desires are held in a perpetual equipoise, and the mind fluctuates between different purposes without determination. I had books of every kind round me, among which I divided my time as caprice or accident directed. I often spent the first hours of the day in considering to what study I should devote the rest; and at last snatched up an author that lay upon the table, or perhaps fled to a coffee-house for deliverance from the anxiety of irresolution and the gloominess of solitude.

Thus my little patrimony grew imperceptibly less, till I was roused from my literary slumber by a creditor whose importunity obliged me to pacify him with so large a sum, that what remained was not sufficient to support me more than eight months. I hope you will not reproach me with avarice or cowardice if I acknowledge that I now thought myself in danger of distress and obliged to endeavour after some certain competence.

There have been heroes of negligence, who have laid the price of their last acre in a drawer, and, without the least interruption of

---

[1] For the sequel see pp. 282-5 and pp. 286-9.

their tranquillity or abatement of their expenses, taken out one piece after another till there was no more remaining. But I was not born to such dignity of imprudence or such exaltation above the cares and necessities of life. I therefore immediately engaged my friends to procure me a little employment which might set me free from the dread of poverty and afford me time to plan out some final scheme of lasting advantage.

My friends were struck with honest solicitude and immediately promised their endeavours for my extrication. They did not suffer their kindness to languish by delay, but prosecuted their inquiries with such success, that in less than a month I was perplexed with variety of offers and contrariety of prospects.

I had, however, no time for long causes of consideration, and therefore soon resolved to accept the office of instructing a young nobleman in the house of his father. I went to the seat at which the family then happened to reside, was received with great politeness, and invited to enter immediately on my charge. The terms offered were such as I should willingly have accepted though my fortune had allowed me greater liberty of choice, the respect with which I was treated flattered my vanity, and perhaps the splendour of the apartments and the luxury of the table were not wholly without their influence. I immediately complied with the proposals and received the young lord into my care.

Having no desire to gain more than I should truly deserve I very diligently prosecuted my undertaking and had the satisfaction of discovering in my pupil a flexible temper, a quick apprehension, and a retentive memory. I did not much doubt that my care would, in time, produce a wise and useful counsellor to the state, though my labours were somewhat obstructed by want of authority and the necessity of complying with the freaks of negligence and of waiting patiently for the lucky moment of voluntary attention. To a man whose imagination was filled with the dignity of knowledge, and to whom a studious life had made all the common amusements insipid and contemptible, it was not very easy to suppress his indignation when he saw himself forsaken in the midst of his lecture for an opportunity to catch an insect, and found his instructions debarred from access to the intellectual faculties by the memory of a childish frolic or the desire of a new plaything.

Those vexations would have recurred less frequently had not his mamma, by entreating at one time that he should be excused from a task as a reward for some petty compliance, and withholding him from his book at another to gratify herself or her visitants with his vivacity, shown him that everything was more pleasing and more important than knowledge, and that study was to be endured rather than chosen, and was only the business of those hours which pleasure left vacant or discipline usurped.

I thought it my duty to complain in tender terms of these frequent avocations, but was answered that rank and fortune might reasonably hope for some indulgence, that the retardation of my pupil's progress would not be imputed to any negligence or inability of mine, and that with the success which satisfied everybody else I might surely satisfy myself. I had now done my duty, and without more remonstrances continued to inculcate my precepts whenever they could be heard, gained every day new influence, and found that by degrees my scholar began to feel the quick impulses of curiosity and the honest ardour of studious ambition.

At length it was resolved to pass a winter in London. The lady had too much fondness for her son to live five months without him, and too high an opinion of his wit and learning to refuse her vanity the gratifications of exhibiting him to the public. I remonstrated against too early an acquaintance with cards and company; but with a soft contempt of my ignorance and pedantry she said that he had been already confined too long to solitary study, and it was now time to show him the world; nothing was more a brand of meanness than bashful timidity; gay freedom and elegant assurance were only to be gained by mixed conversation, a frequent intercourse with strangers, and a timely introduction to splendid assemblies; and she had more than once observed that his forwardness and complaisance began to desert him, that he was silent when he had not something of consequence to say, blushed whenever he happened to find himself mistaken, and hung down his head in the presence of the ladies without the readiness of reply and activity of officiousness remarkable in young gentlemen that are bred in London.

Again I found resistance hopeless, and again thought it proper to comply. We entered the coach, and in four days were placed in the gayest and most magnificent region of the town. My pupil, who had for several years lived at a remote seat, was immediately dazzled with a thousand beams of novelty and show. His imagination was filled with the perpetual tumult of pleasure that passed before him, and it was impossible to allure him from the window or to overpower by any charm of eloquence the rattle of coaches and the sounds which echoed from the doors in the neighbourhood. In three days his attention, which he began to regain, was disturbed by a rich suit in which he was equipped for the reception of company, and which, having been long accustomed to a plain dress, he could not at first survey without ecstasy.

The arrival of the family was now formally notified. Every hour of every day brought more intimate or more distant acquaintances to the door, and my pupil was indiscriminately introduced to all that he might accustom himself to change of faces and be rid with speed of his rustic diffidence.

He soon endeared himself to his mother by the speedy acquisition or recovery of her darling qualities : his eyes sparkle at a numerous assembly and his heart dances at the mention of a ball. He has at once caught the infection of high life, and has no other test of principles or actions than the quality of those to whom they are ascribed. He begins already to look down on me with superiority, and submits to one short lesson in a week as an act of condescension rather than obedience. For he is of opinion that no tutor is properly qualified who cannot speak French ; and having formerly learned a few familiar phrases from his sister's governess, he is every day soliciting his mamma to procure him a foreign footman, that he may grow polite by his conversation. I am not yet insulted, but find myself likely to become soon a superfluous encumbrance. For my scholar has now no time for science or for virtue ; and the lady yesterday declared him so much the favourite of every company, that she was afraid he would not have an hour in the day to dance and fence.

I am, &c.,

EUMATHES

Tuesday, 25th June 1751

Magna quidem sacris quae dat praecepta libellis
Victrix fortunae sapientia.   Dicimus autem
Hos quoque felicis, qui ferre incommoda vitae,
Nec jactare jugum vita didicere magistra.

JUVENAL.

Let stoics ethics haughty rules advance,
To combat fortune, and to conquer chance;
Yet happy those, though not so learn'd are thought,
Whom life instructs, who by experience taught,
For new to come from past misfortunes look.
Nor shake the yoke, which galls the more 'tis shook.

CREECH.

TO THE 'RAMBLER'

SIR,

You have shown by the publication of my letter that you think the life of Victoria not wholly unworthy of the notice of a philosopher. I shall therefore continue my narrative without any apology for unimportance which you have dignified or for inaccuracies which you are to correct.

When my life appeared to be no longer in danger, and as much of my strength was recovered as enabled me to bear the agitation of a coach, I was placed at a lodging in a neighbouring village to which my mother dismissed me with a faint embrace, having repeated her command not to expose my face too soon to the sun or wind, and told me that with care I might perhaps become tolerable again. The prospect of being tolerable had very little power to elevate the imagination of one who had so long been accustomed to praise and ecstasy; but it was some satisfaction to be separated from my mother, who was incessantly ringing the knell of departed beauty, and never entered my room without the whine of condolence or the growl of anger. She often wandered over my face, as travellers over the ruins of a celebrated city, to note every place which had once been remarkable for a happy feature. She condescended to visit my retirement, but always left me more melancholy. For after a thousand trifling inquiries about my diet and a minute examination of my looks she generally concluded with a sigh that I should never more be fit to be seen.

At last I was permitted to return home, but found no great improvement of my condition; for I was imprisoned in my chamber as a criminal whose appearance would disgrace my friends, and condemned to be tortured into new beauty. Every experiment which the officiousness of folly could communicate or the credulity of ignorance admit was tried upon me. Sometimes I was covered with emollients, by which it was expected that all the scars would be filled and my cheeks plumped up to their former smoothness; and sometimes I was punished with artificial excoriations, in hope of gaining new graces with a new skin. The cosmetic science was exhausted upon me; but who can repair the ruins of nature? My mother was forced to give me rest at last, and abandon me to the fate of a fallen toast, whose fortune she considered as a hopeless game, no longer worthy of solicitude or attention.

The condition of a young woman who has never thought or heard of any other excellence than beauty, and whom the sudden blast of disease wrinkles in her bloom, is indeed sufficiently calamitous. She is at once deprived of all that gave her eminence or power, of all that elated her pride or animated her activity, all that filled her days with pleasure and her nights with hope, all that gave her gladness to the present hour or brightened her prospects of futurity. It is perhaps not in the power of a man whose attention has been divided by diversity of pursuits, and who has not been accustomed to derive from others much of his happiness, to image to himself such helpless destitution, such dismal inanity. Every object of pleasing contemplation is at once snatched away, and the soul finds every receptacle of ideas empty or filled only with the memory of joys that can return no more. All is gloomy privation or impotent desire: the faculties of anticipation slumber in despondency, or the powers of pleasure mutiny for employment.

I was so little able to find entertainment for myself, that I was forced in a short time to venture abroad, as the solitary savage is driven by hunger from his cavern. I entered with all the humility of disgrace into assemblies where I had lately sparkled with gaiety and towered with triumph. I was not wholly without hope that dejection had misrepresented me to myself, and that the remains of my former face might yet have some attraction and influence. But the first circle of visits convinced me that my reign was at an end, that life and death were no longer in my hands, that I was no more to practise the glance of command or the frown of prohibition, to receive the tribute of sighs and praises, or be soothed with the gentle murmurs of amorous timidity. My opinion was

now unheard and my proposals were unregarded. The narrowness of my knowledge and the meanness of my sentiments were
easily discovered when the eyes were no longer engaged against the
judgment; and it was observed by those who had formerly been
charmed with my vivacious loquacity that my understanding was
impaired as well as my face, and that I was no longer qualified to
fill a place in any company but a party at cards.

It is scarcely to be imagined how soon the mind sinks to a level
with the condition. I, who had long considered all who approached me as vassals condemned to regulate their pleasures by
my eyes and harass their inventions for my entertainment, was in
less than three weeks reduced to receive a ticket with professions of
obligation, to catch with eagerness at a compliment, and to watch
with all the anxiousness of dependence lest any little civility that
was paid me should pass unacknowledged.

Though the negligence of the men was not very pleasing when
compared with vows and adoration, yet it was far more supportable
than the insolence of my own sex. For the first ten months after
my return into the world I never entered a single house in which
the memory of my downfall was not revived. At one place I was
congratulated on my escape with life; at another I heard of the
benefits of early inoculation; by some I have been told in express
terms that I am not yet without my charms; others have whispered
at my entrance: 'This is the celebrated beauty.' One told me of a
wash that would smooth the skin, and another offered me her chair
that I might not front the light. Some soothed me with the
observation that none can tell how soon my case may be her own;
and some thought it proper to receive me with mournful tenderness, formal condolence, and consolatory blandishments.

Thus was I every day harassed with all the stratagems of well-
bred malignity. Yet insolence was more tolerable than solitude,
and I therefore persisted to keep my time at the doors of my
acquaintance without gratifying them with any appearance of
resentment or depression. I expected that their exultation would
in time vapour away, that the joy of their superiority would end
with its novelty, and that I should be suffered to glide along in my
present form among the nameless multitude whom nature never
intended to excite envy or admiration nor enabled to delight the eye
or inflame the heart.

This was naturally to be expected, and this I began to experience.
But when I was no longer agitated by the perpetual ardour of
resistance and effort of perseverance I found more sensibly the

want of those entertainments which had formerly delighted me. The day rose upon me without an engagement, and the evening closed in its natural gloom without summoning me to a concert or a ball. None had any care to find amusements for me, and I had no power of amusing myself. Idleness exposed me to melancholy, and life began to languish in motionless indifference.

Misery and shame are nearly allied. It was not without many struggles that I prevailed on myself to confess my uneasiness to Euphemia, the only friend who had never pained me with comfort or with pity. I at last laid my calamities before her, rather to ease my heart than receive assistance. 'We must distinguish,' said she, 'my Victoria, those evils which are imposed by Providence from those to which we ourselves give the power of hurting us. Of your calamity a small part is the infliction of Heaven, the rest is little more than the corrosion of idle discontent. You have lost that which may indeed sometimes contribute to happiness but to which happiness is by no means inseparably annexed. You have lost what the greater number of the human race never have possessed, what those on whom it is bestowed for the most part possess in vain, and what you, while it was yours, knew not how to use. You have only lost early what the laws of nature forbid you to keep long, and have lost it while your mind is yet flexible and while you have time to substitute more valuable and more durable excellencies. Consider yourself, my Victoria, as a being born to know, to reason, and to act. Rise at once from your dream of melancholy to wisdom and to piety. You will find that there are other charms than those of beauty and other joys than the praise of fools.'

I am, Sir, &c.,

VICTORIA.

LITERARY COURAGE (137)

Tuesday, 9th July 1751

Dum vitant stulti vitia, in contraria currunt.

HORACE.

Whilst fools one vice condemn,
They run into the opposite extreme.

CREECH.

THAT wonder is the effect of ignorance has been often observed. The awful stillness of attention with which the mind is overspread at the first view of an unexpected effect ceases when we have leisure to disentangle complications and investigate causes. Wonder is a pause of reason, a sudden cessation of the mental progress, which lasts only while the understanding is fixed upon some single idea, and is at an end when it recovers force enough to divide the object into its parts or mark the intermediate gradations from the first agent to the last consequence.

It may be remarked with equal truth that ignorance is often the effect of wonder. It is common for those who have never accustomed themselves to the labour of inquiry nor invigorated their confidence by conquests over difficulty to sleep in the gloomy quiescence of astonishment without any effort to animate inquiry or dispel obscurity. What they cannot immediately conceive they consider as too high to be reached or too extensive to be comprehended. They therefore content themselves with the gaze of folly, forbear to attempt what they have no hopes of performing, and resign the pleasure of rational contemplation to more pertinacious study or more active faculties.

Among the productions of mechanic art many are of a form so different from that of their first materials, and many consist of parts so numerous and so nicely adapted to each other, that it is not possible to view them without amazement. But when we enter the shops of artificers, observe the various tools by which every operation is facilitated, and trace the progress of a manufacture through the different hands that, in succession to each other, contribute to its perfection, we soon discover that every single man has an easy task, and that the extremes, however remote, of natural rudeness and artificial elegance are enjoined by a regular concatenation of effects of which every one is introduced by that which precedes it and equally introduces that which is to follow.

The same is the state of intellectual and manual performances. Long calculations or complex diagrams affright the timorous and unexperienced from a second view; but if we have skill sufficient to analyse them into simple principles it will be discovered that our fear was groundless. 'Divide and conquer' is a principle equally just in science as in policy. Complication is a species of confederacy which, while it continues united, bids defiance to the most active and vigorous intellect, but of which every member is separately weak and which may therefore be quickly subdued if it can once be broken.

The chief art of learning, as Locke has observed, is to attempt but little at a time. The wildest excursions of the mind are made by short flights frequently repeated. The most lofty fabrics of science are formed by the continual accumulation of single propositions.

It often happens, whatever be the cause, that impatience of labour or dread of miscarriage seizes those who are most distinguished for quickness of apprehension, and that they who might with greatest reason promise themselves victory are least willing to hazard the encounter. This diffidence, where the attention is not laid asleep by laziness or dissipated by pleasures, can arise only from confused and general views such as negligence snatches in haste, or from the disappointment of the first hopes formed by arrogance without reflection. To expect that the intricacies of science will be pierced by a careless glance, or the eminences of fame ascended without labour, is to expect a particular privilege, a power denied to the rest of mankind. But to suppose that the maze is inscrutable to diligence, or the heights inaccessible to perseverance, is to submit to the tyranny of fancy and enchain the mind in voluntary shackles.

It is the proper ambition of the heroes in literature to enlarge the boundaries of knowledge by discovering and conquering new regions of the intellectual world. To the success of such undertakings perhaps some degree of fortuitous happiness is necessary, which no man can promise or procure to himself. And therefore doubt and irresolution may be forgiven in him that ventures into the unexplored abysses of truth and attempts to find his way through the fluctuations of uncertainty and the conflicts of contradiction. But when nothing more is required than to pursue a path already beaten, to trample obstacles which others have demolished, why should any man so much distrust his own intellect as to imagine himself unequal to the attempt?

It were to be wished that they who devote their lives to study would at once believe nothing too great for their attainment and consider nothing as too little for their regard, that they would extend their notice alike to science and to life, and unite some knowledge of the present world to their acquaintance with past ages and remote events.

Nothing has so much exposed men of learning to contempt and ridicule as their ignorance of things which are known to all but themselves. Those who have been taught to consider the institutions of the schools as giving the last perfection to human abilities are surprised to see men wrinkled with study yet wanting to be instructed in the minute circumstances of propriety or the necessary forms of daily transaction, and quickly shake off their reverence for modes of education which they find to produce no ability above the rest of mankind.

'Books,' says Bacon, 'can never teach the use of books.' The student must learn by commerce with mankind to reduce his speculations to practice and accommodate his knowledge to the purposes of life.

It is too common for those who have been bred to scholastic professions and passed much of their time in academies, where nothing but learning confers honours, to disregard every other qualification, and to imagine that they shall find mankind ready to pay homage to their knowledge and to crowd about them for instruction. They therefore step out from their cells into the open world with all the confidence of authority and dignity of importance. They look round about them at once with ignorance and scorn on a race of beings to whom they are equally unknown and equally contemptible, but whose manners they must imitate and with whose opinions they must comply if they desire to pass their time happily among them.

To lessen that disdain with which scholars are inclined to look on the common business of the world, and the unwillingness with which they condescend to learn what is not to be found in any system of philosophy, it may be necessary to consider that, though admiration is excited by abstruse researches and remote discoveries, yet pleasure is not given nor affection conciliated but by softer accomplishments and qualities more easily communicable to those about us. He that can only converse upon questions about which only a small part of mankind has knowledge sufficient to make them curious must lose his days in unsocial silence and live in the crowd of life without a companion. He that can only be useful on great occasions may die without exerting his abilities and stand a helpless spectator of a thousand vexations which fret away happiness, and which nothing is required to remove but a little dexterity of conduct and readiness of expedients.

No degree of knowledge attainable by man is able to set him above the want of hourly assistance or to extinguish the desire of fond endearments and tender officiousness; and therefore, no one should think it unnecessary to learn those arts by which friendship may be gained. Kindness is preserved by a constant reciprocation of benefits or interchange of pleasure; but such benefits only can be bestowed as others are capable to receive, and such pleasures only imparted as others are qualified to enjoy.

By this descent from the pinnacles of art no honour will be lost, for the condescensions of learning are always overpaid by gratitude. An elevated genius employed in little things appears, to use the simile of Longinus, like the sun in his evening declination. He remits his splendour, but retains his magnitude, and pleases more though he dazzles less.

SQUIRE BLUSTER (142)

Saturday, 27th July 1751

Ἔνθα δ'ἀνὴρ ἐνίαυε πελώριος, . . . οὐδὲ μετ' ἄλλους
πωλεῖτ', ἀλλ' ἀπάνευθεν ἐὼν ἀθεμίστια ᾔδη.
καὶ γὰρ θαῦμ' ἐτέτυκτο πελώριον, οὐδὲ ἐῴκει,
ἀνδρί γε σιτοφάγῳ.

HOMER.

A giant shepherd here his flock maintains
Far from the rest, and solitary reigns,
In shelter thick of horrid shade reclin'd;
And gloomy mischiefs labour in his mind.
A form enormous! far unlike the race
Of human birth, in stature or in face.

POPE.

TO THE 'RAMBLER'

SIR,
Having been accustomed to retire annually from the town, I lately accepted the invitation of Eugenio who has an estate and seat

in a distant county.   As we were unwilling to travel without improvement we turned often from the direct road to please ourselves with the view of nature or of art.   We examined every wild mountain and medicinal spring, criticized every edifice, contemplated every ruin, and compared every scene of action with the narratives of historians.   By this succession of amusements we enjoyed the exercise of a journey without suffering the fatigue, and had nothing to regret but that by a progress so leisurely and gentle we missed the adventures of a post-chaise and the pleasure of alarming villages with the tumult of our passage and of disguising our insignificancy by the dignity of hurry.

The first week after our arrival at Eugenio's house was passed in receiving visits from his neighbours, who crowded about him with all the eagerness of benevolence, some impatient to learn the news of the court and town, that they might be qualified by authentic information to dictate to the rural politicians on the next bowling day, others desirous of his interest to accommodate disputes or of his advice in the settlement of their fortunes and the marriage of their children.

The civilities which he had received were soon to be returned, and I passed some time with great satisfaction in roving through the country and viewing the seats, gardens, and plantations which are scattered over it.   My pleasure would indeed have been greater had I been sometimes allowed to wander in a park or wilderness alone, but to appear as the friend of Eugenio was an honour not to be enjoyed without some inconveniences.   So much was everyone solicitous for my regard, that I could seldom escape to solitude or steal a moment from the emulation of complaisance and the vigilance of officiousness.

In these rambles of good neighbourhood we frequently passed by a house of unusual magnificence.   While I had my curiosity yet distracted among many novelties it did not much attract my observation; but in a short time I could not forbear surveying it with particular notice.   For the length of the wall which enclosed the gardens, the disposition of the shades that waved over it, and the canals, of which I could obtain some glimpses through the trees from our own windows, gave me reason to expect more grandeur and beauty than I had yet seen in that province.   I therefore inquired as we rode by it why we never, amongst our excursions, spent an hour where there was such an appearance of splendour and affluence.   Eugenio told me that the seat which I so much admired was commonly called in the country the Haunted House, and that no visits were paid there by any of the gentlemen whom I had yet seen. As the haunts of incorporeal beings are generally ruinous, neglected, and desolate, I easily conceived that there was something to be explained, and told him that I supposed it only fairy ground on which we might venture by daylight without danger. 'The danger,' says he, 'is indeed only that of appearing to solicit the acquaintance of a man with whom it is not possible to converse without infamy, and who has driven from him by his insolence or malignity every human being who can live without him.'

Our conversation was then accidentally interrupted; but my inquisitive humour, being now in motion, could not rest without a full account of this newly discovered prodigy. I was soon informed that the fine house and spacious gardens were haunted by Squire Bluster, of whom it was very easy to learn the character, since nobody had regard for him sufficient to hinder them from telling whatever they could discover.

Squire Bluster is descended of an ancient family. The estate, which his ancestors had immemorially possessed, was much augmented by Captain Bluster who served under Drake in the reign of Elizabeth; and the Blusters, who were before only petty gentlemen, have from that time frequently represented the shire in Parliament, been chosen to present addresses, and given laws at hunting-matches and races. They were eminently hospitable and popular till the father of this gentleman died of an election. His lady went to the grave soon after him and left the heir, then only ten years old, to the care of his grandmother, who would not suffer him to be controlled because she could not bear to hear him cry, and never sent him to school because she was not able to live without his company. She taught him, however, very early to inspect the steward's accounts, to dog the butler from the cellar, and to catch the servants at a junket. So that he was at the age of eighteen a complete master of all the lower arts of domestic policy, had often on the road detected combinations between the coachman and the ostler, and procured the discharge of nineteen maids for illicit correspondence with cottagers and chair-women.

By the opportunities of parsimony which minority affords, and which the probity of his guardians had diligently improved, a very large sum of money was accumulated, and he found himself, when he took his affairs into his own hands, the richest man in the county. It has been long the custom of this family to celebrate the heir's completion of his twenty-first year by an entertainment at which the house is thrown open to all that are inclined to enter it, and the whole province flocks together as to a general festivity. On this occasion young Bluster exhibited the first tokens of his future eminence by shaking his purse at an old gentleman who had been the intimate friend of his father, and offering to wager a greater sum than he could afford to venture—a practice with which he has, at one time or other, insulted every freeholder within ten miles round him.

His next acts of offence were committed in a contentious and spiteful vindication of the privileges of his manors and a rigorous and relentless prosecution of every man that presumed to violate his game. As he happens to have no estate adjoining equal to his own, his oppressions are often borne without resistance for fear of a long suit, of which he delights to count the expenses without the least solicitude about the event. For he knows that where nothing but an honorary right is contested the poorer antagonist must always suffer, whatever shall be the last decision of the law.

By the success of some of these disputes he has so elated his insolence, and by reflection upon the general hatred which they have brought upon him so irritated his virulence, that his whole life is spent in meditating or executing mischief. It is his common practice to procure his hedges to be broken in the night, and then to demand satisfaction for damages which his grounds have suffered from his neighbour's cattle. An old widow was yesterday soliciting Eugenio to enable her to replevin her only cow then in the pound by Squire Bluster's order, who had sent one of his agents to take advantage of her calamity and persuade her to sell the cow at an under rate. He has driven a day-labourer from his cottage for gathering blackberries in a hedge for his children, and has now an old woman in the county jail for a trespass which she committed by coming into his ground to pick up acorns for her hog.

Money, in whatever hands, will confer power. Distress will fly to immediate refuge without much consideration of remote consequences. Bluster has therefore a despotic authority in many families whom he has assisted on pressing occasions with larger sums than they can easily repay. The only visits that he makes are to these houses of misfortune, where he enters with the insolence of absolute command, enjoys the terrors of the family, exacts their obedience, riots at their charge, and in the height of his joy insults the father with menaces and the daughters with obscenity.

He is of late somewhat less offensive. For one of his debtors after gentle expostulations by which he was only irritated to grosser outrage, seized him by the sleeve, led him trembling into the court-

yard, and closed the door upon him in a stormy night. He took his
usual revenge next morning by a writ; but the debt was discharged
by the assistance of Eugenio.

It is his rule to suffer his tenants to owe him rent, because by this
indulgence he secures to himself the power of seizure whenever he
has an inclination to amuse himself with calamity and feast his ears
with entreaties and lamentations. Yet as he is sometimes capri-
ciously liberal to those whom he happens to adopt as favourites, and
lets his lands at a cheap rate, his farms are never long unoccupied;
and when one is ruined by oppression the possibility of better
fortune quickly lures another to supply his place.

Such is the life of Squire Bluster, a man in whose power fortune
has liberally placed the means of happiness, but who has defeated
all her gifts of their end by the depravity of his mind. He is
wealthy without followers, he is magnificent without witnesses, he
has birth without alliance; and influence without dignity. His
neighbours scorn him as a brute, his dependants dread him as an
oppressor, and he has only the gloomy comfort of reflecting that
if he is hated he is likewise feared.

I am, &c.,

VAGULUS.

WORTH OF PETTY WRITERS (145)

Tuesday, 6th August 1751

Non si priores Maeonius tenet
Sedes Homerus, Pindaricae latent,
Ceaeque et Alcaei minaces
Stesichorique graves camoenae.

HORACE.

What though the muse her Homer thrones
High above all the immortal quire;
Nor Pindar's rapture she disowns,
Nor hides the plaintive coean lyre:
Alcaeus strikes the tyrant's soul with dread,
Nor yet is grave Stesichorus unread.

FRANCIS.

IT is allowed that vocations and employments of least dignity
are of the most apparent use, that the meanest artisan or manu-
facturer contributes more to the accommodation of life than the

profound scholar and argumentative theorist, and that the public would suffer less present inconvenience from the banishment of philosophers than from the extinction of any common trade.

Some have been so forcibly struck with this observation, that they have in the first warmth of their discovery thought it reasonable to alter the common distribution of dignity, and ventured to condemn mankind of universal ingratitude. For justice exacts that those by whom we are most benefited should be most honoured. And what labour can be more useful than that which procures to families and communities those necessaries which supply the wants of nature or those conveniencies by which ease, security, and elegance are conferred?

This is one of the innumerable theories which the first attempt to reduce them into practice certainly destroys. If we estimate dignity by immediate usefulness, agriculture is undoubtedly the first and noblest science. Yet we see the plough driven, the clod broken, the manure spread, the seeds scattered, and the harvest reaped by men whom those that feed upon their industry will never be persuaded to admit into the same ranks with heroes or with sages, and who, after all the confessions which truth may extort in favour of their occupation, must be content to fill up the lowest class of the commonwealth, to form the base of the pyramid of subordination, and lie buried in obscurity themselves while they support all that is splendid, conspicuous, or exalted.

It will be found upon a closer inspection that this part of the conduct of mankind is by no means contrary to reason or equity. Remuneratory honours are proportioned at once to the usefulness and difficulty of performance, and are properly adjusted by comparison of the mental and corporeal abilities which they appear to employ. That work, however necessary, which is carried on only by muscular strength and manual dexterity is not of equal esteem in the consideration of rational beings with the tasks that exercise the intellectual powers and require the active vigour of imagination or the gradual and laborious investigations of reason.

The merit of all manual occupations seems to terminate in the inventor; and surely the first ages cannot be charged with ingratitude, since those who civilized barbarians and taught them how to secure themselves from cold and hunger were numbered among their deities. But these arts, once discovered by philosophy and facilitated by experience, are afterwards practised with very little assistance from the faculties of the soul. Nor is anything necessary to the regular discharge of these inferior duties beyond that rude observation which the most sluggish intellect may practise, and that industry which the stimulations of necessity naturally enforce.

Yet though the refusal of statues and panegyric to those who employ only their hands and feet in the service of mankind may be easily justified, I am far from intending to incite the petulance of pride, to justify the superciliousness of grandeur, or to intercept any part of the tenderness and benevolence which by the privilege of their common nature one may claim from another.

That it would be neither wise nor equitable to discourage the husbandman, the labourer, the miner, or the smith is generally granted. But there is another race of beings equally obscure and equally indigent, who, because their usefulness is less obvious to vulgar apprehensions, live unrewarded and die unpitied, and who have long been exposed to insult without a defender and to censure without an apologist.

The authors of London were formerly computed by Swift at several thousands, and there is not any reason for suspecting that their number has decreased. Of these only a very few can be said to produce, or endeavour to produce, new ideas, to extend any principle of science, or gratify the imagination with any uncommon train of images or contexture of events. The rest, however laborious, however arrogant, can only be considered as the drudges of the pen, the manufacturers of literature, who have set up for authors, either with or without a regular initiation, and, like other artificers, have no other care than to deliver their tale of wares at the stated time.

It has been formerly imagined that he who intends the entertainment or instruction of others must feel in himself some peculiar impulse of genius; that he must watch the happy minute in which his natural fire is excited, in which his mind is elevated with nobler sentiments, enlightened with clearer views, and invigorated with stronger comprehension; that he must carefully select his thoughts and polish his expressions, and animate his efforts with the hope of raising a monument of learning which neither time nor envy shall be able to destroy.

But the authors whom I am now endeavouring to recommend have been too long hackneyed in the ways of men to indulge the chimerical ambition of immortality. They have seldom any claim to the trade of writing but that they have tried some other without success. They perceive no particular summons to composition except the sound of the clock. They have no other rule than the law or the fashion for admitting their thoughts or rejecting them.

And about the opinion of posterity they have little solicitude, for their productions are seldom intended to remain in the world longer than a week.

That such authors are not to be rewarded with praise is evident, since nothing can be admired when it ceases to exist. But surely, though they cannot aspire to honour, they may be exempted from ignominy, and adopted in that order of men which deserves our kindness though not our reverence. These papers of the day, the ephemerae of learning, have uses more adequate to the purposes of common life than more pompous and durable volumes. If it is necessary for every man to be more acquainted with his contemporaries than with past generations, and rather to know the events which may immediately affect his fortune or quiet than the revolutions of ancient kingdoms in which he has neither possessions nor expectations; if it be pleasing to hear of the preferment and dismission of statesmen, the birth of heirs, and the marriage of beauties, the humble author of journals and gazettes must be considered as a liberal dispenser of beneficial knowledge.

Even the abridger, compiler, and translator, though their labours cannot be ranked with those of the diurnal historiographer, yet must not be rashly doomed to annihilation. Every size of readers requires a genius of correspondent capacity. Some delight in abstracts and epitomes, because they want room in their memory for long details and content themselves with effects without inquiry after causes. Some minds are overpowered by splendour of sentiment, as some eyes are offended by a glaring light. Such will gladly contemplate an author in an humble imitation, as we look without pain upon the sun in the water.

As every writer has his use, every writer ought to have his patrons. And since no man, however high he may now stand, can be certain that he shall not be soon thrown down from his elevation by criticism or caprice, the common interest of learning requires that her sons should cease from intestine hostilities, and, instead of sacrificing each other to malice and contempt, endeavour to avert persecution from the meanest of their fraternity.

AN AUTHOR IN QUEST OF HIS OWN
CHARACTER (146)

Saturday, 10th August 1751

Sunt illic duo, tresve, qui revolvant
Nostrarum tineas ineptiarum:
Sed cum sponsio, fabulaeque lassae
De scorpo fuerint incitato

MARTIAL.

'Tis possible that one or two
These fooleries of mine may view;
But then the bettings must be o'er,
Nor Crab or Childers talk'd of more.

F. LEWIS.

NONE of the projects or designs which exercise the mind of man are equally subject to obstructions and disappointments with the pursuit of fame. Riches cannot easily be denied to them who have something of greater value to offer in exchange. He whose fortune is endangered by litigation will not refuse to augment the wealth of the lawyer. He whose days are darkened by languor, or whose nerves are excruciated by pain, is compelled to pay tribute to the science of healing. But praise may be always omitted without inconvenience. When once a man has made celebrity necessary to his happiness he has put it in the power of the weakest and most timorous malignity if not to take away his satisfaction, at least to withhold it. His enemies may indulge their pride by airy negligence and gratify their malice by quiet neutrality. They that could never have injured a character by invectives may combine to annihilate it by silence, as the women of Rome threatened to put an end to conquest and dominion by supplying no children to the commonwealth.

When a writer has with long toil produced a work intended to burst upon mankind with unexpected lustre and withdraw the attention of the learned world from every other controversy or inquiry he is seldom contented to wait long without the enjoyment of his new praises. With an imagination full of his own importance he walks out like a monarch in disguise to learn the various opinions of his readers. Prepared to feast upon admiration, composed to encounter censures without emotion, and determined not

239

to suffer his quiet to be injured by a sensibility too exquisite of praise or blame, but to laugh with equal contempt at vain objections and injudicious commendations, he enters the places of mingled conversation, sits down to his tea in an obscure corner, and while he appears to examine a file of antiquated journals catches the conversation of the whole room. He listens but hears no mention of his book, and therefore supposes that he has disappointed his curiosity by delay, and that as men of learning would naturally begin their conversation with such a wonderful novelty they had digressed to other subjects before his arrival. The company disperses, and their places are supplied by others equally ignorant or equally careless. The same expectation hurries him to another place from which the same disappointment drives him soon away. His impatience then grows violent and tumultuous. He ranges over the town with restless curiosity, and hears in one quarter of a cricket match, in another of a pickpocket; is told by some of an unexpected bankruptcy, by others of a turtle feast; is sometimes provoked by importunate inquiries after the white bear, and sometimes with praises of the dancing dog. He is afterwards entreated to give his judgment upon a wager about the height of the Monument, invited to see a foot-race in the adjacent villages, desired to read a ludicrous advertisement, or consulted about the most effectual method of making inquiry after a favourite cat. The whole world is busied in affairs which he thinks below the notice of reasonable creatures, and which are nevertheless sufficient to withdraw all regard from his labours and his merits.

He resolves at last to violate his own modesty and to recall the talkers from their folly by an inquiry after himself. He finds everyone provided with an answer. One has seen the work advertised, but never met with any that had read it. Another has been so often imposed upon by specious titles that he never buys a book till its character is established. A third wonders what any man can hope to produce after so many writers of greater eminence. The next has inquired after the author, but can hear no account of him and therefore suspects the name to be fictitious. And another knows him to be a man condemned by indigence to write too frequently what he does not understand.

Many are the consolations with which the unhappy author endeavours to allay his vexation and fortify his patience. He has written with too little indulgence to the understanding of common readers. He has fallen upon an age in which solid knowledge and delicate refinement have given way to low merriment and idle buffoonery, and therefore no writer can hope for distinction who has any higher purpose than to raise laughter. He finds that his enemies, such as superiority will always raise, have been industrious, while his performance was in the press, to vilify and blast it, and that the bookseller whom he had resolved to enrich has rivals that obstruct the circulation of his copies. He at last reposes upon the consideration that the noblest works of learning and genius have always made their way slowly against ignorance and prejudice, and that reputation which is never to be lost must be gradually obtained, as animals of longest life are observed not soon to attain their full stature and strength.

By such arts of voluntary delusion does every man endeavour to conceal his own unimportance from himself. It is long before we are convinced of the small proportion which every individual bears to the collective body of mankind, or learn how few can be interested in the fortune of any single man, how little vacancy is left in the world for any new object of attention, to how small extent the brightest blaze of merit can be spread amidst the mists of business and of folly, and how soon it is clouded by the intervention of other novelties. Not only the writer of books, but the commander of armies and the deliverer of nations will easily outlive all noisy and popular reputation. He may be celebrated for a time by the public voice, but his actions and his name will soon be considered as remote and unaffecting, and be rarely mentioned but by those whose alliance gives them some vanity to gratify by frequent commemoration.

It seems not to be sufficiently considered how little renown can be admitted in the world. Mankind are kept perpetually busy by their fears or desires, and have not more leisure from their own affairs than to acquaint themselves with the accidents of the current day. Engaged in contriving some refuge from calamity or in shortening the way to some new possession, they seldom suffer their thoughts to wander to the past or future. None but a few solitary students have leisure to inquire into the claims of ancient heroes or sages, and names which hoped to range over kingdoms and continents shrink at last into cloisters or colleges.

Nor is it certain that even of these dark and narrow habitations, these last retreats of fame, the possession will be long kept. Of men devoted to literature very few extend their views beyond some particular science, and the greater part seldom inquire, even in their own profession, for any authors but those whom the present mode of study happens to force upon their notice. They desire not to fill their minds with unfashionable knowledge, but contentedly resign to oblivion those books which they now find censured or neglected.

The hope of fame is necessarily connected with such considerations as must abate the ardour of confidence and repress the vigour of pursuit. Whoever claims renown from any kind of excellence expects to fill the place which is now possessed by another. For there are already names of every class sufficient to employ all that will desire to remember them; and surely he that is pushing his predecessors into the gulf of obscurity cannot but sometimes suspect that he must himself sink in like manner and, as he stands upon the same precipice, be swept away with the same violence.

It sometimes happens that fame begins when life is at an end. But far the greater number of candidates for applause have owed their reception in the world to some favourable casualties, and have therefore immediately sunk into neglect when death stripped them of their casual influence and neither fortune nor patronage operated in their favour. Among those who have better claims to regard, the honour paid to their memory is commonly proportioned to the reputation which they enjoyed in their lives, though still growing fainter as it is at a greater distance from the first emission. And since it is so difficult to obtain the notice of contemporaries, how little is it to be hoped from future times? What can merit effect by its own force when the help of art or friendship can scarcely support it?

CRITICISM ON EPISTOLARY WRITINGS (152)

Saturday, 31st August 1751

Tristia maestum,
Vultum verba decent, iratum plena minarum.

HORACE.

Disastrous words can best disaster show;
In angry phrase the angry passions glow.

ELPHINSTON.

'IT was the wisdom,' says Seneca, 'of ancient times, to consider what is most useful as most illustrious.' If this rule be applied to works of genius scarcely any species of composition deserves more to be cultivated than the epistolary style, since none is of more various or frequent use through the whole subordination of human life.

It has yet happened that among the numerous writers which our nation has produced, equal perhaps always in force and genius, and of late in elegance and accuracy, to those of any other country, very few have endeavoured to distinguish themselves by the publication of letters except such as were written in the discharge of public trusts and during the transaction of great affairs; which, though they afford precedents to the minister and memorials to the historian, are of no use as examples of the familiar style or models of private correspondence.

If it be inquired by foreigners how this deficiency has happened in the literature of a country where all indulge themselves with so little danger in speaking and writing, may we not without either bigotry or arrogance inform them that it must be imputed to our contempt of trifles and our due sense of the dignity of the public? We do not think it reasonable to fill the world with volumes from which nothing can be learned, nor expect that the employments of the busy or the amusements of the gay should give way to narratives of our private affairs, complaints of absence, expressions of fondness, or declarations of fidelity.

A slight perusal of the innumerable letters by which the wits of France have signalized their names will prove that other nations need not be discouraged from the like attempts by the consciousness of inability. For surely it is not very difficult to aggravate trifling misfortunes, to magnify familiar incidents, repeat adulatory professions, accumulate servile hyperboles, and produce all that can be found in the despicable remains of Voiture and Scarron.

Yet as much of life must be passed in affairs considerable only by their frequent occurrence, and much of the pleasure which our condition allows must be produced by giving elegance to trifles, it is necessary to learn how to become little without becoming mean, to maintain the necessary intercourse of civility, and fill up the vacuities of actions by agreeable appearances. It had therefore been of advantage if such of our writers as have excelled in the art of decorating insignificance had supplied us with a few sallies of innocent gaiety, effusions of honest tenderness, or exclamations of unimportant hurry.

Precept has generally been posterior to performance. The art of composing works of genius has never been taught but by the example of those who performed it by natural vigour of imagination and rectitude of judgment. As we have few letters, we have likewise few criticisms upon the epistolary style. The observations with which Walsh has introduced his pages of inanity are such as give him little claim to the rank assigned him by Dryden among the critics. 'Letters,' says he, 'are intended as resemblances of conversation, and the chief excellencies of conversation are good humour and good breeding.' This remark, equally valuable for its novelty and propriety, he dilates and enforces with an appearance of complete acquiescence in his own discovery.

No man was ever in doubt about the moral qualities of a letter. It has been always known that he who endeavours to please must appear pleased, and he who would not provoke rudeness must not practise it. But the question among those who establish rules for an epistolary performance is how gaiety or civility may be properly expressed, as among the critics in history it is not contested whether truth ought to be preserved but by what mode of diction it is best adorned.

As letters are written on all subjects, in all states of mind, they cannot be properly reduced to settled rules or described by any single characteristic; and we may safely disentangle our minds from critical embarrassments by determining that a letter has no peculiarity but its form, and that nothing is to be refused admission which would be proper in any other method of treating the same subject. The qualities of the epistolary style most frequently required are ease and simplicity, an even flow of unlaboured diction, and an artless arrangement of obvious sentiments. But these directions are no sooner applied to use than their scantiness and imperfection become evident. Letters are written to the great and to the mean, to the learned and the ignorant, at rest and in distress, in sport and in passion. Nothing can be more improper than ease and laxity of expression when the importance of the subject impresses solicitude or the dignity of the person exacts reverence.

That letters should be written with strict conformity to nature is true, because nothing but conformity to nature can make any composition beautiful or just. But it is natural to depart from familiarity of language upon occasions not familiar. Whatever elevates the sentiments will consequently raise the expression. Whatever fills us with hope or terror will produce some perturbations of images and some figurative distortions of phrase. Whereever we are studious to please we are afraid of trusting our first thoughts, and endeavour to recommend our opinion by studied ornaments, accuracy of method, and elegance of style.

If the personages of the comic scene be allowed by Horace to raise their language in the transports of anger to the turgid vehemence of tragedy, the epistolary writer may likewise without censure comply with the varieties of his matter.   If great events are to be related he may, with all the solemnity of an historian, deduce them from their causes, connect them with their concomitants, and trace them to their consequences.   If a disputed position is to be established or a remote principle to be investigated he may detail his reasonings with all the nicety of syllogistic method.   If a menace is to be averted or a benefit implored he may, without any violation of the edicts of criticism, call every power of rhetoric to his assistance and try every inlet at which love or pity enters the heart.

Letters that have no other end than the entertainment of the correspondents are more properly regulated by critical precepts, because the matter and style are equally arbitrary, and rules are more necessary as there is a larger power of choice.   In letters of this kind some conceive art graceful, and others think negligence amiable.   Some model them by the sonnet, and will allow them no means of delighting but the soft lapse of calm mellifluence.   Others adjust them by the epigram, and expect pointed sentences and forcible periods.   The one party considers exemption from faults as the height of excellence, the other looks upon neglect of excellence as the most disgusting fault.   One avoids censure, the other aspires to praise.   One is always in danger of insipidity, the other continually on the brink of affectation.

When the subject has no intrinsic dignity it must necessarily owe its attractions to artificial embellishments, and may catch at all advantages which the art of writing can supply.   He that, like Pliny, sends his friend a portion for his daughter will, without Pliny's eloquence of address, find means of exciting gratitude and securing acceptance.   But he that has no present to make but a garland, a ribbon, or some petty curiosity, must endeavour to recommend it by his manner of giving it.

The purpose for which letters are written when no intelligence is communicated or business transacted is to preserve in the minds of the absent either love or esteem.   To excite love we must impart pleasure, and to raise esteem we must discover abilities.   Pleasure will generally be given as abilities are displayed by scenes of imagery, points of conceit, unexpected sallies, and artful compliments.   Trifles always require exuberance of ornament; the building which has no strength can be valued only for the grace of its decorations. The pebble must be polished with care which hopes to be valued as a diamond; and words ought surely to be laboured when they are intended to stand for things.

CHOICE OF ASSOCIATES (160)

Saturday, 28th September 1751

Inter se convenit ursis.

JUVENAL.

Beasts of each kind their fellows spare;
Bear lives in amity with Bear.

'THE world,' says Locke, 'has people of all sorts.' As in the general hurry produced by the superfluities of some and necessities of others no man need to stand still for want of employment, so in the innumerable gradations of ability and endless varieties of study and inclination no employment can be vacant for want of a man qualified to discharge it.

Such is probably the natural state of the universe, but it is so much deformed by interest and passion, that the benefit of this adaptation of men to things is not always perceived. The folly or indigence of those who set their services to sale inclines them to boast of qualifications which they do not possess and attempt business which they do not understand; and they who have the power of assigning to others the task of life are seldom honest or seldom happy in their nominations. Patrons are corrupted by avarice, cheated by credulity, or overpowered by resistless solicitation. They are sometimes too strongly influenced by honest prejudices of friendship or the prevalence of virtuous compassion. For, whatever cool reason may direct, it is not easy for a man of tender and scrupulous goodness to overlook the immediate effect of his own actions by turning his eyes upon remoter consequences, and to do that which must give present pain for the sake of obviating evil yet unfelt or securing advantage in time to come. What is distant is in itself obscure, and, when we have no wish to see it, easily escapes our notice or takes such a form as desire or imagination bestows upon it.

Every man might for the same reason, in the multitudes that swarm about him, find some kindred mind with which he could unite in confidence and friendship. Yet we see many straggling single about the world, unhappy for want of an associate and pining with the necessity of confining their sentiments to their own bosoms.

This inconvenience arises in like manner from struggles of the will against the understanding. It is not often difficult to find a suitable companion if every man would be content with such as he is qualified to please. But if vanity tempts him to forsake his rank and post himself among those with whom no common interest or mutual pleasure can ever unite him he must always live in a state of unsocial separation, without tenderness and without trust.

There are many natures which can never approach within a certain distance, and which, when any irregular motive impels them towards contact, seem to start back from each other by some invincible repulsion. There are others which immediately cohere whenever they come into the reach of mutual attraction, and with very little formality of preparation mingle intimately as soon as they meet. Every man whom either business or curiosity has thrown at large into the world will recollect many instances of fondness and dislike which have forced themselves upon him without the intervention of his judgment; of dispositions to court some and avoid others when he could assign no reason for the preference, or none adequate to the violence of his passions; of influence that acted instantaneously upon his mind, and which no arguments or persuasions could ever overcome.

Among those with whom time and intercourse have made us familiar we feel our affections divided in different proportions without much regard to moral or intellectual merit. Every man knows some whom he cannot induce himself to trust, though he has no reason to suspect that they would betray him; those to whom he cannot complain, though he never observed them to want compassion; those in whose presence he never can be gay, though excited by invitations to mirth and freedom; and those from whom he cannot be content to receive instruction, though they never insulted his ignorance by contempt or ostentation.

That much regard is to be had to those instincts of kindness and dislike, or that reason should blindly follow them, I am far from intending to inculcate. It is very certain that by indulgence we may give them strength which they have not from nature, and almost every example of ingratitude and treachery proves that by obeying them we may commit our happiness to those who are very unworthy of so great a trust. But it may deserve to be remarked that, since few contend much with their inclinations, it is generally vain to solicit the goodwill of those whom we perceive thus involuntarily alienated from us. Neither knowledge nor virtue will reconcile antipathy; and though officiousness may for a time be admitted and diligence applauded, they will at least be dismissed with coldness or discouraged by neglect.

Some have indeed an occult power of stealing upon the affections, of exciting universal benevolence, and disposing every heart to fondness and friendship. But this is a felicity granted only to the favourites of nature. The greater part of mankind find a different reception from different dispositions. They sometimes obtain unexpected caresses from those whom they never flattered with uncommon regard, and sometimes exhaust all their arts of pleasing without effect. To these it is necessary to look round and attempt every breast in which they find virtue sufficient for the foundation of friendship, to enter into the crowd and try whom chance will offer to their notice till they fix on some temper congenial to their own, as the magnet rolled in the dust collects the fragments of its kindred metal from a thousand particles of other substance.

Every man must have remarked the facility with which the kindness of others is sometimes gained by those to whom he never could have imparted his own. We are by our occupations, education, and habits of life divided almost into different species which regard one another for the most part with scorn and malignity. Each of these classes of the human race has desires, fears and conversation, vexations and merriment, peculiar to itself; cares which another cannot feel, pleasures which he cannot partake, and modes of expressing every sensation which he cannot understand. That frolic which shakes one man with laughter will convulse another with indignation. The strain of jocularity which in one place obtains treats and patronage would in another be heard with indifference, and in a third with abhorrence.

To raise esteem we must benefit others. To procure love we must please them. Aristotle observes that old men do not readily form friendships because they are not easily susceptible of pleasure. He that can contribute to the hilarity of the vacant hour or partake with equal gust the favourite amusement, he whose mind is employed on the same objects, and who therefore never harasses the understanding with unaccustomed ideas, will be welcomed with ardour and left with regret unless he destroys those recommendations by faults with which peace and security cannot consist.

It were happy if, in forming friendships, virtue could concur with pleasure. But the greatest part of human gratifications approach so nearly to vice, that few who make the delight of others their rule of conduct can avoid disingenuous compliances. Yet certainly he that suffers himself to be driven or allured from virtue mistakes his own interest, since he gains succour by means for which his friend, if ever he becomes wise, must scorn him, and for which at last he must scorn himself.

REVOLUTIONS OF A GARRET (161)

Tuesday, 1st October 1751

Οἴηπερ φύλλων γενεὴ τοίηδε καὶ ἀνδρῶν.

HOMER.

Frail as the leaves that quiver on the sprays,
Like them man flourishes, like them decays.

MR. RAMBLER

SIR,

You have formerly observed that curiosity often terminates in barren knowledge, and that the mind is prompted to study and inquiry rather by the uneasiness of ignorance than the hope of profit. Nothing can be of less importance to any present interest than the fortune of those who have been long lost in the grave and from whom nothing can be hoped or feared. Yet to rouse the zeal of a true antiquary little more is necessary than to mention a name which mankind have conspired to forget. He will make his way to remote scenes of action through obscurity and contradiction, as Tully sought amidst bushes and brambles the tomb of Archimedes.

It is not easy to discover how it concerns him that gathers the produce or receives the rent of an estate to know through what families the land has passed, who is registered in the Conqueror's survey as its possessor, how often it has been forfeited by treason, or how often sold by prodigality. The power or wealth of the present inhabitants of a country cannot be much increased by an inquiry after the names of those barbarians who destroyed one another twenty centuries ago in contests for the shelter of woods or convenience of pasturage. Yet we see that no man can be at rest in the enjoyment of a new purchase till he has learned the history of his grounds from the ancient inhabitants of the parish, and that no nation omits to record the actions of their ancestors, however bloody, savage, and rapacious.

The same disposition, as different opportunities call it forth, discovers itself in great or little things. I have always thought it unworthy of a wise man to slumber in total inactivity only because he happens to have no employment equal to his ambition or genius. It is therefore my custom to apply my attention to the objects before me; and as I cannot think any place wholly unworthy of notice that affords a habitation to a man of letters, I have collected the history and antiquities of the several garrets in which I have resided.

> Quantulacunque estis vos ego magna voco.

> How small to others, but how great to me!

Many of these narratives my industry has been able to extend to a considerable length. But the woman with whom I now lodge has lived only eighteen months in the house and can give no account of its ancient revolutions, the plasterer having, at her entrance, obliterated by his whitewash all the smoky memorials which former tenants had left upon the ceiling, and perhaps drawn the veil of oblivion over politicians, philosophers, and poets.

When I first cheapened my lodgings the landlady told me that she hoped I was not an author, for the lodgers on the first floor had stipulated that the upper rooms should not be occupied by a noisy trade. I very readily promised to give no disturbance to her family, and soon dispatched a bargain on the usual terms.

I had not slept many nights in my new apartment before I began to inquire after my predecessors, and found my landlady, whose imagination is filled chiefly with her own affairs, very ready to give me information.

Curiosity, like all other desires, produces pain as well as pleasure. Before she began her narrative I had heated my head with expectations of adventures and discoveries, of elegance in disguise and learning in distress, and was somewhat mortified when I heard that the first tenant was a tailor, of whom nothing was remembered but that he complained of his room for want of light and, after having lodged in it a month and paid only a week's rent, pawned a piece of cloth which he was trusted to cut out, and was forced to make a precipitate retreat from this quarter of the town.

The next was a young woman newly arrived from the country, who lived for five weeks with great regularity and became by frequent treats very much the favourite of the family, but at last received visits so frequently from a cousin in Cheapside, that she brought the reputation of the house into danger, and was therefore dismissed with good advice.

The room then stood empty for a fortnight. My landlady began to think that she had judged hardly, and often wished for such another lodger. At last an elderly man of a grave aspect read the bill and bargained for the room at the very first price that was asked. He lived in close retirement, seldom went out till evening, and then returned early, sometimes cheerful and at other times dejected. It was remarkable that, whatever he purchased, he never had small money in his pocket, and, though cool and temperate on other occasions, was always vehement and stormy till he received his change. He paid his rent with great exactness, and seldom failed once a week to requite my landlady's civility with a supper. At last, such is the fate of human felicity, the house was alarmed at midnight by the constable, who demanded to search the garrets. My landlady, assuring him that he had mistaken the door, conducted him upstairs, where he found the tools of a coiner. But the tenant had crawled along the roof to an empty house and escaped, much to the joy of my landlady, who declares him a very honest man and wonders why anybody should be hanged for making money when such numbers are in want of it. She, however, confesses that she shall for the future always question the character of those who take her garret without beating down the price.

The bill was then placed again in the window, and the poor woman was teased for seven weeks by innumerable passengers who obliged her to climb with them every hour up five storeys, and then disliked the prospect, hated the noise of a public street, thought the stairs narrow, objected to a low ceiling, required the walls to be hung with fresh paper, asked questions about the neighbourhood, could not think of living so far from their acquaintance, wished the windows had looked to the south rather than the west, and told how the door and chimney might have been better disposed, bid her half the price that she asked, or promised to give her earnest the next day, and came no more.

At last a short meagre man in a tarnished waistcoat desired to see the garret, and, when he had stipulated for two long shelves and a large table, hired it at a low rate. When the affair was completed he looked round him with great satisfaction and repeated some words which the woman did not understand. In two days he brought a great box of books, took possession of his room, and

lived very inoffensively, except that he frequently disturbed the
inhabitants of the next floor by unseasonable noises. He was
generally in bed at noon; but from evening to midnight he sometimes talked aloud with great vehemence, sometimes stamped as in
rage, sometimes threw down his poker, then clattered his chairs,
then sat down in deep thought, and again burst out into loud
vociferations. Sometimes he would sigh as oppressed with misery,
and sometimes shake with convulsive laughter. When he encountered any of the family he gave way or bowed, but rarely
spoke, except that as he went upstairs he often repeated:

Ὃς ὑπέρτατα δώματα ναίει.

This habitant the aerial regions boast.

Hard words, to which his neighbours listened so often that they
learned them without understanding them. What was his employment she did not venture to ask him, but at last heard a printer's boy
inquire for the author.

My landlady was very often advised to beware of this strange
man who, though he was quiet for the present, might perhaps
become outrageous in the hot months. But as she was punctually
paid she could not find any sufficient reason for dismissing him, till
one night he convinced her, by setting fire to his curtains, that it
was not safe to have an author for her inmate.

She had then for six weeks a succession of tenants who left the
house on Saturday, and instead of paying their rent stormed at their
landlady. At last she took in two sisters, one of whom had spent
her little fortune in procuring remedies for a lingering disease and
was now supported and attended by the other. She climbed with
difficulty to the apartment, where she languished eight weeks
without impatience or lamentation, except for the expense and
fatigue which her sister suffered, and then calmly and contentedly
expired. The sister followed her to the grave, paid the few debts
which they had contracted, wiped away the tears of useless sorrow,
and, returning to the business of common life, resigned to me the
vacant habitation.

Such, Mr. Rambler, are the changes which have happened in the
narrow space where my present fortune has fixed my residence.
So true it is that amusement and instruction are always at hand for
those who have skill and willingness to find them, and so just is the
observation of Juvenal, that a single house will show what is done
or suffered in the world.

I am, Sir, &c.

HYMENAEUS'S COURTSHIP

(concluded) (167)

Tuesday, 22nd October 1751

Candida perpetuo reside concordia lecto,
  Tamque pari semper sit Venus aequa jugo.
Diligat ipsa senem quondam, sed et ipsa marito
  Tum quoque cum fuerit, non videatur anus.

MARTIAL.

Their nuptial bed may smiling concord dress,
And Venus still the happy union bless!
Wrinkled with age, may mutual love and truth
To their dim eyes recall the bloom of youth.

F. LEWIS.

TO THE 'RAMBLER'

SIR,

It is not common to envy those with whom we cannot easily be placed in comparison. Every man sees without malevolence the progress of another in the tracks of life which he has himself no desire to tread, and hears, without inclination to cavils or contradiction, the renown of those whose distance will not suffer them to draw the attention of mankind from his own merit. The sailor never thinks it necessary to contest the lawyer's abilities; nor would the Rambler, however jealous of his reputation, be much disturbed by the success of rival wits at Agra or Ispahan.

We do not therefore ascribe to you any superlative degree of virtue when we believe that we may inform you of our change of condition without danger of malignant fascination; and that when you read of the marriage of your correspondents, Hymenaeus and Tranquilla, you will join your wishes to those of their other friends for the happy event of a union in which caprice and selfishness had so little part.

There is at least this reason why we should be less deceived in our connubial hopes than many who enter into the same state, that we have allowed our minds to form no unreasonable expectations, not vitiated our fancies in the soft hours of courtship with visions of felicity which human power cannot bestow or of perfection which

253

human virtue cannot attain. That impartiality with which we endeavoured to inspect the manners of all whom we have known was never so much overpowered by our passion but that we discovered some faults and weaknesses in each other, and joined our hands in conviction that as there are advantages to be enjoyed in marriage there are inconveniencies likewise to be endured, and that, together with confederate intellects and auxiliar virtues, we must find different opinions and opposite inclinations.

We, however, flatter ourselves—for who is not flattered by himself as well as by others on the day of marriage?—that we are eminently qualified to give mutual pleasure. Our birth is without any such remarkable disparity as can give either an opportunity of insulting the other with pompous names and splendid alliances, or of calling in, upon any domestic controversy, the overbearing assistance of powerful relations. Our fortune was equally suitable, so that we meet without any of those obligations which always produce reproach or suspicion of reproach, which, though they may be forgotten in the gaieties of the first month, no delicacy will always suppress, or of which the suppression must be considered as a new favour to be repaid by tameness and submission till gratitude takes the place of love and the desire of pleasing degenerates by degrees into the fear of offending.

The settlements caused no delay, for we did not trust our affairs to the negotiation of wretches who would have paid their court by multiplying stipulations. Tranquilla scorned to detain any part of her fortune from him into whose hands she delivered up her person; and Hymenaeus thought no act of baseness more criminal than his who enslaves his wife by her own generosity, who by marrying without a jointure condemns her to all the dangers of accident and caprice, and at last boasts his liberality by granting what only the indiscretion of her kindness enabled him to withhold. He therefore received on the common terms the portion which any other woman might have brought him, and reserved all the exuberance of acknowledgment for those excellencies which he has yet been able to discover only in Tranquilla.

We did not pass the weeks of courtship like those who consider themselves as taking the last draught of pleasure and resolve not to quit the bowl without a surfeit, or who know themselves about to set happiness to hazard and endeavour to lose their sense of danger in the ebriety of perpetual amusement and whirl round the gulf before they sink. Hymenaeus often repeated a medical axiom, that the succours of sickness ought not to be wasted in health.

We know that, however our eyes may yet sparkle and our hearts bound at the presence of each other, the time of listlessness and satiety, of peevishness and discontent, must come at last, in which we shall be driven for relief to shows and recreations; that the uniformity of life must be sometimes diversified and the vacuities of conversation sometimes supplied. We rejoice in the reflection that we have stores of novelty yet unexhausted, which may be opened when repletion shall call for change, and gratifications yet untasted, by which life, when it shall become vapid or bitter, may be restored to its former sweetness and sprightliness, and again irritate the appetite, and again sparkle in the cup.

Our time will probably be less tasteless than that of those whom the authority and avarice of parents unites almost without their consent in their early years, before they have accumulated any fund of reflection or collected materials for mutual entertainment. Such we have often seen rising in the morning to cards and retiring in the afternoon to doze, whose happiness was celebrated by their neighbours because they happened to grow rich by parsimony, and to be kept quiet by insensibility, and agreed to eat and to sleep together.

We have both mingled with the world, and are therefore no strangers to the faults and virtues, the designs and competitions, the hopes and fears of our contemporaries. We have both amused our leisure with books, and can therefore recount the events of former times or cite the dictates of ancient wisdom. Every occurrence furnishes us with some hint which one or the other can improve; and if it should happen that memory or imagination fail us we can retire to no idle or unimproving solitude.

Though our characters beheld at a distance exhibit this general resemblance, yet a nearer inspection discovers such a dissimilitude of our habitudes and sentiments as leaves each some peculiar advantages, and affords that *concordia discors*, that suitable disagreement, which is always necessary to intellectual harmony. There may be a total diversity of ideas which admits no participation of the same delight, and there may likewise be such a conformity of notions as leaves neither anything to add to the decisions of the other. With such contrariety there can be no peace, with such similarity there can be no pleasure. Our reasonings, though often formed upon different views, terminate generally in the same conclusion. Our thoughts, like rivulets issuing from distant springs, are each impregnated in its course with various mixtures and tinged by infusions unknown to the other, yet at last easily unite into one stream and purify themselves by the gentle effervescence of contrary qualities.

These benefits we receive in a greater degree as we converse without reserve because we have nothing to conceal. We have no debts to be paid by imperceptible deductions from avowed expenses, no habits to be indulged by the private subserviency of a favoured servant, no private interviews of needy relations, no intelligence with spies placed upon each other. We considered marriage as the most solemn league of perpetual friendship, a state from which artifice and concealment are to be banished for ever, and in which every act of dissimulation is a breach of faith.

The impetuous vivacity of youth and that ardour of desire, which the first sight of pleasure naturally produces, have long ceased to hurry us into irregularity and vehemence. And experience has shown us that few gratifications are too valuable to be sacrificed to complaisance. We have thought it convenient to rest from the fatigue of pleasure, and now only continue that course of life into which we had before entered, confirmed in our choice by mutual approbation, supported in our resolution by mutual encouragement, and assisted in our efforts by mutual exhortation.

Such, Mr. Rambler, is our prospect of life, a prospect which, as it is beheld with more attention, seems to open more extensive happiness, and spreads by degrees into the boundless regions of eternity. But if all our prudence has been vain, and we are doomed to give one instance more of the uncertainty of human discernment, we shall comfort ourselves amidst our disappointments that we were not betrayed but by such delusions as caution could not escape, since we sought happiness only in the arms of virtue. We are, Sir, your humble servants,

HYMENAEUS.
TRANQUILLA.

MISELLA DEBAUCHED (170)

Saturday, 2nd November 1751

Confiteor si quid prodest delicta fateri.

OVID.

I grant the charge; forgive the fault confess'd.

TO THE 'RAMBLER'

SIR,

I am one of those beings from whom many that melt at the sight of all other misery think it meritorious to withhold relief, one whom the rigour of virtuous indignation dooms to suffer without complaint and perish without regard, and whom I myself have formerly insulted in the pride of reputation and security of innocence.

I am of a good family, but my father was burthened with more children than he could decently support. A wealthy relation, as he travelled from London to his country seat condescending to make him a visit, was touched with compassion of his narrow fortune, and resolved to ease him of part of his charge by taking the care of a child upon himself. Distress on one side and ambition on the other were too powerful for parental fondness, and the little family passed in review before him that he might make his choice. I was then ten years old, and, without knowing for what purpose, I was called to my great cousin, endeavoured to recommend myself by my best courtesy, sung him my prettiest song, told the last story that I had read, and so much endeared myself by my innocence, that he declared his resolution to adopt me and to educate me with his own daughters.

My parents felt the common struggles at the thought of parting, and some 'natural tears they dropp'd, but wip'd them soon.' They considered, not without that false estimation of the value of wealth which poverty long continued always produces, that I was raised to higher rank than they could give me and to hopes of more ample fortune than they could bequeath. My mother sold some of her ornaments to dress me in such a manner as might secure me from contempt at my first arrival; and when she dismissed me pressed me to her bosom with an embrace that I still feel, gave me some precepts of piety which, however neglected, I have not forgotten, and uttered prayers for my final happiness, of which I have not yet ceased to hope that they will at last be granted.

My sisters envied my new finery and seemed not much to regret our separation. My father conducted me to the stage-coach with a kind of cheerful tenderness; and in a very short time I was transported to splendid apartments and a luxurious table, and grew familiar to show, noise, and gaiety.

In three years my mother died, having implored a blessing on her family with her last breath. I had little opportunity to indulge a sorrow which there was none to partake with me, and therefore soon ceased to reflect much upon my loss. My father turned all his care upon his other children, whom some fortunate adventures and unexpected legacies enabled him, when he died four years after my mother, to leave in a condition above their expectations.

I should have shared the increase of his fortune and had once a portion assigned me in his will; but my cousin, assuring him that all care for me was needless since he had resolved to place me happily in the world, directed him to divide my part amongst my sisters.

Thus I was thrown upon dependence without resource. Being now at an age in which young women are initiated into company, I was no longer to be supported in my former character but at considerable expense. So that, partly lest I should waste money and partly lest my appearance might draw too many compliments and assiduities, I was insensibly degraded from my equality, and enjoyed few privileges above the head servant but that of receiving no wages.

I felt every indignity, but knew that resentment would precipitate my fall. I therefore endeavoured to continue my importance by little services and active officiousness, and for a time preserved myself from neglect by withdrawing all pretences to competition and studying to please rather than to shine. But my interest, notwithstanding this expedient, hourly declined, and my cousin's favourite maid began to exchange repartees with me and consult me about the alterations of a cast gown.

I was now completely depressed; and though I had seen mankind enough to know the necessity of outward cheerfulness, I often withdrew to my chamber to vent my grief or turn my condition in my mind and examine by what means I might escape from perpetual mortification. At last my schemes and sorrows were interrupted by a sudden change of my relation's behaviour, who one day took an occasion when we were left together in a room to bid me suffer myself no longer to be insulted, but assume the place which he always intended me to hold in the family. He assured me that his wife's preference of her own daughters should never hurt me; and, accompanying his professions with a purse of gold, ordered me to bespeak a rich suit at the mercer's, and to apply privately to him for money when I wanted it and insinuate that my other friends supplied me, which he would take care to confirm.

By this stratagem, which I did not then understand, he filled me with tenderness and gratitude, compelled me to repose on him as my only support, and produced a necessity of private conversation. He often appointed interviews at the house of an acquaintance, and sometimes called on me with a coach and carried me abroad. My sense of his favour and the desire of retaining it disposed me to unlimited complaisance; and though I saw his kindness grow every day more fond, I did not suffer any suspicion to enter my thoughts. At last the wretch took advantage of the familiarity which he enjoyed as my relation and the submission which he exacted as my benefactor to complete the ruin of an orphan whom his own promises had made indigent, whom his indulgence had melted, and his authority subdued.

I know not why it should afford subject of exultation to over-power on any terms the resolution or surprise the caution of a girl. But of all the boasters that deck themselves in the spoils of inno-cence and beauty, they surely have the least pretensions to triumph who submit to owe their success to some casual influence. They neither employ the graces of fancy nor the force of understanding in their attempts. They cannot please their vanity with the art of their approaches, the delicacy of their adulations, the elegance of their address, or the efficacy of their eloquence, nor applaud them-selves as possessed of any qualities by which affection is attracted. They surmount no obstacles, they defeat no rivals, but attack only those who cannot resist, and are often content to possess the body without any solicitude to gain the heart.

Many of these despicable wretches does my present acquaintance with infamy and wickedness enable me to number among the heroes of debauchery, reptiles whom their own servants would have despised, had they not been their servants, and with whom beggary would have disdained intercourse, had she not been allured by hopes of relief. Many of the beings which are now rioting in taverns or shivering in the streets have been corrupted, not by arts of gallantry which stole gradually upon the affections and laid prudence asleep, but by the fear of losing benefits which never were intended, or of incurring resentment which they could not escape.

Some have been frighted by masters and some awed by guardians into ruin.

Our crime had its usual consequences, and he soon perceived that I could not long continue in his family. I was distracted at the thought of the reproach which I now believed inevitable. He comforted me with hopes of eluding all discovery, and often upbraided me with the anxiety which perhaps none but himself saw in my countenance, but at last mingled his assurances of protection and maintenance with menaces of total desertion if in the moments of perturbation I should suffer his secret to escape or endeavour to throw on him any part of my infamy.

Thus passed the dismal hours till my retreat could no longer be delayed. It was pretended that my relations had sent for me to a distant country, and I entered upon a state which shall be described in my next letter.

> I am, Sir, &c.,
> MISELLA.

MISELLA DEBAUCHED (*concluded*) (171)

Tuesday, 5th November 1751

Taedet coeli convexa tueri.

VIRGIL.

Dark is the sun, and loathsome is the day.

TO THE 'RAMBLER'

SIR,

Misella now sits down to continue her narrative. I am now convinced that nothing would more powerfully preserve youth from irregularity or guard inexperience from seduction than a just description of the condition into which the wanton plunges herself, and therefore hope that my letter may be a sufficient antidote to my example.

After the distraction, hesitation, and delays which the timidity of guilt naturally produces I was removed to lodgings in a distant part of the town under one of the characters commonly assumed upon such occasions. Here, being by my circumstances condemned to solitude, I passed most of my hours in bitterness and anguish. The conversation of the people with whom I was placed was not all capable of engaging my attention or dispossessing the reigning ideas. The books which I carried to my retreat were such as heightened my abhorrence of myself; for I was not so far abandoned as to sink voluntarily into corruption or endeavour to conceal from my own mind the enormity of my crime.

My relation remitted none of his fondness, but visited me so often that I was sometimes afraid lest his assiduity should expose him to suspicion. Whenever he came he found me weeping, and was therefore less delightfully entertained than he expected. After frequent expostulations upon the unreasonableness of my sorrow and innumerable protestations of everlasting regard he at last found that I was more affected with the loss of my innocence than the danger of my fame, and, that he might not be disturbed by my remorse, began to lull my conscience with the opiates of irreligion. His arguments were such as my course of life has since exposed me often to the necessity of hearing, vulgar, empty, and fallacious. Yet they at first confounded me with their novelty, filled me with doubt and perplexity, and interrupted that peace which I began to feel from the sincerity of my repentance without substituting any other support. I listened awhile to his impious gabble; but its influence was soon overpowered by natural reason and early education, and the convictions which this new attempt gave me of his baseness completed my abhorrence. I have heard of barbarians who, when tempests drive ships upon their coast, decoy them to the rocks that they may plunder their lading, and have always thought that wretches so merciless in their depredations ought to be destroyed by a general insurrection of all social beings. Yet how light is this guilt to the crime of him who, in the agitations of remorse, cuts away the anchor of piety, and when he has drawn aside credulity from the paths of virtue hides the light of Heaven which would direct her to return. I had hitherto considered him as a man equally betrayed with myself by the concurrence of appetite and opportunity; but I now saw with horror that he was contriving to perpetuate his gratification, and was desirous to fit me to his purpose by complete and radical corruption.

To escape, however, was not yet in my power. I could support the expenses of my condition only by the continuance of his favour. He provided all that was necessary, and in a few weeks congratulated me upon my escape from the danger which we had both expected with so much anxiety. I then began to remind him of his promise to restore me with my fame uninjured to the world. He promised me in general terms that nothing should be wanting which his power could add to my happiness, but forbore to release me from my confinement.   I knew how much my reception in the world depended upon my speedy return, and was therefore outrageously impatient of his delays, which I now perceived to be only artifices of lewdness.   He told me at last, with an appearance of sorrow, that all hopes of restoration to my former state were for ever precluded; that chance had discovered my secret and malice divulged it; and that nothing now remained but to seek a retreat more private, where curiosity or hatred could never find us.

The rage, anguish, and resentment which I felt at this account are not to be expressed.   I was in so much dread of reproach and infamy, which he represented as pursuing me with full cry, that I yielded myself implicitly to his disposal, and was removed, with a thousand studied precautions through byways and dark passages to another house, where I harassed him with perpetual solicitations for a small annuity that might enable me to live in the country in obscurity and innocence.

This demand he at first evaded with ardent professions, but in time appeared offended at my importunity and distrust; and having one day endeavoured to soothe me with uncommon expressions of tenderness, when he found my discontent immovable left me with some inarticulate murmurs of anger.   I was pleased that he was at last roused to sensibility, and expecting that at his next visit he would comply with my request, lived with great tranquillity upon the money in my hands, and was so much pleased with this pause of persecution that I did not reflect how much his absence had exceeded the usual intervals till I was alarmed with the danger of wanting subsistence.   I then suddenly contracted my expenses, but was unwilling to supplicate for assistance.   Necessity, however, soon overcame my modesty or my pride, and I applied to him by a letter, but had no answer.   I writ in terms more pressing, but without effect.   I then sent an agent to inquire after him, who informed me that he had quitted his house and was gone with his family to reside for some time upon his estate in Ireland.

However shocked at this abrupt departure, I was yet unwilling to believe that he could wholly abandon me, and therefore, by the sale of my clothes, I supported myself, expecting that every post would bring me relief.   Thus I passed seven months between hope and dejection, in a gradual approach to poverty and distress, emaciated with discontent, and bewildered with uncertainty.   At last my landlady, after many hints of the necessity of a new lover, took the opportunity of my absence to search my boxes, and, missing some of my apparel, seized the remainder for rent, and led me to the door.

To remonstrate against legal cruelty was vain; to supplicate obdurate brutality was hopeless. I went away, I knew not whither, and wandered about without any settled purpose, unacquainted with the usual expedients of misery, unqualified for laborious offices, afraid to meet an eye that had seen me before, and hopeless of relief from those who were strangers to my former condition. Night came on in the midst of my distraction, and I still continued to wander till the menaces of the watch obliged me to shelter myself in a covered passage.

Next day I procured a lodging in the backward garret of a mean house, and employed my landlady to inquire for a service. My applications were generally rejected for want of a character. At length I was received at a draper's; but when it was known to my mistress that I had only one gown, and that of silk, she was of opinion that I looked like a thief, and without warning hurried me away. I then tried to support myself by my needle, and by my landlady's recommendation obtained a little work from a shop, and for three weeks lived without repining. But when my punctuality had gained me so much reputation that I was trusted to make up a head of some value one of my fellow lodgers stole the lace, and I was obliged to fly from a prosecution.

Thus driven again into the streets, I lived upon the least that could support me, and at night accommodated myself under pent-houses as well as I could. At length I became absolutely penniless, and, having strolled all day without sustenance, was at the close of evening accosted by an elderly man with an invitation to a tavern. I refused him with hesitation. He seized me by the hand and drew me into a neighbouring house where, when he saw my face pale with hunger and my eyes swelling with tears, he spurned me from him and bade me cant and whine in some other place; he for his part would take care of his pockets.

I still continued to stand in the way, having scarcely strength to walk farther, when another soon addressed me in the same manner. When he saw the same tokens of calamity he considered that I might be obtained at a cheap rate, and therefore quickly made overtures which I had no longer firmness to reject. By this man I was maintained four months in penurious wickedness, and then abandoned to my former condition, from which I was delivered by another keeper.

In this abject state I have now passed four years, the drudge of extortion and the sport of drunkenness. Sometimes the property of one man, and sometimes the common prey of accidental lewdness; at one time tricked up for sale by the mistress of a brothel, at another begging in the streets to be relieved from hunger by wickedness; without any hope in the day but of finding some whom folly or excess may expose to my allurements, and without any reflections at night, but such as guilt and terror impress upon me.

If those who pass their days in plenty and security could visit for an hour the dismal receptacles to which the prostitute retires from her nocturnal excursions, and see the wretches that lie crowded together, mad with intemperance, ghastly with famine, nauseous with filth, and noisome with disease, it would not be easy for any degree of abhorrence to harden them against compassion, or to repress the desire which they must immediately feel to rescue such numbers of human beings from a state so dreadful.

It is said in France they annually evacuate their streets and ship their prostitutes and vagabonds to their colonies. If the women that infest this city had the same opportunity of escaping from their miseries I believe very little force would be necessary. For who among them can dread any change? Many of us, indeed, are wholly unqualified for any but the most servile employments, and those perhaps would require the care of a magistrate to hinder them from following the same practices in another country. But others are only precluded by infamy from reformation, and would gladly be delivered on any terms from the necessity of guilt and the tyranny of chance. No place but a populous city can afford opportunities for open prostitution, and where the eye of justice can attend to individuals those who cannot be made good may be restrained from mischief. For my part, I should exalt at the privilege of banishment, and think myself happy in any region that should restore me once again to honesty and peace.

I am, Sir, &c.,

MISELLA.

THE MAJORITY ARE WICKED (175)

Tuesday, 19th November 1751

Rari quippe boni, numero vix sunt totidem quot
Thebarum portae, vel divitis ostia Nili.

JUVENAL.

Good men are scarce, the just are thinly sown;
They thrive but ill, nor can they last when grown.
And should we count them, and our store compile;
Yet Thebes more gates could shew, more mouths the Nile.

CREECH.

NONE of the axioms of wisdom which recommend the ancient sages to veneration seems to have required less extent of knowledge or perspicacity of penetration than the remark of Bias, that οἱ πλέονες κακόι—the majority are wicked.

The depravity of mankind is so easily discoverable that nothing but the desert or the cell can exclude it from notice. The knowledge of crimes intrudes uncalled and undesired. They whom their abstraction from common occurrences hinders from seeing iniquity will quickly have their attention awakened by feeling it. Even he who ventures not into the world may learn its corruption in his closet. For what are treatises of morality but persuasives to the practice of duties for which no arguments would be necessary but that we are continually tempted to violate or neglect them? What are all the records of history but narratives of successive villainies, of treasons and usurpations, massacres and wars?

But perhaps the excellence of aphorisms consists not so much in the expression of some rare or abstruse sentiment as in the comprehension of some obvious and useful truth in a few words. We frequently fall in error and folly, not because the true principles of action are not known, but because, for a time, they are not remembered. And he may therefore be justly numbered among the benefactors of mankind who contracts the great rules of life into short sentences that may be easily impressed on the memory and taught by frequent recollection to recur habitually to the mind.

However those who have passed through half the life of man may now wonder that any should require to be cautioned against corruption, they will find that they have themselves purchased their conviction by many disappointments and vexations which an earlier knowledge would have spared them, and may see on every side some entangling themselves in perplexities and some sinking into ruin by ignorance or neglect of the maxim of Bias.

Every day sends out in quest of pleasure and distinction some heir fondled in ignorance and flattered into pride. He comes forth with all the confidence of a spirit unacquainted with superiors and all the benevolence of a mind not yet irritated by opposition, alarmed by fraud, or embittered by cruelty. He loves all because he imagines himself the universal favourite. Every exchange of salutation produces new acquaintance, and every acquaintance kindles into friendship.

Every season brings a new flight of beauties into the world, who have hitherto heard only of their own charms and imagine that the heart feels no passion but that of love. They are soon surrounded by admirers whom they credit because they tell them only what is heard with delight. Whoever gazes upon them is a lover; and whoever forces a sigh is pining in despair.

He surely is a useful monitor who inculcates to these thoughtless strangers that the majority are wicked; who informs them that the train which wealth and beauty draw after them is lured only by the scent of prey; and that, perhaps, among all those who crowd about them with professions and flatteries there is not one who does not hope for some opportunity to devour or betray them, to glut himself by their destruction, or to share their spoils with a stronger savage.

Virtue presented singly to the imagination or the reason is so well recommended by its own graces and so strongly supported by arguments, that a good man wonders how any can be bad. And they who are ignorant of the force of passion and interest, who never observed the arts of seduction, the contagion of example, the gradual descent from one crime to another, or the insensible depravation of the principles by loose conversation, naturally expect to find integrity in every bosom and veracity on every tongue.

It is indeed impossible not to hear from those who have lived longer of wrongs and falsehoods, of violence and circumvention. But such narratives are commonly regarded by the young, the heady, and the confident as nothing more than the murmurs of peevishness or the dreams of dotage; and notwithstanding all the documents of hoary wisdom we commonly plunge into the world fearless and credulous, without any foresight of danger or apprehension of deceit.

I have remarked in a former paper that credulity is the common failing of unexperienced virtue, and that he who is spontaneously suspicious may be justly charged with radical corruption. For if he has not known the prevalence of dishonesty by information, nor had time to observe it with his own eyes, whence can he take his measures of judgment but from himself?

They who best deserve to escape the snares of artifice are most likely to be entangled. He that endeavours to live for the good of others must always be exposed to the arts of them who live only for themselves, unless he is taught by timely precepts the caution required in common transactions, and shown at a distance the pitfalls of treachery.

To youth, therefore, it should be carefully inculcated, that to enter the road of life without caution or reserve, in expectation of general fidelity and justice, is to launch on the wide ocean without the instruments of steerage, and to hope that every wind will be prosperous and that every coast will afford a harbour.

To enumerate the various motives to deceit and injury would be to count all the desires that prevail among the sons of men, since there is no ambition however petty, no wish however absurd, that by indulgence will not be enabled to overpower the influence of virtue. Many there are who openly and almost professedly regulate all their conduct by their love of money, who have no reason for action or forbearance, for compliance or refusal, than that they hope to gain more by one than by the other. These are indeed the meanest and cruellest of human beings, a race with whom, as with some pestiferous animals, the whole creation seems to be at war, but who, however detested or scorned, long continue to add heap to heap, and when they have reduced one to beggary are still permitted to fasten on another.

Others, yet less rationally wicked, pass their lives in mischief because they cannot bear the sight of success, and mark out every man for hatred whose fame or fortune they believe increasing.

Many, who have not advanced to these degrees of guilt, are yet wholly unqualified for friendship and unable to maintain any constant or regular course of kindness. Happiness may be destroyed not only by union with the man who is apparently the slave of interest, but with him whom a wild opinion of the dignity of perseverance, in whatever cause, disposes to pursue every injury with unwearied and perpetual resentment; with him whose vanity inclines him to consider every man as a rival in every pretension; with him whose airy negligence puts his friend's affairs or secrets in continual hazard and who thinks his forgetfulness of others excused by his inattention to himself; and with him whose inconstancy ranges without any settled rule of choice through varieties of friendship, and who adopts and dismisses favourites by the sudden impulse of caprice.

Thus numerous are the dangers to which the converse of mankind exposes us, and which can be avoided only by prudent distrust. He therefore that, remembering this salutary maxim, learns early to withhold his fondness from fair appearances will have reason to pay some honours to Bias of Priene who enabled him to become wise without the cost of experience.

DIRECTIONS TO AUTHORS ATTACKED BY CRITICS (176)

Saturday, 23rd November 1751

Naso suspendere adunco.

HORACE.

On me you turn the nose.

THERE are many vexatious accidents and uneasy situations which raise little compassion for the sufferers, and which no man but those whom they immediately distress can regard with seriousness. Petty mischiefs that have no influence on futurity nor extend their effects to the rest of life are always seen with a kind of malicious pleasure. A mistake or embarrassment which for the present moment fills the face with blushes and the mind with confusion will have no other effect upon those who observe it than that of convulsing them with irresistible laughter. Some circumstances of misery are so powerfully ridiculous that neither kindness nor duty can withstand them. They bear down love, interest, and reverence, and force the friend, the dependant, or the child to give way to instantaneous motions of merriment.

Among the principal of comic calamities may be reckoned the pain which an author, not yet hardened into insensibility, feels at the onset of a furious critic whose age, rank, or fortune gives him confidence to speak without reserve; who heaps one objection upon another, and obtrudes his remarks, and enforces his corrections, without tenderness or awe.

The author, full of the importance of his work and anxious for the justification of every syllable, starts and kindles at the slightest attack. The critic, eager to establish his superiority, triumphing in every discovery of failure, and zealous to impress the cogency of his arguments, pursues him from line to line without cessation or remorse. The critic, who hazards little, proceeds with vehemence, impetuosity, and fearlessness. The author, whose quiet and fame and life and immortality are involved in the controversy, tries every art of subterfuge and defence, maintains modestly what he resolves never to yield, and yields unwillingly what cannot be maintained. The critic's purpose is to conquer, the author only hopes to escape. The critic therefore knits his brow, and raises his voice, and rejoices whenever he perceives any tokens of pain excited by the pressure of his assertions or the point of his sarcasms. The author, whose endeavour is at once to mollify and elude his persecutor, composes his features and softens his accent, breaks the force of assault by retreat, and rather steps aside than flies or advances.

As it very seldom happens that the rage of extemporary criticism inflicts fatal or lasting wounds, I know not that the laws of benevolence entitle this distress to much sympathy. The diversion of baiting an author has the sanction of all ages and nations, and is more lawful than the sport of teasing other animals, because, for the most part, he comes voluntarily to the stake, furnished, as he imagines, by the patron powers of literature with resistless weapons and impenetrable armour, with the mail of the boar of Erymanth and the paws of the lion of Nemea.

But the works of genius are sometimes produced by other motives than vanity; and he whom necessity or duty enforces to write is not always so well satisfied with himself as not to be discouraged by censorious impudence. It may therefore be necessary to consider how they whom publication lays open to the insults of such as their obscurity secures against reprisals may extricate themselves from unexpected encounters.

Vida, a man of considerable skill in the politics of literature, directs his pupil wholly to abandon his defence and, even when he can irrefragably refute all objections, to suffer tamely the exultations of his antagonist.

This rule may perhaps be just when advice is asked and severity solicited, because no man tells his opinion so freely as when he imagines it received with implicit veneration; and critics ought never to be consulted but while errors may yet be rectified or insipidity suppressed. But when the book has once been dismissed into the world and can be no more retouched I know not whether a very different conduct should not be prescribed, and whether firmness and spirit may not sometimes be of use to overpower arrogance and repel brutality. Softness, diffidence, and moderation will often be mistaken for imbecility and dejection; they lure cowardice to the attack by the hopes of easy victory, and it will soon be found that he whom every man thinks he can conquer shall never be at peace.

The animadversions of critics are commonly such as may easily provoke the sedatest writer to some quickness of resentment and asperity of reply. A man who by long consideration has familiarized a subject to his own mind, carefully surveyed the series of his thoughts, and planned all the parts of his composition into a regular dependence on each other, will often start at the sinistrous interpretations or absurd remarks of haste and ignorance, and wonder by what infatuation they have been led away from the obvious sense, and upon what peculiar principles of judgment they decide against him.

The eye of the intellect, like that of the body, is not equally perfect in all, nor equally adapted in any to all objects. The end of criticism is to supply its defects: rules are the instruments of mental vision, which may indeed assist our faculties when properly used but produce confusion and obscurity by unskilful application.

Some seem always to read with the microscope of criticism, and employ their whole attention upon minute elegance or faults scarcely visible to common observation. The dissonance of a syllable, the recurrence of the same sound, the repetition of a particle, the smallest deviation from propriety, the slightest defect in construction or arrangement swell before their eyes into enormities. As they discern with great exactness, they comprehend but a narrow compass, and know nothing of the justness of the design, the general spirit of the performance, the artifice of connection, or the harmony of the parts. They never conceive how small a proportion that which they are busy in contemplating bears to the whole, or how the petty inaccuracies with which they are offended are absorbed and lost in the general excellence.

Others are furnished by criticism with a telescope. They see with great clearness whatever is too remote to be discovered by the rest of mankind, but are totally blind to all that lies immediately before them. They discover in every passage some secret meaning, some remote allusion, some artful allegory, or some occult imitation which no other reader ever suspected. But they have no perception of the cogency of arguments, the force of pathetic sentiments, the various colours of diction, or the flowery embellishments of fancy. Of all that engages the attention of others they are totally insensible while they pry into worlds of conjecture and amuse themselves with phantoms in the clouds.

In criticism, as in every other art, we fail sometimes by our weakness but more frequently by our fault. We are sometimes bewildered by ignorance and sometimes by prejudice; but we seldom deviate far from the right but when we deliver ourselves up to the direction of vanity.

A CLUB OF ANTIQUARIES (177)

Tuesday, 26th November 1751

Turpe est difficiles habere nugas.

MARTIAL.

Those things which now seem frivolous and slight,
Will be of serious consequence to you,
When they have made you once ridiculous.

ROSCOMMON.

TO THE 'RAMBLER'

SIR,

When I was, at the usual time, about to enter upon the profession to which my friends had destined me, being summoned by the death of my father into the country, I found myself master of an unexpected sum of money, and of an estate which, though not large, was in my opinion sufficient to support me in a condition far preferable to the fatigue, dependence, and uncertainty of any gainful occupation. I therefore resolved to devote the rest of my life wholly to curiosity, and without any confinement of my excursions or termination of my views to wander over the boundless regions of general knowledge.

This scheme of life seemed pregnant with inexhaustible variety, and therefore I could not forbear to congratulate myself upon the wisdom of my choice.   I furnished a large room with all conveniencies for study, collected books of every kind, quitted every science at the first perception of disgust, returned to it again as soon as my former ardour happened to revive, and, having no rival to depress me by comparison nor any critic to alarm me with objections, I spent day after day in profound tranquillity, with only so much complacence in my own improvements as served to excite and animate my application.

Thus I lived for some years with complete acquiescence in my own plan of conduct, rising early to read, and dividing the latter part of the day between economy, exercise, and reflection.   But in time I began to find my mind contracted and stiffened by solitude.   My ease and elegance was insensibly impaired, I was no longer able to accommodate myself with readiness to the accidental current or conversation, my notions grew particular and paradoxical, and my phraseology formal and unfashionable.   I spoke on common occasions the language of books.   My quickness of apprehension and celerity of reply had entirely deserted me.   When I delivered my opinion or detailed my knowledge I was bewildered by an unseasonable interrogatory, disconcerted by any slight opposition, and overwhelmed and lost in dejection when the smallest advantage was gained against me in dispute.   I became decisive and dogmatical, impatient of contradiction, perpetually jealous of my character, insolent to such as acknowledged my superiority, and sullen and malignant to all who refused to receive my dictates.

This I soon discovered to be one of those intellectual diseases which a wise man should make haste to cure.   I therefore resolved for a time to shut my books and learn again the art of conversation, to defecate and clear my mind by brisker motions and stronger impulses, and to unite myself once more to the living generation.

For this purpose I hasted to London and entreated one of my academical acquaintances to introduce me into some of the little societies of literature which are formed in taverns and coffeehouses.   He was pleased with an opportunity of showing me to his friends, and soon obtained me admission among a select company of curious men who met once a week to exhilarate their studies and compare their acquisitions.

The eldest and most venerable of this society was Hirsutus, who, after the first civilities of my reception, found means to introduce the mention of his favourite studies by a severe censure of those who want the due regard for their native country.   He informed me that he had early withdrawn his attention from foreign trifles, and that since he begun to addict his mind to serious and manly studies he had very carefully amassed all the English books that were printed in the black character. This search he had pursued so diligently that he was able to show the deficiencies of the best catalogues. He had long since completed his Caxton, had three sheets of Treveris unknown to the antiquaries, and wanted to a perfect Pynson but two volumes, of which one was promised him as a legacy by its present possessor, and the other he was resolved to buy, at whatever price, when Quisquilius's library should be sold. Hirsutus had no other reason for the valuing or slighting a book than that it was printed in the Roman or the Gothic letter, nor any ideas but such as his favourite volumes had supplied. When he was serious he expatiated on the narratives of Johan de Trevisa, and when he was merry regaled us with a quotation from the *Shippe of Foles*.

While I was listening to this hoary student Ferratus entered in a hurry and informed us with the abruptness of ecstasy that his set of halfpence was now complete: he had just received in a handful of change the piece that he had so long been seeking, and could now defy mankind to outgo his collection of English copper.

Chartophylax then observed how fatally human sagacity was sometimes baffled, and how often the most valuable discoveries are made by chance. He had employed himself and his emissaries seven years at great expense to perfect his series of Gazettes, but had long wanted a single paper which, when he despaired of obtaining it, was sent him wrapped round a parcel of tobacco.

Cantilenus turned all his thoughts upon old ballads, for he considered them as the genuine records of the national taste. He offered to show me a copy of *The Children in the Wood*, which he firmly believed to be of the first edition, and by the help of which the text might be freed from several corruptions, if this age of barbarity had any claim to such favours from him.

Many were admitted into this society as inferior members because they had collected old prints and neglected pamphlets or possessed some fragment of antiquity, as the seal of an ancient corporation, the charter of a religious house, the genealogy of a family extinct, or a letter written in the reign of Elizabeth.

Every one of those virtuosos looked on all his associates as wretches of depraved taste and narrow notions. Their conversation was therefore fretful and waspish, their behaviour brutal, their merriment bluntly sarcastic, and their seriousness gloomy and suspicious. They were totally ignorant of all that passes, or has lately passed, in the world, unable to discuss any question of religious, political, or military knowledge, equally strangers to science and politer learning, and without any wish to improve their minds, or any other pleasure than that of displaying rarities of which they would not suffer others to make the proper use.

Hirsutus graciously informed me that the number of their society was limited, but that I might sometimes attend as an auditor. I was pleased to find myself in no danger of an honour which I could not have willingly accepted nor gracefully refused, and left them without any intention of returning. For I soon found that the suppression of those habits with which I was vitiated required association with men very different from this solemn race.

I am, Sir, &c.,

VIVACULUS.

It is natural to feel grief or indignation when anything necessary or useful is wantonly wasted or negligently destroyed; and therefore my correspondent cannot be blamed for looking with uneasiness on the waste of life. Leisure and curiosity might soon make great advances in useful knowledge, were they not diverted by minute emulation and laborious trifles. It may, however, somewhat mollify his anger to reflect that perhaps none of the assembly which he describes was capable of any nobler employment, and that he who does his best, however little, is always to be distinguished from him that does nothing. Whatever busies the mind without corrupting it has at least this use, that it rescues the day from idleness; and he that is never idle will not often be vicious.

THE STUDY OF LIFE (180)

Saturday, 7th December 1751

Ταῦτ' εἰδὼς σοφὸς ἴσθι, μάτην δ'' Επίκουρον ἔασον
ποῦ τὸ κενὸν ζητεῖν, καὶ τίνες αἱ μονάδες.

AUTOMEDON.

On life, on morals, be thy thoughts employ'd;
Leave to the schools their atoms and their void.

IT is somewhere related by Le Clerc that a wealthy trader of good understanding, having the common ambition to breed his son a scholar, carried him to an university, resolving to use his own judgment in the choice of a tutor. He had been taught, by whatever intelligence, the nearest way to the heart of an academic, and at his arrival entertained all who came about him with such profusion, that the professors were lured by the smell of his table from their books, and flocked round him with all the cringes of awkward complaisance. This eagerness answered the merchant's purpose. He glutted them with delicacies, and softened them with caresses till he prevailed upon one after another to open his bosom and make a discovery of his competitions, jealousies, and resentments. Having thus learned each man's character, partly from himself and partly from his acquaintances, he resolved to find some other education for his son, and went away convinced that a scholastic life has no other tendency than to vitiate the morals and contract the understanding. Nor would he afterwards hear with patience the praises of the ancient authors, being persuaded that scholars of all ages must have been the same, and that Xenophon and Cicero were professors of some former university, and therefore mean and selfish, ignorant and servile, like those whom he had lately visited and forsaken.

Envy, curiosity, and a sense of the imperfection of our present state incline us to estimate the advantages which are in the possession of others above their real value. Everyone must have remarked what powers and prerogatives the vulgar imagine to be conferred by learning. A man of science is expected to excel the unlettered and unenlightened even on occasions where literature is of no use; and among weak minds loses part of his reverence by discovering no superiority in those parts of life in which all are unavoidably equal, as when a monarch makes a progress to the remoter provinces the rustics are said sometimes to wonder that they find him of the same size with themselves.

These demands of prejudice and folly can never be satisfied; and therefore many of the imputations which learning suffers from disappointed ignorance are without reproach. But there are some failures to which men of study are peculiarly exposed. Every condition has its disadvantages. The circle of knowledge is too wide for the most active and diligent intellect, and while science is pursued other accomplishments are neglected, as a small garrison must leave one part of an extensive fortress naked when an alarm calls them to another.

The learned, however, might generally support their dignity with more success if they suffered not themselves to be misled by the desire of superfluous attainments. Raphael, in return to Adam's inquiries into the courses of the stars and the revolutions of heaven, counsels him to withdraw his mind from idle speculations and employ his faculties upon nearer and more interesting objects, the survey of his own life, the subjection of his passions, the knowledge of duties which must daily be performed, and the detection of dangers which must daily be incurred.

This angelic counsel every man of letters should always have before him. He that devotes himself to retired study naturally sinks from omission to forgetfulness of social duties. He must be therefore sometimes awakened and recalled to the general condition of mankind.

I am far from any intention to limit curiosity or confine the labours of learning to arts of immediate and necessary use. It is only from the various essays of experimental industry and the vague excursions of minds sent out upon discovery that any advancement of knowledge can be expected. And though many must be disappointed in their labours, yet they are not to be charged with having spent their time in vain. Their example contributed to inspire emulation, and their miscarriages taught others the way to success.

But the distant hope of being one day useful or eminent ought not to mislead us too far from that study which is equally requisite to the great and mean, to the celebrated and obscure—the art of moderating the desires, of repressing the appetites, and of conciliating or retaining the favour of mankind.

No man can imagine the course of his own life or the conduct of the world around him unworthy his attention. Yet among the sons of learning many seem to have thought of everything rather than of themselves, and to have observed everything but what passes before their eyes. Many who toil through the intricacy of complicated systems are insuperably embarrassed with the least perplexity in common affairs. Many who compare the actions and ascertain the characters of ancient heroes let their own days glide away without examination, and suffer vicious habits to encroach upon their minds without resistance or detection.

The most frequent reproach of the scholastic race is the want of fortitude, not martial but philosophic. Men bred in shades and silence, taught to immure themselves at sunset, and accustomed to no other weapon than syllogism, may be allowed to feel terror at personal danger and to be disconcerted by tumult and alarm. But why should he whose life is spent in contemplation, and whose business is only to discover truth, be unable to rectify the fallacies of imagination or contend successfully against prejudice and passion? To what end has he read and meditated if he gives up his understanding to false appearances and suffers himself to be enslaved by fear of evils to which only folly or vanity can expose him, or elated by advantages to which, as they are equally conferred upon the good and bad, no real dignity is annexed?

Such, however, is the state of the world, that the most obsequious of the slaves of pride, the most rapturous of the gazers upon wealth, the most officious of the whisperers of greatness are collected from seminaries appropriated to the study of wisdom and of virtue, where it was intended that appetite should learn to be content with little, and that hope should aspire only to honours which no human power can give or take away.

The student, when he comes forth into the world, instead of congratulating himself upon his exemption from the errors of those whose opinions have been formed by accident or custom and who live without any certain principles of conduct, is commonly in haste to mingle with the multitude and show his sprightliness and ductility by an expeditious compliance with fashions or vices. The first smile of a man whose fortune gives him power to reward his dependants commonly enchants him beyond resistance. The glare of equipage, the sweets of luxury, the liberality of general promises, the softness of habitual affability fill his imagination; and he soon ceases to have any other wish than to be well received, or any measure of right and wrong but the opinion of his patron.

A man flattered and obeyed learns to exact grosser adulation and enjoin lower submission. Neither our virtues nor vices are all our own. If there were no cowardice there would be little insolence. Pride cannot rise to any great degree but by the concurrence of blandishment or the sufferance of tameness. The wretch who would shrink and crouch before one that should dart his eyes upon him with the spirit of natural equality becomes capricious and tyrannical when he sees himself approached with a downcast look and hears the soft address of awe and servility. To those who are willing to purchase favour by cringes and compliance is to be imputed the haughtiness that leaves nothing to be hoped by firmness and integrity.

If, instead of wandering after the meteors of philosophy which fill the world with splendour for a while and then sink and are forgotten, the candidates of learning fixed their eyes upon the permanent lustre of moral and religious truth, they would find a more certain direction to happiness. A little plausibility of discourse and acquaintance with unnecessary speculations is dearly purchased when it excludes those instructions which fortify the heart with resolution and exalt the spirit to independence.

LOVE AND RICHES (192)

Saturday, 18th January 1752

Γένος οὐδὲν εἰς ἔρωτα,
σοφίη, τρόπος πατεῖται.
μόνον ἄργυρον βλέπωσιν.

ANACREON.

Vain the nobest birth would prove,
Nor worth, nor wit avail in love;
Tis gold alone succeeds.

F. LEWIS.

TO THE 'RAMBLER'

SIR,

I am the son of a gentleman whose ancestors for many ages held the first rank in the county, till at last one of them, too desirous of popularity, set his house open, kept a table covered with continual profusion, and distributed his beef and ale to such as chose rather to live upon the folly of others than their own labour, with such thoughtless liberality that he left a third part of his estate mortgaged. His successor, a man of spirit, scorned to impair his dignity by parsimonious retrenchments, or to admit by a sale of his lands any participation of the rights of his manor. He therefore made another mortgage to pay the interest of the former, and pleased himself with the reflection that his son would have the hereditary estate without the diminution of an acre.

Nearly resembling this was the practice of my wise progenitors for many ages. Every man boasted the antiquity of his family, resolved to support the dignity of his birth, and lived in splendour and plenty at the expense of his heir, who, sometimes by a wealthy marriage and sometimes by lucky legacies, discharged part of the encumbrances and thought himself entitled to contract new debts and to leave to his children the same inheritance of embarrassment and distress.

Thus the estate perpetually decayed: the woods were felled by one, the park ploughed by another, the fishery let to farmers by a third. At last the old hall was pulled down to spare the cost of reparation, and part of the materials sold to build a small house with the rest. We were now openly degraded from our original rank, and my father's brother was allowed with less reluctance to serve an apprenticeship, though we never reconciled ourselves heartily to the sound of haberdasher, but always talked of warehouses and a merchant, and when the wind happened to blow loud affected to pity the hazards of commerce and to sympathize with the solicitude of my poor uncle, who had the true retailer's terror of adventure, and never exposed himself or his property to any wider water than the Thames.

In time, however, by continual profit and small expenses, he grew rich and began to turn his thoughts towards rank. He hung the arms of the family over his parlour chimney, pointed at a chariot decorated only with a cipher, became of opinion that money could not make a gentleman, resented the petulance of upstarts, told stories of Alderman Puff's grandfather the porter, wondered that there was no better method for regulating precedence, wished for some dress peculiar to men of fashion, and when his servant presented a letter always inquired whether it came from his brother the esquire.

My father was careful to send him game by every carrier, which, though the conveyance often cost more than the value, was well received because it gave him an opportunity of calling his friends together, describing the beauty of his brother's seat, and lamenting his own folly, whom no remonstrances could withhold from polluting his fingers with a shop-book.

The little presents which we sent were always returned with great munificence. He was desirous of being the second founder of his family, and could not bear that we should be any longer out-shone by those whom we considered as climbers upon our ruins and usurpers of our fortune. He furnished our house with all the elegance of fashionable expense, and was careful to conceal his bounties lest the poverty of his family should be suspected.

At length it happened that, by misconduct like our own, a large estate which had been purchased from us was again exposed to the best bidder. My uncle, delighted with an opportunity of reinstating the family in their possessions, came down with treasures scarcely to be imagined in a place where commerce has not made large sums familiar, and at once drove all the competitors away, expedited the writings, and took possession. He now considered himself as superior to trade, disposed of his stock, and as soon as he had settled his economy began to show his rural sovereignty by breaking the hedges of his tenants in hunting, and seizing the guns or nets of those whose fortunes did not qualify them for sportsmen. He soon afterwards solicited the office of sheriff, from which all his neighbours were glad to be reprieved, but which he regarded as a resumption of ancestral claims and a kind of restoration to blood after the attainder of a trade.

My uncle, whose mind was so filled with this change of his condition that he found no want of domestic entertainment, declared himself too old to marry, and resolved to let the newly purchased estate fall into the regular channel of inheritance. I was therefore considered as heir apparent, and courted with officiousness and caresses by the gentlemen who had hitherto coldly allowed me that rank which they could not refuse, depressed me with studied neglect, and irritated me with ambiguous insults.

I felt not much pleasure from the civilities for which I knew myself indebted to my uncle's industry, till by one of the invitations which every day now brought me, I was induced to spend a week with Lucius, whose daughter Flavilla I had often seen and admired like others, without any thought of nearer approaches. The inequality which had hitherto kept me at a distance being now levelled, I was received with every evidence of respect. Lucius told me the fortune which he intended for his favourite daughter; many odd accidents obliged us to be often together without company, and I soon began to find that they were spreading for me the nets of matrimony.

Flavilla was all softness and complaisance. I, who had been excluded by a narrow fortune from much acquaintance with the world, and never been honoured before with the notice of so fine a lady, was easily enamoured. Lucius either perceived my passion or Flavilla betrayed it. Care was taken that our private meetings should be less frequent, and my charmer confessed by her eyes how much pain she suffered from our restraint. I renewed my visit upon every pretence, but was not allowed one interview without witness. At last I declared my passion to Lucius, who received me as a lover worthy of his daughter and told me that nothing was wanting to his consent but that my uncle should settle his estate upon me. I objected the indecency of encroaching on his life and the danger of provoking him by such an unseasonable demand. Lucius seemed not to think decency of much importance, but admitted the danger of displeasing, and concluded that as he was now old and sickly we might without any inconvenience wait for his death.

With this resolution I was better contented, as it procured me the company of Flavilla, in which the days passed away amidst continual rapture. But in time I began to be ashamed of sitting idle in expectation of growing rich by the death of my benefactor, and proposed to Lucius many schemes of raising my own fortune by such assistance as I knew my uncle willing to give me. Lucius, afraid lest I should change my affection in absence, diverted me from my design by dissuasives to which my passion easily listened. At last my uncle died, and considering himself as neglected by me from the time that Flavilla took possession of my heart, left his estate to my younger brother, who was always hovering about his bed and relating stories of my pranks and extravagance, my contempt of the commercial dialect, and my impatience to be selling stock.

My condition was soon known, and I was no longer admitted by the father of Flavilla. I repeated the protestations of regard which had been formerly returned with so much ardour, in a letter which she received privately but returned by her father's footman. Contempt has driven out my love, and I am content to have purchased by the loss of fortune an escape from a harpy who has joined the artifices of age to the allurements of youth. I am now going to pursue my former projects with a legacy which my uncle bequeathed me, and, if I succeed, shall expect to hear of the repentance of Flavilla.

I am, Sir, yours, &c.,
CONSTANTIUS.

THE YOUNG NOBLEMAN PROGRESSES
IN POLITENESS (194)

Saturday, 25th January 1752

Si damnosa senem juvat alea, ludit et haeres
Bullatus, parvoque eadem quatit arma fritillo.

JUVENAL.

If gaming does an aged fire entice,
Then my young master swiftly learns the vice;
And shakes, in hanging sleeves, the little box and dice.

J. DRYDEN, JUN.

TO THE 'RAMBLER'

SIR,

That vanity which keeps every man important in his own eyes inclines me to believe that neither you nor your readers have yet forgotten the name of Eumathes, who sent you a few months ago an account of his arrival at London with a young nobleman his pupil. I shall therefore continue my narrative without preface or recapitulation.

My pupil in a very short time, by his mother's countenance and direction, accomplished himself with all those qualifications which constitute puerile politeness. He became in a few days a perfect master of his hat, which with a careless nicety he could put off or on without any need to adjust it by a second motion. This was not attained but by frequent consultations with his dancing-master and constant practice before the glass, for he had some rustic habits to overcome. But what will not time and industry perform? A fortnight more furnished him with all the airs and forms of familiar and respectful salutation, from the clap on the shoulder to the humble bow. He practises the stare of strangeness and the smile of condescension, the solemnity of promise and the graciousness of encouragement as if he had been nursed at a levee, and pronounces with no less propriety than his father the monosyllables of coldness and sonorous periods of respectful profession.

He immediately lost the reserve and timidity which solitude and study are apt to impress upon the most courtly genius, was able to enter a crowded room with airy civility, to meet the glances of a hundred eyes without perturbation, and address those whom he never saw before with ease and confidence. In less than a month his mother declared her satisfaction at his proficiency by a triumphant observation that she believed nothing would make him blush.

The silence with which I was contented to hear my pupil's praises gave the lady reason to suspect me not much delighted with his acquisitions. But she attributed my discontent to the diminution of my influence and my fears of losing the patronage of the family; and though she thinks favourably of my learning and morals, she considers me as wholly unacquainted with the customs of the polite part of mankind, and therefore not qualified to form the manners of a young nobleman or communicate the knowledge of the world. This knowledge she comprises in the rules of visiting, the history of the present hour, an early intelligence of the change of fashions, an extensive acquaintance with the names and faces of persons of rank, and a frequent appearance in places of resort.

All this my pupil pursues with great application. He is twice a day in the Mall, where he studies the dress of every man splendid enough to attract his notice, and never comes home without some observation upon sleeves, buttonholes, and embroidery. At his return from the theatre he can give an account of the gallantries, glances, whispers, smiles, sighs, flirts, and blushes of every box, so much to his mother's satisfaction that when I attempted to resume my character by inquiring his opinion of the sentiments and diction of the tragedy, she at once repressed my criticism by telling me that she hoped he did not go to lose his time in attending to the creatures on the stage.

But his acuteness was most eminently signalized at the masquerade, where he discovered his acquaintance through their disguises with such wonderful facility as has afforded the family an inexhaustible topic of conversation. Every new visitor is informed how one was detected by his gait and another by the swing of his arms, a third by the toss of his head, and another by his favourite phrase. Nor can you doubt but these performances receive their just applause, and a genius thus hastening to maturity is promoted by every art of cultivation.

Such have been his endeavours, and such his assistances, that every trace of literature was soon obliterated. He has changed his language with his dress, and instead of endeavouring at purity or propriety has no other care than to catch the reigning phrase and current exclamation, till, by copying whatever is peculiar in the talk of all those whose birth or fortune entitle them to imitation, he has collected every fashionable barbarism of the present winter, and speaks a dialect not to be understood among those who form their style by poring upon authors.

To this copiousness of ideas and felicity of language he has joined such eagerness to lead the conversation, that he is celebrated among the ladies as the prettiest gentleman that the age can boast of, except that some who love to talk themselves think him too forward, and others lament that, with so much wit and knowledge, he is not taller.

His mother listens to his observations with her eyes sparkling and her heart beating, and can scarcely contain in the most numerous assemblies the expectations which she has formed for his future eminence. Women, by whatever fate, always judge absurdly of the intellects of boys. The vivacity and confidence which attract female admiration are seldom produced in the early part of life but by ignorance at least, if not by stupidity; for they proceed not from confidence of right but fearlessness of wrong. Whoever has a clear apprehension must have quick sensibility, and where he has no sufficient reason to trust his own judgment will proceed with doubt and caution because he perpetually dreads the disgrace of error. The pain of miscarriage is naturally proportionate to the desire of excellence; and therefore till men are hardened by long familiarity with reproach, or have attained, by frequent struggles, the art of suppressing their emotions, diffidence is found the inseparable associate of understanding.

But so little distrust has my pupil of his own abilities that he has for some time professed himself a wit, and tortures his imagination on all occasions for burlesque and jocularity. How he supports a character which, perhaps, no man ever assumed without repentance, may be easily conjectured. Wit, you know, is the unexpected copulation of ideas, the discovery of some occult relation between images in appearance remote from each other. An effusion of wit, therefore, presupposes an accumulation of knowledge, a memory stored with notions which the imagination may cull out to compose new assemblages. Whatever may be the native vigour of the mind, she can never form any combinations from few ideas, as many changes can never be rung upon a few bells. Accident may indeed sometimes produce a lucky parallel or a striking contrast; but these gifts of chance are not frequent, and he that has nothing of his own and yet condemns himself to needless expenses must live upon loans or theft.

The indulgence which his youth has hitherto obtained and the respect which his rank secures have hitherto supplied the want of intellectual qualifications; and he imagines that all admire who applaud, and that all who laugh are pleased. He therefore returns every day to the charge with increase of courage, though not of strength, and practises all the tricks by which wit is counterfeited. He lays trains for a quibble, he contrives blunders for his footman, he adapts old stories to present characters, he mistakes the question that he may return a smart answer, he anticipates the argument that he may plausibly object, when he has nothing to reply he repeats the last words of his antagonist, then says: 'Your humble servant,' and concludes with a laugh of triumph.

These mistakes I have honestly attempted to correct; but what can be expected from reason unsupported by fashion, splendour, or authority? He hears me, indeed, or appears to hear me, but is soon rescued from the lecture by more pleasing avocations, and shows, diversions, and caresses, drive my precepts from his remembrance.

He at last imagines himself qualified to enter the world, and has met with adventures in his first sally which I shall by your paper communicate to the public.

I am, &c.,

EUMATHES.

THE YOUNG NOBLEMAN'S INTRODUCTION TO TOWN (195)

Tuesday, 28th January 1752

Nescit equo rudis
Haerere ingenuus puer,
Venarique timet; ludere doctior
Seu graeco jubeas trocho,
Seu malis vetita legibus alea.

HORACE.

Nor knows our youth, of noblest race,
To mount the manag'd steed, or urge the chace;
More skill'd in the mean arts of vice,
The whirling troque, or law-forbidden dice.

FRANCIS.

TO THE 'RAMBLER'

SIR,

Favours of every kind are doubled when they are speedily conferred. This is particularly true of the gratification of curiosity. He that long delays a story and suffers his auditor to torment himself with expectation will seldom be able to recompense the uneasiness, or equal the hope, which he suffers to be raised.

For this reason I have already sent you the continuation of my pupil's history, which, though it contains no events very uncommon, may be of use to young men who are in too much haste to trust their own prudence and quit the wing of protection before they are able to shift for themselves.

When he first settled in London he was so much bewildered in the enormous extent of the town, so confounded by incessant noise and crowds and hurry, and so terrified by rural narratives of the arts of harpers, the rudeness of the populace, malignity of porters, and treachery of coachmen, that he was afraid to go beyond the door without an attendant, and imagined his life in danger if he was obliged to pass the streets at night in any vehicle but his mother's chair.

He was therefore contented for a time that I should accompany him in all his excursions. But his fear abated as he grew more familiar with its objects; and the contempt to which his rusticity exposed him from such of his companions as had accidentally

286

known the town longer obliged him to dissemble his remaining terrors.

His desire of liberty made him now willing to spare me the trouble of observing his motions. But knowing how much his ignorance exposed him to mischief, I thought it cruel to abandon him to the fortune of the town. We went together every day to a coffee-house where he met wits, heirs, and fops airy, ignorant, and thoughtless as himself, with whom he had become acquainted at card-tables and whom he considered as the only beings to be envied or admired. What were their topics of conversation I could never discover. For so much was their vivacity depressed by my intrusive seriousness, that they seldom proceeded beyond the exchange of nods and shrugs, an arch grin, or a broken hint, except when they could retire, while I was looking on the papers, to a corner of the room where they seemed to disburden their imaginations and commonly vented the superfluity of their sprightliness in a peal of laughter. When they had tittered themselves into negligence I could sometimes overhear a few syllables, such as: 'Solemn rascal'—'academical airs'—'smoke the tutor'—'company for gentlemen!' and other broken phrases, by which I did not suffer my quiet to be disturbed, for they never proceeded to avowed indignities, but contented themselves to murmur in secret, and, whenever I turned my eye upon them, shrunk into stillness.

He was, however, desirous of withdrawing from the subjection which he could not venture to break, and made a secret appointment to assist his companions in the persecution of a play. His footman privately procured him a catcall, on which he practised in a back garret for two hours in the afternoon. At the proper time a chair was called. He pretended an engagement at Lady Flutter's, and hastened to the place where his critical associates had assembled. They hurried away to the theatre, full of malignity and denunciations against a man whose name they had never heard and a performance which they could not understand; for they were resolved to judge for themselves, and would not suffer the town to be imposed upon by scribblers. In the pit they exerted themselves with great spirit and vivacity, called out for the tunes of obscene songs, talked loudly at intervals of Shakespeare and Jonson, played on their catcalls a short prelude of terror, clamoured vehemently for the prologue, and clapped with great dexterity at the first entrance of the players.

Two scenes they heard without attempting interruption; but being no longer able to restrain their impatience they then began to exert themselves in groans and hisses and plied their catcalls with incessant diligence, so that they were soon considered by the audience as disturbers of the house, and some who sat near them, either provoked at the obstruction of their entertainment or desirous to preserve the author from the mortification of seeing his hopes destroyed by children, snatched away their instruments of criticism, and by the seasonable vibration of a stick subdued them instantaneously to decency and silence.

To exhilarate themselves after this vexatious defeat they posted to a tavern, where they recovered their alacrity, and after two hours of obstreperous jollity burst out big with enterprise and panting for some occasions to signalize their prowess. They proceeded vigorously through two streets, and with very little opposition dispersed a rabble of drunkards less daring than themselves, then rolled two watchmen in the kennel and broke the windows of a tavern in which the fugitives took shelter. At last it was determined to march up to a row of chairs and demolish them for standing on the pavement. The chairmen formed a line of battle, and blows were exchanged for a time with equal courage on both sides. At last the assailants were overpowered, and the chairmen, when they knew their captives, brought them home by force.

The young gentleman next morning hung his head and was so much ashamed of his outrages and defeat, that perhaps he might have been checked in his first follies had not his mother partly in pity of his dejection and partly in approbation of his spirit, relieved him from his perplexity by paying the damages privately and discouraging all animadversion and reproof.

This indulgence could not wholly preserve him from the remembrance of his disgrace nor at once restore his confidence and elation. He was for three days silent, modest, and compliant, and thought himself neither too wise for instruction nor too manly for restraint. But his levity overcame this salutary sorrow. He began to talk with his former raptures of masquerades, taverns, and frolics, blustered when his wig was not combed with exactness, and threatened destruction to a tailor who had mistaken his directions about the pocket.

I knew that he was now rising again above control and that this inflation of spirits would burst out into some mischievous absurdity. I therefore watched him with great attention; but one evening, having attended his mother at a visit, he withdrew himself unsuspected while the company was engaged at cards. His vivacity and officiousness were soon missed and his return impatiently expected.

Supper was delayed and conversation suspended, every coach that rattled through the street was expected to bring him, and every servant that entered the room was examined concerning his departure. At last the lady returned home and was with great difficulty preserved from fits by spirits and cordials. The family was dispatched a thousand ways without success and the house was filled with distraction, till, as we were deliberating what further measures to take, he returned from a petty gaming-table with his coat torn, and his head broken, without his sword, snuff-box, sleeve-buttons, and watch.

Of this loss or robbery he gave little account, but instead of sinking into his former shame endeavoured to support himself by surliness and asperity. He was not the first that had played away a few trifles, and of what use were birth and fortune if they would not admit some sallies and expenses? His mamma was so much provoked by the cost of this prank that she would neither palliate or conceal it, and his father, after some threats of rustication which his fondness would not suffer him to execute, reduced the allowance of his pocket that he might not be tempted by plenty to profusion. This method would have succeeded in a place where there are no panders to folly and extravagance, but was now likely to have produced pernicious consequences. For we have discovered a treaty with a broker whose daughter he seems disposed to marry on condition that she shall be supplied with present money, for which he is to repay thrice the value at the death of his father.

There was now no time to be lost. A domestic consultation was immediately held, and he was doomed to pass two years in the country. But his mother, touched with his tears, declared that she thought him too much of a man to be any longer confined to his book, and he therefore begins his travels to-morrow under a French governor.

> I am, &c.,
>
> EUMATHES.

MUTABILITY OF HUMAN OPINIONS (196)

Saturday, 1st February 1752

Multa ferunt anni venientes commoda secum
Multa recedentes adimunt.

HORACE.

The blessings flowing in with life's full tide,
Down with our ebb of life decreasing glide.

FRANCIS.

BAXTER, in the narrative of his own life, has enumerated several opinions which, though he thought them evident and incontestable at his first entrance into the world, time and experience disposed him to change.

Whoever reviews the state of his own mind from the dawn of manhood to its decline, and considers what he pursued or dreaded, slighted or esteemed at different periods of his age, will have no reason to imagine such changes of sentiment peculiar to any station or character. Every man, however careless and inattentive, has conviction forced upon him. The lectures of time obtrude themselves upon the most unwilling or dissipated auditor, and by comparing our past with our present thoughts we perceive that we have changed our minds, though perhaps we cannot discover when the alteration happened or by what causes it was produced.

This revolution of sentiments occasions a perpetual contest between the old and young. They who imagine themselves entitled to veneration by the prerogative of longer life are inclined to treat the notions of those whose conduct they superintend with superciliousness and contempt for want of considering that the future and the past have different appearances; that the disproportion will always be great between expectation and enjoyment, between new possession and satiety; that the truth of many maxims of age gives too little pleasure to be allowed till it is felt; and that the miseries of life would be increased beyond all human power of endurance if we were to enter the world with the same opinion as we carry from it.

We naturally indulge those ideas that please us. Hope will predominate in every mind till it has been suppressed by frequent disappointments. The youth has not yet discovered how many evils are continually hovering about us, and when he is set free from the shackles of discipline looks abroad into the world with rapture. He sees an Elysian region open before him, so variegated with beauty and so stored with pleasure that his care is rather to accumulate good than to shun evil. He stands distracted by different forms of delight, and has no other doubt than which path to follow of those which all lead equally to the bowers of happiness.

He who has seen only the superficies of life believes everything to be what it appears, and rarely suspects that external splendour conceals any latent sorrow or vexation. He never imagines that there may be greatness without safety, affluence without content, jollity without friendship, and solitude without peace. He fancies himself permitted to cull the blessings of every condition, and to leave its inconveniencies to the idle and the ignorant. He is inclined to believe no man miserable but by his own fault, and seldom looks with much pity upon failings or miscarriages, because he thinks them willingly admitted or negligently incurred.

It is impossible without pity and contempt to hear a youth of generous sentiments and warm imagination declaring in the moment of openness and confidence his designs and expectations. Because long life is possible he considers it as certain, and therefore promises himself all the changes of happiness, and provides gratifications for every desire. He is, for a time, to give himself wholly to frolic and diversion, to range the world in search of pleasure, to delight every eye, to gain every heart, and to be celebrated equally for his pleasing levities and solid attainments, his deep reflections and his sparkling repartees. He then elevates his views to nobler enjoyments, and finds all the scattered excellencies of the female world united in a woman who prefers his addresses to wealth and titles. He is afterwards to engage in business, to dissipate difficulty and overpower opposition, to climb by the mere force of merit to fame and greatness, and reward all those who countenanced his rise, or paid due regard to his early excellence. At last he will retire in peace and honour, contract his views to domestic pleasures, form the manners of children like himself, observe how every year expands the beauty of his daughters and how his sons catch ardour from their father's history. He will give laws to the neighbourhood, dictate axioms to posterity, and leave the world an example of wisdom and of happiness.

With hopes like these he sallies jocund into life. To little purpose is he told that the condition of humanity admits no pure and unmingled happiness; that the exuberant gaiety of youth ends in poverty or disease, that uncommon qualifications and contrarieties of excellence produce envy equally with applause; that whatever admiration and fondness may promise him he must marry a wife like the wives of others, with some virtues and some faults, and be as often disgusted by her vices as delighted by her elegance; that if he adventures into the circle of action he must expect to encounter men as artful, as daring, as resolute as himself; that of his children some may be deformed and others vicious, some may disgrace him by their follies, some offend him by their insolence, and some exhaust him by their profusion. He hears all this with obstinate incredulity, and wonders by what malignity old age is influenced that it cannot forbear to fill his ears with predictions of misery.

Among other pleasing errors of young minds is the opinion of their own importance. He that has not yet remarked how little attention his contemporaries can spare from their own affairs conceives all eyes turned upon himself, and imagines everyone that approaches him to be an enemy or a follower, an admirer or a spy. He therefore considers his fame as involved in the event of every action. Many of the virtues and vices of youth proceed from this quick sense of reputation. This it is that gives firmness and constancy, fidelity and disinterestedness; and it is this that kindles resentment for slight injuries and dictates all the principles of sanguinary honour.

But as time brings him forward into the world he soon discovers that he only shares fame or reproach with innumerable partners, that he has left unmarked in the obscurity of the crowd, and that what he does, whether good or bad, soon gives way to new objects of regard. He then easily sets himself free from the anxieties of reputation, and considers praise or censure as a transient breath which, while he hears it, is passing away without any lasting mischief or advantage.

In youth it is common to measure right and wrong by the opinion of the world, and in age to act without any measure but interest and to lose shame without substituting virtue.

Such is the condition of life, that something is always wanting to happiness. In youth we have warm hopes which are soon blasted by rashness and negligence, and great designs which are defeated by inexperience. In age we have knowledge and prudence without spirit to exert or motives to prompt them. We are able to plan schemes and regulate measures, but have not time remaining to bring them to completion.

INSOLENCE OF PROSPERO (200)

Saturday, 15th February 1752

Nemo petit modicis quae mittebantur amicis
A Seneca, quae Piso bonus, quae Cotta solebat
Largiri.

JUVENAL.

No man expects (for who so much a sot
Who has the times he lives in so forgot?)
What Seneca, what Piso us'd to send,
To raise, or to support a sinking friend.

BOWLES.

TO THE 'RAMBLER'

MR. RAMBLER,

Such is the tenderness or infirmity of many minds, that when any affliction oppresses them they have immediate recourse to lamentation and complaint, which, though it can only be allowed reasonable when evils admit of remedy, and then only when addressed to those from whom the remedy is expected, yet seems even in hopeless and incurable distresses to be natural, since those by whom it is not indulged imagine that they give a proof of extraordinary fortitude by suppressing it.

I am one of those who, with the Sancho of Cervantes, leave to higher characters the merit of suffering in silence, and give vent without scruple to any sorrow that swells in my heart. It is therefore to me a severe aggravation of a calamity when it is such as in the common opinion will not justify the acerbity of exclamation or support the solemnity of vocal grief. Yet many pains are incident to a man of delicacy, which the unfeeling world cannot be persuaded to pity, and which, when they are separated from their peculiar and personal circumstances, will never be considered as important enough to claim attention or deserve redress.

Of this kind will appear to gross and vulgar apprehensions the miseries which I endured in a morning visit to Prospero, a man lately raised to wealth by a lucky project and too much intoxicated by sudden elevation or too little polished by thought and conversation to enjoy his present fortune with elegance and decency.

We set out in the world together, and for a long time mutually assisted each other in our exigencies as either happened to have money or influence beyond his immediate necessities. You know that nothing generally endears men so much as participation of dangers and misfortunes. I therefore always considered Prospero as united with me in the strongest league of kindness, and imagined that our friendship was only to be broken by the hand of death. I felt at his sudden shoot of success an honest and disinterested joy, but, as I want no part of his superfluities, am not willing to descend from that equality in which we hitherto have lived.

Our intimacy was regarded by me as a dispensation from ceremonial visits; and it was so long before I saw him at his new house, that he gently complained of my neglect and obliged me to come on a day appointed. I kept my promise, but found that the impatience of my friend arose not from any desire to communicate his happiness, but to enjoy his superiority.

When I told my name at the door the footman went to see if his master was at home, and, by the tardiness of his return, gave me reason to suspect that time was taken to deliberate. He then informed me that Prospero desired my company, and showed the staircase carefully secured by mats from the pollution of my feet. The best apartments were ostentatiously set open that I might have a distant view of the magnificence which I was not permitted to approach; and my old friend, receiving me with all the insolence of condescension at the top of the stairs, conducted me to a back room, where he told me he always breakfasted when he had not great company.

On the floor where we sat lay a carpet covered with a cloth of which Prospero ordered his servant to lift up a corner that I might contemplate the brightness of the colours and the elegance of the texture, and asked me whether I had ever seen anything so fine before. I did not gratify his folly with any outcries of admiration, but coldly bade the footman let down the cloth.

We then sat down, and I began to hope that pride was glutted with persecution, when Prospero desired that I would give the servant leave to adjust the cover of my chair, which was slipped a little aside to show the damask. He informed me that he had bespoke ordinary chairs for common use, but had been disappointed by his tradesmen. I put the chair aside with my foot, and drew another so hastily that I was entreated not to rumple the carpet.

Breakfast was at last set, and as I was not willing to indulge the peevishness that began to seize me I commended the tea. Prospero then told me that another time I should taste his finest sort, but that he had only a very small quantity remaining, and reserved it for those whom he thought himself obliged to treat with particular respect.

While we were conversing upon such subjects as imagination happened to suggest he frequently digressed into directions to the servant that waited, or made a slight inquiry after the jeweller or silversmith. And once, as I was pursuing an argument with some degree of earnestness, he started from his posture of attention and ordered that if Lord Lofty called on him that morning he should be shown into the best parlour.

My patience was not yet wholly subdued. I was willing to promote his satisfaction, and therefore observed that the figures on the china were eminently pretty. Prospero had now an opportunity of calling for his Dresden china, 'Which,' says he, 'I always associate with my chased tea-kettle.' The cups were brought. I once resolved not to have looked upon them, but my curiosity prevailed. When I had examined them a little Prospero desired me to set them down, for they who were accustomed only to common dishes seldom handled china with much care. You will, I hope, commend my philosophy when I tell you that I did not dash his baubles to the ground.

He was now so much elevated with his own greatness that he thought some humility necessary to avert the glance of envy, and therefore told me with an air of soft composure that I was not to estimate life by external appearance, that all these shining acquisitions had added little to his happiness, that he still remembered with pleasure the days in which he and I were upon the level, and had often in the moment of reflection been doubtful whether he should lose much by changing his condition for mine.

I began now to be afraid lest his pride should, by silence and submission, be emboldened to insults that could not easily be borne, and therefore coolly considered how I should repress it without such bitterness of reproof as I was yet unwilling to use. But he interrupted my meditation by asking leave to be dressed, and told me that he had promised to attend some ladies in the park, and, if I was going the same way, would take me in his chariot. I had no inclination to any favours, and therefore left him without any intention of seeing him again unless some misfortune should restore his understanding.

I am, &c.,

ASPER.

Though I am not wholly insensible of the provocations which my correspondent has received, I cannot altogether commend the keenness of his resentment nor encourage him to persist in his resolution of breaking off all commerce with his old acquaintance. One of the golden precepts of Pythagoras directs that 'a friend should not be hated for little faults'; and surely he upon whom nothing worse can be charged, than that he mats his stairs, and covers his carpet, and sets out his finery to show before those whom he does not admit to use it, has yet committed nothing that should exclude him from common degrees of kindness. Such improprieties often proceed rather from stupidity than malice. Those who thus shine only to dazzle are influenced merely by custom and example, and neither examine, nor are qualified to examine, the motives of their own practice or to state the nice limits between elegance and ostentation. They are often innocent of the pain which their vanity produces, and insult others when they have no worse purpose than to please themselves.

He that too much refines his delicacy will always endanger his quiet. Of those with whom nature and virtue oblige us to converse some are ignorant of the arts of pleasing and offend when they design to caress; some are negligent and gratify themselves without regard to the quiet of another; some perhaps are malicious and feel no greater satisfaction in prosperity than that of raising envy and trampling inferiority. But whatever be the motive of insult, it is always best to overlook it; for folly scarcely can deserve resentment, and malice is punished by neglect.

ART OF LIVING AT THE COST
OF OTHERS (206)

Saturday, 7th March 1752

Propositi nondum pudet, atque eadem est mens,
Ut bona summa putes, aliena vivere quadra.

JUVENAL.

But harden'd by affronts, and still the same,
Lost to all sense of honour and of fame,
Thou yet can'st love to haunt the great man's board,
And think no supper good but with a lord.

BOWLES.

WHEN Diogenes was once asked what kind of wine he liked best, he answered: 'That which is drunk at the cost of others.'

Though the character of Diogenes has never excited any general zeal of imitation there are many who resemble him in his taste of wine, many who are frugal though not abstemious, whose appetites, though too powerful for reason, are kept under restraint by avarice, and to whom all delicacies lose their flavour when they cannot be obtained but at their own expense.

Nothing produces more singularity of manners and inconstancy of life than the conflict of opposite vices in the same mind. He that uniformly pursues any purpose, whether good or bad, has a settled principle of action, and, as he may always find associates who are travelling the same way, is countenanced by example and sheltered in the multitude. But a man actuated at once by different desires must move in a direction peculiar to himself, and suffer that reproach which we are naturally inclined to bestow on those who deviate from the rest of the world even without inquiring whether they are worse or better.

Yet this conflict of desires sometimes produces wonderful effects. To riot in far-fetched dishes or surfeit with unexhausted variety, and yet practise the most rigid economy, is surely an art which may justly draw the eyes of mankind upon them whose industry or judgment has enabled them to attain it. To him, indeed, who is content to break open the chests or mortgage the manors of his ancestors that he may hire the ministers of excess at the highest price gluttony is an easy science. Yet we often hear the votaries of luxury boasting of the elegance which they owe to the taste of others, relating with rapture the succession of dishes with which their cooks and caterers supply them, and expecting their share of praise with the discoverers of arts and the civilizers of nations. But to shorten the way to convivial happiness by eating without cost is a secret hitherto in few hands, but certainly deserves the curiosity of those whose principal enjoyment is their dinner, and who see the sun rise with no other hope than that they shall fill their bellies before it sets.

Of them that have within my knowledge attempted this scheme of happiness the greater part have been immediately obliged to desist.   And some, whom their first attempts flattered with success, were reduced by degrees to a few tables, from which they were at last chased to make way for others; and having long habituated themselves to superfluous plenty growled away their latter years in discontented competence.

None enter the regions of luxury with higher expectations than men of wit, who imagine that they shall never want a welcome to that company whose ideas they can enlarge or whose imaginations they can elevate, and believe themselves able to pay for their wine with the mirth which it qualifies them to produce.   Full of this opinion, they crowd, with little invitation, wherever the smell of a feast allures them, but are seldom encouraged to repeat their visits, being dreaded by the pert as rivals and hated by the dull as disturbers of the company.

No man has been so happy in gaining and keeping the privilege of living at luxurious houses as Gulosulus, who, after thirty years of continual revelry, has now established by uncontroverted prescription his claim to partake of every entertainment, and whose presence they who aspire to the praise of a sumptuous table are careful to procure on a day of importance by sending the invitation a fortnight before.

Gulosulus entered the world without any eminent degree of merit, but was careful to frequent houses where persons of rank resorted.   By being often seen he became in time known, and from sitting in the same room was suffered to mix in idle conversation or assisted to fill up a vacant hour when better amusement was not readily to be had.   From the coffee-house he was sometimes taken away to dinner; and as no man refuses the acquaintance of him whom he sees admitted to familiarity by others of equal dignity, when he had been met at a few tables he with less difficulty found the way to more, till at last he was regularly expected to appear wherever preparations are made for a feast within the circuit of his acquaintance.

When he was thus by accident initiated in luxury he felt in himself no inclination to retire from a life of so much pleasure, and therefore very seriously considered how he might continue it. Great qualities or uncommon accomplishments he did not find necessary. For he had already seen that merit rather enforces respect than attracts fondness; and as he thought no folly greater than that of losing a dinner for any other gratification, he often congratulated himself that he had none of that disgusting excellence which impresses awe upon greatness and condemns its possessors to the society of those who are wise or brave and indigent as themselves.

Gulosulus, having never allotted much of his time to books or meditation, had no opinion in philosophy or politics, and was not in danger of injuring his interest by dogmatical positions or violent contradiction. If a dispute arose he took care to listen with earnest attention, and when either speaker grew vehement and loud turned towards him with eager quickness and uttered a short phrase of admiration, as if surprised by such cogency of argument as he had never known before. By this silent concession he generally preserved in either controvertist such a conviction of his own superiority as inclined him rather to pity than irritate his adversary, and prevented those outrages which are sometimes produced by the rage of defeat or petulance or triumph.

Gulosulus was never embarrassed but when he was required to declare his sentiments before he had been able to discover to which side the master of the house inclined; for it was his invariable rule to adopt the notions of those that invited him.

It will sometimes happen that the insolence of wealth breaks into contemptuousness, or the turbulence of wine requires a vent; and Gulosulus seldom fails of being singled out on such emergencies as one on whom any experiment of ribaldry may be safely tried. Sometimes his lordship finds himself inclined to exhibit a specimen of raillery for the diversion of his guest, and Gulosulus always supplies him with a subject of merriment. But he has learned to consider rudeness and indignities as familiarities that entitle him to greater freedom: he comforts himself that those who treat and insult him pay for their laughter, and that he keeps his money while they enjoy their jest.

His chief policy consists in selecting some dish from every course and recommending it to the company with an air so decisive that no one ventures to contradict him. By this practice he acquires at a feast a kind of dictatorial authority, his taste becomes the standard of pickles and seasoning, and he is venerated by the professors of epicurism as the only man who understands the niceties of cookery.

Whenever a new sauce is imported or any innovation made in the culinary system he procures the earliest intelligence and the most authentic receipt, and by communicating his knowledge under proper injunctions of secrecy gains a right of tasting his own dish whenever it is prepared, that he may tell whether his directions have been fully understood.

By this method of life Gulosulus has so impressed on his imagination the dignity of feasting, that he has no other topic of talk or subject of meditation. His calendar is a bill of fare: he measures the year by successive dainties. The only common places of his memory are his meals; and if you ask him at what time an event happened he considers whether he heard it after a dinner of turbot or venison. He knows, indeed, that those who value themselves upon sense, learning, or piety speak of him with contempt; but he considers them as wretches envious or ignorant, who do not know his happiness or wish to supplant him; and declares to his friends that he is fully satisfied with his own conduct since he has fed every day on twenty dishes and yet doubled his estate.

THE RAMBLER'S FAREWELL (208)

Saturday, 14th March 1752

'Ηράκλειτος ἐγώ. Τί μ' ὦ κάτω ἕλκετ' ἀμουσοις;
οὐχ ὑμῖν ἐπόνουν, τοῖς δέ μ' ἐπισταμένοις.
Εἷς ἐμοὶ ἄνθρωπος τρισμύριοι. Οἱ δ' ἀνάριθμοι
οὐδείς· ταῦτ' αὐδῶ καὶ παρὰ Περσεφόνη.

DIOGENES LAERTIUS.

'Begone, ye blockheads,' Heraclitus cries,
'And leave my labours to the learn'd and wise.
By wit, by knowledge, studious to be read,
I scorn the multitude, alive and dead.'

TIME, which puts an end to all pleasures and sorrows, has likewise concluded the labours of the Rambler. Having supported for two years the anxious employment of a periodical writer, and multiplied my essays to four volumes, I have now determined to desist.

The reasons of this resolution it is of little importance to declare, since justification is unnecessary where no objection is made. I am far from supposing that the cessation of my performances will raise any inquiry; for I have never been much of a favourite of the public, nor can boast that in the progress of my undertaking I have been animated by the rewards of the liberal, the caresses of the great, or the praises of the eminent.

But I have no design to gratify pride by submission or malice by lamentation, nor think it reasonable to complain of neglect from those whose regard I never solicited. If I have not been distinguished by the distributors of literary honours I have seldom descended to the arts by which favour is obtained. I have seen the meteors of fashion rise and fall, without any attempt to add a moment to their duration. I have never complied with contemporary curiosity, nor enabled my readers to discuss the topic of the day. I have rarely exemplified my assertions by living characters. In my papers no man could look for censures of his enemies or praises of himself; and they only were expected to peruse them, whose passions left them leisure for abstracted truth, and whose virtue could please by its naked dignity.

To some, however, I am indebted for encouragement, and to

others for assistance.   The number of my friends was never great, but they have been such as would not suffer me to think that I was writing in vain; and I did not feel much dejection from the want of popularity.   My obligations having not been frequent, my acknowledgments may be soon dispatched.   I can restore to all my correspondents their productions, with little diminution of the bulk of my volumes, though not without the loss of some pieces to which particular honours have been paid.

The parts from which I claim no other praise than that of having given them an opportunity of appearing, are the four billets in the tenth paper, the second letter in the fifteenth, the thirtieth, the forty-fourth, the ninety-seventh, and the hundredth papers, and the second letter in the hundred and seventh.

Having thus deprived myself of many excuses which candour might have admitted for the inequality of my compositions, being no longer able to allege the necessity of gratifying correspondents, the importunity with which publication was solicited, or obstinacy with which correction was rejected, I must remain accountable for all my faults, and submit without subterfuge to the censures of criticism; which, however, I shall not endeavour to soften by a formal deprecation, or to overbear by the influence of a patron. The supplications of an author never yet reprieved him a moment from oblivion; and, though greatness has sometimes sheltered guilt, it can afford no protection to ignorance or dullness.   Having hitherto attempted only the propagation of truth, I will not at last violate it by the confession of terrors which I do not feel. Having laboured to maintain the dignity of virtue, I will not now degrade it by the meanness of dedication.

The seeming vanity with which I have sometimes spoken of myself would perhaps require an apology, were it not extenuated by the example of those who have published essays before me, and by the privilege which every nameless writer has been hitherto allowed.

'A mask,' says Castiglione, 'confers a right of acting and speaking with less restraint, even when the wearer happens to be known.   He that is discovered without his own content may claim some indulgence, and cannot be rigorously called to justify those sallies or frolics which his disguise must prove him desirous to conceal.

But I have been cautious lest this offence should be frequently or grossly committed; for, as one of the philosophers directs us to live with a friend as with one that is some time to become an enemy, I have always thought it the duty of an anonymous author to write as if he expected to be hereafter known.

I am willing to flatter myself with hopes that, by collecting these papers, I am not preparing for my future life either shame or repentance. That all are happily imagined, or accurately polished, that the same sentiments have not sometimes recurred, or the same expressions been too frequently repeated, I have not confidence in my abilities sufficient to warrant. He that condemns himself to compose on a stated day will often bring to his task an attention dissipated, a memory embarrassed, an imagination overwhelmed, a mind distracted with anxieties, a body languishing with disease. He will labour on a barren topic till it is too late to change it, or, in the ardour of invention, diffuse his thoughts into wild exuberance which the pressing hour of publication cannot suffer judgment to examine or reduce.

Whatever shall be the final sentence of mankind, I have at least endeavoured to deserve their kindness. I have laboured to refine our language to grammatical purity, and to clear it from colloquial barbarisms, licentious idioms, and irregular combinations. Something, perhaps, I have added to the elegance of its construction, and something to the harmony of its cadence. When common words were less pleasing to the ear, or less distinct in their signification, I have familiarized the terms of philosophy by applying them to popular ideas, but have rarely admitted any word not authorized by former writers; for I believe that whoever knows the English tongue in its present extent will be able to express his thoughts without further help from other nations.

As it has been my principal design to inculcate wisdom or piety, I have allotted few papers to the idle sports of imagination. Some, perhaps, may be found, of which the highest excellence is harmless merriment; but scarcely any man is so steadily serious as not complain that the severity of dictatorial instruction has been too selbom relieved, and that he is driven by the sternness of the Rambler's philosophy to more cheerful and airy companions.

Next to the excursions of fancy are the disquisitions of criticism, which, in my opinion, is only to be ranked among the subordinate and instrumental arts. Arbitrary decision and general exclamation I have carefully avoided, by asserting nothing without a reason, and establishing all my principles of judgment on unalterable and evident truth.

In the pictures of life I have never been so studious of novelty or surprise as to depart wholly from all resemblance: a fault which writers deservedly celebrated frequently commit that they may raise, as the occasion requires, either mirth or abhorrence. Some enlargement may be allowed to declamation, and some exaggeration to burlesque; but as they deviate further from reality they become less and less useful because their lessons will fail of application. The mind of the reader is carried away from the contemplation of his own manners; he finds in himself no likeness to the phantom before him; and, though he laughs or rages, is not reformed.

The essays professedly serious, if I have been able to execute my own intentions, will be found exactly conformable to the precepts of Christianity, without any accommodation to the licentiousness and levity of the present age. I therefore look back on this part of my work with pleasure, which no blame or praise of man shall diminish or augment. I shall never envy the honours which wit and learning obtain in any other cause if I can be numbered among the writers who have given ardour to virtue and confidence to truth.

Αὐτῶν ἐκ μακάρων ἀντάξιος εἴη ἀμοιβή.

Celestial powers, that piety regard,
From you my labours want their last reward.

EVERYMAN'S LIBRARY: A Selected List

BIOGRAPHY

Baxter, Richard (1615–91).
THE AUTOBIOGRAPHY OF RICHARD BAXTER. 868

Boswell, James (1740–95). *See* Johnson.

Brontë, Charlotte (1816–55).
LIFE, 1857. By *Mrs Gaskell.* Introduction by *May Sinclair.* (*See also* Fiction.) 318

Burns, Robert (1759–96).
LIFE, 1828. By *J. G. Lockhart* (1794–1854). With Introduction by *Prof. James Kinsley*, M.A., PH.D. (*See also* Poetry and Drama.) 156

Byron, Lord (1788–1824).
LETTERS. Edited by *R. G. Howarth*, B.LITT., and with an Introduction by *André Maurois.* (*See also* Poetry and Drama.) 931

Canton, William (1845–1926).
A CHILD'S BOOK OF SAINTS, 1898. (*See also* Essays.) 61

Cellini, Benvenuto (1500–71).
THE LIFE OF BENVENUTO CELLINI, written by himself. Translated by *Anne Macdonell.* Introduction by *William Gaunt.* 51

Cowper, William (1731–1800).
SELECTED LETTERS. Edited, with Introduction, by *W. Hadley*, M.A. 774
(*See also* Poetry and Drama.)

Dickens, Charles (1812–70).
LIFE, 1874. By *John Forster* (1812–76). Introduction by *G. K. Chesterton.* 2 vols.
(*See also* Fiction.) 781–2

Evelyn, John (1620–1706).
DIARY. Edited by *William Bray*, 1819. Intro. by *G. W. E. Russell.* 2 vols. 220–1

Fox, George (1624–91).
JOURNAL, 1694. Revised by *Norman Penney*, with Account of Fox's last years.
Introduction by *Rufus M. Jones.* 754

Franklin, Benjamin (1706–90).
AUTOBIOGRAPHY, 1817. With Introduction and Account of Franklin's later life by *W. Macdonald.* Reset new edition (1949), with a newly compiled Index. 316

Goethe, Johann Wolfgang von (1749–1832).
LIFE, 1855. By *G. H. Lewes* (1817–78). Introduction by *Havelock Ellis.* Index.
(*See also* Poetry and Drama.) 269

Hudson, William Henry (1841–1922).
FAR AWAY AND LONG AGO, 1918. Intro. by *John Galsworthy.* 956

Johnson, Samuel (1709–84).
LIVES OF THE ENGLISH POETS, 1781. Introduction by *Mrs L. Archer-Hind.* 2 vols.
(*See also* Essays, Fiction.) 770–1
BOSWELL'S LIFE OF JOHNSON, 1791. A new edition (1949), with Introduction by *S. C. Roberts*, M.A., LL.D., and a 30-page Index by Alan Dent. 2 vols. 1–2

Keats, John (1795–1821).
LIFE AND LETTERS, 1848. By *Lord Houghton* (1809–85). Introduction by *Robert Lynd.* Note on the letters by Lewis Gibbs. (*See also* Poetry and Drama.) 801

Lamb, Charles (1775–1834).
LETTERS. New edition (1945) arranged from the Complete Annotated Edition of the Letters. 2 vols. (*See also* Essays and Belles-Lettres, Fiction.) 342–3

Napoleon Buonaparte (1769–1821).
HISTORY OF NAPOLEON BUONAPARTE, 1829. By *J. G. Lockhart* (1794–1854). 3
(*See also* Essays and Belles-Lettres.)

Nelson, Horatio, Viscount (1758–1805).
LIFE, 1813. By *Robert Southey* (1774–1843). (*See also* Essays.) 52

Outram, General Sir James (1803–63), 'the Bayard of India.'
LIFE, 1903. Deals with important passages in the history of India in the nineteenth century. By *L. J. Trotter* (1827–1912). 396

Pepys, Samuel (1633–1703).
DIARY. Newly edited (1953), with modernized spelling, by *John Warrington*, from the edition of Mynors Bright (1875–9). 3 vols. 53–5

Plutarch (46?–120).
LIVES OF THE NOBLE GREEKS AND ROMANS. Dryden's edition, 1683–6. Revised, with Introduction, by *A. H. Clough* (1819–61). 3 vols. 407–9

Rousseau, Jean Jacques (1712–78).
CONFESSIONS, 1782. 2 vols. Complete and unabridged English translation. New Introduction by *Prof. R. Niklaus*, B.A., PH.D., of Exeter University. 859–60
(*See also* Essays, Theology and Philosophy.)

Scott, Sir Walter (1771–1832).
LOCKHART'S LIFE OF SCOTT. An abridgement by *J. G. Lockhart* himself from the original 7 volumes. New Introduction by *W. M. Parker*, M.A. 39

ESSAYS AND BELLES-LETTRES

FICTION

HISTORY

ORATORY

11

REFERENCE

ROMANCE

Aucassin and Nicolette, with other Medieval Romances. Translated, with Introduction, by *Eugene Mason.*   497

Boccaccio, Giovanni (1313–75).
DECAMERON, 1471. Translated by *J. M. Rigg*, 1903. Introduction by *Edward Hutton*, 2 vols. Unabridged.   845–6

Bunyan, John (1628–88).
PILGRIM'S PROGRESS, Parts I and II, 1678–84. Reset edition. Introduction by *Prof. G. B. Harrison*, M.A., PH.D.   (*See also* Theology and Philosophy.) 204

Cervantes, Saavedra Miguel de (1547–1616).
DON QUIXOTE DE LA MANCHA. Translated by *P. A. Motteux.* Notes by *J. G. Lockhart.* Introduction and supplementary Notes by *L. B. Walton*, M.A., B.LITT. 2 vols.   385–6

Chrétien de Troyes (fl. 12th cent.).
ARTHURIAN ROMANCES ('Erec et Enide'; 'Cligés'; 'Yvain' and 'Lancelot'). Translated into prose, with Introduction, notes and bibliography, by *William Wistar Comfort.*   698

Kalevala, or The Land of Heroes. Translated from the Finnish by W. F. Kirby. 2 vols.   259–60

Mabinogion, The. Translated with Introduction by *Thomas Jones*, M.A., D.LITT., and *Gwyn Jones*, M.A.   97

Malory, Sir Thomas (fl. 1400?–70).
LE MORTE D'ARTHUR. Introduction by *Sir John Rhys.* 2 vols.   45–6

Marie de France (12th century), LAYS OF, AND OTHER FRENCH LEGENDS. Eight of Marie's 'Lais' and two of the anonymous French love stories of the same period translated with an Introduction by *Eugene Mason.*   557

Njal's Saga. THE STORY OF BURNT NJAL (written about 1280–90). Translated from the Icelandic by *Sir G. W. Dasent* (1861). Introduction (1957) and Index by *Prof. Edward Turville-Petre*, B.LITT., M.A.   558

Rabelais, François (1494?–1553).
THE HEROIC DEEDS OF GARGANTUA AND PANTAGRUEL, 1532–5. Introduction by *D. B. Wyndham Lewis.* 2 vols. A complete unabridged edition of Urquhart and Motteux's translation, 1653–94.   826–7

SCIENCE

Boyle, Robert (1627–91).
THE SCEPTICAL CHYMIST, 1661. Introduction by *M. M. Pattison Muir.*   559

Darwin, Charles (1809–82).
THE ORIGIN OF SPECIES, 1859. The sixth edition embodies Darwin's final additions and revisions. New Introduction (1956) by *W. R. Thompson*, F.R.S.   811
   (*See also* Travel and Topography.)

Eddington, Arthur Stanley (1882–1944).
THE NATURE OF THE PHYSICAL WORLD, 1928. Introduction by *Sir Edmund Whittaker*, F.R.S., O.M.   922

Euclid (fl. c. 330–c. 275 B.C.).
THE ELEMENTS OF EUCLID. Edited by *Isaac Todhunter*, with Introduction by *Sir Thomas L. Heath*, K.C.B., F.R.S.   891

Faraday, Michael (1791–1867).
EXPERIMENTAL RESEARCHES IN ELECTRICITY, 1839–55. With Plates and Diagrams, and an appreciation by *Prof. John Tyndall.*   576

Harvey, William (1578–1657).
THE CIRCULATION OF THE BLOOD. Introduction by *Ernest Parkyn.*   262

Howard, John (1726?–90).
THE STATE OF THE PRISONS, 1777. Intro. and Notes by *Kenneth Ruck.*   835

Marx, Karl (1818–83).
CAPITAL, 1867. Translated by *Eden* and *Cedar Paul.* 2 vols. Introduction by *Prof. G. D. H. Cole.*   848–9

Mill, John Stuart (1806–73). *See* Wollstonecraft.

Owen, Robert (1771–1858).
A NEW VIEW OF SOCIETY, 1813; and OTHER WRITINGS. Introduction by *G. D. H. Cole.*   799

Pearson, Karl (1857–1936).
THE GRAMMAR OF SCIENCE, 1892.   939

Ricardo, David (1772–1823).
THE PRINCIPLES OF POLITICAL ECONOMY AND TAXATION, 1817. Introduction by *Prof. Michael P. Fogarty*, M.A.   590

Smith, Adam (1723–90).
THE WEALTH OF NATIONS, 1766. Intro. by *Prof. Edwin Seligman.* 2 vols. 412–13

White, Gilbert (1720–93).
A NATURAL HISTORY OF SELBORNE, 1789. New edition (1949). Introduction and Notes by *R. M. Lockley.*   48

Wollstonecraft, Mary (1759–97), THE RIGHTS OF WOMAN, 1792; and **Mill, John Stuart** (1806–73), THE SUBJECTION OF WOMEN, 1869. New Introduction by *Pamela Frankau.*   825

THEOLOGY AND PHILOSOPHY

15

TRAVEL AND TOPOGRAPHY